# Thousand Autumns

QIAN QIU

3

# Thousand Autumns

## QIAN QIU

WRITTEN BY
**Meng Xi Shi**

TRANSLATED BY
**Faelicy**

ILLUSTRATED BY
**Me.Mimo**

BONUS ILLUSTRATION BY
**Ning**

Seven Seas

*Seven Seas Entertainment*

THOUSAND AUTUMNS: QIAN QIU VOL. 3

Published originally under the title of 《千秋》(Qian Qiu)
Author © 梦溪石 (Meng Xi Shi)
English edition rights under license granted by 北京晋江原创网络科技有限公司
(Beijing Jinjiang Original Network Technology Co., Ltd.)
English edition copyright © 2023 Seven Seas Entertainment, Inc.
Arranged through JS Agency Co., Ltd
All rights reserved

Illustrations by Me.Mimo
Bonus Illustration by Ning

Seven Seas press and purchase enquiries can be sent to Marketing Manager Lianne Sentar
at press@gomanga.com. Information regarding the distribution and purchase of digital
editions is available from Digital Manager CK Russell at digital@gomanga.com.

Follow Seven Seas Entertainment online at
sevenseasentertainment.com.

TRANSLATION: Faelicy
ADAPTATION: Harry Catlin
COVER DESIGN: M. A. Lewife
INTERIOR DESIGN & LAYOUT: Clay Gardner
PROOFREADER: Stephanie Cohen, Hnä
COPY EDITOR: Jade Gardner
EDITOR: Laurel Ashgrove
PREPRESS TECHNICIAN: Melanie Ujimori, Jules Valera
MANAGING EDITOR: Alyssa Scavetta
EDITOR-IN-CHIEF: Julie Davis
ASSOCIATE PUBLISHER: Adam Arnold
PUBLISHER: Jason DeAngelis

ISBN: 978-1-63858-941-9
Printed in Canada
First Printing: January 2024
10 9 8 7 6 5 4 3 2 1

# TABLE OF

## CONTENTS

# Meeting Bai Rong Again

T HROUGH THE RED HILLS I MEANDER; *around the sand dunes I wind. Frigid ice seeps into my flesh; the wind's chill throbs within my bones.*[1]

By the time Shen Qiao re-entered Chang'an, his state of mind had changed.

He entered the city alone. He was carrying a sword and dressed in Daoist garb, but with his sickly appearance, his poor eyesight, and how slowly he walked, he bore little resemblance to a martial artist from the jianghu. Instead, he looked more like a wandering Daoist priest who was only carrying a sword out of fear for the chaos of the times. Nothing about him seemed threatening in the least.

Chang'an was bustling with officials, people streaming through the streets like rivers, just like it'd always been every time he visited. But this time, it felt even livelier than before.

With some asking around, he learned that most of these people were preparing to head to Tuyuhun's capital to attend the Coiling Dragon Assembly on the ninth of September. All because some busybody had spread news that a scroll of the *Zhuyang Strategy* would appear this year, and that the Tai'e sword, a treasure that had been buried with the First Emperor of Qin and later unearthed by the Tyrant of Western Chu, would also be present.

---

1    From 白馬篇, or *Song of the White Horse, by Shen Yue.*

Everyone already knew that Northern Zhou, Tiantai Sect, and Xuandu Mountain each held a volume of the *Zhuyang Strategy*—they had already been claimed. Still, there were always more people trying to get their hands on them, though to this day no one had managed to plunder those volumes from the factions that safeguarded them. It was clear that such a feat must be enormously difficult, so much that even the average martial expert couldn't pull it off. The scroll at Tiantai Sect, for example—even if they tried to steal it, grandmasters like Yan Wushi and Ruyan Kehui might find themselves unable to leave unscathed, never mind anyone with lesser skills.

The two remaining volumes had been scattered to the wind, their whereabouts unknown. The Liuhe Guild had managed to obtain one and wanted to transport it south with some other cargo, but Yan Wushi ruined things along the way. The scroll had been destroyed, gone from the world forevermore.

If a *Zhuyang Strategy* scroll really did appear at the Coiling Dragon Assembly, then, it must be the last volume that remained adrift—and unclaimed. Obtaining this scroll would be much simpler than hunting down the ones from Tiantai Sect or Xuandu Mountain, never mind taking on the martial artists within the Inner Palace of Northern Zhou. Everyone in the jianghu would covet it.

Wealth might move most people's hearts, but to those from the jianghu, all the gold and silver in the world couldn't compare to the temptation of peerless martial prowess. Qi Fengge had once been able to freely roam the jianghu because of his status as the strongest in the land, and all had to quail beneath his every breath. What awe-inspiring might! Wasn't that how a true man should be?

As for the Tai'e sword, it had once been the priceless national treasure of Chu and was later obtained by the Emperor of Qin. The sword had always been regarded as a symbol of benevolent rule, so although it was an outstanding blade in its own right, its significance went far beyond that of a mere weapon. Legend said that those who held this sword would rule the world; it was equivalent in meaning to the Qin Dynasty's famous Heirloom Seal of the Realm.[2] So both Southern Chen and Northern Zhou were paying close attention to this year's Coiling Dragon Assembly—they'd even sent men to monitor the situation.

Regardless of their objectives, one thing was certain: there were quite a few people on the same journey as Shen Qiao. There wasn't a vacancy to be found in any of the city's inns. Seeing this, Shen Qiao decided to hurry along his way and rest in a town outside the city instead.

To his surprise, however, notable men from all over the land were everywhere. Not only did he see practitioners from the many major sects, but even the ordinary, little-known sects had all sent dispatches. Some of them were here to watch the bustle and broaden their knowledge while others wanted to see if they could profit off the commotion. As Shen Qiao walked onward and the curtain of night fell, even the small towns outside Chang'an seemed to be packed full of travelers.

He went to inn after inn, and each one told him that even the woodsheds were occupied, leaving him at a loss. With his poor eyesight, though he could make out some vague approximations by the light of day, the moment night arrived, he couldn't see a thing. This made camping in the wilderness difficult. How unexpected that the long journey from Mount Tai to Chang'an had gone so smoothly, and it was only once he reached a large city like Chang'an that he was plagued with troubles.

---

2    传国玉玺. *The fabled imperial seal from the Qin Dynasty.*

"Apologies to the Daoist master—we're currently completely booked. We even have guests sleeping in the woodshed. We truly cannot make more room for your esteemed self!" The inn's concierge wrung his hands, a pained smile on his face.

Shen Qiao was just about to ask again when a sweet voice came from beside him. "This one has already reserved a main room—it's quite spacious enough. If the Daoist master doesn't mind, he can share a bed with me."

The interior of the inn was jostling with people. Those who were close to him raised their heads to see a gorgeous beauty gazing flirtatiously at a sickly priest and were instantly displeased.

Someone mockingly said, "If the young maiden is feeling lonely, she should at least find a stronger man! That priest looks like he'd be blown over by a stiff breeze. Are you sure he'll be able to manage?"

At these words, a smattering of laughter rose from beside them.

The beauty smiled sweetly. "But this one likes handsome priests like this Daoist master and not perverted, rotten men!"

She had barely finished talking when the man who'd been mocking them cried out. He grabbed his head, too shocked to speak—half of his hair had suddenly gone missing.

The beauty laughed. "This one is in a good mood today, having encountered an old friend. I'd rather not see any bloodshed. You lot should really try to behave yourselves. Otherwise, if my old friend ignores me for this, you'll be in big trouble."

While this conversation was unfolding, Shen Qiao had already left the inn without looking back.

"Who the hell are you?!" shouted the man who'd lost half his hair, full of false bravado.

But the beauty had no interest in bothering with them any longer.

She vanished with a flash, leaving behind only a fragrant aroma where she'd once stood.

"This one is Little Peony; is it not a lovely name?"

Her voice still lingered in their ears. Everyone looked at each other, appalled. "Hehuan Sect's Bai Rong?! Why has that demoness come here?!"

Leaving the inn, Bai Rong saw that the man ahead of her had already become a silhouette in the distance. She gritted her teeth despite herself and chased after him with her qinggong. "Shen Qiao! You stay right there!" she yelled.

Perhaps he'd heard her because that silhouette finally stopped moving.

Shen Qiao turned around and sighed quietly. "What advice do you have for me?"

Bai Rong had grown up in Hehuan Sect, where she had seen the deepest treacheries of the human heart, the vilest faces of human beings. She'd believed she'd turned her heart into stone a long time ago, that nothing could move her anymore. But at this moment, faced with Shen Qiao's grudging and reluctant expression, a strong burst of indignation surged through her heart.

"Daoist Master Shen is so callous in his relationships!" she spat. "The day you were hiding in Bailong Monastery, we searched for you on my master's orders. If I hadn't bought you time then, you wouldn't be standing here today! Is this how you repay others for their kindness?!"

When Shen Qiao didn't respond, she couldn't help but give an icy laugh. "Or does Daoist Master Shen blame me for the deaths of those two priests? Back then, one of our elders was right there, and Xiao Se was even more hostile, ready to jump on any mistakes I made. Did you want me to implicate myself for two strangers I'd never met before?"

Shen Qiao shook his head. "I indeed must thank you for what happened that day. But it's also true that Zhu-xiong and Chuyi died, and this was an evil committed by Hehuan Sect. All grudges have their sources, and debts their debtors. I'll have them repay it sooner or later. What has already happened cannot be undone; it's meaningless to mire ourselves in who was right or wrong."

Bai Rong bit her lip and remained quiet for a moment.

"I heard that you destroyed all your martial arts in the hope of taking my master down with you," she said, "and that you were gravely injured by him and almost lost your life. Are...are you all right now?"

"I'm well," said Shen Qiao. "Thank you for your concern."

"Shizun also suffered grievous injuries," said Bai Rong. "He's afraid that Yuan Xiuxiu will take the chance to finish him off, so he's hidden himself somewhere to cultivate. No one knows where he is."

"Not even you?"

Bai Rong gave a wan smile. "What? Did you think he really trusted me?"

Shen Qiao knew that there was a good chance she was affecting this expression to win his sympathy, but he truly couldn't bring himself to castigate her.

"I know you want to take revenge on Shizun," said Bai Rong softly. "However, even if I did know where he was, I couldn't let you go to your death like that. Right now, you're not his match at all."

Shen Qiao nodded. "Thank you for telling me. However, I have no plans to look for him at the moment."

"Then who are you looking for?" said Bai Rong. "Are you going to attend the Coiling Dragon Assembly in Tuyuhun's royal capital? You wish to save Yan Wushi?"

She'd always been enormously intelligent—naturally she'd already guessed what Shen Qiao had come for.

When Shen Qiao didn't answer, Bai Rong sighed. "Shen-lang, do you know what you're doing? True, Yan Wushi might have attained the pinnacle of martial arts. Few people in the world can take him on. But a joint assault from five of the land's most powerful martial artists? Even if he were a god from Daluo's immortal realm, he would have no chance of surviving. And remember what he did to you! How can you just put that behind you? Even a cat or dog would keep their distance from someone who hurt them over and over, wouldn't they? Do your feelings for him truly run that deep?"

Shen Qiao frowned. "Am I only allowed to save him out of personal feelings?"

"Then why must you risk your life for him if you don't feel anything?" pressed Bai Rong. "No matter how strong you are, you can't win if it's one against five. It's not just you: Yan Wushi can't, my shizun can't, and even if Qi Fengge were revived, he couldn't! The Coiling Dragon Assembly is on the ninth of September, but the ambush is on the eighth, and today is already the fifth! Even if you rush there now, you won't make it in time!"

Shen Qiao was silent. When she saw this, even the unflagging smile on Bai Rong's face took on a touch of anger. "Don't you get it?" she begged. "I don't want to see you throw away your life!"

Bai Rong had feelings for him. Shen Qiao wasn't made of wood; naturally, he knew.

Bai Rong was the type to care only for her own interests—she would never risk her life or betray her sect simply because she loved Shen Qiao. She wouldn't even disobey her master or elders for his sake. The most she'd do was extend Shen Qiao some slight conveniences, lift a finger or two, as long as it didn't hurt her interests. This much was already remarkable for her.

But she didn't understand Shen Qiao, and Shen Qiao had no inclination to explain any further. He didn't want Bai Rong to misunderstand—it was best for her if he drew a clear line between them right here and now.

"Thank you for your advice, but I still must go." He stared at Bai Rong. "In the eyes of outsiders, Hehuan Sect is ruthless and treacherous, consuming even the bones of those they destroy. But you take to it like a fish to water."

"So, in the end, a demoness like me is only worth your disdain."

Shen Qiao shook his head. "You've misunderstood. All I mean is that I know you'd never be content to stay an ordinary disciple in Hehuan Sect. I have no right to demand anything of you, but I hope that you'll take good care of yourself and avoid becoming someone like Huo Xijing or Sang Jingxing. You're different from them."

*You're different from them.* Bai Rong's eyes prickled at those simple words, but she showed no trace of it, smiling sweetly instead. "Then you should come see me from time to time. Supervise me to make sure I don't end up like them!"

"I'm sorry," was all Shen Qiao said, and he turned right around and left.

Bai Rong stamped her foot. "Shen Qiao!"

But with a "Rainbow Stretches across the Heavens," Shen Qiao was already like a distant swan, with nary a trace of dust left in his wake. In the blink of an eye, he was already dozens of yards away, the wide sleeves of his Daoist robe fluttering as he glided farther and farther, never looking back.

• • •

The eighth of September. Fuqi, the royal capital of Tuyuhun.

Throughout the year, the Western Regions saw more windblown sands than rain, but this year had been somewhat unusual: there was a continuous drizzle since the beginning of autumn. Even the buildings of the royal capital, normally caked in dust year-round, now looked refreshed beyond recognition.

With the influence of the culture of the Central Plains, the nobles and royals of Tuyuhun all spoke and wrote using Han characters, and even the Han style of dress was widely adopted. Furthermore, as the Coiling Dragon Assembly drew near, it brought many people from the Central Plains to the city. At first glance, it was almost like being back in Chang'an.

Outside the city was a pavilion, meant as shelter from the rain. It was called Yinyang Pavilion. No one knew when it'd been constructed, but with mountains on the left and waters on the right, and the pavilion directly in the middle, it was exactly like a boundary between the Yin and the Yang.

The pavilion was in the style of the Central Plains. Only in the corners of its eaves could one find a hint of a more exotic aesthetic. With the passing of so many years, even the words "Yinyang Pavilion" had mostly peeled off, revealing the wood's original texture and color beneath the fading black paint.

Yan Wushi stood at the center of the pavilion, his hands clasped behind him. It was unclear how long he'd been standing there.

He gazed out of the pavilion, his posture languid and carefree. He seemed to be watching the rain, but also like he was waiting for someone.

In the distance, a single man emerged from the wet trees and brush.

The man wore a black monk's robe, and his head was completely smooth and bare. Though his face was extraordinarily handsome, faint lines showed at the corners of his eyes. With an umbrella in hand, he walked toward Yan Wushi at a sedate pace.

"Amitabha. Has Sect Leader Yan been well?"

He spoke casually, as if he were having an everyday conversation, but his voice rang crisp and clear across the landscape, unwaning despite the distance.

"You haven't grown a single hair since we parted at Chuyun Temple," Yan Wushi said coolly. "Truly, your days must be full of troubles and worries—a vexing and unhappy life. Is the contented life of an ordinary monk that difficult for you?"

Buddhist Master Xueting forced a smile at Yan Wushi's cutting sarcasm. "Sect Leader Yan's words are as unforgiving as always!"

"The one who invited me was Duan Wenyang, so why have you appeared instead? Unless the great and mighty former State Preceptor of Zhou has abandoned himself to the point of colluding with the Göktürks?"

"Sect Leader Yan's reappearance in the jianghu has stirred up a storm of violence and bloodshed," said Buddhist Master Xueting. "You've disturbed all peace. In this humble monk's opinion, you should find a place to direct your energies toward meditating on your martial arts, lest more murder and evil arises from your hands."

Yan Wushi burst into noisy laughter. "I've always hated how you do nothing but spew Buddhist doctrines, you bald donkey. But today you've smartened up; you've dropped all the nonsense and cut straight to the chase. Good!"

Buddhist Master Xueting lowered his head and lashes. "Buddha urges us toward kindness, to drop our cleavers and seek enlightenment. But for those who refuse to repent despite repeated teachings, he can also demonstrate the thunderous might of Vajrapani. What use is there in preaching the truths of Buddhism to someone like

Sect Leader Yan? We can only subdue you with force and stop a killer by killing you ourselves."

"Let me guess the reason you agreed to ambush me together with Duan Wenyang," said Yan Wushi. "Yuwen Yong refuses to elevate Buddhism, so you sent men to infiltrate the Göktürks, day after day. Eventually, even Taspar Khagan converted to Buddhism, but the Göktürks have the dispositions of wolves and tigers: fierce and ruthless. The influence of Buddhism remained limited, and your only option was to return your attention to Northern Zhou.

"Yuwen Yong is incredibly wary of Buddhism. Even if you destroyed Huanyue Sect, he'd never re-elevate Buddhism. So your best bet was to kill me first, then kill Yuwen Yong, then have the crown prince Yuwen Yun ascend, and, finally, you'd pledge allegiance to him. Yuwen Yun is different from his father—he's very fond of Buddhism. The years you spent constantly appealing to him weren't in vain! The moment he comes to power, Buddhism will once again regain its former glory in Northern Zhou."

Buddhist Master Xueting invoked one of Buddha's names. "Yuwen Yong revels in war and slaughter," he said. "He exploits the people and squanders wealth; he's not an enlightened ruler in the slightest. His war on Qi this time has taxed the entire country even further. It's only a matter of time before the masses collapse beneath the strain."

"So, you're saying that you believe the crown prince Yuwen Yun to be the true enlightened ruler instead?" asked Yan Wushi, deeply amused.

Buddhist Master Xueting replied simply, "The crown prince both deeply reveres and understands Buddhism. It is in his destiny to become a buddha."

A smile slowly spread over Yan Wushi's face. "To think you could lie through your teeth when Yuwen Yun is like that! Amazing.

You just want to kill me, right? Well then, bring it on! Where's Duan Wenyang? Tell him to get over here!"

As his words fell, a bright laugh pierced through the air. "How egotistical of Sect Leader Yan. Has he never thought that today might become the day he dies?"

# 54

# Yan Wushi's Death

"**B**ALD OLD DONKEY**,**" sneered Yan Wushi. "You've been praised as one of the world's three best martial artists, yet you have to rope in Duan Wenyang to kill me? Aren't you ashamed of yourself?"

Buddhist Master Xueting's expression remained indifferent. "As long as Sect Leader Yan dies today, my reputation is of little importance. You're too superficial, Sect Leader Yan."

Yan Wushi burst out laughing. "If you had to find a helper from the Göktürks, why didn't you just summon Hulugu's ghost here instead? What can a sad little Duan Wenyang do to my venerable self?"

"Sect Leader Yan really shouldn't boast too much," Duan Wenyang warned him. "Otherwise, if you end up losing your life here today, you'll be left with no face even in the underworld."

Speaking didn't hinder his attacks in the slightest. In the blink of an eye, the silhouettes of his whip were already blotting out the sky as they descended, sealing off all of Yan Wushi's escape routes from above.

Duan Wenyang's first whip had long since been destroyed during his fights against Li Qingyu and Shen Qiao. The one he held now was newly made, named Shizhang Ruanhong.[3] No less time had

---

3  十丈软红. Literally "Thirty Yards of Gentle Red." Here, the "red" refers to the secular world.

been spent on the crafting of this whip than on the first, and perhaps it was even more durable. With a slight flick of Duan Wenyang's wrist, its shape flowed and transformed, giving rise to thousands of mirages, enough to dazzle the eye and leave onlookers confounded.

It was obvious: his strength had grown immensely since his duels with Li Qingyu and Shen Qiao at the Su residence.

No matter who it was, as long as they weren't mediocre, no one was content to be ordinary; they would strive to continually improve themselves. This might be true for oneself, but it would hold true for one's enemies as well.

Duan Wenyang's whip techniques were the uncanny and un-predictable type, and the saber techniques of the Western Regions had been woven in as well. These two sets of techniques combined into a raging sandstorm: boundless and never-ending, engulfing its opponent from the front and suffocating them in despair until they lost all will to fight.

But his opponent was Yan Wushi.

Yan Wushi was unarmed. However, his fingers became as a sword before the two great martial artists of this generation, and under the command of his true qi, the petals and leaves fluttering around them transformed into thousands of razor-sharp knives, obliterating every single one of Duan Wenyang's attacks.

Buddhist Master Xueting was a man of little expression. He appeared even godlier than the buddha statues within the temples: devoid of joy or anger and completely unmoved by the outside world.

At this moment, even as he saw Duan Wenyang thwarted, he expressed neither surprise nor fury. Instead, he pushed his palms out evenly away from him. As his true qi condensed, those ten fingers, already exceptionally pale, seemed to faintly glow with the brilliance of colored glaze. Xueting's face, too, seemed to tint with the slight shimmer of moonlight, as beautiful as a jade carving.

His "Acala Seals" totaled six. Just before, he'd struck with three of them, one after another, yet they were ineffective on Yan Wushi. Now he was using the fourth and fifth gestures: "Immovable as a Mountain" and "Plucking a Flower, a Tacit Smile."

The former was a defensive move in place of an attack; the latter focused on countering strength with softness. Within his hands, the complicated, ever-changing strikes became extraordinarily beautiful and pleasing to the eye, enough to make one drop their guard unconsciously.

When he sent out the "Immovable as a Mountain" seal, a buzzing whine sounded in everyone's ears, and their minds blanked momentarily—even the whip in Duan Wenyang's hands unknowingly stilled for an instant. Yan Wushi, however, remained completely unaffected and even gave a cold laugh. Ignoring Xueting's mudra, its pose like plucking a flower as it swept toward him from behind, he reached out for Duan Wenyang's whip as before. His hand passed through the thickly woven mesh of afterimages like it was nothing and actually caught the whip barehanded. Then, with a yank and a twist, he turned around, redirecting the force and sending every ounce of Duan Wenyang's true qi toward Buddhist Master Xueting!

Xueting pushed off the ground with a tap of his foot, and his body instantly drifted several yards back. Despite fighting two against one, Yan Wushi didn't retreat and actually chased after him, and, as they came face-to-face, their palms met.

A strong force against a strong force. The true qi from two martial artist grandmasters came into inevitable confrontation with a devastating conclusion: a split second later came a roaring explosion, and a vortex swept up around the two combatants, one that hungered to swallow all of creation within it. Duan Wenyang only felt a powerful turbulence engulf him from the front, and he was forced to withdraw his whip and retreat five or six steps back. Only then did he escape its terrifying impact.

But neither of the two people within moved a single step. The fallen leaves beneath their feet were pulled into the air by their true qi and left dancing in the wind.

Xueting gazed at Yan Wushi, expressionless, when suddenly a powerful truth swelled up within his heart: if he couldn't kill this man today, he'd probably never have the chance again!

As a grandmaster, Xueting naturally had a grandmaster's pride. If possible, he'd of course prefer a fair and honorable one-on-one duel with Yan Wushi, but upon him weighed a heavy duty: the renewal of Buddhism. And Yan Wushi was his greatest obstacle; only with Yan Wushi gone could Buddhism return to its previous standing within Northern Zhou. He absolutely could not lose this battle!

Yan Wushi suddenly smiled at him. It was an inexplicable and uncanny smile, and Xueting couldn't help but furrow his brow.

The next moment, instead of continuing to engage him, Yan Wushi turned right around and dove at Duan Wenyang.

At this time, Duan Wenyang's Shizhang Ruanhong was held high above him as he brought it down toward Yan Wushi's head.

The whip's momentum was like a thousand-ton weight, and, suffused with Duan Wenyang's true qi, it became an arc of white light.

But he hadn't expected that Yan Wushi would suddenly drop Buddhist Master Xueting and walk toward him instead.

And he really did walk. His steps were as calm and unhurried as if he were taking an idle stroll. But within a few short steps, he'd already moved from next to Buddhist Master Xueting to where Duan Wenyang stood. Then he reached out, grabbing that white arc directly.

It was a bizarre movement—it looked slow, but he grasped the whip's body with precise accuracy. And just like that, Shizhang Ruanhong was clutched within his hand while the hand itself remained completely unharmed.

Duan Wenyang's expression shifted. Before he could react, the other man's fingers clamped down, and the whip that Duan Wenyang had spent so much painstaking effort to create was crushed to fragments within his grip!

"Did your shifu never teach you that all weapons will amount to nothing before a true expert?" A savage smile hung at the corner of Yan Wushi's lips. As he spoke, his hand was already sliding down the crushed whip toward Duan Wenyang's arm.

That hand would have been able to grab a normal person, but Duan Wenyang was no ordinary man. He didn't waste any time mourning his whip—the moment it was destroyed, he'd already released it, and he struck at Yan Wushi's chest with his other hand.

At the same time, Buddhist Master Xueting's attack had also arrived: his "Acala Seal" was already approaching the center of Yan Wushi's back. He'd begun after Duan Wenyang, yet somehow, he was even faster!

Yan Wushi didn't move his feet, but his body vanished into thin air right before Duan Wenyang. But Duan Wenyang knew this was only a misdirection—it was impossible for a person to disappear without a trace in such a short amount of time, so he didn't slow his attack in the slightest.

Yet still, his palm actually missed!

How could there be a qinggong of such incredible speed?

Duan Wenyang was in complete disbelief.

On the other end, Yan Wushi and Xueting's palms met a second time.

The force behind this clash was even stronger. The trees nearby shuddered with the force of their true qi, cracks snaking up their trunks at a speed visible to the naked eye.

This time, both Yan Wushi and Buddhist Master Xueting fell back three steps.

*Is that man a monster?!* was the thought that flashed through Duan Wenyang's mind as he witnessed Yan Wushi's skills firsthand.

He'd always boasted of himself as being supremely talented, that even his master Hulugu couldn't have been better than him at the same age, but after encountering the almost-inhuman entity known as Yan Wushi, he'd been beset with continuous setbacks. Back then, when he'd heard of the wretched picture his shidi Kunye had made as Yan Wushi chased him around, he'd even laughed at Kunye's incompetence. But looking at himself now, it seemed he wasn't faring much better.

And he was even working together with a top-class grandmaster like Xueting, one of the top three in the world. Yet they still couldn't kill one single Yan Wushi?!

"The technique he just used was 'Body to Shadow, Phase and Replace.'" This voice rang within Duan Wenyang's ears—the speaker had sent the sound directly to him so that only he could hear, but it wasn't an unfamiliar voice. "When one achieves ultimate mastery over it, even a horizon-spanning distance will appear to be little more than a few feet. He may seem to be very close to you, but in reality, he never approached you at all. His focus has always been on that monk Xueting over there. Don't let him confuse you."

The voice had just finished when a sword suddenly materialized to the left of Yan Wushi.

And together with that sword came a few sporadic notes from a zither.

Purple sword glares fell like a shroud, their light flooding everywhere in perfect harmony with the zither. Using the zither's notes as a medium, the player tore right through the dense armor of true qi Yan Wushi had constructed, taking advantage of Yan Wushi's focus on fighting Xueting. This attack was sourced from the same branch of demonic arts as Yan Wushi's, and thanks to that commonality, it found a tiny crack within his defenses.

The instant that crack was revealed, the piercing sword glares arrived, directly targeting Yan Wushi!

"The *Fenglin Scriptures* have a flaw. The stronger one grows, the more devastating this flaw becomes. Yan Wushi has reached the ninth stage, and because of this flaw, he's unable to progress any further to achieve the highest echelon of true perfection. If we wish to kill him, now is the time!"

It was Guang Lingsan's voice, bright and clear, but his actual person was nowhere to be found. Perhaps he'd arrived a long while ago and remained in hiding this entire time, waiting for the right moment to maximize the confounding effect of his zither.

Out of all present at the scene, the one most qualified to remark on Yan Wushi's martial arts could only be another practitioner of the demonic discipline, and the Fajing Sect Leader.

Indeed, the purple sword glares surged forth with unstoppable momentum and pierced right through Yan Wushi's clothes. His back was instantly dyed with a bloom of crimson.

Yan Wushi snorted a laugh. "A bunch of trash! My venerable self has no interest in playing with you lot anymore!"

With that, he turned and sent a strike at Yu Ai's Junzi Buqi. Its sword glare wavered a little but continued its rush toward him.

The zither's melody suddenly transformed, escalating from sedate to fervently impassioned!

Guang Lingsan yelled, "The flaw in his demonic core has appeared!"

Before he'd even finished his words, someone appeared close by and sent a swift gust from his palm at Yan Wushi!

Meanwhile, Xueting's hands came together to form the last seal, his hands twisting and turning: this was the final form of his "Acala Seals," the "Crimson Lotus of Fiery Retribution"!

The flames of retribution came forth in the shape of crimson lotuses, as vast as the sea or the sky, boundless and unending. They surged like raging tides, blazing intensely, incinerating away all the world's delusions.

A small crack finally appeared in Yan Wushi's true qi, so dense and perfect in its construction.

The flames of retribution licked inside, wave upon wave. They forced the crack to expand, then finally ripped it open completely, went straight for his demonic core, and tore it out, roots and all!

The next moment, five slender, pale fingers slammed hard into Yan Wushi's chest.

A small trickle of blood seeped from the corner of his mouth.

But with this, his expression, too, became vicious. His sleeve flapped toward Buddhist Master Xueting, sending along a powerful blast of internal energy and forcing him to evade its edge. Buddhist Master Xueting swept half a step back.

That half step was enough. Yan Wushi turned around and grabbed the blade stabbed into his body in a barehanded grip, then gave it a forceful twist. And just as he'd crushed Duan Wenyang's whip before, Junzi Buqi's blade actually shattered into pieces. Then he crooked his fingers and went straight for Yu Ai's face. The two of them exchanged dozens of blows in an instant, and right at that moment, Dou Yanshan struck forth with another palm, slamming it right into an unguarded spot in the center of Yan Wushi's back.

*Success!*

Dou Yanshan hadn't dared to get his hopes up, and so he was delighted by this unexpected turn of events. He'd put all his strength into this strike, and Yan Wushi had taken it straight on—it was impossible for him to endure unscathed.

With these two strikes from Buddhist Master Xueting and Dou Yanshan, the pressure on Duan Wenyang and Yu Ai was greatly reduced.

Though Guang Lingsan hadn't shown himself at all, the contribution of his zither music wasn't insignificant. He was the one who'd discovered the flaw left behind by Yan Wushi's qi deviation through his duel with Ruyan Kehui, and taking advantage of it, they struck right at the root.

Noticing Buddhist Master Xueting's lack of follow-up—instead he only stood at the side, watching—Dou Yanshan also stayed his hand and asked, "Why did the Great Master stop?"

"Though Yan Wushi and I stand on opposing sides, there is no personal grudge between us. We had no choice but to conduct this ambush, but regardless, an opponent like him deserves to be respected. He doesn't deserve to die here, not like this."

Dou Yanshan sneered internally. *If you were truly virtuous, then why participate in this ambush?* But he didn't express his feelings, only smiled. "The Great Master is truly a man of noble character!"

As if he could see into his thoughts, Buddhist Master Xueting said coolly, "Guild Leader Dou should know this: even if Yan Wushi dies, the *Zhuyang Strategy* scroll he destroyed will not return."

Dou Yanshan gave a chuckle. "Yan Wushi alone has set the entire world astir. If he dies, everyone will be at peace, and Buddhism can flourish—I must congratulate you, Great Master!"

As the two of them spoke, Yan Wushi was struck by another palm.

He needed to leave, but with his weakness revealed, the zither's notes were now clouding his mind. Combined with the internal injuries he'd accumulated—caused by the two palm strikes from before, and the way Yu Ai and Duan Wenyang continued to press their attacks—his defensive true qi had finally collapsed completely. Then, two more blows struck him.

Of course, Yu Ai and Duan Wenyang weren't doing much better either: Yu Ai's sword was broken, and he'd taken three strikes to the chest. His face was ghastly pale as he stumbled back several steps, then finally fell to the ground. Duan Wenyang's whip had been destroyed, and he was suffering from internal injuries. Several of his ribs were broken, and he coughed up many mouthfuls of blood.

And yet, under these circumstances, Yan Wushi still had the strength to escape, and his body became a blur of afterimages. Both Dou Yanshan's and Guang Lingsan's faces twisted in alarm, but it was already too late for them to stop him.

At that moment, Xueting vanished from where he was standing. Pushing his qinggong to the utmost, he blocked Yan Wushi directly. The power of his "Acala Seals" forced Yan Wushi to take the attack head-on, and with this he lost his last chance to escape. However, this time Xueting fell back more than five steps, and his face instantly went bright red, then swiftly changed to a ghastly white—he'd forced himself to swallow down the blood bubbling up in his mouth.

Yan Wushi burst into laughter.

But then that laughter ceased abruptly, and he hacked up a huge mouthful of fresh blood.

And Dou Yanshan flung himself at him, striking a palm right against the Baihui acupoint on the crown of Yan Wushi's head!

With this strike, Yan Wushi finally toppled to the ground, unmoving.

Buddhist Master Xueting furrowed his brows, but in the end said nothing. He watched as Yan Wushi's eyes slowly slid closed, then quietly chanted one of Buddha's names. Putting his hands together, he bowed in the fallen man's direction, then simply turned and left without another glance.

Yu Ai and Duan Wenyang were both seriously injured. Seeing that Yan Wushi had no hope of surviving, they left one after the other to treat their wounds.

Dou Yanshan crouched to examine the body carefully. After confirming that there was no breath, he finally revealed a smile and turned to Guang Lingsan as he walked out holding his zither. "Congratulations, Sect Leader Guang! The day you unify the three sects is just around the corner."

"Thank you for your kind words, Guild Leader Dou. Are you certain that Yan Wushi is dead?"

"Of course. I shattered his skull with that blow. Plus, all his internal organs are ruptured and bleeding from those strikes earlier. His life has ended; there's no way he can survive."

Guang Lingsan smiled. "The demonic discipline has a technique called 'From the Heavens Above to the Earth Below,'" he said. "Right before the practitioner's life is about to end, they destroy their body and enter a state of false death while preserving a small chance of survival for themselves. The only issue is that learning this technique is terribly painful, and normally, it has limited usefulness. Hence, few people try to learn it."

"Is Sect Leader Guang worried that Yan Wushi has also learned this technique?" asked Dou Yanshan.

"Since we've already gone this far, it's better if we take the time to thoroughly confirm things. There is no harm in being certain."

He walked toward Yan Wushi and reached for his wrist.

A sheathed sword appeared, held lengthwise before him.

This sword was plain to the point of being crude: there was nothing extraordinary about it, save for the four characters engraved next to the hilt—"Shanhe Tongbei."

Guang Lingsan's expression flickered. He didn't even know when the other party had appeared.

"He may have made enemies everywhere when he was alive, their numbers uncountable, but he was still a grandmaster of his generation," said this new arrival. "The dead are to be revered above all. Isn't it rather inappropriate to be doing this to an opponent who deserves your respect?"

Dou Yanshan narrowed his eyes and ground out the newcomer's name, syllable by syllable: "Shen! Qiao!"

# To Repay Evil with Virtue

**S**HEN QIAO NODDED at the two of them. "Have you both been well?"

After his initial surprise, Guang Lingsan composed himself and scrutinized Shen Qiao carefully. "I heard that Daoist Master Shen fought with Sang Jingxing and injured him gravely. I didn't expect you to recover so quickly. What wonderful news!"

No one else had been present at their fight, and, having been seriously wounded by Shen Qiao, of course Sang Jingxing wouldn't have gone around announcing what had happened. But Guang Lingsan was a member of the demonic sects, so naturally he could obtain news others couldn't.

Hearing this, Dou Yanshan was also secretly astonished, and he re-evaluated Shen Qiao's strength.

Shen Qiao shook his head. "I can't say that I've fully recovered."

These words were completely true, but it was hard to believe him. Though martial arts placed heavy emphasis on arduous training, every sect and discipline had their own carefully guarded secrets. Furthermore, Shen Qiao was Qi Fengge's disciple—who knew if Qi Fengge had passed down some sort of divine martial arts manual to him?

Guang Lingsan smiled. "When it comes to how Sect Leader Yan treated you, Daoist Master Shen, others might know little, but I do know some. I heard it was all thanks to Sect Leader Yan that your duel with Sang Jingxing happened in the first place."

"That is correct," said Shen Qiao.

"He was cold and callous toward you, just like he was to everyone else."

"Yes."

"I'm sure you didn't cross such great distances just to retrieve his body—you must have come to rescue him. Unfortunately, you're a step too late."

Shen Qiao answered each of his questions. "Correct."

Guang Lingsan finally showed a trace of surprise. "Exactly what about Yan Wushi deserves you going this far? Is it really like the rumors say? That the two of you have another, more private relationship?"

"I'm not acting out of personal feelings," Shen Qiao said coolly. "I'm saving Yan Wushi for the greater good."

Dou Yanshan began laughing, unable to hold back his expression of contemptuous amusement. "This is the first time I've heard Yan Wushi's name in the same sentence as the words 'greater good'! Are you saying that the moment Yan Wushi dies, the greater good will cease to exist?"

"Yan Wushi isn't a good person," said Shen Qiao, "but as he assists the Lord of Zhou, he can be considered one of his supporters. Each of you might have killed him for your own reasons, but in the end, isn't that at the core of it all? His support for Yuwen Yong's Northern Zhou conflicts with all of your interests, hence you must eliminate him. But I believe that the only one who can put an end to this chaos is Yuwen Yong, and that is where we disagree."

Dou Yanshan shook his head. "Shen Qiao, you are one of the Han, yet you support one of the Xianbei? No wonder Xuandu Mountain judged you unsuitable for sect leader."

Shen Qiao gave a smile. "I take it Guild Leader Dou has never found himself in a situation where countless others oppose your views. As long as I believe something's worth doing, why does it matter what others see or think? Anyone with true fondness for you, the friends and family who have your best interests at heart, will eventually understand where you're coming from."

"Since Yan Wushi is already dead," said Guang Lingsan, "there's nothing for you to do here. How we wish to deal with his corpse shouldn't hinder you in any way, so why must you interfere?"

Shen Qiao frowned. "Once someone dies, everything dies with them, just like a lamp flame being extinguished. No matter what, he was a grandmaster of his generation. As his acquaintance, I wish to retrieve his body for a proper burial. I hope that the two of you will grant me this."

Guang Lingsan shook his head. "We put all our strength and effort into killing Yan Wushi, so naturally we wish to confirm that he's truly dead, with no chance of coming back. Let me cut off his head first—you can still take his body with you later."

"And if I say no?" said Shen Qiao.

"Daoist Master Shen is indeed a handsome man, but unfortunately, neither Guild Leader Dou nor I are interested in men," he said, a smile remaining on his face. "I'm afraid we won't show you any tender feelings."

With a toss of his hand, the zither in his arms flipped over, and he drew a longsword from it with his other hand. In a flash, the blade's point was already before Shen Qiao's face!

Shen Qiao drifted back and drew Shanhe Tongbei.

Two streams of sword qi clashed in an unavoidable confrontation. At once, a white ray pierced the sun, like the herald for a grand omen, sharp enough to slice right through metal and as harsh as snow and frost. It was only the beginning of autumn, yet Dou Yanshan suddenly felt the slam of cutting wind and freezing rain against his face, and he shivered internally, taking an unconscious step back. He realized quickly how shameful his actions were, but soon he felt another burst of intense alarm.

When this former sect leader of Xuandu Mountain became your opponent, he wouldn't be the weak pushover kind of opponent.

In fact, it wasn't only Dou Yanshan who was shocked. Within Guang Lingsan's heart, too, a tempestuous storm had long begun brewing.

He'd met Shen Qiao only a few times—strictly speaking, only twice. The first time was when Shen Qiao had exhausted his strength in repelling Bai Rong, so he'd been completely powerless by the time Guang Lingsan had appeared. Furthermore, he'd been blind, so it was obvious how severe his injuries were—on the brink of being irreparable. But now he saw him again, though Shen Qiao still looked feeble as before, the moment he drew his sword, his entire person transformed like a sickly tree that had suddenly begun glowing with new splendor, its withered branches returning to life. It was oppressively dazzling, brilliant and magnificent.

No, at this moment, Shen Qiao himself was a sharp sword!

The sword intent undulated like shimmering ripples—it appeared soft, but it was endless and everywhere, omnipresent. Not only did it shatter Guang Lingsan's sword glare, it weaved itself into a dense net, enveloping both Guang Lingsan and Shen Qiao within.

If you can conquer the hardest of all things in the world with the softest, then nothing in the world will be your match. Man and sword finally became one and the same; never again would any flaws be found.

Was this the true power of Xuandu Mountain's sect leader, of Qi Fengge's disciple?!

Guang Lingsan didn't often wield a sword—he was used to his zither—but his skill with the sword was still effortlessly superior to most. However, at this moment, faced with Shen Qiao's airtight defenses and offense, a sense of helplessness suddenly welled up within him—he didn't even know where to begin striking.

He was willing to make a bet: forget about him. Even if a true sword master were here, they would feel exactly the same as he did!

Guang Lingsan decisively abandoned his sword for his zither. Taking advantage of the brief time he'd bought by retreating from the sword net, he crooked his fingers and grabbed behind his back. In the blink of an eye, the zither he'd been carrying on his back appeared within his hand. Its clanging notes surged toward Shen Qiao with the force of a thundering storm.

Dou Yanshan seemed to have noticed his impatience, for he no longer stood on the sidelines watching. Instead, he leapt into the air and aimed a strike at Shen Qiao.

Shen Qiao wasn't Yan Wushi, after all. There was no need to tirelessly strive for his death. Dou Yanshan's palm strike was only intended to overwhelm Shen Qiao, to fluster and confuse him, and in doing so force a loss.

But to his surprise, he found that when the harsh blast from his palm came within three feet of Shen Qiao, it was completely swallowed by his sword glare. It was like tossing a pebble into the ocean—when compared to the waves that already raged, the ripples from the pebble were smaller than small, practically negligible!

Instead, it was the sword glare that surged, expanding until it was about to reach Dou Yanshan's nose.

Both his and Guang Lingsan's martial arts were good enough to rank within the top ten. Even without using their full strength, the two of them working together were already more than enough to murder any regular man. However, Shen Qiao had been contending with them for a while, yet showed no signs of falling behind. It was clear just how terrifying and unfathomable his strength was. With his reappearance in the jianghu this time, he was truly someone you could not afford to offend.

If they continued the fight, a grudge was sure to form. The Liuhe Guild's business enterprises encompassed the entire land, and they believed that amiability was the key to prosperity. Dou Yanshan had participated in the ambush on Yan Wushi this time because there were others spearheading the assault and all he had to do was follow their lead. But Shen Qiao was different. Since there was no need to kill him, a martial expert like him could naturally give the Liuhe Guild countless headaches in the future.

Dou Yanshan weighed the pros and cons, then decisively chose to give up. Yan Wushi was almost certainly dead, and even Buddhist Master Xueting and Duan Wenyang had left. Don Yanshan had only participated to exact revenge on Yan Wushi for destroying the *Zhuyang Strategy* scroll, so giving his all here would mean heavy losses with little gain.

Having deliberated all of this, he gave a bright laugh, then resolutely retreated.

"Fighting two-on-one is a bit dishonest of us, so I won't interfere with Sect Leader Guang's entertainment any longer. I'll be taking my leave first; we'll meet some other day!"

Guang Lingsan had no right to denigrate Dou Yanshan's dishonesty. The five of them didn't have much of a relationship in the first place, and on top of that, they each held their own positions and interests. They could only gather together because of their shared goal of killing Yan Wushi. Now that Yan Wushi was dead and their goal achieved, their temporary cooperation had also come to an end.

But since everyone else was already gone, why was he still here, fighting so desperately against Shen Qiao when it was so strenuous and thankless?

Guang Lingsan glanced to the side. Yan Wushi was still lying there, bleeding from all the apertures of his face, unconscious and insensible. There was probably less chance of him surviving than of Qi Fengge coming back to life.

Thinking this, he too lost all interest in continuing with Shen Qiao. The zither's melody suddenly rose to a pitch. Shen Qiao's senses weren't blocked, and the momentum of his sword couldn't help but slow just a little. Guang Lingsan used this opportunity to extricate himself, sending a palm strike at Shen Qiao before swiftly gliding away.

"Daoist Master Shen is benevolent and kind. Yan Wushi may have had countless enemies, but having you as a friend is surely enough to let him rest in peace. What harm is there in assisting you in accomplishing your kind deeds?"

As soon he heard these words, Shen Qiao also withdrew his sword and stepped back. "My deep thanks to Sect Leader Guang!"

Guang Lingsan smiled and nodded at him, then turned and retreated.

After today's battle, news of Yan Wushi's death would soon spread throughout the jianghu. Having lost their backbone, Huanyue Sect would be unable to hold on for long with only Bian Yanmei and Yu Shengyan, and the balance of power between the three demonic sects would certainly change as well. Fajing Sect could take this chance to return to the Central Plains; there were still many things he had to do.

Shen Qiao remained standing in place, watching Guang Lingsan walk into the distance. Only then did he release a long sigh. Holding his chest, he forced the salty sweetness that had surged up into his throat back down.

No matter how incredible the *Zhuyang Strategy*'s true qi was, Shen Qiao hadn't been practicing it for long. It was already unbelievably fortunate that he'd been able to recover more than half his former martial prowess. Then he'd tried to fight one against two, and both his opponents were martial experts who ranked within the top ten. He'd already pushed his spent strength to the limit—a little more and he'd have given it away to Guang Lingsan. Luckily, neither Guang Lingsan nor Dou Yanshan had any interest in continuing the fight, and Shen Qiao's pre-emptive attack had dominated them so much that they'd believed his strength unfathomable.

Shen Qiao gave a bitter smile. After circulating his true qi for a long moment, his situation finally, slowly stabilized. He walked over to Yan Wushi and bent at the waist, reaching for his wrist.

His hand was cold and lifeless to the touch, without even the whisper of a pulse.

The pain and dismay he had felt at Yan Wushi tossing him to Sang Jingxing was still vivid in his mind. Carrying the blood debts of the abbot and Chuyi's lives, Shen Qiao had used all his strength to crawl inch by inch out of the netherworld. Trapped in a field of death, he'd fought his way to survival, like a phoenix passing into Nirvana. When he'd heard of the great danger this man was in, he finally came to the decision to discard all personal feelings between them and rushed here to his rescue. Yet in the end, he'd still been a step too late.

Shen Qiao gave a sigh and whispered, "Very well. Take care of yourself on your way to the netherworld."

No sooner had the words left his lips when the wrist he'd been loosely holding suddenly shifted, the movement almost imperceptible.

Shen Qiao froze for a moment. Before he realized what was going on, something grabbed *his* wrist!

# 56

# Rescue

THE MOVEMENT WAS TOO SUDDEN—even Shen Qiao was thoroughly stunned.

Since even Guang Lingsan had been so assured as to stroll off, it was obvious that Yan Wushi's chances of survival had been slim to none. In truth, he shouldn't still be alive at all. Shen Qiao was already prepared to bury him and erect a grave marker— he'd never expected something like this.

There was little force in Yan Wushi's grip, and it was as if he'd exhausted all his strength with that one action. As soon as his hand landed in Shen Qiao's, he let go and made no further movements. His eyes were still tightly closed, a lifeless gray pallor cast over his pale face. Blood still trickled from his body. Shen Qiao had never seen such a wretched state before; it was as if that motion just now was only his final struggle against the clutches of death.

Shen Qiao felt for Yan Wushi's heart. Just as he expected, the entire expanse beneath his palm was as cold as ice, without a shred of warmth. Shen Qiao attempted to pass a wisp of true qi into his body, but it immediately vanished into nothingness, as if he'd cast a clod of mud into the sea.

He untied Yan Wushi's hair and ran his fingers through the strands. Very quickly, he arrived at the area around the Baihui acupoint, and there he found an obvious crack.

An ordinary person would have certainly perished from an injury like this, but one could not argue that Yan Wushi was ordinary, after all. He'd fought one against five, and his opponents were five of the greatest martial artists in the world. There was even Buddhist Master Xueting, yet Yan Wushi had been able to hold his own even with a grandmaster like that among them. Though Shen Qiao had arrived a step too late to personally witness that fierce battle himself, he could imagine how marvelously incomparable it must have been.

The crack wasn't long, but it was very deep. The attacker must have used all of their strength. He pondered that blow: even though it was Yan Wushi, even if it hadn't ruptured his brain itself, it must have shattered his skull, leaving him no chance of survival.

Shen Qiao wasn't a doctor—he was completely helpless when faced with such a severe injury. He could only release Yan Wushi's hand, then begin probing the meridians of his body while carefully supporting the back of his neck.

His bones weren't broken, his meridians were intact. The fatal injury had been caused by the sword piercing through his chest, together with those palm strikes that had gravely damaged his internal organs. Finally, there was the wound on his head—the straw that broke the camel's back.

The more Shen Qiao examined him, the lower his heart sank.

Was there really no way to save him?

Then suddenly, he gave a sound of surprise.

A sound so faint, only he could hear it.

But it was a sound that betrayed just how surprised Shen Qiao was inside.

For he'd discovered that within Yan Wushi's Dantian, which should have long gone cold and been shattered, there was a tiny, almost imperceptible wisp of qi still quietly circulating there.

He thought for a moment, then decided to simply pull Yan Wushi's arm up, tug the man right onto his back, and head forward, step by step.

To Shen Qiao, the royal capital of Tuyuhun was an unfamiliar location. Wind carrying sand was said to blow here all year around, while the Gobi Desert stretched in all directions. The only city of any scale within dozens of miles of this area was the oasis where the royal capital was located. However, as one had to pass through here on the way to various nations of the Western Regions like Qocho and Khotan, it was impossible for the population to be entirely concentrated within the royal capital. Upon leaving the capital and heading west, if they looked down and into the distance, they'd find thinly scattered villages and houses everywhere.

The Gobi Desert was boundless, and even caverns to shelter from the sandstorms were rare. Not to mention that Shen Qiao was carrying what was basically a living corpse. Even resolving the issue of food and water was a massive problem. It was impossible to just search for a concealed cavern to hide in like in the Central Plains. No matter how much he didn't want to be found, he had no choice but to first find a place where people lived, yet which was far removed from the jianghu, and stay there.

Shen Qiao squinted for a long moment beneath the blinding sunlight, then finally chose a location in the distance. He headed in that direction, carrying Yan Wushi.

The royal capital of Tuyuhun, being populated with all sorts of people, was absolutely not somewhere they could remain. His only nearby options lay in the small, scattered villages around it.

Shen Qiao brought Yan Wushi to a village next to Zhaling Lake. Several dozen households were established there, and a main road used often by traveling merchants lay nearby—the occasional traveler would come and stay. Hence, it wasn't too bustling, but it also wasn't too remote, at least not so much that they'd be hostile to an outsider like Shen Qiao.

Shen Qiao chose this location primarily out of consideration for Yan Wushi's current state. If he still had a chance of survival, and Shen Qiao managed to save him, then for the time being such news could not be leaked. Yan Wushi had enemies everywhere—if someone like Guang Lingsan knew that Yan Wushi had survived, he'd definitely rush over to kill them both. Even Qi Fengge wouldn't be able to fend off that many martial experts by himself, let alone Shen Qiao, who'd only recovered a little more than half of his martial arts.

As night crept close, the village houses all lit lamps one after another, and Shen Qiao, carrying Yan Wushi, knocked on the door of one such house.

A young lady answered it. She wore a red dress, and a long braid draped over her shoulder. As was common for locals, long years beneath the sun had tanned her skin a soft bronze, but her features were neither rough nor ugly. She must have been prone to smiling, for whenever the corners of her lips pulled up, two dimples would appear on her cheeks. It was quite adorable.

Shen Qiao told her of his reason for knocking: his friend was injured, so he wished to stay here for a while to let him recuperate, and once he was better, they'd leave—they absolutely wouldn't give the host any trouble.

Though currency from the Central Plains was also accepted here, on the outskirts, people were more accustomed to bartering. So Shen Qiao took out a large chunk of salt and a small, delicately wrought flower of gold. Within the Central Plains, an ornament like this could be purchased at any jewelry shop, but it was a rare sight here. Zhao Zhiying had gotten the disciples at her sect to prepare it for Shen Qiao before he'd left, and, unexpectedly, it really did come in handy.

It was obvious the girl was used to merchants asking for lodging, but she hadn't expected the door knocker this time to be such a handsome man. As she listened to him speak, his expression pleasant and smiling, her face grew a little hot and her gaze was captured by the golden flower. But she still didn't agree right away. Using a mix of her local Qiang language and some awkward Mandarin, along with a few hand gestures, she told Shen Qiao that she lived together with her grandfather, so she had to ask him first.

Shen Qiao expressed his understanding and waited outside with Yan Wushi on his back. He'd thought that he'd have to wait a long time, but not long after, the door opened again. An old man with silvery hair came out, with the girl following behind him.

The old man was fluent in Mandarin. He asked Shen Qiao a couple of questions before opening the door to let them in. After a brief conversation, Shen Qiao learned that this old man had once lived in the Central Plains when he was young. While there, he'd saved some money, then built the largest house within this city. Unfortunately, his son and daughter-in-law had passed early, leaving him with only a granddaughter to live with.

Shen Qiao had chosen this family because of their large courtyard and many rooms. This way, even if he needed to pass qi to heal Yan Wushi's injuries, they could avoid unnecessary attention from others.

The old man had seen and learned much in his long life. He showed no surprise at the sight of a weapon carrier like Shen Qiao. Instead, it was the girl, Banna, who showed deep curiosity in Shen Qiao's Daoist clothing. She stood behind her grandfather, staring intently, but every time Shen Qiao looked over at her, she'd lower her head, a little bashful.

After exchanging a few courteous words, the old man hesitantly said, "My old self often receives traveling merchants for a stay, and as a guest, you've come from afar, so of course we welcome you. But this friend of yours seems to be injured quite badly. I fear his enemies must be terribly strong? My granddaughter and I are but ordinary people, and we've never done anything to invite trouble upon ourselves. Please, I ask that the Daoist Master tell me the truth so that I can make my decision."

"I'll be honest with you," said Shen Qiao. "This friend of mine has indeed invited quite a bit of trouble upon himself. Currently, all his enemies think him dead, but I wish to save him. Unfortunately, the Central Plains are too far away so we won't be able to get back right away. Hence, we have no choice but to ask your esteemed self for hospitality. As long as no one knows he's here, my friend will be safe. If anything goes wrong, I'll leave with him immediately; we definitely won't bring you any trouble."

The old man continued to hesitate, but Banna tugged on the corner of his clothes. "Grandpa, this gentleman doesn't look like a bad man. They're in a bad spot; if we're able to help, we should help!"

When he saw his granddaughter speaking up for them, the old man sighed. "Very well. If that's the case, the two of you may stay here. We will also keep your identities secret from everyone else. I'll just tell them that you're traveling scholars from the Central Plains. I also ask the Daoist master not to make too many trips outside unless it's absolutely necessary—that way, there will be less trouble for us."

Shen Qiao was deeply grateful. Ever since the tragedy that befell the abbot and Chuyi, he was completely adamant about not involving innocent people unless there was truly no other choice, so he naturally thanked the man profusely. He only intended to stay a short while—once the Coiling Dragon Assembly was over and those martial artists left, he could take Yan Wushi back to Chang'an and hand him to Bian Yanmei.

Banna was a little taken with Shen Qiao and wanted to speak to him more. When she saw him walking to the side yard carrying Yan Wushi, she took the initiative to help him open the door, but her finger accidentally brushed Yan Wushi's arm in the process. The chilling cold of his body startled her immediately, and she stumbled back a few steps, then pointed to him in shock.

"Shen...Shen-langjun, the person you're carrying...is he really alive?"

Shen Qiao smiled wryly to himself, thinking that he also didn't know whether he was still alive. But he could only comfort her and say, "It's just a very serious injury, one which has caused him to stop breathing for the time being. He's not dead."

Banna left, not quite convinced. The few times she saw Yan Wushi afterward, he always appeared well and truly dead. Even though his body didn't rot or stink like normal corpses, it was ice-cold from head to toe, and there was no sign of life to be seen. The most terrifying thing was that once, when Shen Qiao wasn't paying attention, she'd placed her finger beneath his nose, yet she couldn't feel the slightest breath at all.

She almost suspected that Shen Qiao was so grief-stricken by his friend's death that he refused to accept reality. But this served as an advantage to Shen Qiao: it meant that other than delivering him meals twice a day, she no longer paid their side yard any periodic visits. This saved Shen Qiao some trouble as, given his disposition, he really had no idea how he'd wave her off otherwise.

With everything settled, Shen Qiao could give his full attention to examining Yan Wushi's situation.

Day after day, little by little, the true qi in Yan Wushi's Dantian seemed to grow—it truly seemed he had a chance. It was obvious this was the *Zhuyang Strategy*'s true qi working its magic within Yan Wushi's body, just like it'd done for Shen Qiao. But the difference was that Yan Wushi hadn't lost his martial arts, so he couldn't do as Shen Qiao had: destroy everything and rebuild from scratch. His fatal injuries weren't the result of ruined foundations either—one could rebuild their foundations, but to repair one's skull after cracking it open? Now that was unheard of. If Yan Wushi remained like this, in the end, he'd still be unable to escape death.

Shen Qiao thought and thought, and he could only come up with one solution.

# Royal Capital

DOU YANSHAN HAD PUT his full strength into that strike; it was out of the question for him to show any mercy. Not only had it split Yan Wushi's skull, but also the bigger problem was that the contents had suffered severe damage. After mulling it over, the only route open to Shen Qiao was to first use his internal energy and true qi to dissolve the blood clots within Yan Wushi's brain, then slowly reorient the injured meridians all over his body, as well as repair his organs. Whether Yan Wushi would really wake up again, or if he'd linger in this half-dead state for the rest of his life, would be up to heaven.

As he sat there racking his brains for a solution, that man remained completely unconscious, his eyes closed and breaths faint, totally unaware of the day and time. Shen Qiao glanced at him, sighed quietly, and again smiled bitterly.

A small, foreign village was naturally limited when it came to food—it was two meals a day, mostly lamb and fried flatbread. But Shen Qiao had always been adaptable. He ate whatever they sent and never complained.

Yan Wushi's situation was more complicated. Insensate as he was, at most he could only drink some soup. However, his jaw was tightly clenched, and his tongue blocked the entrance to his throat. Spoon-feeding him the soup was futile: even if Shen Qiao forcefully poured it into his mouth, it would just dribble out from the corners. Special tools existed for feeding medicine, but finding one in a small Tuyuhun village was impossible. Left with no other choice, Shen Qiao could only take a sip of soup first, then pry open Yan Wushi's jaw and feed it to him, mouth-to-mouth. He used his tongue to hold the other man's down and forced the soup into him. Like this, he managed to make him drink one or two mouthfuls with great difficulty.

Yan Wushi was recovering at an incredibly slow pace. The true qi in his Dantian never vanished, but it was latent and feeble, sometimes discernible, sometimes hidden, like a candle flame flickering in the wind that could be snuffed out at any moment. And Shen Qiao's own martial prowess had yet to fully recover, so he could only channel qi for Yan Wushi once a day. He was at the end of his rope with Yan Wushi's situation; at this point, he was mostly just trying anything and everything to see what would stick.

This once-willful, once-egotistical man, who'd been overflowing with arrogance, could now only lie upon a bed, completely at the mercy of others. Even that shadow of a smile that always hung at the corner of his lips was gone. All that remained of his handsome face was just that, the handsome beauty—all those other quirks that people associated with him as a grandmaster of the demonic discipline had completely vanished. There was only still the white peppering his temples, impossible to wipe away, and the docility upon his face, incongruous enough to make others mistake his identity.

How the tables had turned. Even Yan Wushi himself had probably never thought that he could fall into such dire straits.

That being said, from what Shen Qiao knew about this man, even if Yan Wushi had long anticipated an ambush, there was a high chance he'd show up to that battle anyway. To others, an ambush like that was a calamity they'd avoid like the plague, but to Yan Wushi, it was a rare and exciting fight.

His miscalculation lay in his overconfidence. He'd believed there was no way he could lose, and that even if he were outmatched, he could still leave easily. He hadn't foreseen that Guang Lingsan, another demonic practitioner like him, was so determined to involve himself, to eliminate Yan Wushi, that he'd even divulge the flaw in the *Fenglin Scriptures'* demonic core to outsiders.

There were no medicinal ingredients to brew. All Yan Wushi could rely on was the wisp of true qi Shen Qiao had passed to him, but on the fourth day, his breaths suddenly weakened to the point of being inaudible. Shen Qiao, too, thought that continuing like this was hopeless: even if the other man still had a chance to survive, dragging out this half-dead state would still conclude with his life being extinguished.

Shen Qiao held the soup bowl, his brows slightly furrowed as he pondered for a long while. Then he suddenly saw that Yan Wushi's eyelids seemed to tremble.

It was such a tiny motion, he almost thought he'd seen wrong.

"Sect Leader Yan?" Shen Qiao tried calling his name several times, but sure enough, there was no response.

He picked up the other man's wrist—the pulse was so faint it was almost imperceptible. If Shen Qiao hadn't probed carefully, he would have seemed no different than a corpse.

For some reason, a feeling of absurdity suddenly surged within Shen Qiao.

That day, Yan Wushi had personally delivered him to Sang Jingxing and forced him to the edge of a precipice. He'd probably never thought then that he'd end up where he was today, and definitely not that he'd end up completely at someone else's mercy. If Shen Qiao hadn't shown up, with how Guang Lingsan and Dou Yanshan handled matters, Yan Wushi would have long been decapitated. Not even the great immortals of Daluo Mountain could come back to life after that.

Even at this moment, Shen Qiao only needed to land another palm strike on the crown of his head, or his heart, and that would be enough to transform this half-dead man into a fully dead one.

But finally, after quietly staring at him for a long while, Shen Qiao only gave a sigh, then raised his head to take another mouthful of soup. Supporting Yan Wushi by the nape of his neck, he gripped his chin and forced his mouth open, then slowly passed the broth to him, bit by bit.

Having repeated these actions for several days, Shen Qiao was already carrying them out with practiced ease. As he was a pure-hearted Daoist, and he was doing it to save a life, he naturally felt not the slightest bit of embarrassment or inappropriateness.

However, another person seeing this might not feel the same way.

Banna was taken with Shen Qiao. Even if she was terrified of Yan Wushi's corpselike state, she still stubbornly insisted on delivering their two daily meals herself, all so that Shen Qiao could open the door, and they could exchange a couple of words there. Though there was a language barrier, she was satisfied with this.

Today she brought over lunch as usual, but for some reason—perhaps because the plates were a bit heavy—she didn't feel like knocking. Instead, she carefully shouldered the door open and walked the familiar path through the side yard and into the inner room.

The door to the inner room was open, and the result was that she saw a scene that left her gaping and tongue-tied: Shen Qiao was bent at the waist, gripping the alive-dead man's chin as he pressed their mouths together. He was completely unconcerned that Banna had walked in. Beneath the blinding sunlight, she could even see their tongues briefly intertwine.

To be more precise, Shen Qiao's tongue was prying apart Yan Wushi's teeth, then pushing inside as far as it could go, all so that he could successfully pass the soup into Yan Wushi's mouth.

But the other party was basically a living corpse, completely insensate; even with his efforts, some broth and saliva still dribbled down from the corner of Yan Wushi's mouth.

The people of the Western Regions were more open-minded, and Banna was both beautiful and young. She was very popular with the boys in the village, but in all the years of her life, she'd never had such an intimate interaction with a man. Now she stared at them, her face burning and heart thumping, her mouth dry. For a long time, she was frozen stiff.

Having been in the middle of feeding Yan Wushi soup, Shen Qiao hadn't expected Banna to suddenly come in at all. He could only finish passing him that mouthful before putting the bowl down, and then he greeted Banna's flushed, crimson face.

Banna's lovely eyes were faintly red, and she asked him in her awkward Mandarin, "So you liked him, and that's why you refused to let me come close and refused to accept my affections?"

This misunderstanding was really too massive! Shen Qiao gave a strained smile. "You don't have any feeding tools here, so I could only feed him soup this way. We don't even count as friends. I ask the maiden not to misunderstand us."

Dubious, Banna said, "Then why won't Shen-langjun accept me? Is it because I'm not as pretty as the girls from your Central Plains? Or is it because I am not as gentle and ladylike as them? Please tell me; I can learn!"

Shen Qiao had never thought that he could attract another bout of romantic troubles just by staying here for a couple of days. If it'd been a woman from the Central Plains instead, she'd never have said it so frankly even if she'd fallen in love at first sight. But Banna had no such considerations. If she liked someone, she naturally had to confess early. Otherwise, once the man returned to the Central Plains, they'd never be able to meet again, and then it'd be too late to even cry.

Shen Qiao patiently explained to her: "As a Daoist priest, I must remain unmarried my entire life."

Banna wasn't swayed. "Grandpa said that Daoist priests can return to the secular world."

She'd actually come well prepared.

Shen Qiao didn't know whether to laugh or to cry. All he could say was, "You're fourteen years old this year, but I'm already past my prime. The gap between our ages is too large."

"What does that mean, 'prime'?" asked Banna.

"Around thirty years old."

Banna gasped. "You're already thirty years old? I couldn't tell at all!"

"The life spans of martial artists will always be somewhat longer," said Shen Qiao.

Banna bit her lip. "Then when I am fifty years old, will you still look like this?"

Shen Qiao shook his head and pointed to Yan Wushi. "How can that be? I'm not an ageless immortal. At that point I'll probably look like him."

Banna looked at Yan Wushi. Other than the peppering of white at his temples, she only saw a fantastically handsome face. There was no trace of aging to speak of.

She asked in a trembling voice, "How old is he?"

Shen Qiao thought for a moment, then said doubtfully, "Less than fifty, probably?"

Banna was shocked stiff, as if she'd been struck by lightning on a clear day. The Western Regions were full of wind and sand, so all the village men who were in their forties or fifties possessed faces that were creased and weather-beaten. How could they even compare to Yan Wushi? Putting aside men, women aged even faster—once they passed thirty, they'd begin to put on weight, their wrinkles deepening. Banna knew that she was young and beautiful now, but what about ten or twenty years later? The idea of her beloved remaining as handsome as ever while she was already old and gray... it was unbearable.

The poor girl had just experienced her first bout of adolescent love and already run into this kind of unresolvable problem. She was immediately beside herself with distress, and her sheer dejection went without saying.

With tears in her eyes, Banna shoved the plates of food into his arms and sniffled. "It's fine. Buddha sent you to me, but he refused to bring us together. It's obvious that we're not meant to be. I hope his esteemed self blesses the two of you, so that you can grow old together!"

Shen Qiao did not know how to respond.

Despite being stuck in this awkward situation, he was forced to call back Banna, who was hiding her face and about to leave, ready to find somewhere to soothe her emotional wounds. "I need to leave for half a day and will be taking a trip to the city," he said. "If someone comes asking questions, you can just pretend that you know nothing. But if his enemies come knocking for him and there's really nothing you can do, just hand him over to them.

Prioritize protecting yourselves first—there's no need to risk your lives for him."

Banna wiped at her tears. "Does he have a lot of enemies?"

Shen Qiao nodded. "He does have quite a few."

Banna was full of worry. "Then isn't being together with him terribly dangerous for you?"

This girl was pure and sincere—she spoke whatever came to her mind. She liked Shen Qiao, so she told him directly. She'd been deeply hurt by his rejection, but when she heard that Yan Wushi had many enemies, she immediately began worrying for Shen Qiao instead.

The hearts of those in the secular world were treacherous, more frightening than the gods and demons themselves. But it was because there was sincerity to be found within the treachery that the sincerity became all the more precious.

Warmth flooded Shen Qiao's heart, and he consoled her. "I know my limits, so I'll be fine. But I'm afraid of dragging you two into this, so you must be careful."

He and Yan Wushi had been staying in this small village for the past few days. They received little news here, so he had to take a trip to the royal capital. If those jianghu practitioners were gone, he could also take Yan Wushi to Chang'an and hand him to Bian Yanmei soon. The demonic sects had many secret techniques, so perhaps Bian Yanmei had a method to save his shizun.

After saying his temporary farewells to Banna and her grandfather, Shen Qiao returned to the capital. It was as bustling as ever, with people coming and going. The Coiling Dragon Assembly had just finished yesterday, and the emotions of many were still running high—the inn was full of people discussing this year's assembly. Shen Qiao sat in a corner without anyone's notice, a cloak ubiquitous to the desert over his Daoist robes, its hood concealing his face and hair.

In his search for information, he'd specially chosen the largest and most active inn in the capital. He ordered a jar of wine and several taels of meat, then quietly listened to the great assortment of voices.

"Did you hear? The Tai'e sword has an owner now! Someone purchased it for twenty thousand gold!"

With those words, a flood of exclamations rose all around him.

"That person must be mad! Or they have nowhere to spend their money! Tai'e may be a famous sword, but it's only a little sharper than average! How could it be worth that much money?"

The first person laughed. "Of course there's a reason. The buyer was Qi's Duke of Pengcheng County, Chen Gong."

The others immediately understood. "Then that's no surprise. Tai'e was once Chu's symbol of benevolent rule. He must want to give it to the Emperor of Qi."

Hearing this, someone else gave a mocking laugh. "Qi is about to be destroyed! Will Tai'e grant them divine protection?"

"Who knows! I heard that Chen Gong is a sycophant who won his seat by flattering the Lord of Qi. If Qi's destroyed, he'll likely lose both his life and possessions. He's probably just clutching at whatever straw he can, making some last-ditch efforts in hopes that they'll save him!"

These words had just fallen when a group of people walked in. The leader was tall and dressed in splendid finery. Though his face wasn't particularly handsome, there was a bold vigor about him that even his clothes couldn't conceal. He glanced around him after entering, gave a slight nod, and his attendants smoothly came up to arrange for his seating and dishes. His pomp and mannerisms immediately differentiated him from the jianghu practitioners crowding the place.

*Speak of the devil and he will appear.* The people who'd been excitedly talking about him just a moment ago all felt a little awkward, and they immediately quieted down.

Among the people peeking at Chen Gong, Shen Qiao shot him a glance from the corner too, without any change in his expression.

If not for the fact that he could vaguely make out the profile he'd once known from his face, or the whispers buzzing beside him, going, "The man himself is here, keep quiet," Shen Qiao would never have made the connection between this young noble, so arrogant and reserved, and the boy from that dilapidated temple in the past.

Even without knowing his identity, the innkeeper understood that this was an important customer whom he must not offend. Together with his waiters, he deftly cleaned up several tables previous customers had used, then led Chen Gong to his seat with a face full of smiles.

As soon as Chen Gong and his men were seated, another group of people entered the door.

Shen Qiao took a quick glance and frowned. Feeling this was really too much of a coincidence, he pulled the hood lower over his forehead.

Yu Ai and Dou Yanshan sat at the same table. The former had come alone—there were no disciples of Xuandu Mountain with him—but the latter had brought several members of the Liuhe Guild. Two of them looked somewhat familiar: they seemed to be the Hu brothers Shen Qiao had met by chance back in Chuyun Temple.

But his vision was still lacking, and he was afraid that they'd notice if he looked too long, so he quickly lowered his head to savor his alcohol, patiently waiting for everyone to leave.

The inns outside the Great Wall were less particular—even the royal capital's best and biggest relay station didn't have private rooms. Instead, everyone was crammed into one hall, which made for quite a noisy scene. Everyone spoke at once, so naturally those with loud voices would be heard more.

Chen Gong was here, and he'd brought a great many attendants. Even the martial artists of the jianghu wouldn't want to make enemies for themselves for no reason, beyond a scant few troublemakers. So the topic of Tai'e sword was over, and it was natural for everyone to bring up the other piece of shocking news, one that had already been mentioned countless times in the past few days.

"Say, do you think that Yan Wushi is really dead?"

Judging from his voice, the speaker wasn't a noteworthy martial artist, nor was he from a powerful sect. When he uttered the name "Yan Wushi," he'd subconsciously lowered his volume, like he was terrified that Yan Wushi would do as Chen Gong had and suddenly materialize before them in the flesh.

It was obvious that Yan Wushi's name carried extraordinary impact. The moment that first man brought it up, their surroundings fell into a temporary silence, just like when Chen Gong had entered. It was a few moments before someone replied, "It should be true. I heard that Sect Leader Yu and Guild Leader Dou were also part of the ambush, and they're here right now. If you don't believe it, you can ask them."

In the past, whenever those from the jianghu heard Yan Wushi's name, their hearts would give an inevitable tremble. But these days, after the news of him being ambushed and killed by five martial experts had spread, it'd actually incurred more dissent.

A single man had been ambushed and killed by five experts. What did that mean? In other words, those five had doubted their ability in beating him one-on-one; to kill one Yan Wushi, they had to go as far as joining forces. "The strong is king" was the law of the jianghu. Though many were relieved at the news, there were also many who secretly admired Yan Wushi because of it. They thought that if he hadn't died, he probably could have succeeded Qi Fengge as the foremost martial artist in all the land.

Most people didn't dare say such things, but there were a few who couldn't stop running their mouths. One such person immediately declared loudly, "A victory through superior numbers goes against the morals of the jianghu! What a pity that a grandmaster like Yan Wushi would die in such an unjust way!"

Yu Ai shot him a cold glance but said nothing. However, Dou Yanshan lightly flicked his finger, and the speaker yelped, then covered his mouth, his expression twisting in pain.

His friend went pale with shock and leapt to his feet. "Wulang, are you all right?!" Then he cupped his hands at Dou Yanshan. "I beg Guild Leader Dou's pardon. This brother of mine is always running his mouth. After a couple of drinks, he starts babbling nonsense, so I ask you to not hold it against him!"

Dou Yanshan chortled. "What you eat is your business, but what you say is ours. I only knocked out one of his front teeth as a small lesson. I've already shown him mercy."

Sure enough, as Dou Yanshan spoke, the man in question spat out a mouthful of bloody foam, along with a tooth. Dissatisfied anger was written all over his face and he looked about to retort, but his friend quickly covered his mouth and snapped, "Wulang, stop causing trouble!"

That man could only shut his mouth awkwardly. His companion forcefully hauled him up, and the two of them left in a hurry.

After this little interlude, no one dared to speak carelessly again. The Liuhe Guild conducted business across the entire land. Offending Chen Gong would at most net you a beating and an entry ban from Qi, but offending the Liuhe Guild? You never knew when you might have entered their territory or used the items they'd escorted.

However, it was impossible to suppress that many mouths. After a brief silence, some people rose and left, then new customers entered through the door. Noise and clamor once again rose, and the topic of Yan Wushi's death was an unavoidable one. And this was still a location outside the Great Wall—once it spread to the Central Plains, who knew how many waves and problems it would stir up there.

"Since Yan Wushi is dead, isn't Shen Qiao in trouble?" This voice came from close to Shen Qiao, and it wasn't loud. The speaker was likely talking to their friend.

"Why do you say that?"

"Didn't Shen Qiao lose all his martial arts and end up forced to rely on Yan Wushi? He became his kept man, right. Now that he's lost his backer, what good awaits a cripple like him? Surely he doesn't have the face to return to Xuandu Mountain and beg them to take him back?"

These people obviously didn't know that it'd been a long time since Shen Qiao and Yan Wushi had showed up together. Their information was still frozen in time back at the Su residence's banquet, when Shen Qiao had attended it on Yan Wushi's behalf.

"That's true. He probably doesn't have the guts to go back. Didn't Xuandu Mountain already put out the notice that Shen Qiao is no longer their sect leader?"

"But they never announced Shen Qiao's expulsion. They must still care about their old relationship. Say, why do you think he went as far as to disgrace himself by staying with the Demon Lord instead of returning to his sect?"

"Maybe Yan Wushi gave him a pleasure that no one else could?"

At this point in the conversation, the two of them snickered in unison, their faces revealing their unspoken thoughts.

They had no idea that the person they were gossiping about was sitting at the table behind them, currently listening to their conversation without a twitch in expression. Shen Qiao even had the mood to place two pieces of beef on some flatbread to make a beef roll, before placing it in his mouth and chewing slowly.

"Since Huanyue Sect and Hehuan Sect came from the same source, then Huanyue Sect must know Hehuan Sect's techniques. What you said is completely possible: the Demon Lord was skilled in martial arts, but he must have been even more skilled in bed. After getting a taste, Shen Qiao couldn't stop himself from wanting more. Maybe the Demon Lord was already tired of him, and it was Shen Qiao who was unable to let go!"

The last word was barely out of his mouth when he suddenly screamed. He slapped his hands over his mouth and keeled over, then writhed on the floor in pain.

This sudden episode gave everyone a huge shock. They all turned to gaze at him as one.

Naturally, the person who'd hurt him couldn't have been sitting behind him.

Shen Qiao was somewhat surprised too. He looked to the front of that person.

Yu Ai sat there, his posture and manner severe. He slowly put down the chopstick in his hand and said coldly, "Since when does an outsider have the right to humiliate a member of our Xuandu Mountain?"

# Expulsion

EVEN IF SOME PEOPLE had been ignorant of Yu Ai's identity beforehand, after what he'd just said, it was near impossible for them to not realize.

The reason they'd judged Shen Qiao without fear was because they thought that, to Xuandu Mountain, he was only a discarded disciple. Having long lost his martial arts and his glory, he posed no threat to them, and Xuandu Mountain protecting him was even more impossible. They'd never thought that Yu Ai would step in.

After his brief shock, Shen Qiao slowly put down his roll. He understood what was going on.

No matter how much of a failure he was, he was still from Xuandu Mountain. When others criticized him, they were also staining Xuandu Mountain's reputation, and Yu Ai naturally wouldn't stand for that.

But if Yu Ai cared that much about Xuandu Mountain's reputation, wasn't collaborating with the Göktürks and receiving titles from them even more shameful?

Shen Qiao inwardly shook his head, clearing such thoughts from his mind. He had no interest in watching the farce in front of him any longer. He was only waiting for them to drink and eat their fill before leaving, then he could get up and leave himself.

The man whose teeth Yu Ai had shattered was in an uncontrollable rage. He said something garbled, then grabbed the longsword beside him and leapt at Yu Ai.

But Yu Ai didn't even unsheathe his sword. With only the remaining chopstick in his hand, he knocked the other man to the ground.

The man in question was called Ji Jin. Though he carried the moniker of "Nine-Tailed Divine Fox," people called him "Bigmouthed Ji" behind his back because he was always running his mouth and offending others. Ji Jin wasn't too shabby a martial artist—not first-rate, but his skills were enough to be second-rate. Normally he had more restraint and wouldn't talk smack about others right to their face, but who knew what he was thinking this time. Somehow, he'd failed to realize the obvious fact that the sect leader of Xuandu Mountain himself was sitting right before him, so in a bout of terrible misfortune, he'd managed to humiliate himself and his entire family line.

His friend didn't dare back him up before Yu Ai, he only helped Ji Jin up and smiled apologetically in Yu Ai's direction. "Please forgive him, Sect Leader Yu. This brother of mine has had too much to drink, and he really said some shameful things!"

Yu Ai didn't reply. His gaze swept right over the man to fall on the one behind him. "A-Qiao, it's been such a long time, and you won't even say a word of greeting?"

Shen Qiao sighed to himself. They'd grown up together since childhood and knew each other like the back of their own hands. Even if he covered his face, his mannerisms and figure would still evoke that sense of familiarity. Yu Ai wasn't a fool; he'd eventually realized it was him.

Shen Qiao pulled down his hood, and someone near him said, "It really is Shen Qiao!" This voice instantly drew in a wave of low, shocked responses.

Quite a few of them felt somewhat guilty—the man they'd just been loudly discussing had been right next to them, sitting and listening.

What sort of ill fortune was blowing about today? They spoke of Chen Gong, and Chen Gong came; now they spoke of Shen Qiao, and Shen Qiao was also here. Would Yan Wushi show up in a moment too?

Several of them thought this and couldn't help but shiver, glancing around themselves.

"It's been a while. Has Sect Leader Yu been well?"

Since he'd already been discovered, Shen Qiao didn't bother pretending anymore. He nodded to Yu Ai, his voice mild, as if they were no more than distant acquaintances meeting again after many years.

For a moment, to Yu Ai, the noise and commotion of the inn seemed to ebb like the tide. Only Shen Qiao's voice remained in his ears.

He stared at Shen Qiao, scrutinizing him, as if trying to determine whether Shen Qiao really was doing well. It was a long while before he replied, "You've lost weight."

Shen Qiao didn't reply to his comment. He was only here to gather information—now that he'd been discovered, he had no reason to continue staying.

"I still have some important matters to attend to, so I'll be leaving first. Please enjoy your meals, Sect Leader Yu and Guild Leader Dou."

Of course, Yu Ai wouldn't let him leave so easily. His foot moved, and then he was in front of Shen Qiao. "A-Qiao, come back to Xuandu Mountain with me."

Shen Qiao's expression didn't so much as flicker. "Surely Sect Leader Yu jests. I am no longer a disciple of Xuandu Mountain, so why would I go back there?"

Yu Ai was faintly enraged. "I never ordered your expulsion, so you're still a disciple of Xuandu Mountain. Are you unwilling to acknowledge even Shizun now?"

Shen Qiao shook his head. "I believe you're mistaken on one thing. I am Qi Fengge's disciple. This point will never change, no matter what. But you colluded with Kunye to poison me, had me lose to him on Banbu Peak, then took the chance to steal the position of sect leader—and furthermore, you even began to collaborate with the Göktürks. Ever since then, Xuandu Mountain is no longer the Xuandu Mountain I know. Even without you ordering my expulsion, I will not acknowledge myself as a disciple of Xuandu Mountain."

Shen Qiao had spoken these staggering, unnerving words in a mild and placid tone, which made what he said feel all the more convoluted and jarring.

No one had anticipated that there was this kind of tale behind Shen Qiao's fall from the cliff back then. They were all stunned into silence, frozen in place. When their wits returned, a roaring clamor immediately erupted in the hall.

Yu Ai, too, hadn't expected for Shen Qiao to choose to spill the details here, in public, at this moment. His face immediately flushed crimson—not from shame but indignation.

Of course, Shen Qiao had no evidence. Even if he'd said it, he couldn't do anything to Yu Ai, but Yu Ai still felt like his clothes had been stripped off, leaving him naked.

He tamped down on his rage and said evenly, "A-Qiao, come back with me."

"Yu Ai, the Göktürks are savage and ambitious," Shen Qiao said coolly. "Everyone knows this. Yet for the sake of your own prospects and interests, you willingly went to ask a tiger for its skin. You even forced all of Xuandu Mountain onto your ship. Right now, I can't stop you, but that doesn't mean that I approve of this outcome, nor that I'll enter the mire with you."

"You..."

"Since it's come to this point, with so many people here, let us ask them to be our witnesses. As Qi Fengge's mantle disciple, I hereby declare this: from now on, you are no longer Qi Fengge's disciple. We shall walk our own paths, cross our own bridges, and have nothing to do with each other!"

Shen Qiao stood in place, his expression as indifferent as ever, as if he were completely unaware of the massive wave his words would incite. His Daoist robe fluttered faintly beneath his cloak despite the lack of wind, a powerful presence around him, yet no trace of anger. At this moment, his handsome face, once so gentle and harmless, carried with it a fierceness that made others unable to look at him directly. He was like a sword kept within a box—even unsheathed, he already radiated a piercing brilliance.

Yu Ai was both shocked and outraged. "How dare you! Shizun has already passed! How can you speak for his esteemed self like that?!"

"I was the only one around when Shizun passed, and I am Shizun's only mantle disciple," Shen Qiao replied. "My will is his will! I only quietly endured it before out of consideration for the greater picture—I didn't want to see Xuandu Mountain divided by internal strife. But you've pushed and pushed, and you even accepted titles from the Göktürks! As you've gone against Shizun's teachings, I naturally must expel you on his behalf!"

Even buddhas knew wrath. His face had lost all traces of gentleness—it was now replaced by a stormy rage. "Yu Ai, listen to me. You have no right to punish me because none of Xuandu Mountain's forefathers will ever acknowledge you as sect leader! I hope you can finish what you've started. If you insist on obstinately clinging to your ways, unwilling to repent, one day I will return to punish you!"

The hall was a graveyard of silence. Everyone was staring at Shen Qiao, completely unable to connect him with the man the rumors claimed had willingly disgraced himself and cozied up with the Demon Lord.

Once Shen Qiao was finished, he walked toward the entrance without another glance back.

Yu Ai stopped wavering. He grabbed Junzi Buqi, wanting to stop him, but Shen Qiao was faster—bystanders only saw a flash of black knocking Yu Ai's sword away. With a closer look, they realized that Shen Qiao hadn't even unsheathed his sword.

At this moment, Dou Yanshan moved.

At first, he'd only wanted to enjoy this family quarrel between sect siblings as a bystander. However, looking at how indecisive Yu Ai's moves were, the hesitation within his heart clear, Dou Yanshan knew he probably wouldn't be able to stop his shixiong. So, in this situation, he had no choice but to lend his hand.

"I haven't known Sect Leader Yu for long, but I know he is a sentimental person who cares for old friendships and is unwilling to be harsh with Daoist Master Shen. I ask Daoist Master Shen to cool down a little. Why don't we all sit down and have a long conversation?"

But Shen Qiao didn't move to fight Dou Yanshan. Instead, his gait shifted, and using "A Rainbow Stretches across the Heavens," he circled around him and immediately arrived at the exit of the inn.

"A-Qiao, don't force my hand!" Yu Ai snarled. Junzi Buqi was already unsheathed.

Before Shen Qiao could respond, a mocking remark came from the side. "Fighting the few with many, achieving victory through superior numbers. Are the two of you planning to do to Daoist Master Shen what you did to Yan Wushi?"

Chen Gong, who had been looking on this entire time, now finally stood. This matter was unrelated to him, but for some reason he'd stuck his hand in.

Dou Yanshan laughed. "The Duke of Pengcheng County has just obtained the Tai'e sword. Shouldn't you return quickly and report back to the Lord of Qi? Why are you idling about here and meddling in unrelated affairs?"

Coming from his mouth, the words "Duke of Pengcheng County" was tinged with subtle taunting. Chen Gong might have been a new noble of Qi, but he had nothing to do with the jianghu, so the Liuhe Guild had no reason to take him seriously.

Chen Gong didn't reply to Dou Yanshan's words. Instead, he looked at Shen Qiao and said warmly, "If Daoist Master Shen finds it difficult to extricate himself, I've rented an entire relay station within the capital. You can follow me there for some rest."

"I'm deeply grateful for the Duke of Pengcheng County's kindness," said Shen Qiao, "but this lowly Daoist must decline your hospitality."

Saying this, he cupped his hands at him, then turned to leave.

Yu Ai naturally couldn't let him leave so easily. "Wait!" he said, reaching out toward Shen Qiao.

Shen Qiao didn't even glance back. Like eyes had sprouted on the back of his head, he slid a couple of steps forward, as light as a feather, then turned around with his sword across his chest, blocking Yu Ai's outstretched hand. He'd channeled true qi into the sheath— Yu Ai felt a slight jolt and was forced to release it.

But Yu Ai reacted quickly. With his other hand, he drew Junzi Buqi, and its sword glare poured forth, airy and graceful. It swept toward Shen Qiao's face, and even Dou Yanshan was a little shocked to see it. He thought to himself that Yu Ai probably hadn't used his full strength during their ambush on Yan Wushi, that he'd only appeared seriously injured, when in truth, he just hadn't wanted to lead the charge.

Regardless of which it was, Yu Ai was determined to keep Shen Qiao here. This time, now that there was no Yan Wushi to thwart him, he absolutely refused to allow him to escape before his very eyes again. He knew that Joyful Reunion's poison was matchlessly potent. With how sickly and feeble Shen Qiao had been on Xuandu Mountain, a full recovery in such a short period of time was impossible.

But he hadn't realized that, with a long separation, a reappraisal was due. Yu Ai's sword glare flowed through a myriad of shapes and descended upon Shen Qiao, but the man who should have been enveloped by the sword screen vanished. He reappeared behind Yu Ai, his footwork indescribably swift and uncanny, but his sword remained sheathed as before. Instead, he stretched out his right hand and tapped a finger upon the sword screen.

True qi poured into the screen, and it immediately shattered, reduced to fine powder and scattering in all directions!

A trace of disbelief surfaced on Yu Ai's face. The tip of his sword quivered, then he twirled it a couple dozen times. It wove toward Shen Qiao, rippling with light.

It made for a resplendent and otherworldly scene, the jeweled rays piercing the heavens like light spilling over colored glaze. Dazzling, splendid, and radiant.

These were the last set of moves from the Azure Waves Sword Technique, but somewhat changed. None of Qi Fengge's disciples were incompetent, naturally, and Yu Ai had made several alterations to them for himself. Most days, his disposition was frosty, and he rarely smiled, but he loved using this kind of gorgeous, brilliant swordplay. Even his sword qi carried with it a thunderous, seething viciousness. As it hurtled forth with the sword glares, a great rumble roared in the ears of everyone present. Even those somewhat lacking in martial arts could already feel their blood and qi roiling, and they couldn't help but back up a few steps.

But Shen Qiao didn't retreat.

He actually didn't retreat!

This went completely against everyone's expectations, including those who'd once looked down on him, taking him for Yan Wushi's kept man and subordinate.

Shen Qiao finally unsheathed his sword!

Shanhe Tongbei flashed forth like silk, its sword qi soaring to the heavens. It spread forth from Shen Qiao, rich and mellow, until one couldn't help but want to drown themselves in its comfortable warmth. But many people were still distracted from earlier and failed to notice that Shen Qiao's sword was already thrusting before him.

It took no time at all—everything happened in a blink of an eye. Both parties were already in the air, their sword tips pointed at each other. Yu Ai moved as swiftly as lightning, but Shen Qiao was even faster—he became one with his sword, then suddenly vanished from Yu Ai's line of sight.

In the world of martial arts, speed is everything!

At once, Yu Ai's guard rose. He immediately turned and swung his sword behind him, but it was already too late. Shen Qiao's sword intent was only inches away, and there was no escape. He only had the time to see that glimpse of white sword glare, and his heart sank. Lacking the time for careful thought, he retreated with an unprecedented swiftness, pushing his "A Rainbow Stretches across the Heavens" to the utmost. His entire person disappeared into thin air, then reappeared three feet away.

Shen Qiao could have pursued and caught him—his white sword intent had already been perfected. The next step up would be to achieve sword heart. Even if he only had half of his internal energy, his white sword intent was more than enough to terrify many out of their senses.

But Shen Qiao didn't press his advantage, and Yu Ai came to a stop as well. The two of them stared at each other, each lost in their own emotions. They both knew that they could never return to the past.

Shen Qiao stood there, back as straight as a pine, his sword pointed toward the ground. He said sternly, "You should understand now that if we fight, neither your victory nor my defeat are guaranteed. Stop thinking that you have me at your mercy, that you can manipulate me as you please. Even if I'm no longer the sect leader of Xuandu Mountain, I'm still Shen Qiao, still Qi Fengge's disciple!"

There was a complicated expression on Yu Ai's face. "Yuan Ying and Hengbo miss you very much. They wish for your return..."

"Yu Ai, after you poisoned me with Joyful Reunion, I no longer believe anything you say."

Yu Ai's expression darkened. Something billowed within his eyes, as if raging waves were soon to come. "I was wrong then. But starting from now, I'll never hurt you again."

Shen Qiao shook his head. "What's the point of saying this now? What's done cannot be undone, that which is broken cannot be repaired, and no reparations can make up for the wrongs inflicted. What people call reparations is only a way to deceive themselves and others. The reason I won't return to Xuandu Mountain is because

I don't want a Xuandu Mountain rent by strife and, even more, because I don't want the efforts of our forefathers to vanish like smoke. Since you've already taken that step together with the disciples of Xuandu Mountain, you must brace yourself for the consequences. When the day comes that you can no longer bear them, I will come find you myself."

Yu Ai's chest heaved erratically. After a long moment, he gave a frosty laugh and said, "Very well. Very well..."

As he repeated those words, his icy tone was tinged with a hint of despair, but it quickly faded, as if it were a mere illusion.

He slid his sword back into his sheath without another word, then turned and left. Not once did he glance back at Shen Qiao.

Dou Yanshan rubbed his nose. Now that Yu Ai was gone, he'd lost his excuse to intervene. Even more, he was still wary and fearful of Shen Qiao's martial arts, so naturally he wasn't too eager to throw himself into the muck.

"Congratulations on recovering your martial arts, Daoist Master Shen," he said. "As someone who is friendly with Sect Leader Yu, I was obligated to speak up for him earlier. I ask you not to take offense."

The reason Dou Yanshan was able to lead the largest guild in all the land was his incredible cunning. He wasn't easy to deal with. Just before he'd attacked without hesitation, and now he'd apologized right away. Quick and decisive, a shrewd and formidable man to the end.

It was hard to strike a smiling face, and for someone of Shen Qiao's upbringing, it was even more impossible. He nodded and said, "We all have our own positions; this I understand. Guild Leader Dou is too generous."

Dou Yanshan said, "Previously, Daoist Master Shen took Yan Wushi's body away with him. I trust that the man has already been interred? It's unfortunate that a grandmaster of his generation had to lose his life outside the Great Wall. The dead must be revered above all else, and to the people of the Central Plains, a burial at home is highly important. If Daoist Master Shen does not object, the Liuhe Guild is willing to lend our help. We can transport Sect Leader Yan's corpse back to Chang'an, then deliver it to Huanyue Sect."

Shen Qiao responded coolly, "I'm grateful to Guild Leader Dou for his kindness. However, the body was already interred; unearthing it again would be inauspicious. The people of the jianghu place less importance in these customs, and since he had countless enemies, he should have already anticipated this kind of end. I only retrieved his remains due to the small bit of friendship we shared in the past."

Dou Yanshan tried to probe further, but Shen Qiao's defenses were watertight. There wasn't even the slightest hint of a leak.

Shen Qiao looked at the people around him, then said slowly, "Your mouths are yours alone. You can speak about me as you wish— I won't interfere. If you're dissatisfied with me, you only need to come and find me—I'll be humbly waiting. But if I hear anyone insult Xuandu Mountain or my master, then please excuse my sword for its lack of mercy."

Right as these words fell, a white light flashed in everyone's eyes. Before they could react, the bamboo banner pole in front of the inn's door fell to the ground in six neat pieces. Even the banner at the top had been reduced to fine powder by the sword glare.

Everyone gaped, completely astounded. The ones who'd denigrated and slandered him to his back earlier felt their hearts tremble.

They knew very well that just this sword glare itself was far beyond what most of them could ever achieve in their lives, and it was obvious Shen Qiao meant this as a warning and a threat. It wasn't only for them, it was also for Dou Yanshan.

But Dou Yanshan was all smiles. He seemed perfectly at ease and even clapped his hands. "Daoist Master Shen must have perfected his swordplay already!" he exclaimed.

"It's but a small trick; nothing worth showing off," said Shen Qiao. "I've embarrassed myself before Guild Leader Dou."

If this had been in the past, with his disposition, Shen Qiao would never make a display of his martial arts like this. But things had changed: some people would never listen to reason and only understood if you spoke with your fist. They fully believed that the strong were king; to them, kindness was no more than a weakness.

After wandering the jianghu for a year, Shen Qiao had finally learned to deal with different people using different means.

He paid the waiter for the damaged banner together with his meal, then turned to leave the inn.

Of course, this time, no one stopped him.

Since Dou Yanshan and Yu Ai were here, Shen Qiao couldn't leave the city rashly, let alone look for a pharmacy to purchase medicine, otherwise the other party's astuteness would immediately let them realize that something was amiss. So, he found another inn and pretended to settle down there. Once night fell and curfew arrived, he silently left the city at last and ran toward the village.

The move he'd showed the crowd earlier that day was no more than an empty display of strength. He knew better than anyone else that with his current abilities, fighting Yu Ai was already pushing it. Yu Ai hadn't suspected anything due to his own guilty conscience and the psychological blow he'd taken from Shen Qiao's words, but Dou Yanshan was different. As a bystander, he could see clearly, and he likely still held some doubts about Shen Qiao's martial arts. Right now, there was a millstone with the surname Yan waiting for him in the village, so Shen Qiao absolutely couldn't afford any mistakes.

The moon was already high in the sky when he arrived in the village, its gentle glow spilling over the river. Shen Qiao finally slowed his steps and walked toward Banna's house.

The village at night was cloaked in an eerie silence, broken only by the occasional baying of dogs in the distance.

Shen Qiao gave the courtyard gate a few light taps. They sounded clearly in the dead of the night, easily loud enough for the people inside to hear.

A candle flame still burned within the building, evidence that the residents had yet to sleep.

After a moment, he heard the patter of footsteps, and the courtyard gate opened. Banna's frightened face appeared by the entrance.

Shen Qiao's eyes didn't work very well at this time of day, but he was accustomed to being blind. He'd long been able to tell someone's emotions by their breathing, footsteps, and tone, and his heart sank a little straight away. "Did something happen?"

"Shen-langjun, you've finally returned!" Banna held her chest. "Grandpa isn't home, and I was so scared being here by myself. That... that...living dead man is awake!"

# Awakening

**S**HEN QIAO GRABBED Banna's shoulder. With this, she calmed down slightly.

"He's awake? You entered and saw him?"

Banna nodded. "I heard some noise coming from that room earlier in the day and went to check. At first, when I saw him open his eyes, I was happy and wanted to ask if he'd like to eat something. But then he suddenly grabbed my neck. I was terrified I'd attract others over, so I didn't dare call for help. Then he suddenly let go and fell back down..."

She saw that Shen Qiao was continuing inside and quickly grabbed him. "You must be careful! He's crazy; it's like he can't recognize anyone! He almost strangled me to death earlier, look! The marks are still here!"

Shen Qiao hadn't noticed before she brought them up. His eyes had been thoroughly damaged by the poison, and everything appeared blurry and vague. Now, as he gave her a careful look by the light of the moon, he could see five dark, finger-shaped bruises over one side of her neck. It was a dreadful sight.

Banna then rolled up her sleeve. Similar bruises dotted her wrist.

Shen Qiao was deeply apologetic. Their temporary stay had already brought her a great deal of trouble, and now she'd even been injured because of them. "I'm terribly sorry. There's ointment for bruising in the room; I'll go get some for you."

Banna said vivaciously, "No need! This kind of injury is nothing. I've gotten far worse while outside with Grandpa!"

She had locked Yan Wushi's room from the outside. She pulled out the key and handed it to Shen Qiao. "If he's still crazy, just run out and lock him inside!"

"No need to worry," said Shen Qiao, giving her a consoling smile. "I know what I'm doing." While they were talking, he'd already opened the door and walked in.

The houses beyond the Great Wall were designed with fewer considerations. Their rooms lacked partition screens—a single glance was enough to survey the entire room.

Banna gave a low gasp of surprise despite herself.

For that living dead man was sitting on the bed and staring at them.

"Sect Leader Yan?" asked Shen Qiao.

There was no reaction. Not only did he fail to speak, he didn't even blink. He looked like a wooden puppet—it made for an eerie sight.

Banna whispered, "He wasn't like this before..."

Shen Qiao nodded, then approached him slowly. Banna was both scared and intrigued as she followed behind Shen Qiao, occasionally poking her head out to look at the puppet.

"Sect Leader Yan, can you hear me?"

Yan Wushi only looked at him, his eyes filled entirely with Shen Qiao's reflection.

"I'll be taking your pulse." Shen Qiao lifted his wrist, and Yan Wushi didn't respond to that either, letting Shen Qiao handle him as he wished. But his eyes remained fixed on Shen Qiao—whether Shen Qiao was hunched over or sitting upright, Yan Wushi's gaze never left him.

His pulse was feeble, almost flickering. His damaged internal organs had yet to recover, and there was a disordered wisp of qi scuttling through his entire body. His situation really didn't look too good.

Shen Qiao recalled what Yan Wushi had said to him, that there was a flaw in the demonic core within the *Fenglin Scriptures*. The higher one progressed, the more evident the flaw's impact on the body became. In the end, the practitioner's martial arts would stagnate entirely and even their life span would be affected.

Since Guang Lingsan was also a demonic practitioner as well as the leader of a sect, he must have discovered the existence of this flaw. Last time, during the five-man ambush on Yan Wushi, he'd first used music to distract Yan Wushi mentally, then tore open that breach while the others attacked, thus increasing the damage he'd sustained.

One could say that without Guang Lingsan's help, even if Yan Wushi couldn't have defeated the other four, escaping wouldn't have been an issue for him. Yet the presence of an enemy who knew him far too well became the source of his crushing defeat.

Even though he was awake now, that flaw didn't disappear or mend just because of that. Instead, it had gradually spread to his organs and the meridians of his foundations. In other words, whether or not he'd woken up made no real difference.

Just as Shen Qiao was furrowing his brows and pondering, Yan Wushi suddenly smiled at him.

This smile was different from those faint half smiles from the past, and lacked any sense of sarcasm, ridicule, or unbridled arrogance. It was simply a smile, nothing more, as if it weren't Shen Qiao in front of him, but a beautiful flower.

Shen Qiao stilled.

He felt no joy at this smile, but rather an indescribable horror and disquiet.

Banna, too, was frightened. She stammered, "What's...what's wrong with him? He wasn't like this during the day!"

Shen Qiao looked back at her. "What was he like during the day? Did he do anything else besides grab your throat? Like speaking, for example?"

Banna shook her head. "He didn't. He was terribly vicious then. But now...now..."

She wasn't very fluent in Mandarin; after a long period of mulling, she finally forced out a line. "But now he's very docile."

Using "docile" to describe Yan Wushi? Anyone would find it comical. Even Shen Qiao felt a flicker of laughter welling up inside him, but he couldn't find any rebuttal.

Because right now, Yan Wushi was indeed very docile.

He did nothing beyond smiling at Shen Qiao.

Shen Qiao pulled out some ointment and gave it to Banna. "It's late; you should hurry up and rest. Today was hard on you. If you apply this, the marks should no longer be visible tomorrow."

"How about you sleep in my grandpa's room?" asked Banna. "What if he goes crazy again in the middle of the night?"

Shen Qiao shook his head. "No need to worry."

When she saw him unwilling to say more, Banna could only leave, looking back three times with every step she took.

After sending her off, Shen Qiao finally realized that no lamps had been lit yet. However, the moonlight was bright tonight, and though it spilled in through the window, Shen Qiao had failed to notice anything amiss.

He walked over to light the lamp, but the moment he turned, someone suddenly wrapped their arms around his waist.

Shen Qiao startled. Before he could push the hands away, he heard a voice from behind him, muffled and stilted. "Don't...go..."

Each word was forced out with great effort, as if his tongue were stiff in his mouth. If it hadn't been for their closeness, Shen Qiao might have failed to understand him.

Shen Qiao believed that Banna wasn't lying, which meant that Yan Wushi's current situation was somewhat unusual.

But whether he was truly insane, or only faking insanity, none of that had anything to do with him.

Shen Qiao flicked his finger, and Yan Wushi let go despite himself. He walked to the window side and lit his lamp before finally turning around.

"Sect Leader Ya..."

He never finished the word "Yan," for he saw the other man's scared, anxious gaze. As if he were afraid that Shen Qiao was about to leave, he was struggling to get up and walk, but his weak limbs almost sent him tumbling to the ground.

Shen Qiao watched where Yan Wushi lay flat on the ground. The hand that had been about to reach over stopped in midair, then moved no further.

"Are you all right?" asked Shen Qiao.

"Don't...go..." Yan Wushi only repeated these words.

Shen Qiao stood there and watched him for a long time, then sighed. He went over to help the man up anyway.

"Do you still remember your name? Who you are?" he asked.

Confusion washed over Yan Wushi's face. He didn't respond; instead he sent Shen Qiao another gentle smile.

Shen Qiao's hand felt along the top of Yan Wushi's head. The crack was still there, so the damage to the insides must remain as well. He didn't know how deep that injury ran either; it wasn't like he could open up the man's skull to check, and he also had no way of knowing how severe the damage to his brain was, or whether he'd really become an idiot.

"My name is Shen Qiao. You should have some impression of me, no?"

Yan Wushi repeated, "Shen...Qiao..."

"Your name is Yan Wushi."

Yan Wushi didn't answer, as if he were still digesting Shen Qiao's words. Only after another long moment did he give a soft sound of assent. "Shen...Qiao..."

Shen Qiao smiled. "If I were the one who'd fallen to the ground, you definitely wouldn't have helped me up. On the contrary, you'd stand there, watching to see how long it'd take for me to struggle to my feet myself. Isn't that right?"

Yan Wushi again revealed a bewildered expression, as if he didn't understand what Shen Qiao was saying.

Shen Qiao gave a soft sigh, then gently pried his hands away.

"Your injuries are too serious; a single day won't be enough to heal them. After a couple of more days, when your situation isn't as critical, I'll take you back to Chang'an. Sleep for now. Everything else can wait until tomorrow morning."

Without waiting for Yan Wushi to respond, he walked over to the side, sat cross-legged on a blanket, closed his eyes, and began regulating his breathing.

Yan Wushi's situation being what it was, even though Shen Qiao was meditating and circulating his internal energy, he didn't dare bring his entire mind and body into that special state where he blurred the boundaries between one and all. He left a small part of his awareness to watch for outside disturbances.

The night quickly passed, and light crept forth, far in the east.

Shen Qiao circulated his true qi through the meridians of his entire body for several rounds. Every time the qi returned to the origin, it accumulated and was refined within the Dantian, cycling endlessly, while his three energies—the essence, the qi, and the spirit—gathered within his skull, full of vigor and life. It was as if his entire person had entered a new echelon that was wonderful beyond words.

It was as though he could see within himself, watch every meridian in his body slowly stretch forth, the once-clogged vessels now clear and open. Warm true qi washed away all residual impurities, and his foundations, now newly repaired and rejoined, were even stabler than they'd been in the past. Even though he'd overextended himself previously, ignoring the difference in strength as he charged into a fight, all he'd suffered was a roiling of his blood and qi. He no longer hacked up blood at the drop of a hat as he did before.

Perhaps his eyes would never return to a state where he could see everything clearly, but every cloud had a silver lining, and Shen Qiao didn't regret what had happened. The past was the past; people could only continue looking ever forward. If he hadn't been poisoned with Joyful Reunion, if he hadn't fallen from Banbu Peak, perhaps he'd never have been able to comprehend the true wonders of the *Zhuyang Strategy*, and his martial progress would have stopped there for all eternity.

At this moment, Shen Qiao seemed to have broken free of his shell of a body, his conscious mind now wandering the boundless expanse of primordial chaos. The myriad of stars in the sky, the thousands of phenomena spread across the earth, the land itself akin to a chessboard. The mountains and rivers, the grass and the trees, the wind and the moon. All of them were distinct, every detail clear beyond compare.

As if in the entire passage of time, he was the only person to ever exist.

*There is something undefined yet complete, born before Heaven and Earth. It is soundless and formless; independent and eternal; cyclical and inexhaustible.*[4]

*The Dao is chaos, the Dao is nature, the Dao is contained within the subtleties; it rises from the inner self, and it is in everything.*

*That is the Dao!*

In that instant, before Shen Qiao's eyes, everything became clear at once. He seemed to glimpse a glittering, transparent Daoist core, a perfect construction of nature, roaming a short distance away from him. But before he had the chance to reach out and touch it, he heard a voice from afar, its direction unclear.

"Shen Qiao."

He jolted, and everything went dark before his eyes. All the brilliance dissolved into nothingness, like a high tower suddenly collapsing and shattering, its fragments scattered.

Shen Qiao abruptly coughed up a mouthful of blood!

He slowly opened his eyes.

Yan Wushi was sitting on the bed, his back to the wall, disheveled hair hanging loose around him. Like before, he was staring at Shen Qiao, but his gaze was different from last night's.

*I was still careless,* Shen Qiao thought dryly. He wiped the blood from the corner of his mouth.

He'd left a small shred of awareness to watch the outside, but his sudden enlightenment partway through had caused him to lose himself entirely, without his realization.

"How does Sect Leader Yan feel?"

"You...truly went beyond my expectations," Yan Wushi said.

---

4    From Chapter 25 of the *Daodejing*.

He wore a fatigued, sluggish expression, but there was none of the bewilderment from last night. The person who'd smiled gently at Shen Qiao, who'd hugged him and refused to let go, had been like a flash in a pan: there and gone within a night.

But Shen Qiao's heart, originally on tenterhooks, calmed down instead. This was the Yan Wushi he knew: callous and coldhearted, who thought everyone beneath himself.

"I'd thought...that you'd be crushed after Sang Jingxing..." His words came very slowly, and they were feeble and empty of vitality. It was probably due to the injury, but after waking up, he hadn't leapt to ask about his own situation and instead began talking about Shen Qiao, calm and composed.

"I'm very sorry for disappointing Sect Leader Yan," Shen Qiao said coolly. "I'm still alive and well."

The corner of Yan Wushi's mouth tugged upward. "No...I'm not... disappointed... I'm actually pleasantly surprised... You destroyed... the demonic core...I planted within you...correct?"

Shen Qiao looked at him. "You should have known. At that time, I was absolutely no match for Sang Jingxing. My only option was to destroy my foundations and martial arts to perish together with him."

Yan Wushi nodded. "Yes. That was...your only choice."

"Yan Wushi," said Shen Qiao. "I know you want to ruin me. You believe that there is no kindness in the world, that a softhearted person like me has no reason to exist. You want me to open my eyes and see the cruelty within human hearts, to plunge me into hell, sinking and struggling, until I become a part of that hell myself."

A hint of a smile emerged at the corner of Yan Wushi's lips. He slowly continued speaking, pausing after each word. "But I... never imagined...that even in that hopeless situation...you could still...stand up again."

Shen Qiao closed his eyes, then opened them again. The ripples within him from before had completely vanished, leaving only complete calm. "If not for the *Zhuyang Strategy*, I truly would have died then. Your assumptions were correct. With the *Zhuyang Strategy*, a person really can rebuild their foundations. In other words, it indeed possesses the power to bring one back to life, truly proving itself the world's most remarkable book. But to do so, first you must destroy everything you've learned, dozens of years' worth of knowledge. Right now, you may be gravely injured, but your demonic core is still intact. If you wish to learn the *Zhuyang Strategy*, you must shatter your demonic core and experience what I did back then."

Yan Wushi stared at him unswervingly and gave no reply. Instead, he asked, "Was it...very painful?"

Like someone tempering his bones and smelting his tendons; like someone peeling his skin and paring away his flesh. Like he'd gone through all eighteen levels of hell.

But Shen Qiao was no longer willing to think about it, because instead of remembering the suffering of his body, he'd recall Bailong Monastery's abbot and Chuyi. He'd recall their tragic deaths, and he'd recall his own self-righteousness, his unrequited and wishful beliefs. He could have scarcely imagined that a heart of stone could never be moved, that the man he'd considered a friend had only seen him as an object for an experiment.

Shen Qiao withdrew all those thoughts and spoke, his tone very steady. "Yesterday, when I went to the capital, Dou Yanshan was still there. We need to wait a few more days for those martial artists to leave, then I will take you back to Chang'an."

Yet Yan Wushi shook his head. Even this little motion taxed him terribly. "It's already too late..."

*What's too late?* Shen Qiao was about to ask, but then he saw that Yan Wushi had closed his eyes and gone still.

His heart thumped, and he stepped forward to test for Yan Wushi's breathing.

It was still there. He'd only fallen into a deep sleep.

But his pulse seemed to be even more erratic than before. If he were to personify the man's true qi, it was like Yan Wushi had dozens of people brawling inside his body right now.

Shen Qiao tried to channel a small trickle of true qi into him, but it soon rebounded, together with the chaotic streams of qi within his body. Their violent retaliation forced Shen Qiao to quickly withdraw.

Yan Wushi slept until the afternoon.

The old man had yet to return. According to Banna, some traveling merchants had hired him as their guide yesterday, so he'd be gone for quite a few days. It wasn't his first time—heading west from here mostly led to the endless golden sands of the Gobi Desert. The routes through it were long and difficult to discern. People often got lost or went astray in its depths, never to return again. But the locals were familiar with the roads and knew what directions to take to leave the desert.

The bruises on Banna's neck and wrist had mostly healed. Shen Qiao talked to her for some time, then she went to set the sheep to pasture while he took the lamb broth she'd made with him back to the side yard.

Just as he returned, Yan Wushi's eyelashes trembled, as if he were about to wake.

Shen Qiao ladled the soup into two bowls and waited for him to wake up so he could ask about those words he'd said before he lost consciousness.

Yan Wushi opened his eyes, staring hazily at the muslin canopy above him.

"Do you feel any discomfort?" asked Shen Qiao. "I took your pulse just now. Several streams of true qi inside your body..."

"Meiren...gege."[5]

Shen Qiao paused.

A bizarre silence settled over the room. Even the faint aroma of the lamb soup seemed to be mocking Shen Qiao's speechlessness.

"It...hurts..."

He sounded nothing like the Yan Wushi whom Shen Qiao knew; it was as if someone else had taken over his body and spoken through it. Shen Qiao stared at him. He almost suspected that the great and mighty Huanyue Sect Leader had been possessed.

Shen Qiao pulled himself together. "What happened to you?"

"Hurts..." Yan Wushi looked at him. A hint of indignation came over his gaze—he seemed to be condemning Shen Qiao for standing over there instead of coming to him.

Shen Qiao had lived for thirty years and experienced all sorts of difficulties and dilemmas, but never had he been at such a loss on how to react as he was now.

Was Yan Wushi acting pitiful on purpose?

That was impossible. The way he'd acted before passing out was really the most consistent with his character.

Shen Qiao once again recalled the gentle, harmless smile Yan Wushi had shown him earlier.

But this wasn't quite the same as back then either.

Shen Qiao said, "You still remember your name, don't you?"

Yan Wushi blinked a couple of times. This expression made Shen Qiao's mouth twitch.

5    美人哥哥. *Meaning "beautiful older brother."*

"I'm...Xie Ling..."

Xie Ling... Xie?

Shen Qiao suddenly remembered what Kunye told him, that Yan Wushi's surname was once Xie—he'd descended from that great noble family of a bygone dynasty. And he'd come to this Coiling Dragon Assembly for the purpose of retrieving an item from his deceased mother.

Even just recalling this much, Shen Qiao still found it hard to believe.

He furrowed his brows a little, falling into a contemplative silence.

The lamb soup was starting to cool; a film of oil had congealed atop it.

Yan Wushi's gaze wandered back and forth between the soup and Shen Qiao, then he said hesitantly, "I'm hungry..."

Before this moment, no matter how downtrodden Yan Wushi became, Shen Qiao could never imagine that he'd look at him with such a lost, imploring expression and say, "I'm hungry."

Even when the other man had been remorseless, sarcastic, and taunting earlier, Shen Qiao had thought it normal, because *that* was Yan Wushi.

So how had he ended up like this?

Shen Qiao kneaded his forehead despite himself, thinking the entire thing an absolute pain.

"What else do you remember, other than the name Xie Ling?"

Yan Wushi's limbs were so weak, he couldn't even keep the bowl steady, so Shen Qiao could only spoon-feed him, little by little.

"Nothing..."

"Do you remember the name Yan Wushi?"

Yan Wushi shook his head, his bemused expression genuine.

Shen Qiao couldn't help but sigh again. "You really don't remember anything?"

When he combined Banna's words with Yan Wushi's various actions before and after the few times he'd woken up, Shen Qiao managed to grasp a bit of a lead.

In short, the chaotic true qi and head injury might be the reason for the massive changes in Yan Wushi's disposition.

He spent most of his time asleep, but every time he woke, he'd display a different type of behavior. Sometimes, it was a personality derived from fragmented memories; sometimes, he'd return to normal, like previously; sometimes, he'd be the way Banna had described him: violent and completely unable to control himself.

But Shen Qiao wasn't a doctor. He could come to these conclusions, but he had absolutely no idea on how to return Yan Wushi to normal.

He also didn't know if Yan Wushi would show further personalities beyond the ones he'd already demonstrated.

"I do remember..." With a bowl of soup in his belly, Yan Wushi licked his lips.

"Hm?" Shen Qiao was about to get up, but hearing this, he looked back at him.

"While...I was asleep...you kissed me... It also...tasted of lamb soup."

He had no words to respond to that.

Shen Qiao, who'd always been outstandingly good-tempered, suddenly had an urge. An urge to upend the other bowl of soup in his hand over that man's head.

Yan Wushi seemed to have sensed his thoughts and shrank back despite himself. Once again, he looked at Shen Qiao with that hurt expression.

Shen Qiao held his forehead and looked to the heavens, speechless.

# Onward to Ruoqiang

W HEN THE SUN SLIPPED low in the west, Banna returned with the sheep. As always, she first herded them into the pen, but kept the lamb she was holding in her arms and brought it with her to Shen Qiao's room. There she knocked.

Shen Qiao quickly came to open the door. On seeing Banna, he smiled at her. "You're back."

He turned to the side, but Banna didn't enter, instead only poking her head in. She was still afraid that Yan Wushi would go insane like he had yesterday.

But that man merely sat on the bed, quietly watching her. His expression didn't seem as violent as yesterday either.

"He's already fully recovered?" asked Banna.

Shen Qiao gave a wry smile and shook his head. "I fear he's gotten worse."

"Oh," said Banna. Now she was even more afraid to go in.

Shen Qiao didn't know how to explain the complicated situation Yan Wushi was in; he could only try to summarize it in a few words: "He's suffering from a head injury, so sometimes he's clear-minded, other times he isn't. Most of the time, he isn't."

"Is he clear-minded now?" Banna looked at Yan Wushi curiously, and he looked back at her too. His dark, tranquil eyes made her shiver inexplicably.

"...He's not."

Banna's fear returned. "Will he still grab people by the neck?"

"He probably won't," said Shen Qiao. "Right now, his mind seems to be close to that of a young child's. He can't even speak clearly. I was too careless last time; in the future I'll make sure he never hurts the two of you ever again."

Banna had never heard of this kind of situation before. She blinked a couple of times, watching Yan Wushi.

And Yan Wushi blinked back at her.

Banna and Shen Qiao fell silent, then Shen Qiao kneaded his temples.

Banna thought for a moment before putting the lamb she was holding on the ground. She urged it toward Yan Wushi and smiled. "Why don't we let him play with the lamb? The village children all love lambs."

The little lamb was a spotless white. Just the sight of it made one want to squeeze and pet it. Even Shen Qiao thought it adorable.

Yet Yan Wushi's brows pinched as he watched the lamb totter toward him. It lowered its head to sniff at his robe when he suddenly reached out and gave it a vicious shove.

The little lamb bleated, stumbling a few steps before falling to its knees.

Throwing her fear of Yan Wushi to the side, Banna quickly ran over to pick up the lamb.

Shen Qiao frowned at Yan Wushi, but he only gazed back with an innocent expression.

"Banna, let me deal with this. Go ahead and finish your tasks."

After that little interlude, there was obviously some lingering fear in Banna's heart. She nodded and obediently left with the lamb without another word.

"Why did you push the lamb just now?" asked Shen Qiao.

Yan Wushi only looked at him without reply.

But Shen Qiao faintly realized something.

No matter how much someone's personality changed, or how confused their memories became, everyone had some intrinsic qualities etched deep into their bones that couldn't be changed. Yan Wushi had always been a distrustful man, and even if he only possessed a few scattered memories now, that point would not change.

Shen Qiao said, "Give me your hand. I'll take your pulse."

Yan Wushi held out his hand.

There was a clear contrast between his attitude toward Shen Qiao and the way he treated Banna.

But Shen Qiao knew that it was because Yan Wushi possessed an uncanny instinct that told him that Shen Qiao would never hurt him.

Shen Qiao placed three fingers on his pulse and asked, "Can you move your hands and feet now? How about standing and walking?"

Yan Wushi nodded. "I can...but I get dizzy..."

Shen Qiao tried to probe. "This morning, you told me that it was too late to go back to Chang'an. Do you remember that?"

Yan Wushi gave him a blank stare.

Shen Qiao couldn't help but heave a long sigh.

"Why don't you lie down and rest?" Perhaps he'd return to normal again after sleeping? Even a sarcastic, mocking Yan Wushi was far better than his current state of complete ignorance.

But Yan Wushi refused. "Don't want to."

So, he didn't want to sleep.

If it'd been an ordinary child, there would have been many ways to coax him. But this was no child. Asking Shen Qiao to say gentle and tender words, the kind you'd use on a child, to Yan Wushi's face? It was impossible.

As the two of them stared at each other, at an impasse, a knock sounded at the door.

As though he'd been granted amnesty, Shen Qiao let out an imperceptible sigh of relief, then stood to open the door.

It was Banna. She'd fried some flatbread and brought it over with the lamb soup.

The two of them exchanged a couple of words by the door. Shen Qiao thanked her and closed the door after she left, heading back inside.

Shen Qiao placed the lamb soup and flatbread in front of Yan Wushi. "Are you hungry? Eat."

Yan Wushi glanced at Shen Qiao, then quickly dropped his head and mumbled, "Feed me."

Shen Qiao fell silent.

After a long time with no reply, Yan Wushi raised his head to look at Shen Qiao, then said hesitantly, "Like last time... Kis..."

*If I knock him unconscious right now, will he wake up with a more normal personality?* Shen Qiao contemplated this with all seriousness.

Yan Wushi seemed to have sensed the impending danger; he swallowed down the "kiss" that was halfway out of his mouth and huddled in a corner of the bed.

Shen Qiao gave another sigh, pushing the lamb soup to him while he picked himself up some flatbread. He tore off a small piece and popped it into his mouth, chewing slowly.

Only then did Yan Wushi scoot back from the bed's corner. He reached for the soup.

His meridians were injured, his bones damaged. His hands still trembled slightly as he held the bowl, but nowhere near as much as when he'd first woken up. It was obvious that he'd recovered quite a bit.

Shen Qiao watched as he lowered his head and sipped the soup, little by little. Something occurred to him, and he suddenly asked, "You were worried about the soup? That's why you wanted me to feed you?"

That way, the soup would have to enter Shen Qiao's mouth first, and if it were poisoned, he'd collapse first as well.

Yan Wushi didn't reply, but his silence itself was already an answer.

Shen Qiao should have been furious, but he answered calmly, "I don't know how much you remember, and even if I say I have no intention of hurting you, you might not believe me. However, Banna and her grandfather are good people. Since we must stay here for now, you should restrain yourself a little, lest you hurt their feelings. I also won't allow you to hurt anyone else anymore."

Yan Wushi remained silent. Shen Qiao didn't know what else to say, so he also fell quiet.

Once he'd believed that, given enough time, even someone like Yan Wushi could be moved, that fullhearted sincerity could wear down even metal and stone. Only just now did he realize how ridiculously wrong he'd been.

No matter how Yan Wushi changed, the only person he'd ever trust was himself.

The two of them sat by themselves, one on the bed and the other at the table. Though there was only a short distance between them, their gazes never met.

More precisely speaking, Shen Qiao was eating with his head lowered while Yan Wushi was watching Shen Qiao.

After a long time, Yan Wushi finally spoke. "Meiren-gege…"

This address instantly elicited a full-body shudder from Shen Qiao. He was about to correct him when a burst of noise came from outside.

He listened attentively for a moment, then abruptly stood and began heading out. He didn't forget to look back and tell Yan Wushi, "You stay here. Don't come out."

Elsewhere, Banna had also heard the noise. She thought little of it and assumed her grandfather had returned. With a cheer, she ran out to greet him.

The moment she opened the gate, however, she saw a troop of men on horses galloping toward her, dust rolling behind them.

Her grandfather wasn't among them at all.

Banna immediately remembered that Shen Qiao and Yan Wushi were still here. Suspecting that the other party had come for them, she tried to close the gate, ready to turn and inform Shen Qiao.

However, the men were faster than she was. One of them reined in his horse and dismounted, then strode up and kicked open the courtyard gate. It all happened so quickly that Banna had no time to react.

Banna gasped as the impact from the gate being kicked open forced her to stumble back several steps, and she almost fell to the ground. But a hand landed on her lower back as she staggered, immediately stopping her from teetering back further.

Once she'd found her footing, Shen Qiao let go and turned to the newcomer. "Who is this gentleman?"

Another man in the back dismounted his horse. He strode up to them, pulling down the scarf that covered his face, and then cupped his hands at Shen Qiao. "I apologize for my subordinate's rudeness and how he scared this young lady," he said. "I came to find you. There were too many people back at the inn, so we didn't have the chance for a real discussion. Have you been doing well, Daoist Master Shen?"

After a long separation, a reappraisal was due. The man's speech was courteous and refined, and even his smiled brimmed with confidence. A glance was enough to know that he'd been among the elites for a while, living in luxury. He was no longer that Chen Gong from the past, who'd been uneducated, a little coarse, and yet keen in his own way.

Looking again at the men who'd come with Chen Gong, Shen Qiao unexpectedly saw some familiar faces among them, one being the patriarch of Qi's Murong family, Murong Qin. The same Murong Qin who'd appeared at Chuyun Temple to seize the cargo the Liuhe Guild had been escorting. Things really had changed—the martial expert who'd once sold himself to the imperial court of Qi had become Chen Gong's subordinate. One couldn't help but marvel at the vagaries of fate.

Shen Qiao withdrew his gaze from Murong Qin, Tuoba Liangzhe, and the others. He looked at Chen Gong and said harshly, "This place is remote and distant, yet County Duke Chen managed to find it anyway. How did you know where I was?"

Chen Gong glanced at Banna and smiled. "I met an old man. I believe he's this young lady's grandfather?"

Banna was alarmed but also still somewhat confused. However, Shen Qiao's face fell. "If there's something you want, just bring it to me! Why involve innocent bystanders?"

Contrary to expectations, Chen Gong's tone was consoling: "Don't be so nervous. I only wished to ask him your whereabouts; now that I know, I naturally won't do anything to him. The wind is harsh out in the open, which makes it hard to talk. Won't you invite me inside?"

Hearing that her grandfather had been captured, Banna's entire body grew weak. Shen Qiao reached out to support her. After a brief moment of silence, he said, "This way, please."

Murong Qin and the others were about to follow, but Chen Gong stopped them. "Daoist Master Shen is an upright gentleman; he won't do anything to me. You can just wait outside."

The mighty Murong Qin was the foremost martial artist in the imperial court of Qi, and he'd held himself with great arrogance that night at Chuyun Temple. Yet at this moment, in front of Chen Gong, he was as docile as a mouse before a cat, following each order with the appropriate action and without an extra word. He cupped his hands at Chen Gong, then brought the others to stand guard outside.

Chen Gong followed Shen Qiao inside. He gave a surprised sound and then smiled brightly. "Where's Sect Leader Yan?"

He'd probably received quite a bit of information interrogating the old man. Shen Qiao didn't reply as they each sat down. Then he cut straight to the chase: "What does County Duke Chen require from his visit this time?"

Chen Gong smiled. "In the end, we still count as old friends. You showed me kindness before; what kind of person would I be if I repaid that with evil? So, you need not look at me like that, Daoist Master Shen."

Shen Qiao said coolly, "This humble Daoist dares not claim the credit. County Duke Chen has already repaid that trifling favor with several chests full of sandwiches. If County Duke Chen can show great magnanimity and release the old man, I will be endlessly grateful."

"Nothing's happened to him," said Chen Gong. "He'll be released sooner or later; you need not worry. Previously at the capital, I had something I wanted to discuss with you, but you left in such a rush and vanished in the blink of an eye. So, I had no choice but to do something like this."

Shen Qiao had no reply.

Chen Gong was unconcerned with his coldness. After a pause, he continued, "I indeed came here today due to a certain matter. I wish to cooperate with Daoist Master Shen on something."

He suddenly changed the topic. "Outside, rumor has it Sect Leader Yan is already dead. I never thought that he'd still be alive, or that you were the one who saved him. From what I know, Yan Wushi was rather unkind to you, yet you repaid evil with virtue, letting bygones be bygones. Such breadth of mind is truly admirable!"

Shen Qiao wasn't someone who liked mocking others, but he was enraged at Chen Gong threatening him with the old man. He couldn't help but reply, "People who repay kindness with treachery are everywhere in his world, so why would repaying evil with virtue be any stranger?"

It was a line full of implications, and Chen Gong's expression flickered. But in the next moment, he again smiled as if nothing were wrong. "It's been a while since our last meeting; Daoist Master Shen's tongue has grown quite sharp. I wonder what those experts who ambushed Yan Wushi would do if they knew he was still alive. Daoist Master Shen is an exceptional martial artist, true, but even if you can deal with Yu Ai, can you deal with Guang Lingsan and Duan Wenyang? Let alone that old monk Xueting."

"Are these words the cooperation that County Duke Chen was referring to?"

"Of course not," said Chen Gong. "Does Daoist Master Shen know of Ruoqiang?"

*Ruoqiang.*

Shen Qiao repeated the word twice in his mind—it sounded like a person's name. He shook his head.

Chen Gong said, "*The Book of Han—Memoir of the Western Regions* says thus: on exiting the Southern Pass, the closest location is a country named Ruoqiang. And this small country was destroyed by Shanshan."

Only last year, Chen Gong had been completely illiterate, yet now he could recite *The Book of Han* with perfect ease. The Lord of Qi might have been a capricious fool, but if he were to favor someone, they'd have to possess something extraordinary. Looking at this, Chen Gong was indeed worthy of the emperor's fondness.

Shen Qiao didn't speak; he quietly waited for him to continue.

"Pardon me for being blunt," said Chen Gong. "Ruoqiang mined jade. Though now destroyed, the ruins of the ancient city are still there. It used to be rich in a special kind of carnelian[6] that can't be found anywhere else, and that's what I'm looking for. As for why I wish for your cooperation, it's because your martial prowess would be a great boon to me, but there's something in it for you as well. That thing is called jade cistanche, and it grows near the carnelian deposits. It can rejoin bones, regenerate muscles, and is miraculously effective on internal injuries. I believe that Sect Leader Yan might have need of it."

After that, he spoke no more and waited for Shen Qiao's response.

The room was quiet, except for Banna's occasional sniffles. The rims of her eyes were red.

Shen Qiao was silent for a long moment. "You're afraid that I'll refuse to go, so you're holding Banna's grandfather elsewhere and threatening me with him."

Chen Gong remained undaunted. "Correct. I don't know why you saved Yan Wushi after what he did to you, so I can't be certain

---

6    Carnelian, while not actually jade, was considered by those in ancient China to be a kind of jade.

that you'd be willing to take such a risk for him. But I know the kind of person you are. You could never stand by and let an innocent man suffer because of you."

"Thank you, you've truly understood me well," said Shen Qiao coolly.

"In that case, Daoist Master Shen has agreed?"

"Do I have any other choice?"

Chen Gong smiled. "Indeed, you do not. Worry not, the old man is unharmed. I'll have someone release him upon our return."

"Release him first, then I'll go with you."

Chen Gong shook his head, still smiling. "I can't do that. Why would you say that, Daoist Master Shen? The only way you'd earnestly come on this trip is if I held the old man above you. Oh, that's right, since Sect Leader Yan is probably in poor health, I've already ordered some men to prepare sufficient quantities of food and medicine for him. You can be at ease in bringing him."

These words were a test. Chen Gong suspected that even if Yan Wushi hadn't died in the ambush by five martial experts, he'd still be injured, so it'd be difficult for him to return to his previous strength.

But Shen Qiao neither confirmed or denied it—he had no intention of replying at all. So Chen Gong could only say, "If there are no issues, let's leave tomorrow morning. I'm certain Murong Qin has already found me a place to stay for the night. I'll go and rest first, then come find you tomorrow. You should get some rest too. Ruoqiang is a long way from here. We must properly use this respite and conserve our strength."

With that, Chen Gong stood and left.

"Shen-langjun..." Banna gazed at Shen Qiao, as if pleading for help.

Shen Qiao finally gave a wry smile. "I don't know what I can do to apologize. This all happened because of me. I promise that

I'll come back soon. I'll see that your grandfather returns safely as well."

He took out all the meager money he still had on him. "Here, take it. In case it's necessary."

Banna shook her head. "I don't want it."

"Be good," said Shen Qiao gently. "Stay at home, and unless you must, don't stray too far. I will definitely return your grandpa to you, safe and sound."

Few people could resist this "be good" from Shen Qiao. Banna's heart had been in a desperate panic, but now she slowly began to calm down. She didn't blame Shen Qiao for bringing trouble to her family, because this girl was very considerate, and she knew that Shen Qiao must feel hundreds or thousands of times more awful than she did at this moment.

She nodded. "You...have to be careful."

Shen Qiao gave her a comforting smile and said only four words: "Everything will be fine."

Murong Qin really had used some unknown method to seize a relatively comfortable house within the village. The original owner had been forced to stay at someone else's place, and the entire village kept a wide berth from these sudden newcomers, as if they were venomous scorpions. Fortunately, Chen Gong had no interest in staying long—early the next morning, Murong Qin arrived on orders and knocked.

After the third knock, the gates opened, and Shen Qiao walked out with Yan Wushi.

It'd been a while since Yan Wushi had stood and walked, so his limbs were a little stiff. Furthermore, he was still suffering from serious internal injuries—every step that he took aggravated his wounds. Hence, he moved at a very slow pace.

That night at Chuyun Monastery, Yan Wushi had practically dropped down from the sky and completely destroyed the *Zhuyang Strategy*, and he'd humiliated Murong Qin's party quite a bit with his poisonous tongue. Now they saw him as a fallen tiger, his face pale and body plagued by illness, and Murong Qin couldn't help the burst of schadenfreude that came from his lips. "I trust that Sect Leader Yan remembers his old friends from Chuyun Temple," he sneered. "You truly don't look too well."

Now that Yan Wushi had become a public enemy across the entire land, with all sorts of factions raring to kill him, Murong Qin thought Yan Wushi beneath himself.

Yan Wushi's face was impassive. Even his eyes looked like they'd been soaked in well water and were bone-chillingly cold.

For some reason, these eyes staring at him caused Murong Qin to swallow back his more spiteful words.

Chen Gong walked over, his movements confident and easy. A number of people followed behind him.

His presence was magnificent—no longer that of the helpless youth who'd been mistreated by his stepmother and left the house in anger. Environment influences demeanor, upbringing influences base character. When someone's status and position in society change, so, too, will their personality.

"Ready to go now, Daoist Master Shen?"

Shen Qiao nodded.

"We'll ride horses first. There's a small town right before we enter the desert; we'll switch to fresh mounts there."

He was languid and carefree, completely unworried about the prospect of Shen Qiao turning hostile. Ignoring that he still had Banna's grandfather, even if Shen Qiao took Chen Gong hostage, his party still had the advantage of numbers. All they needed to do then was capture a villager to use as a hostage, and Shen Qiao's hands would be tied.

Shen Qiao knew this as well, so he made no rash actions.

"What do you need the carnelian for?"

Chen Gong smiled. "I expected you to ask me this yesterday instead of waiting until now. That carnelian has a certain ability that's highly important to me, but the ancient ruins have been deserted for many years. I don't know what kind of dangers we'll be facing this time. Every additional ally means additional strength. I didn't think about asking you in the beginning, but after seeing your moves in the capital, my confidence has increased greatly. With Daoist Master Shen here, we'll be many times more powerful!"

Shen Qiao didn't respond. When he saw Chen Gong lead two horses over, he said, "I'll ride together with him."

Chen Gong glanced at Yan Wushi. "What kind of injury ails Sect Leader Yan? He looks a little vacant—can he no longer even recognize people?"

Yan Wushi answered coldly, "My venerable self can recognize people just fine. I just can't be bothered to waste words on you. Do you think you're all that just because you've latched on to Gao Wei? In this venerable one's eyes, you're still nothing more than an insect."

Chen Gong's expression twisted, but he reached out to stop Tuoba Liangzhe behind him from drawing his sword.

"Sect Leader Yan is truly a great man—still using words as bold as these when in such dire straits. I hope you can still say these things once the Göktürks and Buddhist factions know you're still alive."

Yan Wushi sneered. "Did Gao Wei only teach you how to mouth off while you were in his bed? If you're dissatisfied, feel free to come at me."

Chen Gong frowned. He was a little perturbed, wondering if his information was wrong, that perhaps Yan Wushi wasn't only alive but wholly uninjured? Could he have managed to fool all five of those great martial experts?

Despite knowing this was terribly unlikely, when the subject was a monster like Yan Wushi, even the strangest and most impossible things seemed to become logical.

Not only Chen Gong, but even Murong Qin, Tuoba Liangzhe, and the others still held some fear in their hearts.

A person's reputation was akin to the shadow cast by a tree. Even if the Huanyue Sect Leader was only standing there, it was enough to make everyone question themselves.

As it was said: only an evil person could torment other evil people. No matter how powerful Shen Qiao was, he could never pull this off.

Chen Gong didn't waste too much time. He waved his hand, and everyone mounted their houses, ready to depart.

Shen Qiao had Yan Wushi mount first, then he moved to sit in front of him in order to steer the horse.

Everyone set off. Several dozen horses trotted along the road, the wind and sand muffling everyone's voices. At this time, even speaking became an arduous task, since sand would get in the moment they opened their mouths. No one was willing to eat any sand, so they just hung their heads and continued onward, communicating with each other through gestures.

Arms wrapped tightly around Shen Qiao's waist, and a chest pressed right up against his back. Yan Wushi leaned close to his ear and said quietly, "A-Qiao, how did I do earlier?"

As soon as Shen Qiao heard that gentle tone, he was certain that this Yan Wushi was not the "normal" Yan Wushi.

He noticed that he'd been sighing more often the last few days than he'd ever done in the past. "Xie Ling?"

Yan Wushi was a little surprised. "How did you know that my old name was Xie Ling?"

Shen Qiao's only answer was silence.

# Discoveries

I F TALKING WITH Yan Wushi in the past had him raging himself to an early death, then talking to Yan Wushi right now was like raging to death and then being brought back to life by the force of that same rage. Those who lacked a strong will would surely be unable to continue the conversation.

Shen Qiao sighed and decided just to shut his mouth, refusing to speak further.

But when the man in the back saw him refusing to talk, his arms tightened as he placed his chin on Shen Qiao's shoulder. "A-Qiao, why are you ignoring me?"

*Because right now I'm contemplating whether to knock you out before we keep going,* Shen Qiao thought. He tilted his head a little to the side and lowered his voice. "Since you still remember who you are, then do you know why Chen Gong is looking for carnelian in Ruoqiang's ancient city?"

"I don't know," said Yan Wushi. "But I've heard about jade cistanche before. It usually grows deep inside the Gobi Desert and is normally hidden within rocky crevices. It's incredibly difficult to find and indeed a rare treasure. But it's clear that Chen Gong is only looking for the carnelian. He just brought up jade cistanche as bait so he could get us to run here and there for him."

Even in the past, when he hadn't been injured, Shen Qiao had rarely heard him analyze anything in such a placid tone.

"Yes, I noticed as well," said Shen Qiao. "But even if there is no jade cistanche, he's holding Banna's grandfather hostage, so I was forced to take this trip with him. However, if we can find the jade cistanche, you'll be able to fully recover from your wounds."

"In truth, my real wound lies in the flaw within my demonic core. The jade cistanche can only cure external wounds, so it won't be of much help."

Shen Qiao was amused. "You have a crack in your skull. The jade cistanche can spur muscle growth and rejoin bones, so it'll have its uses, no? Surely, you must heal the external injuries first?"

"Actually, I don't wish to heal." Yan Wushi sounded dejected.

Shen Qiao frowned. "Why not?"

He sensed that Yan Wushi's current personality was different from all the previous ones. Rather, it felt a little like the one who'd smiled gently at him several days ago.

"Because once I'm healed, I won't be able to talk to you anymore," said Yan Wushi. "Don't tell me that you prefer the Yan Wushi who ignored your sincerity and delivered you to Sang Jingxing?"

"You are him," said Shen Qiao.

"I am not."

Shen Qiao was at a loss. "Then who are you?"

Yan Wushi was silent for a moment. "You can call me A-Yan."

Shen Qiao did not respond.

"Won't you call me that just once? Please? I've never heard you say my name before."

Shen Qiao was stupefied. "When I look at your face, I can't bring myself to say it."

Yan Wushi complained, "A face is just the surface, a shell. Why put so much stock in appearances? I know everything he did to you. Yan Wushi might be a fickle ingrate, but I'd never turn my back on you. A-Qiao, it's impossible to find a second person as kind as you in this world. He might not cherish you, but I will. Won't you let me?"

Shen Qiao stopped talking and refused to respond further, but Yan Wushi didn't give up. He was about to say something more, but then he saw Chen Gong's horse suddenly slow. The other man turned his head to glance at them. Seeing the two of them whispering to each other, he couldn't help but jab at them. "Looks like the rumors were untrue; Daoist Master Shen and Yan Wushi get along quite well! That puts me at ease too. With the kind support from the two of you, I need not worry about failing to find the carnelian on this trip!"

Shen Qiao looked up at the sky. Having lived here for several days, he'd also gained some understanding of the local weather. "Is there a sandstorm coming?"

Chen Gong naturally didn't know, but he'd brought along people who did. Murong Qin said, "Correct. There's a small town right ahead of us. My Lord, why don't we rest there for the night and then continue the journey tomorrow? We can take the opportunity to change our mounts as well."

Once, this man had been full of arrogance, but now he was perfectly happy to call Chen Gong his lord. Shen Qiao couldn't help glancing at him. Murong Qin's expression remained the same as ever, as though he didn't find this master-servant relationship insulting to himself in the slightest. He should have venerated the Emperor of Qi, Gao Wei, as his lord, yet now he was honoring Chen Gong...

As if he'd sensed his feelings, Yan Wushi leaned over behind Shen Qiao to speak into his ear. "The Murong family has already pledged their loyalty to Chen Gong in secret."

Yan Wushi's hot breath fanned over his ear, making it so Shen Qiao couldn't help but lean forward himself.

After a short journey, they arrived at the little town. With Chen Gong's retinue blaring their wealth and presence, they booked the best inn in town the moment they entered—though in truth it was the town's only inn. Its lodgings were quite a bit worse compared to Banna's house, let alone that of the royal capital. But they were in a remote location, after all, so just finding a place to rest was already quite remarkable. No one had any complaints, and after dinner, everyone returned to their rooms without a word.

The inn had a limited number of rooms, so Shen Qiao and Yan Wushi shared one.

Shen Qiao wasn't a curious person by nature, but he still found himself concerned at the way Chen Gong had gone from a perfectly ordinary youth to someone so full of mysteries on their next meeting. Especially when these mysteries were likely related to the goal of this trip and their safety—Shen Qiao couldn't afford to be lax.

"If we're talking about power, Chen Gong derives all of his from the Lord of Qi," he mused. "So, if the Lord of Qi perishes, Chen Gong will be left with nothing. Murong Qin was the best martial artist in Qi's imperial court, but he willingly became Chen Gong's subordinate and addresses him as lord. On a fundamental level, this is incredibly odd."

Ever since Yan Wushi's massive shift in personality, his eyes would always follow Shen Qiao. Whether Shen Qiao stood up or sat down, his gaze remained fixed on him, and Shen Qiao of course felt it—he wasn't a corpse. It just made him feel terribly awkward. After he finished speaking, he couldn't help but frown. "Why do you keep staring at me?"

"Because you're good-looking." Yan Wushi smiled at him, and it was as if ten miles of peach blossoms were blooming in the spring breeze, their branches glittering like gems as the moon's crystal glow seeped through them.

Shen Qiao sighed, realizing that even though this Yan Wushi still wasn't very normal, he was still somewhat better than the ones prior. "Talk about proper things."

"Did Chen Gong know martial arts before?" Yan Wushi suddenly asked.

With this reminder, Shen Qiao suddenly realized where that sense of disconnect had come from.

Before, not only did Chen Gong not know martial arts, he could barely read more than a handful of characters. Where had he learned martial arts from? There'd been the couple of moves he'd learned from Shen Qiao for self-defense, but those were only enough to deal with a bandit or two at most. But the current Chen Gong moved with restraint, his steps limber—it was obvious he'd already passed a certain stage in his martial arts journey. Perhaps not a first-rate martial artist, but at least second-rate, enough to enter into the top ranks of the jianghu.

How could he have progressed by such leaps and bounds in such a short period of time? Most people had to start their training at a young age, yet Chen Gong was like a tower that had been erected overnight. It was terribly suspicious.

"Also, previously when I said to return to Chang'an, you said that it was too late," Shen Qiao said. "Did something happen over there? Will the Lord of Zhou be all right?"

Yan Wushi shook his head. Having spent most of the day on horseback, his face was heavy with fatigue. Even though he'd only been sitting, spared the need to focus on the road, he was still heavily injured. Just the bumps and jolts along the way had been enough to aggravate those wounds.

"My head hurts a little..." A pained expression surfaced on his face, and he reached toward his head to touch the injury.

Shen Qiao saw this right away and grabbed his hand. "Don't move."

He placed his hand on Yan Wushi's back and channeled a few wisps of true qi inside.

Shen Qiao's present internal cultivation came from the *Zhuyang Strategy* and was neutral and gentle. But when it entered Yan Wushi's body, it only aggravated his pain, and his expression twisted in agony.

Shen Qiao had no choice but to quickly stop what he was doing.

Yan Wushi's body was boiling, as if he were standing inside a blazing furnace. Nothing like this had ever happened before.

"Sect Leader Yan?" called Shen Qiao softly.

Yan Wushi grabbed his hand. Despite his stupor, he still remembered to say, "Call me A-Yan..."

Shen Qiao said not a word.

"A lot of things you said are a mess in my mind, so I can't explain. Perhaps Yan Wushi knows, but I don't..."

*Does that mean that each personality has limited access to his memories?* Shen Qiao pondered with a frown.

"Let me sleep a bit first..." Yan Wushi said. His voice grew quieter and quieter; by the end of his sentence, his eyes were already closed.

In truth, Buddhist Master Xueting and the others wanting to kill Yan Wushi wasn't because his death would make the world right again. They'd wanted to stop Huanyue Sect from expanding its authority in Northern Zhou, and furthermore, they wanted to stop Huanyue Sect from assisting the Lord of Zhou in uniting the lands. Hence, their final target was Yuwen Yong. Now that Yan Wushi was already dead in the eyes of outsiders, Huanyue Sect was without a leader. Bian Yanmei would be struggling to stabilize the sect, so he'd definitely be remiss on his protection of Yuwen Yong. With this, an opportunity arose for others to take advantage of.

So, Yan Wushi's "too late" probably meant that something was about to happen to Yuwen Yong.

But they'd already arrived in Tuyuhun, which was thousands of miles away from Chang'an, and they were about to enter the vast, desolate desert where few people trod. Even without taking Yan Wushi into consideration, Banna's grandfather was still in Chen Gong's hands, so Shen Qiao couldn't just turn and leave. The only thing he could do now was continue onward and help Chen Gong obtain the carnelian first.

Early the next morning, Chen Gong sent his men over to wake them up. Yan Wushi was still in a deep sleep—no matter how they called him, he wouldn't wake.

Shen Qiao had no choice but to place Yan Wushi at the front of the horse while he sat behind him. He wrapped his arms around Yan Wushi to hold the reins, thus preventing him from tumbling off along the way.

Seeing this, Chen Gong handed him a bottle of medicine. "Inside are pills that can increase alertness and replenish qi. Give Sect Leader Yan a couple—perhaps they'll help."

"Thank you," said Shen Qiao, "but I don't know what his condition is, so rashly giving him medicine might not be the best decision."

Chen Gong smiled. "Don't worry. They're concocted of mild ingredients, like wolfberry and wild sage. In the case they're ineffective, they won't kill him. If my guess is correct, he's like this due to the severe injuries he suffered from the fight with Dou Yanshan's group. Normally, I'd be happy to just laugh at him from the sidelines, but right now we're all in the same boat. If something happens to Yan Wushi, you'll be distracted, which doesn't benefit me at all."

He'd spoken the truth. Yan Wushi's situation wasn't looking too hopeful—his body's true qi was in disorder, leaving him unable to accept any from outside sources. Shen Qiao was completely at the end of his rope.

He took the bottle and tipped out two pills, then fed them to Yan Wushi.

Not long after, the man suddenly moved. He hacked up a large mouthful of blood before slowly opening his eyes.

Shen Qiao suddenly realized something. If the pills really only contained mild ingredients, they couldn't have been this effective.

"What other things are in these pills?" he asked Chen Gong.

This time, Chen Gong was honest. "Ginseng and snow lotus. I didn't tell you before because I was afraid that you wouldn't let him take any, thinking they'd be too potent."

Shen Qiao then asked Yan Wushi, "How do you feel?"

He didn't reply, but his drooping eyelids fluttered a little, as if giving him a glance. Then they slid closed again, and he arduously straightened himself while on the horse.

But his face was a chilly white, and a faint sheen of sweat covered his forehead.

"Looks like it won't be an issue to keep going. Let's go."

Chen Gong seemed to be in a hurry to reach his destination. Though he didn't show it too much, Shen Qiao could sense it.

The little town didn't have any camels they could switch to, so the group could only continue on horseback. Fortunately, the area wasn't completely covered in sand; scattered rocks could be seen, meaning that they were still in the Gobi Desert.

Yan Wushi didn't speak to Shen Qiao again for the rest of the journey; he only drowsily leaned against Shen Qiao's back.

The fact that he was still alive was already enough to attract much attention, but Chen Gong's men paid little heed to him, even Murong Qin. They seemed to have another goal in mind, and this goal was far more important than Yan Wushi.

It was difficult for horses to travel in the Gobi Desert. As the sandstorm blew harder, they were forced to dismount and walk while leading the horses. Martial artists traveled quickly; after walking for over a half a day, from dawn to dusk, they were already far from that little town. Only a sea of golden sand lay around them, and even martial experts were helpless against it. Fortunately, they'd long prepared for this and covered their faces with cloaks and heads with scarves. That way, they managed to avoid getting sand in their mouths.

The one who walked in front was a rather homely middle-aged man. Shen Qiao didn't know him, and Chen Gong had no intention of introducing him either. But it was obvious he didn't know any martial arts and wasn't part of Murong Qin's group. Chen Gong had brought him to scout out their path.

The man held a compass in hand as he rode high astride a horse. Since he was in charge of discerning their direction, someone led the horse for him.

Then suddenly, he raised his hand.

Immediately, Murong Qin yelled, "Halt!"

Everyone stopped in their tracks and stared at the middle-aged man's back.

For a long time, the man watched the compass with his head lowered. Then he turned and jogged over to Chen Gong, wiping haphazardly at the sweat on the face with his scarf. "My Lord...something's strange... Once we got here, the compass stopped working!"

Chen Gong's brow furrowed. "Didn't you say before that we should walk in this direction?"

Faced with Chen Gong's blazing stare, the man was almost unable to finish his sentence. "Yes...yes! But now...please look at this!"

He passed the compass to Chen Gong, who looked at it. The needle was spinning wildly with no sign of rest.

Naturally, Chen Gong didn't understand. "What does this mean?"

The man smiled apologetically. "If this lowly one's guess is correct, the ancient city of Ruoqiang that your esteemed self is looking for must be right underneath, and it indeed has something inside it. That something is interfering with the compass needle. Perhaps it's the carnelian you're after! But, because of this interference, this lowly one is unable to find the entrance to the city!"

Everyone raised their heads and looked around, but all they could see was an ocean of yellow sand, blurring even the boundary between heaven and earth. Occasionally they could spot a few bare rocks nearby, but not even a hint of the so-called ancient ruins.

Chen Gong asked Murong Qin, "What do you think?"

Murong Qin thought for a while. "Why don't we wait for the sandstorm to stop first, my Lord?"

Chen Gong frowned. "But there's no place to use as shelter here."

He turned back to the guide. "Should we keep going, or should we stop here and wait? Give me a definite answer."

Chen Gong's words were flippant, but the man dared not reply recklessly. He hesitated, unable to decide, fearful that they'd make the wrong decision due to his answer, which would cost him his head. He scratched at his face anxiously. "That...it's..."

"Think carefully before you answer," said Chen Gong coldly.

The man shuddered hard, then blurted, "We should keep going!"

"Are you sure?"

"Yes! Of course! This lowly one will lead the way. Judging from the compass's response, it should be around here somewhere! We'll find it eventually if we keep looking!"

"Let's go, then," said Chen Gong.

Everyone continued onward, and Shen Qiao followed behind them. He looked back at Yan Wushi, now sprawled prone on horseback, then hesitated for a moment. "Are you Yan Wushi? Or someone else?"

The man quietly extended a hand from beneath his robe and grabbed Shen Qiao's wrist, still holding the reins. "It's me, A-Yan."

Shen Qiao had no words, but he internally breathed a sigh of relief.

Though he'd saved Yan Wushi, deep inside his heart, he didn't want to have too much contact with him.

After Yan Wushi's massive change in disposition, both personalities born from him—"A-Yan" and "Xie Ling"—were much easier to speak with than the original. At least, when he was with them, Shen Qiao could manage to pretend that they were two other people entirely instead of Yan Wushi.

Suddenly, a man in front yelled in surprise, "My Lord, he's gone!"

# The Only One
# in the World

THE MOMENT HE SAID THIS, everyone looked over. Sure enough, they could find no trace of the middle-aged man, and the yellow sands before them grew increasingly turbid, whipped into whirling eddies over the flat ground. Visibility had dropped to the lowest: Shen Qiao couldn't even see which silhouette was Chen Gong, let alone the middle-aged man.

Murong Qin arduously made his way to the front and grabbed Chen Gong. He yelled, "The sandstorm is too strong! My Lord, please take shelter over there!"

Chen Gong gritted his teeth. "No, none of us know our way around here. We must follow him closely!"

Just as he spoke, the sandstorm grew even fiercer. Lifting their heads, they could see the yellow sands being blown by the darkened skies. Tears sprang up as sand blew into their eyes, blurring their vision. In this kind of situation, even the strongest of martial artists was no match for nature. They could only wind their scarves tighter, but the sandstorm made it near impossible for anyone to continue forward.

Shen Qiao clutched Yan Wushi's wrist in a tight grip while doing his best to hunch over, reducing the force of the wind against his body.

Frightened, the horses began to struggle. The moment Shen Qiao's attention slipped, the reins were yanked out of his hands. By the time he looked back, the horse was nowhere to be found.

The wind shrieked within his ears, and the haze of endless yellow was all he could see.

"My Lord, this way..."

Shen Qiao dimly heard Murong Qin's words, and he quickly hurried in their direction. But then his next step landed on empty air, and his entire person slid downward!

Beneath him seemed to be a bottomless abyss, the sloped walls treacherously steep. Shen Qiao felt like he'd been falling for ages, yet there was still nowhere for his feet to secure himself.

Another couple of moments passed before he felt the incline lessen, if only slightly. With one hand on the boulder behind him, Shen Qiao steadied himself, then managed to straighten while standing on the slope.

Inky darkness filled his eyes—he couldn't see his hand before his face. But this actually gave him a sense of nostalgic familiarity.

The wind that had been howling into his ears had vanished, leaving his surroundings as silent as the grave.

Except for the sounds of breathing that came from below—rapid yet feeble.

"Who's there?" asked Shen Qiao.

Those breaths paused, then after a long silence, they weakly replied, "...It's me."

Shen Qiao groped his way down the slope, leaping and jumping to where the voice was coming from. "How did you end up down here?"

He clearly remembered letting go of Yan Wushi's hand before he fell.

"A-Qiao, my arm seems to be dislocated, and my head hurts..."

Shen Qiao took in Yan Wushi's words silently.

He'd already had that crack in his skull, and now he'd fallen from such a high place. How could his head not hurt?

Shen Qiao could only walk over to him. "Which arm?"

"Right arm," said Yan Wushi.

Shen Qiao felt along the arm and set the joint. Yan Wushi gave a muffled grunt, but he didn't cry out in pain.

"Wait for me here," said Shen Qiao. "I'm going ahead to take a look."

But just as he was about to step forward, Yan Wushi grabbed the edge of his robe.

"Won't your head hurt even more if you stand and walk now?" asked Shen Qiao.

"...No," said Yan Wushi.

Shen Qiao didn't want to waste too much time on conversation. He was also afraid that he might end up unable to find Yan Wushi even if he tried to come back, due to their lack of bearings here. "Very well. Let's walk slowly and find Chen Gong first."

Even though they were speaking in hushed tones, an echoing emptiness still lingered around them. It was obvious that they were somewhere underground, and it was somewhere quite spacious, perhaps like a cavern.

But these happenings had been so strange and bizarre that they couldn't afford to drop their guard.

Uneven stones lay beneath their feet—a moment of carelessness would be enough for them to trip. But these stones didn't seem to be randomly placed. In fact, it was the opposite. When Shen Qiao bent over to touch a couple, he found that they'd been neatly cut, their edges uniform. There were even faint patterns on their surface, a sure sign that they were man-made.

"Ruoqiang?" said Yan Wushi.

His voice quavered, and he did his best to speak as little as possible, condensing the sentence "Is this place the Ruoqiang they were speaking of?" into just two syllables. Perhaps the fall had given him another concussion.

Shen Qiao made a sound of assent. "It's possible."

He fished out a torch from his lapels and lit it.

The torch's glow was only enough to illuminate a small area around them, but when Shen Qiao managed to discern where they were, his heart involuntarily gave a thump.

They weren't standing at the true bottom, because only a couple of steps away, the ground abruptly dropped again, forming another massive pit of depths unknown. If they hadn't fallen here earlier, if their momentum had been just a little greater, they'd have fallen into that abyss instead, and who knew how that would have ended up.

Right at this moment, Yan Wushi spoke next to his ear. "A-Qiao, I think I saw someone ahead of us just now."

Shen Qiao asked, "Did you make out who it was?"

Yan Wushi's next words were hair-raising. "It didn't look like a person."

The flaming stick in their hands made them very conspicuous in this darkness. If Chen Gong and his men had seen them, they should've said something.

But there was only one path beneath their feet. If they didn't continue onward, they'd have to turn back.

"Let's go in the opposite direction, then," said Shen Qiao.

The path was narrow. Only one person could pass at a time.

The firelight flickered, as if about to go out, yet the darkness was both vast and endless. In a situation like this, the presence of humans became tiny and insignificant, something the darkness could engulf at any moment.

Yan Wushi suddenly said, "How did you feel, back when you were blind?"

Shen Qiao started slightly, then was silent for a moment. "Nothing in particular. It was fine after I got used to it."

"Why didn't you feel any hatred?"

Shen Qiao thought for a moment. "I did feel resentment. But not hatred. It's exhausting to hold on to too many things. Of course, there are many people with evil intentions in this world, but there are even more people willing to lend a helping hand. I wish to remember those people, not the things that will only bring me despair and suffering."

Yan Wushi sighed. "But all the people I've seen have treated you poorly. If not for you, Chen Gong could never have the glory he possesses today, but not only did he forget the kindness you showed him, he even returned it with further animosity by threatening you into exploring Ruoqiang with him."

Shen Qiao countered coolly, "There were good people, you just didn't see them. Back when you delivered me to Sang Jingxing, leaving me no choice but to forsake my own martial arts so he would perish with me, there was a young Daoist priest at Bailong Monastery, and he just happened to be the little boy we saved outside Xiang Province's city. If not for his timely rescue, I wouldn't be standing here and talking to you right now. Afterward, Hehuan Sect came for me, and though the abbot of Bailong Monastery knew that he could save himself by handing me over, he chose to give up his own life instead. When people like them exist, how can I possibly let myself sink into hatred? Shen Qiao's heart is very small; there's only room enough for good people like them. As for those who don't deserve to be remembered, I won't spare them anything—not even hatred."

"Then what about Yan Wushi? Do you not hate him either?"

"If not for the fact that your death might affect the state of both Northern Zhou and the world itself, we wouldn't be standing here having this conversation."

Yan Wushi laughed. "In truth, you do hold hatred. But you're too forgiving and softhearted, so even your hatred doesn't last for long. A-Qiao, your weaknesses are too obvious. That's why anyone can use them to coerce you, just like Chen Gong did. You could have seized Chen Gong and threatened him into releasing Banna's grandfather. Even that would've been better than following him all the way here."

"True," said Shen Qiao. "I could have done that. But if I did, you'd have no way of escape. You're saying that I should have just left you behind, correct?"

Yan Wushi answered softly, "No, but I understand why my previous self treated you the way he did. He's a paranoid person at heart, someone who'd never trust anyone else. No matter how good you are, he'd always want to bring out the darkness hidden within you. But he doesn't know that you are you. There may be hundreds of thousands of Chen Gongs in this world, but there is only one Shen Qiao."

Shen Qiao sighed. "Now I really do somewhat believe that you're not him because Yan Wushi would never say something like that."

Yan Wushi said gently, "Of course I'm not him. I'm A-Yan."

"...Don't you have a headache? How can you still talk so much?"

Yan Wushi went quiet; he no longer made a peep.

In the span of their conversation, the two of them had already walked for about fifteen minutes, one in front and the other in the back.

Shen Qiao suddenly stopped.

The torch, down to its last embers, finally flickered out in the darkness.

His voice carried some bewilderment. "We seem to have come full circle."

At the end of the path was a pitch-black cave, exactly the same as the one they'd seen earlier.

"Was this place a circle all along? So, we only walked from one end to the other?"

He'd just said this when someone's voice came from up ahead. "Is that Daoist Master Shen?"

It was Tuoba Liangzhe.

Shen Qiao raised his voice in reply. "It is! Where are you?"

"I also fell down from above earlier. I hit my head and fainted. I woke up just now. May I ask if Daoist Master Shen has seen our Lord and his men?"

"I haven't," said Shen Qiao. "We've been unable to find our way out since we fell down. Did you find anything?"

"There's a door here," said Tuoba Liangzhe. "There seem to be stairs behind it, but it's too dark for me to see. When I fell, my torches went missing as well. Do you have more?"

"I do," said Shen Qiao. "There's one left."

They might have each had their own goals and sides, but they were in a cooperative relationship at the moment, and if they wanted to break through, they'd have to work together.

Shen Qiao lit the torch and walked over. Sure enough, Tuoba Liangzhe was waiting for them at the cavern entrance. As they came closer, it was easy to see the large bloodstain on his forehead.

"Did you find any other passages earlier?"

"No," said Shen Qiao.

"Then it seems that we can only try going down."

Right at this moment, Shen Qiao suddenly saw a hairy hand materialize behind Tuoba Liangzhe. It had five fingers tipped in reddened nails—and was about to land on Tuoba Liangzhe's shoulder!

The thing had approached so silently that they'd actually failed to notice it. He had no idea whether it was even human.

Before Shen Qiao could open his mouth, Tuoba Liangzhe, too, sensed something wrong. He turned abruptly and thrust his sword at it.

But the sword didn't pierce the newcomer's body. Instead, as if it'd encountered an iron wall, the tip of the sword actually bent a little.

Tuoba Liangzhe retreated at top speed. Shen Qiao shoved the torch into Yan Wushi's hand, then drew Shanhe Tongbei while rushing forward.

The thing was tall and heavyset—it didn't look like anyone from the entourage. Shen Qiao remembered Yan Wushi's suggestion that it wasn't human, and he didn't dare be reckless. He channeled true qi into his sword, causing it to glow a faint white. Even if the newcomer was a bronze or iron wall, this thrust would still be able to pierce it through.

But though that monster looked clumsy, it was actually incredibly agile. Jumping left and right, it managed to evade Shen Qiao's sword. It seemed entirely focused on Tuoba Liangzhe as it spread its fingers and grabbed at him.

Now that he was close to it, Shen Qiao could feel a heavy stench strike him in the face. The monster's body was covered in hair, and its eyes shone a dim green—it looked like an ape.

Everything happened in the span of a blink. Tuoba Liangzhe had thought that Shen Qiao would take most of the pressure off him; he didn't expect the creature's relentless pursuit as it pounced on him. To his right was a bottomless abyss, behind him was Yan Wushi.

There was no space to dodge, so he could only clamber onto the wall on his left. With a couple of leaps, he was already several yards off the ground.

But the ape continued to chase him, and it even followed him up the wall at a speed even greater than them, the martial artists. It was just about to grab Tuoba Liangzhe, who leapt to the side and down, but then he did something Shen Qiao could never have expected.

He reached out toward Yan Wushi, preparing to grab him and toss him at the ape, thus extricating himself from the situation.

But his hand missed as he extended it forward, and he caught nothing but empty air!

# Several Yan Wushis

THE APE POUNCED ATOP OF Tuoba Liangzhe, and together they fell into the abyss. Only Tuoba Liangzhe's shocked cry lingered, echoing through the empty space around them.

Yan Wushi, who'd almost become a human shield courtesy of Tuoba Liangzhe, was currently pressed against the stone wall as he gasped. His face was as pale as a ghost, and the flickering, feeble firelight seemed to suffuse it in an almost apathetic, stony coldness.

Shen Qiao breathed a sigh of relief, then went up to take his pulse. "Are you all right?"

Yan Wushi stiffened a little at first, but he soon relaxed and let him press down on his wrist.

Shen Qiao's brows were tightly pinched, but it wasn't due to his reaction. "Why is your true qi growing increasingly chaotic? It's like it's brawling within your body!"

Yan Wushi said, "I used my true qi just now."

Shen Qiao could hear just how exhausted and spent he was from those couple of words—it was a shock.

Before he could react, Yan Wushi was already collapsing toward him, his entire body falling against Shen Qiao. Shen Qiao was forced to catch him. Unprepared for the icy cold of his skin, Shen Qiao jolted, shuddering.

This situation was a little similar to what had happened in Chen, during Yan Wushi's qi deviation after dueling Ruyan Kehui.

And the seeds of his current illness had also been planted that day.

Yan Wushi was trembling as well. It made him unconsciously try to press closer to Shen Qiao, wanting to draw some warmth.

Due to what had happened last time, Shen Qiao didn't dare to pass true qi to him carelessly. "How are you feeling? If you can't walk, let's rest here for a moment first."

Yan Wushi forced two words out through gritted teeth. "Let's go..."

Shen Qiao sighed. He bent at the waist, pulled Yan Wushi onto his back, and then walked toward the cavern exit, using his sword as support.

Sect Leader Yan, who'd once been unrivaled throughout the jianghu, who'd disdained all great heroes as unworthy, had probably never dreamed that he'd see such a day.

They didn't have any torches left, but before the last one died, Shen Qiao had indeed spotted stairs beneath the cavern exit. They were incredibly steep, but the existence of stairs meant that people had once lived down there in the past. Most likely it was there that the ancient city of Ruoqiang that Chen Gong was looking for waited.

The man on Shen Qiao's back continued to shiver, but his will was so strong that he refused to let out a single moan.

The ape that had attacked them earlier must have lived here for a long time. It'd grabbed Tuoba Liangzhe and fallen down with him, so did that mean that below them wasn't the bottomless abyss they'd imagined but a passage leading somewhere else?

Shen Qiao walked down the stairs, step by step, thinking as he went.

Yan Wushi said hoarsely, "I'm not A-Yan."

Shen Qiao grunted in reply. "I know."

The man's expression when he'd watched Tuoba Liangzhe fall, and the way he'd reacted when Shen Qiao touched his gate of life, was enough to tell Shen Qiao that the personality within Yan Wushi's body had changed again.

After interacting with him for several days, Shen Qiao had roughly inferred what was going on.

One of the personalities was his original one, which he'd tentatively refer to as Yan Wushi.

Another was the one who called him "Meiren-gege," "Xie Ling." Though this personality was somewhat innocent, his guard was just as high, and he disliked speaking. However, he trusted Shen Qiao, probably because Shen Qiao had been the first person he'd seen upon waking up, or perhaps because he could sense that Shen Qiao didn't have any malice. In any case, Xie Ling did anything he was told to do, which made dealing with him fairly painless. The real Yan Wushi would never do something like that.

And the last personality was the one who'd been conversing with him earlier. This personality had a much milder temper, and you could discuss some things with him. Out of all of Yan Wushi's personalities, he was the easiest to get along with.

Shen Qiao asked, "Then who are you right now?"

But Yan Wushi's answer was paradoxical: "I'm him, but I'm also not him."

The true qi within his body was rampaging, so he must have been in extreme agony at this moment. But if he didn't want to focus on the pain, he could only distract himself by talking.

"So, you aren't Yan Wushi, or Xie Ling, or A-Yan?"

"I don't know, my head is a mess. Sometimes I'll recall certain things, sometimes I feel like those things didn't actually happen to me. Maybe I don't even know the things I did just a moment ago..."

Shen Qiao was already used to this kind of situation. "Once we find the jade cistanche, your situation should take a turn for the better."

"The jade cistanche can only heal external injuries. It's ineffective against internal ones."

"Then what must you do to fully recover?"

"Wait until I patch the flaw in the *Fenglin Scriptures*."

"Didn't you say that it's impossible to repair the flaw in the demonic core?" Tinged with surprise, Shen Qiao's voice echoed down the passage.

Yan Wushi couldn't remember much at the moment, but he still recalled how "he" had treated Shen Qiao. How, when he'd personally delivered him to Sang Jingxing, he had almost been able to see Shen Qiao's heart withering within his eyes. How Shen Qiao had said to "him": "The reason I'm met with betrayal after betrayal isn't because I'm naive. It's because I believe that kindness will always exist. If there were no fools like me, where would Sect Leader Yan find your pleasure?"

And it hadn't been long since then.

Just how had Shen Qiao felt when he'd faced "him" anew?

"I've already found the method," he said coolly.

There was still a hint of remaining warmth within his chest, left there by Xie Ling and A-Yan, from their feelings whenever they thought about Shen Qiao.

But at this moment, Yan Wushi forcefully wiped it away, and his gaze fell a short distance in front of Shen Qiao.

"Someone's there," he said.

At practically the same moment, Shen Qiao stopped.

He'd also heard it—that fleeting yet heavy sound of breathing.

"Who's there?" Shen Qiao asked.

In the darkness, a pair of glowing green eyes shone like ghost fire lamps, suspended in midair as they stared at the two.

At the same time, the thick, heavy stench of blood spread through the area.

The ancient city of Ruoqiang, decrepit and neglected for ages, was indeed full of dangers.

# Exhausted

SHEN QIAO STOOD STILL and didn't move. The other party didn't approach either. The two of them stared each other down in a stalemate, making for a rather eerie atmosphere.

Shen Qiao had already seen those dim green eyes on the other ape, so seeing them again didn't come as much of a surprise. He only thought it somewhat strange. Why were there so many apes in this desolate, sealed-off ruin?

Could they really survive down here for hundreds of years without any food or water?

Watching Shen Qiao bide his time, showing no signs of rashness, those eyes couldn't restrain themselves any longer. They flashed briefly in the dark, then the green glow faded, and everything was engulfed in darkness once more. The stench of blood quickly faded as well, disappearing into the distance.

It had left, just like that?

The stairway was incredibly long, and as Shen Qiao groped along the walls, he found that they were more or less all carved on both sides with engravings. It was clear that this had been a flourishing city in the past. After Loulan[7] annexed Ruoqiang, the country had disappeared from historical records, together with all its people and

---

7   楼兰. Also known as Kroän, an ancient kingdom located along the Silk Road. It was later renamed Shanshan during the Han Dynasty.

countless treasures. Perhaps Loulan had plundered it all, or perhaps it had just been buried and lost to time. In any case, the slow flow of history had nothing to say about them anymore.

Step by step, Shen Qiao descended the stairs while carrying Yan Wushi. Within the expansive, far-reaching darkness, his pace seemed to slow, each step stretching out infinitely. Because of his injuries, Yan Wushi was unable to suppress his breathing, which made his breaths sound somewhat heavy as they lingered by Shen Qiao's ear together with the faint puffs of hot air. Then there were the sounds of Shanhe Tongbei as it tapped against the ground, probing out a path. It all gave Shen Qiao the illusion that this staircase was a never-ending one.

Since there was no end to it, why not stop and rest for a moment?

No matter how much farther they walked, they wouldn't be able to leave anyway.

Suddenly, he felt an icy coldness against his nape. Yan Wushi's hand had touched him there, and Shen Qiao couldn't help but shudder.

The place had been stale and airless for many long years. Staying here for an extended time would cause someone to feel stifled—their minds would grow dull, and they'd become dazed and lethargic.

Just before, Shen Qiao's mind had been completely focused on the ape. His attention had slipped, and he'd almost fallen into that trap.

"Many thanks," he said.

Yan Wushi didn't reply.

Shen Qiao was already used to this. The true qi of Yan Wushi's body was in disorder; he couldn't even control himself and was constantly switching between personalities. The current one probably didn't like to talk.

The two of them walked some distance when, suddenly, Shen Qiao felt that the stairs beneath him had disappeared, only to be replaced by flat ground. The walls on either side of the staircase had also vanished. But this only made him more discomfited as he had no idea just how large this open space was, nor what traps might suddenly spring up beneath his feet.

A sword soundlessly thrust toward Shen Qiao's face. The blade, as cold as autumn water, didn't even glint within the darkness.

But Shen Qiao had stayed in the dark for a long time—he was accustomed to using his ears to discern everything, and they were exceptionally sensitive. The sharp blade point was still a mere inch from his eyes, but he'd already leapt into the air, sweeping backward with his sword across his chest. With a loud clang, the attack was dissipated.

Before Shen Qiao could speak, the other party began questioning him. "What demon goes there? Tell me your name!"

Finding the situation awkward, Shen Qiao countered, "And who is this distinguished gentleman?"

Whoever it was, they managed to recognize his voice. "Daoist Master Shen?"

"And you are?" asked Shen Qiao.

"I'm Chu Ping," said the man. "I came together with our Lord."

Chen Gong had brought around a dozen men with him. Other than the likes of Murong Qin, whom Shen Qiao already knew, Shen Qiao had almost no interactions with the rest of them.

Shen Qiao made a sound of assent. "Where's Chen Gong?"

"My Lord and the others are in front of us. Just now, a monkey-like monster carried off two of our men, so I thought you were also... Forgive my rudeness. Please come with me, Daoist Master Shen!"

His voice was shaking with fear, and he was panting as he spoke. It was evident that he'd just gone through a treacherous battle.

"Are there any traps here?" asked Shen Qiao.

"No," said Chu Ping. "This place should be a terrace, but we'll be turning a corner just up ahead. My Lord and the others are right beyond that corner."

Shen Qiao used the sound of Chu Ping's footsteps to discern the direction they were heading and followed after him. After walking for a while, he heard someone ahead of them say, "Who is it?"

"It's me, Murong Patriarch," said Chu Ping. "I've found Daoist Master Shen and his friend."

Murong Qin's voice sounded a little strained. "Hurry over here!"

Chu Ping grew nervous as well. "What happened? Did that monkey return?"

Murong Qin didn't respond. Then there was a hiss in the dark, and a flame burst to life above his hand.

With the help of the firelight, Shen Qiao could see that there were other people standing beside Murong Qin, but their numbers had clearly decreased from before.

Upon seeing Shen Qiao and Yan Wushi, an expression of relief washed over Chen Gong's face. "I'm glad the two of you are fine."

"What happened here?" asked Shen Qiao.

"The gale blew away the sand and revealed a deep pit, which led down to Ruoqiang's ancient city, so we dropped down. However, this place is quite large, and we didn't all drop down together, so some of our men got separated."

"Then where should we go now?"

Chen Gong answered each of his questions. "We just scouted the area. If our guess is correct, we should be inside the walls of the original city. Jade cistanche grows underground, so we must find the passage that leads below ground within the city, then continue down from there."

"This city has been buried beneath the sand for hundreds of years," Shen Qiao pointed out. "Even if there were a passage, it's probably been blocked for a long time. We might not be able to find it even after consuming all our supplies."

"No need to worry," said Chen Gong. "Before coming here, I saw a rough depiction of the city layout from Ruoqiang's time, so I have some idea of where that passage might be. Back then, Ruoqiang's people constructed an altar on the north side of the capital. The passage should be beneath it, so we only need to find that northern altar.

"There are some monsters here; you may have met them earlier. Likely a kind of ape that's been dwelling here for a while. They have sharp eyes and ears, and they're used to the dark. Their physical capabilities are comparable to those of martial artists, so we must be careful, so as not repeat our mistakes."

He hadn't only said these words for Shen Qiao—they were more directed to the subordinates with him, probably because they'd lost a couple of people earlier. The men immediately agreed in unison, then, with Murong Qin leading the way, they followed the fire glow deeper inside.

Their increased numbers gave everyone a sense of security, and they were suddenly much more at ease, especially now that Shen Qiao had joined them. After they'd personally witnessed how he'd been a match for both Dou Yanshan and Yu Ai together, their hearts had all placed him in the ranks of first-rate martial artists.

Currently, few people knew of Kunye's death. Once this news spread, likely no one would dare look down upon Shen Qiao anymore.

The jianghu was simply that pragmatic. Concealed beneath the lofty sentiments and ideals, beneath the blades, were the same beliefs as everywhere else: survival of the fittest, and the strong were king.

The apes hiding low in the dark also seemed to fear their numbers, for none came out, and they traveled smoothly for quite a while. Logically speaking, since Ruoqiang was a small country even before its destruction, the capital couldn't be that large either. The distance they'd walked should have been more than enough to take them from the south side of the city to the north.

Though everyone had their doubts, considering the gap in social status, they dared not recklessly question Chen Gong. Only Shen Qiao asked, "How much longer will it be?"

Chen Gong was also a little uncertain. After all, what he'd seen inside the imperial palace of Qi was only an incomplete map left behind from the Han Dynasty. "We should be almost there."

However, no sooner than he'd said this, someone within their group suddenly called quietly, "Liulang has disappeared!"

Soon after was a shout of surprise: "What is this?!"

To conserve their torches, Murong Qin was the only person who'd lit one. Before he could shine it over, someone was already fumbling about his lapels, trying to find another one to light, but, perhaps due to his panic, his trembling hands dropped the torch, and it fell right to the ground.

Murong Qin rushed over and directed his firelight at the ground. On top of the torch that'd just fallen was a hairy spider—its entire body was dark gray, and even excluding its legs, it was the size of a full-grown man's palm. Three white stripes marked its back, giving the impression of a person with their eyes closed. Once the spider began to crawl, the "eyes" opened, as if it were blinking.

None of them had ever seen something so eerie. They weren't scared, exactly, but they all felt indescribably disgusted, and their hair stood on end.

Someone couldn't take it anymore and swung his sword at the

spider, slicing it right in half. However, as soon as he did, many more baby spiders burst out of its abdomen, and one after another, they all crawled toward the men's feet.

"Liulang! That's Liulang!"

Someone had lit up a new torch. As the light it cast flickered around a spot far away, they saw a corpse collapsed there, still wearing familiar robes. But the body itself was shriveled, the skin stretched tightly over the bones. It was horrific.

"Don't let those things close!" yelled Murong Qin. He unsheathed his sword as he spoke, and a couple of sword glares flashed, instantly killing all the spiders that had been crawling toward him and Chen Gong.

But the others weren't so lucky. The baby spiders crawled at an astonishing speed, climbing up their feet and legs. They slipped into any crevice they could find, and the moment they touched warm skin, they injected their venom, paralyzing their victims. Those victims didn't feel anything even as their blood was sucked dry— they couldn't even make a sound.

In the blink of an eye, two or three more men collapsed. As lackeys responsible for odd jobs who ran back and forth for Chen Gong, they only knew a couple of moves and were completely unable to react in time. Like Liulang, they fell silently to the ground.

The others were horrified. They dared not be careless anymore; they all drew their weapons and began hacking at those spiders. But the spiders were too small, and more continued to pour from some unknown source. The surrounding darkness combined with their nervousness meant it was easy to overlook some. And when they sliced open a couple of large ones, more small ones would crawl out. It was impossible to kill them all, and impossible to guard themselves completely.

The only exception was Shen Qiao, standing beneath Shanhe Tongbei's sword screen. No spiders approached him, and he kept Yan Wushi shielded behind him. His sword qi wrapped around them, watertight, a white waterfall within the darkness, so brilliant and dazzling that no one could look away.

The spiders targeted the weak and feared the strong. When they realized they couldn't get close to Shen Qiao, they all turned around and surged toward the others.

Chen Gong angrily lambasted his men. "Don't pierce their abdomens! Use fire! Burn them with fire!"

He kept himself occupied as well: a sword in one hand, a torch in the other as he swung it toward the ground. The spiders were afraid of the firelight and dared not come closer. He took the opportunity to burn some, but the torches were limited. As he watched the spiders rush forth in endless waves, crawling over several of his men who had already fallen, Chen Gong was forced to command the remaining men: "Run forward!"

But when it rained, it poured. Right at that moment, everyone felt a cool breeze blow behind them. Before they could react, someone screamed while collapsing forward.

"The demon monkeys!" someone yelled, white with terror. "The demon monkeys are back!"

Caught between a rock and a hard place, they couldn't run even if they wanted to. In their panic, they subconsciously gathered where Murong Qin and Shen Qiao were, for those two were the strongest of their group. So far, they'd been handling the situation with ease, completely unscathed.

But things weren't easy for Shen Qiao either. Two apes leapt toward him at the same time. He had to deal with spiders in front of him while taking on those two apes—and he needed to protect

Yan Wushi as well. Forced to juggle three things at once, he could barely keep up.

It was exactly like Chen Gong had said: having lived in the dark for a long time, the apes had developed night vision. Like cunning hunters hiding in the shadows, they'd coldly watched as the spiders' assault drove everyone into a panic, then took the best opportunity to attack, wanting to fell them in a single blow.

The clang of weapons sounded incessantly, but many of them realized that whenever they thrust out their swords, even if it seemed like they should be able to pierce right through those creatures' chests, they'd either be blocked by the hard, steely hide beneath the apes' fur or the ape would evade at the last moment. They had to worry about those blood-sucking spiders while dealing with the tireless apes, and within a couple of rounds, they were thoroughly exhausted from the fighting, their bodies all sporting various injuries.

The nails of those apes seemed to be tipped in a kind of poison as well, for the cuts they left began to burn with pain.

Yan Wushi suddenly spoke up. "The apes are the spiders' natural enemies. The moment they appeared, the spiders retreated."

His voice was weak and hoarse, devoid of his old arrogance that proclaimed that everything was beneath his concern. But there was a strange power in his words—the moment he spoke, everyone found themselves listening to him attentively.

Everyone who heard what he said froze. In what little time they could spare while fighting the apes, many of them looked at the ground. Indeed, those disgusting spiders had all vanished.

Without the spiders hampering them, it was as if a huge load had been lifted, and everyone's spirits rose immediately. For a time, true qi flooded forth while swords swept up gusts of wind, forcing those apes to retreat a couple of paces.

But it didn't last for long. A loud, drawn-out howl rose in the darkness, like a woman's wailing, and the apes' attacks grew fierce once more. Some of them pounced forward despite being wounded by the group's sword qi, as if ready to fight to the end.

Shen Qiao said to Yan Wushi, "That should be the apes' leader commanding them. We must capture it, or we'll have no peace. Go hide by Murong Qin; I'll go look for the leader. I probably won't be able to protect you for a while."

Yan Wushi grunted in assent but said nothing else. After all, the two of them had never been friends in the first place. Of course, they couldn't be considered enemies now, but while Yan Wushi's current personality might be different from the original one, it was just as callous. If he'd told Shen Qiao something like "be careful," that would have surprised him more.

He watched as Yan Wushi pressed himself against the cavern wall and quickly vanished into its protruding cracks. The apes wouldn't be able to find him for now. Then Shen Qiao leapt up the wall, using those jutting rifts as footholds. With a few ups and downs, he vaulted toward the source of that howl and then quickly slipped into the darkness.

Shen Qiao's Daoist robes fluttered as he landed, light and agile, sword in hand. Under the broad daylight, he'd have appeared full of immortal poise and drawn countless eyes. Unfortunately, in this place, everyone could barely look after themselves. Only Yan Wushi sent a keen look at his disappearing figure. Then, instead of going to Chen Gong and Murong Qin for protection like Shen Qiao had told him to, he circled around everyone and went further into the darkness.

No one noticed his disappearance, least of all Shen Qiao. His eyes were closed as he used his ears to discern the leader's location.

But ever since that scream, it'd made no sound, so Shen Qiao could only grope forward based on his impressions.

The clanging of weapons from below grew farther and farther away. Shen Qiao held his breath as he melded into the ruins and broken tiles behind his back. There, he could keenly feel the endless quiet and unknowns brought by the darkness.

Suddenly, the scream rang out again!

It was long and mournful before suddenly turning shrill, like a bugle call or alarm. Below them, the herd of apes once again began attacking Chen Gong and his men in a frenzy.

Now was the time!

*Clang—!*

With a cry like a fledgling phoenix, Shanhe Tongbei sprang from its sheath!

Shen Qiao pushed off the ground and leapt into the darkness.

There was no support to be found within the dark, but he glided through the air. This strike of his wasn't flashy in the slightest, but it was impossibly fast. His sword glare seemed to engulf him completely, turning him into a white arc as he swept through the void. Tinged with purple, as if heralding a propitious result, it shot straight toward the source of that sound!

The sword glare surged as it traveled. The ape was a living creature, so naturally it must have sensed the danger. But it was the leader, the ruler over this ancient ruin, and had commanded absolute power for so long. When it saw that someone dared to challenge its authority, its first instinct wasn't to run but to pounce at Shen Qiao in a rage.

With it illuminated by the sword glare, Shen Qiao realized that the ape in question was different from the rest: it had the face of a man. Even more unsettling were the pair of flashing green eyes within that hairy human face, glaring balefully at Shen Qiao.

Its claws carried the stench of blood along with another strange, unidentifiable smell. It completely ignored Shen Qiao's sword glare and slammed upon him like a mountain crashing down!

Shen Qiao suddenly realized what that smell was: it was the smell the spiders released as they lay dead on the ground. Having lived for so long underground and lacking any other source of food, they must have fed on the spiders, and over time, they became the spiders' natural enemies. That was why the spiders had all fled the moment they appeared.

But, to the apes, the sudden appearance of so many people was a huge new food source. This drew them over, and they began their relentless pursuit.

The ape had no idea of the sword glare's power. It thought its hide tough like bronze and iron, and so it fearlessly swiped at him, the attack ferocious and carrying that same reek. If that blow scored a solid hit, Shen Qiao's brains would definitely splatter all over the ground.

The two clashed head-on. Wrapped in true qi, the sword glare tore the ape's skin right open, and the blade sank a few inches into its flesh.

The leader of the apes was both shocked and enraged. It immediately shrieked. Hearing this, the apes tirelessly surrounding Chen Gong's group abandoned them. They leapt up the cavern walls, changing their target to Shen Qiao!

The apes weren't only agile and capable of powerful attacks, they also possessed hides as strong as steel. Normal weapons couldn't scratch them at all. Even Shanhe Tongbei could only harm them when infused with true qi. If it had been a one-on-one match, Shen Qiao could have fought without fear, but with a dozen of them pouncing upon him instead, even a grandmaster the likes of Buddhist Master Xueting would have been overwhelmed.

He immediately withdrew his sword and retreated. But now that he'd wounded the leader of the apes, making his escape wouldn't be so easy. Not only did it pounce at Shen Qiao, it commanded the remaining apes to surround him as one.

When Murong Qin saw that Shen Qiao had drawn the apes away, he quickly said to Chen Gong, "My Lord, let's hurry and leave!"

But Chen Gong said, "No, go help him!"

Murong Qin was a little dismayed. "My Lord?"

Chen Gong frowned. "We're all in the same boat. Shen Qiao has been of great help to us, so we should help him if we can!"

With that, he leapt upward with his sword.

Having no choice, Murong Qin and the others gritted their teeth and followed.

However, the ape leader loathed Shen Qiao for injuring it and was determined to rip him into pieces. Under the threat of their leader, the other apes were also uninterested in fighting Chen Gong's group—they all rushed toward Shen Qiao. If anything, Chen Gong's interference only made them more frenzied and agitated, completely unafraid of death, so much so that the moment Chen Gong's attention slipped, a slash deep enough to show the bone was gored into his arm.

When he saw this, Murong Qin yelled out in a panic, "My Lord!"

He rushed over to administer medicine to Chen Gong while the others shrank back at the sight of his injury.

Shen Qiao had no connections with them in the first place. Even though he was in a tight spot now due to wanting to capture the leader first, it also happened to resolve their crisis as well.

Murong Qin spoke to Chen Gong in a hushed voice, "My Lord, there's no time to lose. Once those demon apes kill Shen Qiao, they'll turn to us, and we'll be in trouble. Let's leave, quickly!"

Chen Gong was silent for a moment. Then, having made up his mind, he yelled, "Retreat!"

Before they left, he turned his head back and up. In the midst of the apes' frenzied, frightening shrieks, those few blazing sword glares shone fiercely, but they also gave the impression of stranded helplessness. It was impossible to say how much longer Shen Qiao would last.

Chen Gong withdrew his gaze, then left with Murong Qin and the others, never glancing back.

As Shen Qiao killed two of the apes, he indeed began to grow fatigued.

After all, his martial abilities hadn't fully recovered; furthermore, these apes seemed to have gone mad—one after another, they threw themselves at the sword qi without any sense of self-preservation. But his sword qi couldn't last forever. Shen Qiao slashed open a long cut in the chest of one ape, and its blood splattered his face, the nauseating stench slamming into him alongside. Even Shen Qiao's movements couldn't help but pause at this.

While the other apes were attacking Shen Qiao, the leader had been biding its time, waiting for its chance. Now that it'd managed to glimpse one, it howled and leapt at Shen Qiao, grabbing him while shoving him backward!

The ape was holding him tightly; Shen Qiao couldn't struggle free. His entire body was forced to fall back, and he lost his footing, falling into a deep pit.

Right at this moment, the leader of the apes released him. As the other apes grabbed it by the tail, it viciously shoved Shen Qiao into that pit, then gave a loud roar as if it were celebrating its victory!

Carrying Shen Qiao's weight, Shanhe Tongbei scored a long trail of sparks in the wall, but Shen Qiao still couldn't stop his descent.

The pit seemed like a real abyss—he had no idea how long it'd take to reach the bottom. His arm grew numb and sore, and every single wound upon his body was hurting. He'd been injured while fighting those apes; at this point he could feel a burning, excruciating agony.

Shen Qiao looked down. Below him glowed a faint red. He didn't know what it was.

He'd already lost all feeling within his arm. In a moment of carelessness, Shanhe Tongbei left the wall, and his entire person plummeted downward!

But this plummet had just started when someone firmly grabbed him by the other arm.

Shen Qiao lifted his head and saw that Yan Wushi had somehow appeared. In order to grab onto Shen Qiao, his entire upper half was over the edge.

"Hold on tight!" he said to Shen Qiao, his voice severe.

# Poisoned

WITH THIS BUFFER, Shen Qiao was able to catch his breath. He forcefully jammed Shanhe Tongbei into the wall while his feet caught a jutting crack. Drawing a deep breath, he flipped himself upward to where Yan Wushi was hiding.

This place wasn't a true cave. Instead, it was a crack in the stone wall that had become a fissure due to its age. Buried by wind and sand, baptized by the slow march of years, the city had long become part of the underground itself.

Before he could ask, Yan Wushi said, "Down there should be the red carnelian that Chen Gong is after."

Earlier, Shen Qiao had his hands full trying to secure himself, so he hadn't paid much attention. Now, as he looked down, he realized that there was a sea of glimmering red beneath him. If they'd been in broad daylight, the red shine wouldn't have been particularly dazzling, as it was only the light from the ore itself. But it was lustrous, translucent, and beautiful, and in the darkness, it was enough to cast their faces in a crimson glow.

From here all the way to the front, the winding passage twisted and turned. Carnelian deposits illuminated their surroundings on the left and right, but they were all buried deep within the rocks. There was no way to dig them out.

They were indeed beautiful, but what did Chen Gong need them for? The emperor of Qi favored him greatly, showering him with endless riches and glory; even Murong Qin was willing to serve him, loyal and steadfast. To say nothing of the money and treasures he must possess. The Chen Gong of the past had nothing, so perhaps he'd have been willing to risk his life for the carnelian, but the current Chen Gong had too much. Why would he still come here despite all the dangers?

Could he have another goal?

Shen Qiao thought that the Chen Gong he'd reunited with had long changed completely as a person. He couldn't use his old insight to appraise his schemes and cunning now.

He withdrew his gaze and looked back. "Many thanks. Why are you here?"

Yan Wushi didn't answer the question. "There's a path here that leads underground."

Shen Qiao was surprised. "You already went down?"

"I didn't get too close. There were two apes guarding it nearby."

"Then, did you see the jade cistanche?"

Yan Wushi gave an affirmation.

Shen Qiao briefly inspected his own condition. He had about a dozen wounds, both large and small, scattered over his body. Most of them were cuts inflicted by the apes back when he'd been protecting Yan Wushi, but there were also scrapes and bruises from his fall. However, these were all flesh wounds. The poison on those apes' claws was also only a mild one, and he quickly expelled it by circulating his true qi.

In comparison, the injuries Chen Gong's group had suffered were quite a bit more severe.

"Those apes have lived here for hundreds of years without seeing the light of day, all while consuming the human-face spiders and jade cistanche. Their hides are like iron—weapons cannot hurt them unless infused with true qi, and their bodies are as light as a swallow. That's what makes them so difficult to deal with."

But Shen Qiao's spirits actually rose. "Let's go, then. Since we're already here, we might as well go the full way. Once we have the jade cistanche, we'll soon be able to heal your external injuries!"

Yan Wushi glanced at him. "Do you need to rest?"

Shen Qiao shook his head. "Let's grab the jade cistanche first, lest we meet with Chen Gong's group again and more problems arise."

Yan Wushi nodded and didn't add more. "Come with me."

He stood and began walking, leading the way as Shen Qiao followed behind him.

As they left that stretch of carnelian, the red glow faded, and their path was once again plunged into darkness. They moved as lightly as possible, the sound of their breaths mingling with the rustling of their clothes. But their actual silhouettes remained separate, with one in the front and the other in the back—intimate in impression yet estranged in reality.

It wasn't a short distance, and there were quite a few twists and turns along the way, but as Yan Wushi had already walked it once, his pace was fairly brisk. After about fifteen minutes, he suddenly halted. Fortunately, Shen Qiao reacted quickly and came to a stop immediately, otherwise he would have run into him.

Yan Wushi looked back and said quietly, "Right in front is..."

However, before he could finish, a stench assailed them from the front. Shen Qiao yanked Yan Wushi behind himself, then raised the sword in his right hand to block.

A massive weight suddenly slammed down from above. Taken by surprise, Shen Qiao was forced back three steps, but he quickly drew his sword and slashed at it. The ape shrieked and leapt back, then quickly pounced over again. At the same time, another ape also leapt into the fray.

Entrenched within the darkness, Shen Qiao couldn't see, but his other senses sharpened. He backed up a few steps, waiting until those apes leapt over together, then he channeled true qi into the blade and transformed it into a white arc. Caught off guard, the apes screamed in pain as they were slashed by its edge before immediately attacking Shen Qiao with even more vehemence.

Shen Qiao said to Yan Wushi, "I'll hold them here. Go get the jade cistanche!"

Even before he'd said so, Yan Wushi had already bent over and was pulling up multiple bunches of those white, palm-shaped fruit growing within the narrow fissure above the carnelian. They looked a little like aloe vera, and though they should have been white, the light from the carnelian cast them in a faint red glow. When they were snapped, a milky white liquid flowed out, accompanied by a subtle fragrance.

Legend said that jade cistanche was incredibly precious, miraculous at healing wounds. Even the imperial palaces might not have any. But after plucking a couple, Yan Wushi didn't give the rest a single glance. Instead, he turned to look at the carnelian beneath the cliff, before doing something entirely unexpected: he pulled out all the jade cistanche that had already fruited and destroyed them, then threw them off the cliff. The cistanche quickly vanished amid the sea of red light.

The sound of hurried footsteps came from the other end of the passage. Chen Gong's party had managed to rid themselves of the apes with great difficulty only to encounter more human-faced spiders. After another brief struggle, the apes had caught up, and they were forced to dash onward while fighting. Now they'd arrived, believing that they'd found the light at the end of the tunnel, but they'd never imagined a reunion with old friends.

"Daoist Master Shen?!"

Chen Gong's tone was both astonished and doubtful. He'd thought that there was no way Shen Qiao could survive the apes' group assault, but not only had he not died, he'd arrived here faster than they had.

However, there was no time for guilty feelings or interrogation, for the apes had already caught up, and there were still two in the front. Chen Gong's appearance caused those two to switch targets: they instantly took everyone to be invaders, which actually helped remove some of the burden from Shen Qiao.

Chen Gong's party silently bemoaned their misfortune. They'd thought that they'd finally be able to obtain the carnelian after all their hardships—they hadn't imagined that there was another fierce battle up ahead. The apes were unrelenting and ferocious. If they didn't eliminate them completely, they wouldn't even be able to leave, let alone get their hands on the carnelian.

Everyone had no choice but to draw their weapons and tussle with the apes. However, there was one small stroke of fortune: the apes weren't indestructible. Having fought with Chen Gong and his men for so long, they were also getting fatigued. Soon, Shen Qiao and Murong Qin each sliced open an ape's throat, killing them.

The apes had long gained a humanlike disposition. Grieved by the deaths of their own, they were also a little afraid and tried to retreat. Only the ape leader flew into a rage, attacking them in an even greater frenzy.

Despite its fury, the leader was already in disarray, and after fighting the apes for so long, everyone had slowly begun to grasp some tricks, instead of merely trying to muscle through with force. The neck was the softest and weakest part of the ape—as long as one could find the chance to pierce it with their sword, even if the blow didn't decapitate the ape, it would still slice open its throat and kill it.

Within half an hour, a fair number of apes had died by their blades. Seeing their victory imminent, Chen Gong slowly left the circle of battle and walked toward the cliff.

The carnelian lay only thirty or so yards below the cliff—to those skilled in qinggong, the height was no trouble at all. Chen Gong had journeyed a great distance here from Qi's capital just for this, and he'd even almost lost his life along the way. Now that he could see his final goal right before his eyes, he couldn't help but grow excited.

He composed himself, tossing aside all his useless emotions, then turned back to glance at Murong Qin and the others.

Out of everyone who'd followed him here, there were only three people left, not counting Chen Gong himself. They were Murong Qin and his nephew Murong Xun, as well as a man named Sa Kunpeng. The three of them had been the best martial artists out of the bunch, but they were all still fighting the apes and barely able to keep up. Chen Gong lacked the patience to wait until they could take a look, so he jumped down along the cliff wall himself.

There were no apes or spiders down below; it was all carnelian, sprouting in clusters of crystals. Their red glow wasn't blinding, nor did it remind him of blood. Instead, they actually gave off a faint sense of harmonious peace. Chen Gong couldn't contain his excitement; he reached out to touch them. The crystal surface was smooth and translucent, reflecting even the outline of his fingers.

Only after a moment did his excited feelings slowly calm down.

Chen Gong looked around himself. These naturally formed crystals were incomparably hard and couldn't be easily removed. To do so would probably require dozens, even hundreds of men chipping away at them with an axe.

But Chen Gong had no intention of taking the carnelian with him. It was true that they were priceless, but that had never been his goal.

He untied the Tai'e sword upon his back, then looked for the carnelian crystal with the sharpest edge. He pressed the sword to the carnelian, right where the hilt connected to the blade.

With a quiet click, the hilt separated from the blade. Just like that, he'd broken a legendary sword that had been passed down the generations into two.

But an expression of joy came over Chen Gong's face. He threw the blade aside, then carefully removed a small piece of silk from a hollow within the hilt.

The silk was crammed full of words. Chen Gong looked at it for a while, and the joy on his face became brighter and brighter. He simply stood among the carnelian as he began to carefully read.

However, after a moment, his expression suddenly filled with alarm. He looked down to see the palm of his right hand had already turned a bruised purple without his notice, and it was slowly spreading up his arm. A prickling pain accompanied it as it traveled, an itchiness within the agony that made him want to scratch at it. And Chen Gong did, but it didn't stop the itchiness—he scratched until it bled, to no avail.

Beneath the skin, it felt like thousands of insects were biting at him, painful and itchy beyond enduring. His veins began to protrude, sprawling upwards in the direction of the blood flow, all while slowly spreading toward his wrist.

Chen Gong didn't need someone to tell him to know that he'd been poisoned.

There was no time to be concerned about anything else; he climbed back up the cliff wall in a few leaps and returned to the original passage. At this time, Murong Qin and Shen Qiao had managed to kill over half of the apes, forcing the leader to retreat, while Yan Wushi had somehow found a mechanism within the wall. A massive boulder came crashing down to seal off the passage, and everyone took the chance to back up. The boulder separated them from the apes, letting the entire group pause to catch their breaths.

But Chen Gong was completely preoccupied with the fact that he'd been poisoned; he had no time to spare for the apes. Murong Qin saw his terrified expression and quickly ran over to support him.

"Quick! Hurry! Do you have any antidotes on you?"

Murong Qin's gaze landed on his palm, and he couldn't conceal his alarm. "My Lord, this is...?!"

The purplish-blue color had already begun to creep over his wrist.

Chen Gong was practically roaring by now. "Antidote!"

He'd taken quite a few at the bottom of the cliff, but they were all ineffective. Now he could only place all his hopes on Murong Qin.

But no antidote could cure everything. Anything Murong Qin had on him, Chen Gong certainly also had. After swallowing down a great many pills to no avail, Chen Gong was already on the brink of despair.

He didn't expect that, after staking everything on achieving his goal, he would lose his life over something like this.

"Does Daoist Master Shen have a method to cure this poison?" he said hoarsely. As if Shen Qiao were his final hope, his gaze on him was full of desperate anticipation.

Shen Qiao didn't even have any idea of how he'd been poisoned in the first place. All he'd seen was Chen Gong jumping down the cliff, and next thing he knew, he'd returned, poisoned. "Is there something poisonous down there?"

"It's the carnelian! The carnelian is incredibly toxic! Do you know how to save me? I heard that Xuandu Mountain was also peerless when it came to refining medicine, and you were the sect leader! You must know about all sorts of cures. If you can save me, I'll give you everything I have in return!"

Shen Qiao shook his head. "I left in a hurry and came here under duress. There was no time for me to bring anything like an antidote."

But Chen Gong only thought him unwilling. He fished out a piece of jade from his lapels and tossed it to Shen Qiao. "In truth, back when you agreed to travel with us, I ordered someone to free that old man. By now he must already be back home with his granddaughter. If you're still worried, once you get back, you can take this jade to Yunlai Inn within the capital and ask for him. I paid the innkeeper to hold the old man there temporarily. Even if he hasn't let him go, if you bring this piece of jade to the innkeeper, you can have him released. I know that you're an upright gentleman; you've saved my life many times before as well. I only had you come on the trip this time because I had no other choice. I never intended to hurt anyone! Please, for the sake of our old friendship, save me!"

He spoke incredibly quickly; one could imagine just how panicked he was.

Shen Qiao said helplessly, "I truly don't have an antidote."

The moment he said this, Chen Gong's face turned the color of ash.

He tried to expel the poison through circulating his true qi, but that only seemed to hasten its encroachment further. Seeing that the bluish color was already about to reach his elbow, Chen Gong gritted his teeth, then said to Murong Qin, "Quick, cut off my arm!"

But right at that moment, Yan Wushi suddenly spoke up from where he'd been silently hiding in the dark the entire while. "Why don't you ask me if I have any ideas?"

# Fellow Travelers

CHEN GONG STARED DEAD-EYED at Yan Wushi. "Does Sect Leader Yan have a method?"

"You probably noticed back when fighting those apes. Their nails are both sharp and poisonous, so the moment they scratch you, the wound will begin to swell and itch."

His words came neither fast nor slow; it was obvious he was completely unmoved by Chen Gong's poisoning. There was even a leisurely tone to his speech, as if this had nothing to do with him.

"Claws that sharp must be honed from time to time. There aren't a great variety of rocks to choose from here, so the carnelian those apes guarded were their best choice. Occasionally, they'll file their claws against it, yet they're never poisoned. That's because within a mile of every toxic substance must be something else that neutralizes it, just like the spiders and apes within this ancient city."

Murong Qin had found a key within his words. "Sect Leader Yan means that there's antidote to my Lord's poison?"

But understanding suddenly flashed through Chen Gong's mind. "The jade cistanche! Is it the jade cistanche?! Hurry, can you go see if there's any jade cistanche nearby?!"

Murong Qin and the others quickly ran to the cliff and looked around. And sure enough, they discovered jade cistanche.

"My Lord, there's indeed some here!" said Murong Xun happily.

Shen Qiao glanced at Yan Wushi despite himself. The latter stood with his hands in his sleeves, body still half-hidden in the shadows. It was clear he had no intention of speaking.

Chen Gong was overjoyed. "Bring it here!"

Murong Qin and his nephew sliced off those sprigs of jade cistanche and brought them back. Without so much as a glance, Chen Gong quickly shoved them into his mouth and gulped them down.

But a miracle did not occur. Fifteen minutes later, his hand was still unbearably painful and itchy, and the purplish-blue color even began to darken. It'd already traveled up from his elbow and was nearly at his shoulder.

Chen Gong's face was ashy pale, almost blue—a near match for the color of his arm.

Only then did Yan Wushi slowly say, "The jade cistanche is indeed the antidote, but its leaves and branches have no effect. The only part that can cure the poison is the fruit. Those apes must have consumed the fruit for generations, and that's why they fear neither the poison from the carnelian nor the spiders. That's why they can live here. As this place was once Ruoqiang's altar, these apes might have been trained by the people of Ruoqiang back then in order to guard the jade cistanche. Did you look at the leader? It'd already begun to develop a human face; it obviously possessed an exceptional amount of wisdom and cunning."

Originally, these words should have been fascinating. Unfortunately, their speaker's tone was dry and flat, making them rather dull.

Of course, Chen Gong was not in the mood to listen to his detailed explanation on the apes' origins. On a normal day, he'd have already flown into a rage and commanded Murong Qin to seize him, but Yan Wushi held his life in his hands, so he could only swallow down his anger. "It seems that Sect Leader Yan has already picked all the fruit? I don't know what you want from me, but as long as I'm capable of it, I will do as you say. Please give me the fruit from the cistanche."

"You know what I want."

Yet Yan Wushi refused to say.

Chen Gong understood Shen Qiao. He knew that Shen Qiao was an upright gentleman, and that you could cheat a gentleman by using their sentimentalities against them. So, during all his confrontations with Shen Qiao, he'd always held the upper hand, but this wasn't effective against Yan Wushi. Everyone knew that Yan Wushi was willful and did as he pleased. It was impossible to use common sense to infer anything about him. Chen Gong knew that even news of his survival couldn't be used to threaten him. Instead, it was Yan Wushi who held the cistanche fruit and had become his last hope of survival.

"If Sect Leader Yan doesn't clarify, how can I know?" He still refused to give up, putting up a final, life-and-death struggle.

Yan Wushi said coldly, "Why don't you guess if I can destroy these fruits before your dogs take action? If you're willing to take the risk, I'm not against giving it a go."

The moment he said this, Murong Xun, though enraged, could only stop his movements, having intended to approach him.

Chen Gong gritted his teeth. "You want what's within Tai'e?"

Yan Wushi didn't reply.

Chen Gong had no choice. He could only fish out the piece of silk hidden inside his lapel with his other hand, then pass it to Yan Wushi.

"Where's the cistanche?"

Yan Wushi took the piece of silk, then retrieved a fruit from somewhere about his person and tossed it to Chen Gong.

Bitter about his defeat, Chen Gong couldn't resist asking, "You'd already guessed my goal, so you specially rushed here before us, then used the fruit to threaten me?"

Perhaps he was in a good mood after obtaining the piece of silk because Yan Wushi finally showed him great clemency and answered his question. "The Tai'e sword once belonged to Chen Commandery's Xie family. Its hilt was always hollow, but an exceptionally rare metal was used when forging it. That metal is abnormally hard, so the only way to hide something inside the hilt is to break it open using some kind of extraordinary rock, then put great effort into reforging it again. That sword later vanished, never to be heard of again until it resurfaced in Tuyuhun."

Having eaten the jade cistanche's fruit, Chen Gong finally found some relief. It would take quite some time for the toxins to subside, though, so he could only distract himself by talking.

"So, the moment you saw me with this sword, you knew that it'd already been opened and reforged," he said. "And because I ran straight to Ruoqiang looking for the carnelian, you were also able to guess that I wanted to break open the sword and retrieve the item inside. Hence, you threw away the cistanche fruit in advance, leaving only a couple for yourself. All so that you could threaten me into handing over the item after I was poisoned!"

With this sudden realization, Chen Gong couldn't help but taunt, "Even when Sect Leader Yan is suffering from such severe injuries, his scheming and calculations can still leave us in the dust!"

Meanwhile, Murong Xun angrily rebuked: "How despicable and shameless of you! Reaping the fruits of others' work!"

Yan Wushi gave a cold laugh. To him, squabbling with them was beneath him.

Murong Qin flashed forward, wanting to seize Yan Wushi, but he didn't expect Shen Qiao to suddenly interfere. With his sword across his chest, he blocked Murong Qin.

The two of them exchanged several blows, and Murong Qin realized he couldn't gain an upper hand over Shen Qiao. Surprise welled up within him, unbidden.

In just a year, the blind man who'd still been too weak to truss a chicken back in Chuyun Temple had managed to recover to this extent. No one could afford to underestimate him.

In the time it took for Shen Qiao to block the attack, Yan Wushi had already swiftly slipped into the darkness. "He's gone!" Murong Xun yelled in surprise. At his voice, everyone turned to look.

Sa Kunpeng leapt forward to investigate. Sure enough, he could find no trace of Yan Wushi.

"My Lord, there appears to be a mechanism here. But nothing happened when I pulled it!" he cried.

"He must have shut it down from the other side!" said Murong Xun angrily.

Behind them was the passage-sealing boulder. Apart from the fact that there was a thousand-pound rock blocking their path of retreat, even if they did manage to lift it again, there was still the ape leader and venomous spiders waiting for them on the other side. It wasn't that they couldn't defeat them but that it would exhaust far too much energy. Just thinking about those spiders and their ability to slip through every crack gave everyone goosebumps.

Before them was a cliff, and beneath that cliff was a sea of carnelian crystals. They might have been beautiful, but they weren't edible, and they were even highly toxic. Having seen the awful condition Chen Gong had been in, none of them would be willing to bring trouble on themselves by coveting that carnelian.

Which meant that they were currently trapped here, without any paths to take and unable to leave.

"Are you satisfied now, Shen Qiao?!" Murong Xun roared, full of rage that had nowhere to go.

Shen Qiao's eyes were closed as he rested. He didn't respond at all.

Chen Gong said sternly, "All of you, go look to see if there are any other exits. If Yan Wushi could leave this place, certainly we can as well."

While Murong Qin and the other two searched for an exit, he looked at Shen Qiao. "Daoist Master Shen, forgive my bluntness. Previously, Yan Wushi was gravely injured after those five martial experts ambushed him. You didn't need to bring him on the current trip, but because I said that there might be jade cistanche here, you still brought him in. Forget a friend, even a stranger receiving such benevolence would be moved to tears. But now he's obtained both the jade cistanche and my silk piece, and he didn't take you with him but abandoned you here and left by himself. Even I feel that this is an injustice to you, even if you yourself don't feel it."

"If I expect to be repaid for my kindness, then how much do you owe me right now?" Shen Qiao replied coolly. "What repayment should you give me? If I hadn't stepped in at the broken-down temple back then, how could you have defeated those local hoodlums? Later, at Chuyun Temple, if I weren't there, you'd have died at Murong Qin's hands long ago. How could you be here ordering them around like so? But how did you repay me? By leading Mu Tipo to me? Or by threatening me with Banna's grandfather so that I'd come with you to Ruoqiang?"

Chen Gong was unable to answer. Suddenly, none of the provocative words in his head could leave his lips.

"You and I do not walk the same path," said Shen Qiao. "We never did, and we never will."

At first, Chen Gong felt a little guilty, but hearing these words, he actually grew angry. "True, you are noble and virtuous beyond compare," he sneered. "But what good did that bring you? I earned everything I have today through my own efforts. What's so shameful about that? I might as well tell you. I was born with the ability to remember everything I see and hear. Though I was mostly illiterate back at Chuyun Temple, I still managed to memorize everything you recited. There were so many martial experts at the scene; who would have imagined that an insignificant nobody could pull off what they couldn't? Mu Tipo is cruel and ruthless. The people he favors never last beyond a month, and most of them suffer horrific fates. But I was able to make him recommend me to the Lord of Qi through my own abilities, and that was my true stepping stone to greater heights."

Murong Qin and the others had indeed chosen Chen Gong, but they still couldn't help the awkwardness hearing him talk about his experience as a kept man. But Chen Gong himself had no such feelings, and he continued to speak with ease, calm and composed.

"Obtaining the favor of the Emperor of Qi isn't my final goal. There's no man in the world who's willing to serve others with his body, even if he's the one taking initiative in bed. Using the Lord of Qi's favor, I had him find me a teacher so that I could learn to read. I know very well that those great aristocratic families will never acknowledge people with my background, but I don't need their approval. There are only two things in the world that allow you to rule over people's hearts: one is the book, and the other is the sword. So, I needed to learn as many words as possible, read as many books as possible, all in the shortest amount of time. And I succeeded.

"Shen Qiao, why do you think Murong Qin and the others chose me? Just due to riches and glory? That's not it. Are kings and generals made in the womb? The kingdom of Qi is destined to fall, and they know that as soon as Qi suffers a crushing defeat, everyone will leave like rats from a sinking ship. There's no future in following the Lord of Qi, so they follow me instead. At least I know myself and my abilities well, unlike the Lord of Qi and most of his aristocrats.

"But what about you, Shen Qiao? You are indeed noble and virtuous—an upright gentleman. To be honest, I admire you greatly, because I can never be like you, to repay evil with virtue without resentment or regret. But a gentleman like you cannot survive in this world; you'll only be swallowed up, consumed until not even your bones remain. Just like now. Yan Wushi has betrayed you again and again. In the end, you can only await your death together with an 'enemy' like me. Isn't that ridiculous?"

Shen Qiao remained silent and calm until he finished. Then he said slowly, "Chen Gong, ever since I met you, I knew that you were different from the others in your hometown. You are smart and full of energy; you have ambition. You're ruthless to both yourself and others. Within these troubled times, you have the ability to become someone truly formidable. You were able to climb up the ladder of success called Mu Tipo, then use him to obtain the Emperor of Qi's favor on your own merits; I won't look down on you for that. The reason you always think me noble and virtuous is because deep within your heart, your conscience is still alive. You know that your methods are wrong, and that's why you subconsciously compare yourself to me, why you're concerned about how I see you. Otherwise, everyone has their own Dao, their own path, so you need only focus on moving forward. Why stop to look at others?"

For a long time, Chen Gong was at a loss for words. Then he suddenly burst out laughing. "You're right! You're completely right! I'm grateful to you! You've resolved my complexes and doubts. From this point forth, I'll be able to climb even higher."

"Congratulations, then," said Shen Qiao flatly.

He closed his eyes once more, leaning back against the chilly stone. Then he let himself thoroughly sink into the darkness, both in body and in mind.

From the moment Yan Wushi had handed him to Sang Jingxing, Shen Qiao had learned to drop all expectations. Without expectations, there'd be no disappointment, let alone despair. So, when Yan Wushi had abandoned him and left him by himself, though he'd been a little surprised in the beginning, even that surprise had quickly become trifling and insignificant.

Yan Wushi had always been like this. Even if his personality had changed greatly, the selfishness and callousness innate to him wouldn't lessen in the slightest.

For many things, just because you gave, didn't mean you'd receive anything in return.

He was already used to it, so why would he still be sad or disappointed?

Murong Qin and the others searched everywhere but slowly began to feel hopeless. It was true that they still had rations with them, and that the daily needs of martial artists were far less than that of a normal person's, meaning that the rations could last them a long time, but they couldn't stay here forever. Furthermore, this place was deep underground, lacking sun or sky, and it was airless. Even if they didn't starve to death, they'd eventually suffocate.

At this moment, Sa Kungpeng suggested, "What if this subordinate goes to search at the bottom of the cliff? Perhaps there's another exit there?"

Chen Gong thought for a moment. "Very well. Carnelian is down there, but that doesn't mean there's nowhere to stand. Just be careful not to touch the carnelian."

Sa Kungpeng agreed. As Murong Xun was young and energetic, he'd grown bored after sitting around for so long, so he rose and went down with him.

Pretty much everyone had some scratches from the apes; those wounds were burning and swollen, but it wasn't anything serious, only flesh wounds. They didn't even need to eat the cistanche fruit—applying juice squeezed from the cistanche roots to the wounds was enough to relieve the swelling and itching.

Chen Gong sent Murong Qin to go down to help them search, then asked Shen Qiao, "If we manage to get out, what will you do?"

Shen Qiao slowly opened his eyes. Within this darkness, no one could see the bewilderment in his gaze.

Based on his pace and the amount of time that had passed, Yan Wushi should be almost back on the surface. With his abilities, even if he couldn't confront the Buddhist and Confucian sects directly for now, he could quickly contact the people from Huanyue Sect, which would at least save him from getting trapped in dangerous situations. In other words, even without Shen Qiao, Yan Wushi could still have a good life.

Shen Qiao suddenly thought of something. "What you obtained just now, that was one of the *Zhuyang Strategy* scrolls?"

"Correct," said Chen Gong.

"Was there anything special about that scroll compared to the others?"

Chen Gong was silent for a moment. "How much do you know about the *Zhuyang Strategy*?"

"The *Zhuyang Strategy* is composed of five volumes and combines the strengths of the three schools of thought," said Shen Qiao. "It's the product of Tao Hongjing's lifelong efforts."

"You've also read a couple of the other volumes yourself. Any thoughts?"

"It is indeed the most remarkable martial arts book in the world. I've greatly benefited from it."

"It seems your information is incomplete," said Chen Gong. "It's true that the *Zhuyang Strategy* has five volumes, and that it combines the strengths of the three schools, but that only applies to the contents of four of the volumes. There's one more volume that has been lost for many years. No one knows where it is, but it's said that its contents are related to the martial arts of the demonic discipline."

Shen Qiao startled, but after thinking closely, he found Chen Gong's words quite logical.

In the past, Yan Wushi had attempted many times to use the *Zhuyang Strategy*'s true qi for himself, and he'd even experimented with Shen Qiao for it, repeatedly trying to bring out his potential. But reality had proven that because his martial foundations were his demonic core, it was incompatible with Shen Qiao's Daoist core. Hence, the *Zhuyang Strategy* ended up being of little value to him, like a chicken rib that was still edible: tasteless, but a waste to throw away.

If the *Zhuyang Strategy* only wrote about the martial arts of the Three Schools, Yan Wushi could never have said something like "he already had a way to patch the flaw." With how capable he was, he'd likely already deduced that there was a *Zhuyang Strategy* volume hidden within Tai'e, and that this was exactly the one he needed.

Having deduced the entire sequence of events, Shen Qiao slowly exhaled, a trace of fatigue in his expression. Suddenly, he felt a little tired.

But his voice remained as calm as before. "So that's how it is. Tao Hongjing was indeed a man of great learning. No wonder the demonic practitioners have constantly sought the *Zhuyang Strategy* as well. It sounds like that piece of silk was exactly what they were after. And since you were also chasing it so anxiously, does that mean you're practicing the martial arts of the demonic discipline? Did you join Hehuan Sect?"

"What a joke," said Chen Gong. "With my current rank and status, why would I need to join Hehuan Sect and get ordered around? If anything, it's Hehuan Sect who requires all the conveniences I can provide, so our relationship is just one of business and mutual cooperation. It benefits us both."

However, saying this much was useless as well. In reality, they were still trapped here with no method of escape.

Having searched around the cliff bottom once, Murong Qin and the others returned empty-handed. Everyone was a little disheartened, and Chen Gong spoke no more. Instead, he took the opportunity to meditate and preserve his energy while reciting the contents of the silk scrap he'd hastily memorized earlier, wanting to integrate it within himself.

He'd never been the type to wait around for his death. Even in this kind of situation, he still did his absolute best to create a favorable environment for himself. That was why, in these troubled times, Chen Gong had been able to rise from a penniless commoner to where he was today. To the point that even the imperial court of Qi's foremost martial artist, Murong Qin, was willing to obey his commands and dispatches.

After an unknown length of time, a sound suddenly came from the stone wall. Everyone had just been nodding off and immediately opened their eyes; they turned toward that sound and saw a silhouette reappear where Yan Wushi had originally vanished.

Murong Xun reacted first. He leapt up, ready to charge over with his sword. "Yan Wushi?!"

The name was uttered through clenched teeth, his voice brimming with hatred.

# Escape from Trouble

HOWEVER, Yan Wushi only needed one line to freeze him in his place.

"The path branches off outside. Without me, you won't be able to leave."

"Sanlang!" Chen Gong stopped Murong Xun, who reluctantly sheathed his weapon and returned to his place behind Chen Gong.

Chen Gong cupped his hands, his manner courteous. "Many thanks to Sect Leader Yan for coming back; we are deeply grateful. If Sect Leader Yan is willing to show us the way out, I promise to happily leave the piece of silk to him and never ask for it again."

Yan Wushi glanced at him but didn't say anything. He simply turned to head out from where he'd entered.

Murong Qin looked at Chen Gong and asked, "My Lord, should we follow?"

Chen Gong nodded. "I'll lead; just follow behind me."

"My Lord!"

Chen Gong smiled. "Stop the nonsense and follow me!"

Murong Qin and Murong Xun were both a little moved. They spoke no further and strode after Chen Gong.

Naturally, Chen Gong hadn't won over the likes of Murong Qin for no reason. Even if he'd leapt up and become the Emperor of Qi's favorite, he'd still been a poor youth with neither background nor family properties. It wasn't enough to make an arrogant martial expert like Murong Qin serve him happily. In truth, Shen Qiao had already hit the nail on the head earlier: Chen Gong was tremendously talented. The ability to remember everything he saw and heard had allowed him to seize his stroke of fortune in encountering the *Zhuyang Strategy*. Furthermore, he'd spent great efforts honing himself, and he hadn't been satisfied with becoming the Lord of Qi's favored official. Judging from his actions, he indeed possessed the potential to become a formidable leader.

If they dug a bit deeper, someone like Murong Qin, who came from the royal family of the earlier Yan Dynasty, would have already lost all their authority within this new era if not for their martial arts. They weren't from a powerful, aristocratic family, so the emperor wouldn't give them too much authority either. Their only choice was to become hounds and falcons for the true heavyweights. Even the ordinary nobles of Qi could look down on them. Under these circumstances, Chen Gong had given them a new option, and he'd won them over with his own performance. They were naturally willing to pledge their loyalty to a better, more enlightened master in Chen Gong.

Of course, Shen Qiao didn't know the details of the situation, but he'd also spent quite some time in the secular world himself. Thanks to Yan Wushi's influence, he now had some understanding of the politics and mindsets it was built on. Chen Gong had managed to climb this high in such a short period of time and win over many people—he was indeed someone incredible. If it had been Yan Wushi instead, even if he understood all those mindsets and logic, his arrogant, willful nature meant that he might not be able to bend when necessary like Chen Gong had.

The entire passage had been carved from the mountain. Chen Gong still had some torches with him. Once he lit one, they could see candlesticks lining both sides of the hall. The entire capital of Ruoqiang had sunken and collapsed sometime in the past, which might have caused part of the mountain to cave in as well. Certain points along the tunnel were blocked by boulders that had fallen from above, leaving only a tiny gap through which to pass. They were forced to carefully squeeze through after clearing away some of the rocks.

Murong Xun was a little worried. "There aren't any spiders here, right?"

"Those spiders reek of rotten flesh, but I don't smell that here, so there shouldn't be any around."

As they were talking, the path suddenly branched into two separate ones.

Everyone halted and looked at Yan Wushi's back.

"Go left," he told them.

Murong Xun was suspicious. "Wait! How do you know to go left?"

"I went right earlier. There were spiders."

"Why should we trust you?" asked Murong Xun. "And how are you unscathed after encountering the spiders?"

Yan Wushi ignored him and continued walking.

Murong Qin held Murong Xun's shoulder and whispered, "He has the jade cistanche."

Murong Xun immediately understood as well. *That's right, since the jade cistanche can counteract the spiders' venom, it should also keep the spiders away.*

But in that case, why would Yan Wushi return to guide them out? He couldn't have suddenly found his conscience, could he?

The mighty Huanyue Sect Leader suddenly growing a conscience? Forget about convincing others, even Murong Xun refused to believe it.

The entire path was angled up gently, which proved that they were heading toward the surface. No one said anything, but they all gradually began to believe Yan Wushi. They followed him until they found another split in the path some distance later.

And this time, there were three branches.

Yan Wushi stopped. "This is as far as I came before turning back." Meaning, he also didn't know which path to take from now on.

But everyone now understood as well. When they'd entered in the beginning, they hadn't taken the proper roads, so currently they were mainly retreading the capital's inner passages. These splits led to all sorts of different directions. It was just like the hallways within the Central Plains' palaces: some would lead to a different palace, while one would lead to the capital itself. And it was the latter that would lead to the true exit. If they chose any of the others, not only might they end up taking a detour, they might even run into spiders or apes and suffer the consequences.

Chen Gong asked Yan Wushi, "Which path would you take?"

Yan Wushi didn't answer.

Shen Qiao had been silent the entire time, but now he suddenly spoke. "Since we don't know, we can just leave a mark here and choose a random path. It'll all depend on our luck anyhow. If we pick the wrong one, we can only blame our own bad luck."

"That works," said Chen Gong.

He picked up a rock and scored several marks into the stone wall.

Shen Qiao couldn't help but do a double take.

He'd known Chen Gong's martial ability was fair, but he'd been busy fighting the apes earlier and couldn't spare the time to observe. Each stroke Chen Gong made now was obviously infused with true qi—the white marks were scored deep into the walls, showing his level of mastery.

Once the marks were made, Chen Gong said, "Why don't we take the middle one? Perhaps that leads outside."

Naturally, no one had any objections.

Seeing that Yan Wushi wasn't moving, Murong Xun couldn't resist asking, "Why aren't you walking?"

"This path...I've never taken it before, so I won't lead."

There were slight pauses between his words. The others hadn't noticed, but Shen Qiao did.

Murong Xun sneered, "Who knows if you've taken it or not. Now that you refuse to take the lead, how can we trust you've not set some kind of ambush for us along the way?"

In the past, Murong Xun wouldn't have dared to say such things to Yan Wushi even if he'd had a hundred times the number of guts. But this was just how humans were: now that they'd seen him defeated and downtrodden, their idea of his standing also plummeted, to the point that they'd think that they could defeat him too and that he was unworthy of even a mention.

Yan Wushi didn't answer, taking action instead.

Murong Xun was standing beside him. Yan Wushi moved so quickly that before he could draw his sword, the man had already grabbed him by the throat and slammed him into the wall!

Murong Qin struck a palm at Yan Wushi, but this was blocked by a light and graceful sword sheath.

"We're not even out of danger yet, and you're all raring to kill each other?" Shen Qiao said flatly.

Murong Xun tried to claw at Yan Wushi, but before he could even raise his hand, Yan Wushi released him and retreated behind Shen Qiao.

"Everyone, stop!" yelled Chen Gong.

Turning to Murong Xun, he said, "Sect Leader Yan didn't need to come back and find us. But since he did, we should be grateful. You must not be rude to him again." Then he cupped his hands at Yan Wushi. "Let me apologize to Sect Leader Yan on Sanlang's behalf. Since I was the one who chose this path, I'll take the lead!"

After he spoke, he walked forward while carrying the torch.

Despite his show of courage in walking at the forefront, Chen Gong's every step was exceedingly careful. Whenever he felt that something was even slightly amiss, he'd stop and observe the situation for a long while.

But perhaps the heavens really did favor him—their gamble actually paid off. Their entire journey was free of obstacles, even as they left the tunnel, walked through the capital, and returned to the place they'd originally fallen from.

Finding the exit from here might have been difficult for a normal person, but all they needed to do was leap upward with their qinggong, secure their positions, and then clamber upward, step by step.

The moment the sun and sky greeted them again, everyone was almost blinded by the fierce light. But at the same time, anyone who'd spent three days underground and almost lost their life down there would find this sunlight precious beyond compare.

Shen Qiao wound his scarf over his eyes, lest they be blinded by the sudden, intense stimulation. After a moment, once his eyes had slowly adjusted, he removed the cloth and noticed Yan Wushi standing behind him. He'd somehow lost his scarf and could only use his hand to shield his eyes, but he also stuck close to Shen Qiao, as if afraid he'd run away. It inexplicably looked a little silly.

"What are Daoist Master Shen and Sect Leader Yan's plans afterward?" asked Chen Gong. "We'll be passing through Chang'an as we return to Qi, so if the two of you don't mind, I can see you there. That way Sect Leader Yan's identity won't be exposed, and you won't draw any unnecessary trouble."

His original goal for this trip had been to open up Tai'e and extract the silk within, but now, even though he knew the silk was with Yan Wushi, he didn't mention it at all; it was clear he'd memorized the contents. His words to Shen Qiao weren't simply to express his goodwill and magnanimity, but also to tell Shen Qiao and Yan Wushi that he had no intention of revealing Yan Wushi's whereabouts.

With a long separation came time for a reappraisal. Chen Gong as he was now, could no longer be judged with the eyes of the past.

Shen Qiao glanced at Yan Wushi. "Thank you for your kindness, but I have somewhere else to go. As for Sect Leader Yan, he should be left to make his own decisions."

"I'll go with you," said Yan Wushi.

Chen Gong smiled, seemingly indifferent. "That's fine. Then we'll part ways here. The mountains and rivers forever remain unchanged, and the world is limited in size, so we'll definitely see each other again. I hope that next time we meet, Sect Leader Yan will have made a full recovery, and Daoist Master Shen will be leading Xuandu Mountain once more."

Shen Qiao gave no answer to that, simply cupping his hands instead. "No need to see us off."

If they wanted to leave Tuyuhun, they had to follow their original road, back to that small town to rest and purchase horses. Only afterward could they return to the royal capital before traveling on. But Chen Gong and Shen Qiao had different objectives in the first place. Shen Qiao still had many things he wished to ask Yan Wushi, so he had no plans to travel with them.

They watched as the others left, leaving behind footprints both deep and shallow in the fine sand. Then a gust of wind blew past, and those prints vanished without a trace. Shen Qiao turned to

Yan Wushi. "Chen Gong isn't a generous person," he said. "You took his silk piece, so even if he remembers the contents, he'll still hold a grudge against you deep down. This will cause you trouble in the future."

Yan Wushi stared at him unswervingly, then suddenly said in a hurt voice, "It wasn't me, Meiren-gege."

Shen Qiao held his forehead. "I know. It was the previous...the previous Yan Wushi. But the silk is still on you, isn't it?"

"You can tell us apart?" asked Yan Wushi happily.

Shen Qiao was silent for a moment. "If it were one of your other personalities, you could never have returned after leaving."

"I'm so happy," said Yan Wushi. "You recognized me. I know he abandoned you... I was so worried. I had to use all my strength to take control and head back." He tugged on Shen Qiao's hand. "Don't be mad, all right?"

Shen Qiao gave a long sigh. "If he didn't do that, he wouldn't be Yan Wushi. The real Yan Wushi would also never say such things to me. I just never thought that a man with his personality could give birth to someone like you. That should be impossible."

A trace of imperceptible cunning surfaced in Yan Wushi's smile. "That's not true."

Shen Qiao didn't understand. "What?"

"Nothing. When can we head back? Should we wait until they're a long way off? I'm hungry."

# Rebirth after Death

THEY'D FOUGHT TOGETHER beneath the ancient city of Ruoqiang, but that was only because they'd shared a common enemy. Now that they were back on the surface, Chen Gong's party of four might not be able to take the upper hand against Shen Qiao, but they held a piece of very important information that they could use against him: Yan Wushi had survived the ambush by those five martial experts, and Shen Qiao had been the one to rescue him.

If this information was revealed, the five powers that had ambushed Yan Wushi would definitely not let it go. Right now, Shen Qiao was alone; it was impossible for him to fight off that many people. Yes, Chen Gong had implied that he wouldn't reveal their whereabouts, but Shen Qiao couldn't trust him so easily now. He naturally chose to be as careful as possible—better safe than sorry—lest he commit the same mistakes.

In order to return to Tuyuhun, they first had to pass through the small town they'd stopped in before, but Shen Qiao didn't want to encounter Chen Gong again, so he didn't rest at an inn within the town. Instead, he found a household to stay in for a few days.

This household's conditions were even worse than those of Banna's. They couldn't even offer lamb soup, only fried flatbread, and they didn't have many vacant rooms. They could only spare one.

"Previously, you said that the jade cistanche is miraculously effective on external injuries," said Shen Qiao. "As you took that much cistanche with you, isn't there hope that we can fully heal your head injury?"

Yan Wushi groped around in his sleeve for a cistanche, then passed it to Shen Qiao. "Here."

Shen Qiao was surprised. "Why me?"

"You were scratched by the apes back underground in Ruoqiang, right? The cistanche's juice is limited and its curative effects mediocre. The fruit is much better."

Shen Qiao took the cistanche, then suddenly said, "You're A-Yan, not Xie Ling, aren't you?"

Yan Wushi was quiet for a moment. "How did you know?"

Shen Qiao shook his head. "You talk too much. Xie Ling goes most of the day without saying anything. And from what I know about Yan Wushi, he'd never inconvenience himself in the slightest. Though your personalities all have their differences, some intrinsic qualities never change. When we were at Banna's place, if there was lamb soup to eat, Xie Ling wouldn't touch the flatbread. And if there was only flatbread, Xie Ling would still endure and refuse to eat while remaining silent. But just now, though your face betrayed your displeasure, you still partook of the flatbread."

Yan Wushi sputtered a laugh. "A-Qiao, I had no idea that you paid so much attention to our every move. I'm truly overwhelmed and flattered!"

"If I don't pay close attention, I fear that a fool like myself will get duped again, and I won't even know it." His tone was leisurely and placid as he spoke these words, without even a shred of resentment. How much treachery had he suffered in this world, had been hammered down upon him, in order for him to forge such a chivalrous and sentimental heart?

Yan Wushi gave a slight sigh. "If you're a fool, A-Qiao, then no intelligent people exist in this world!"

Shen Qiao burst out laughing. "Thank you for your praise."

Then Yan Wushi asked sweetly, "Who do you like more: me or Xie Ling?"

Shen Qiao froze a little, then knit his brows and said mildly, "Whether it's you, Xie Ling, or some other personality, you're all just a fragment of Yan Wushi's inner demons. Since you've already obtained the silk piece, it'll just be a matter of time before he repairs the flaw in his demonic core. Once that happens, all of you will disappear, while Yan Wushi will still be Yan Wushi. Who I like isn't important."

Yan Wushi smiled. "You're correct. In the end, we were all born from Yan Wushi and are joined to him, so it's impossible for us to exist separate from this body. So you must like Xie Ling the most, because Xie Ling is the least like Yan Wushi, correct?"

Shen Qiao didn't answer his question. Instead, he sighed. "Back in Ruoqiang, we never got a good night's rest. Let's sleep first. I'm tired as well."

He didn't wait for a reply, just closed his eyes and crossed his legs as he began to meditate.

In the days he'd spent inside Ruoqiang's ancient city, though every step had been fraught with danger, Shen Qiao had also gained new experiences. Those apes weren't as sly and calculating as humans, but they were inexhaustible and far more aggressive. While fighting them, Shen Qiao had often felt like he was wandering between life and death, and every time he escaped a grisly fate, his comprehension of martial arts would rise to the next level.

His initial defeat at Banbu Peak had been wholly unexpected. The moment he'd fallen from the cliff, Shen Qiao's heart had been full of anger and disbelief, just like any other person's would be. But after witnessing all sorts of people and affairs, he'd tempered himself a true tender heart, and he could even face life-and-death situations calmly. This type of mindset was reflected in his swordplay. When he'd used the Azure Waves sword techniques in the past, even if he could endlessly change and wield them with ease, they lacked the confidence born from experience with life and death. But when he used them now, the moves poured out with a transcendental grace.

As the *Zhuyang Strategy*'s true qi rebuilt his meridians, it and his personality quietly and subtly actualized each other.

*Only when a person's mind is truly detached and tranquil could they understand the subtlest, most wondrous aspects of nature's beauty. The endless red dust of the human world sees a lone crane soaring high and far. The heavenly Dao is unfeeling, and I alone have obtained it.*

An outsider might notice that his aura grew more transcendental day after day. Even dressed in an ordinary Daoist robe, he looked more divine than the gods or immortals themselves.

To Shen Qiao, this sensation brought him into a deeply profound state: awake yet asleep, in between dream and reality. He could unconsciously sense and know everything around him.

The sleeping households, the cold moon that hung outside, the dogs asleep by the fences, the breeze as it rustled the branches, and even inside his room...Yan Wushi.

Shen Qiao suddenly opened his eyes.

The man who was supposed to be asleep was staring at him, eyes wide open.

Shen Qiao was somewhat uncertain and asked, "Xie Ling?"

Yan Wushi made a sound of confirmation and didn't blink.

"How come it's you?"

"I wanted to come out, so I did," said Yan Wushi.

Though this answer was a little cryptic, Shen Qiao actually understood him. He meant that the Xie Ling personality's strong obsessive tendencies had allowed him to take over for now.

Words that were brief yet complete, with intermittent pauses. This was indeed Xie Ling's style.

"I should thank you," said Shen Qiao, "for coming back to bring me out of Ruoqiang. But you'd already switched to A-Yan by the time we were out, so I had to wait until now to tell you."

"No need," said Yan Wushi.

So he said, but his eyes remained on Shen Qiao.

Lacking the erratic moods, without the icy aloofness hidden within mocking smiles, Xie Ling's personality actually became more distinctive.

Shen Qiao felt that if Yan Wushi had been Xie Ling from the start, many things probably wouldn't have happened. But there were no "what-ifs" in life. Yan Wushi was Yan Wushi; Xie Ling was a part of Yan Wushi, but Yan Wushi would never be Xie Ling.

"When I was training with the *Zhuyang Strategy* on Xuandu Mountain in the past," Shen Qiao said, "it always felt like I was looking at a beauty through a veil: I knew that she was beautiful, but I couldn't see her clearly, and there was nothing I could do about it. Only after I lost all my martial arts in my battle with Sang Jingxing did I realize what it truly meant to fight your way out of certain death and be reborn. By starting over, I was able to use the *Zhuyang Strategy* to its greatest effect. But in this world, giving up everything is easier said than done. Even if they knew that the *Zhuyang Strategy* is capable of reshaping one's meridians, would the likes of Dou Yanshan and Duan Wenyang be willing to give up all the prowess they'd cultivated over the decades and start again?"

Yan Wushi didn't reply.

Shen Qiao didn't need him to either. He smiled, then continued, "Even without hearing it from them personally, I know that very few people would be willing to do so. Leaving aside others to talk about myself, even my past self, before I was forced to give up all my martial arts, would have been plagued with misgivings. But if your heart is full of worries, even if you were forced to destroy all your martial arts, you wouldn't be able to properly cultivate with the *Zhuyang Strategy*. There's a Buddhist verse that says, 'one must throw away their life and embrace death before they can give up everything and achieve true peace.'

"But demonic and Daoist cores are fundamentally different. You haven't lost your martial arts either—you only need to repair the flaw, so it should be much easier for you than it was for me."

"Why...are you saying...this?"

Shen Qiao said, "You once said that only an evenly matched opponent was qualified to be your equal. Back then, I didn't have those qualifications. Even my current self cannot compare to your past self. With your abilities, repairing the demonic core's flaw is only a matter a time, and you will certainly recover your martial arts one day. What I said just now were the insights I had while cultivating with the *Zhuyang Strategy*. I hope they can benefit you. As one who follows the martial path, I also hope for a day when we can have a proper and straightforward battle."

"I'm...Xie Ling," said Yan Wushi.

"I know," said Shen Qiao. "But you're not the only one who can hear these words. Your other personalities can hear them too."

Yan Wushi gazed at him silently.

Shen Qiao was already used to this. It matched the reaction he expected of Xie Ling.

He patted the other man's shoulder. "It's late. Sleep."

After another long moment, that person finally listened and closed his eyes.

Shen Qiao also closed his eyes, then returned to resting cross-legged.

After a few days, Shen Qiao reckoned that Chen Gong's party should have been in a hurry to return to Qi, so they likely wouldn't stay in Tuyuhun for too long. By this point, they might have already reached the royal capital or even left Tuyuhun entirely. So he left the small town and returned to the royal capital of Tuyuhun together with Yan Wushi. It'd been a while since they last saw it.

Sure enough, they didn't meet Chen Gong's party along the way. The Coiling Dragon Assembly had ended quite some time ago, so the Central Plains' martial artists had already departed, greatly lowering the risk of Yan Wushi being discovered. But Shen Qiao still felt their characteristics were too distinct and conspicuous. If they continued south, they might end up with more troubles. Hence, he exchanged his Daoist robe for common Han ones and brought back a set of women's clothes together with some cosmetics. He placed them before Yan Wushi.

Yan Wushi just stared at him silently.

Shen Qiao gave a light cough. "Your appearance is too striking. It's better to disguise yourself."

Yan Wushi didn't answer, but his expression was clearly asking, *Then why aren't you putting on the outfit?*

"You can wear a veil once you change into women's clothes. If others think you're a woman, they'll avoid looking at you so as not to arouse suspicions. But if you continue to dress as a man, the moment you meet observant types like Dou Yanshan and Duan Wenyang, they'll still be able to pick up some clues. In order to keep from stirring up trouble before you meet up with Huanyue Sect, women's clothing is the safest choice."

The two of them stared awkwardly at each other for a while.

Shen Qiao frowned. "Will you wear it or not?"

Yan Wushi shook his head. "If I don't wear it...what will you do?"

"I'll seal your acupoints, help you into the outfit, and then rent a carriage and take you that way. That might be somewhat more painful, but it'll at least save me quite a bit of trouble."

Yan Wushi lowered his lashes. "I'll wear it."

"Good boy." Shen Qiao was pleased, thinking that Xie Ling was really the easiest to persuade.

The white hair peppering his temples had to be dyed black, but his hair could remain in a bun—no change was required here, since many women also wore this hairstyle. His eyebrows had to be trimmed slightly, his cheeks and lips dabbed with rouge. A general look was good enough—they didn't need to be particular about the details. Then he changed into the outfit and embroidered shoes. Though his figure looked somewhat strange and his expression was stiff and cold, an air of handsome beauty remained about his features, which had its own charm.

Shen Qiao saw how tense he was and laughed. "Don't be afraid. In the past, whenever the portraits of our forefathers at Xuandu Mountain began to fade, I was the one who'd touch them up. Touching up portraits and touching up makeup—though not the same, they still share certain similarities."

Once he was finished, he stood and gave Yan Wushi a once-over, then nodded. "Not bad. Would you like to see yourself in the mirror?"

But the other man had no interest in even glancing at the bronze mirror. He went and put the veil on straight away.

What you couldn't see couldn't hurt you.

# Tangren

**B**Y THE TIME the two of them returned to Tuyuhun's royal capital, winter had already arrived. There were far fewer merchants passing through here to the other countries of the Western Regions now, and the entire capital seemed completely different from when they'd left—assuming a cold and lonely appearance.

"This is only temporary," said a street peddler selling tangren.[8] "Traveling west in the winter is difficult, so many merchants set off during autumn and return the following spring. Once winter is over, more people will show up again!"

He was a Han, but ten years ago he'd met a Tuyuhun maiden while passing by this place with a group of traveling merchants. Afterward, he'd married and settled down here to have a family.

Shen Qiao had a natural approachability—the power to make everyone around him extremely comfortable, as if they were basking in the spring breeze. Previously, Yan Wushi had been standing in front of his tangren stall for a while, but the peddler hadn't spoken to him. Then Shen Qiao had walked over and asked a couple of questions, and just like that, the peddler started chatting with him like he'd met an old friend from his hometown.

---

"There are actually quite a few Han people in the city," the peddler told him. "Even the royal and noble families of Tuyuhun speak the Han language and wear Han clothing. But since we're in the Western Regions, most people aren't willing to leave their native land and come here."

Shen Qiao smiled. "That's true. Your wife must have been amazingly beautiful and wise to make you stay. From the way you talk, you have to be a fairly well-read scholar, yet you were willing to stay in this distant land for her, thousands of miles away from your hometown. Seeing such deep love between spouses truly makes one jealous!"

Hearing Shen Qiao's praise, the peddler scratched his head, both embarrassed and proud. "Thank you for your compliments. I just went through a couple of years' worth of private tutoring when I was young. I'm not much of a scholar at all! And where did you return from? You look all worn from travel. Was it with some traveling merchants to spend the winter?"

Shen Qiao said, "We've been on the road for a while, traveling west. We saw how the weather was growing colder and didn't dare to keep going, so we returned. We heard that a Coiling Dragon Assembly took place in the capital some days ago. I imagine it's already over?"

"It's been over for a while," said the peddler. "Everyone's already left. Thought it was busy this year—a lot of people from the jianghu came with their swords and sabers. Since I make tangren, I didn't get much business from them. In fact, during the days after they arrived, people would draw their swords against each other from time to time! I was so scared I hid at home for a couple of days!"

"In that case, the city no longer has any jianghu practitioners?"

"None! After the Coiling Dragon Assembly ended, they all left.

Did you see those inns? They were all jam-packed before! It's much better now. Even after lowering their prices, they can't fill their rooms! However, I heard that Qi was destroyed by Zhou. Maybe the number of traveling merchants heading west next year will drop even further!"

At first, Shen Qiao had been worried that once news of "Yan Wushi's death" spread, Yuwen Yong's life would be in danger. But he hadn't anticipated that such a huge development would have taken place in the few months since they'd left Chang'an. He couldn't resist throwing a glance at the man beside him.

Yan Wushi was wearing a veil, concealing his expression, so Shen Qiao couldn't see it clearly.

"Qi was destroyed?" asked Shen Qiao. "That quickly? Did they not put up any resistance?"

The peddler sighed. "Who knows. Perhaps the Zhou army was simply too strong. Hah, thinking about it now, my old home was in Qi. It's unfortunate—even though I've been living far away in Tuyuhun for years, I still heard news about how capricious and foolish our ruler was. But I could have never imagined that such a large nation could really disappear, just like that!"

"The unification of the north will still be beneficial to the people," said Shen Qiao. "Once things quiet down, the number of merchants traveling to and from the Western Regions will only increase, not decrease."

Another smile spread over the peddler's face. "That's true. I'll take your word for it, then. I'll be waiting for the day the Central Plains know true peace, then I'll take my wife and children back to see my hometown!"

He kept Shen Qiao in a conversation for quite a while and still wished to continue, but then he saw how Yan Wushi was silently standing to the side, seemingly staring at the tangren. Only then did he remember his business, and he quickly laughed. "This lady must be your wife, then? Is she also from Tuyuhun?"

"She's my younger sister," said Shen Qiao.

"Wife," said Yan Wushi.

Shen Qiao and Yan Wushi's eyes met.

Shen Qiao guessed that Yan Wushi had done it on purpose due to his dissatisfaction at being made to dress up like a woman, but he couldn't say too much in front of an outsider. He could only give a light cough and throw in a belated explanation: "This is my cousin. She's a bit immature, so please don't take offense."

It would have better if he hadn't explained. The moment he did, the peddler instantly imagined a story about a pair of cousins in forbidden love eloping to a faraway land. He quickly nodded repeatedly. "I understand! I understand!"

Shen Qiao was completely baffled. *What do you understand? Even I don't understand.*

Beside him, Yan Wushi pointed at a tangren. "I want this."

His voice was deep, completely unlike a woman's, but the peddler didn't think too much of it. After all, sandstorms were rampant outside the Great Wall. Some Tuyuhun maidens also had hoarse voices because of it.

The peddler's spirits rose after hearing Yan Wushi's words. "What would your esteemed self like? I can make anything!"

"Horse, cow, sheep…" said Yan Wushi.

Shen Qiao didn't know whether to laugh or cry. "Just one should be enough? What are you going to do with so many?"

"Then I want one," said Yan Wushi.

The peddler smiled. "All right, of course! Would you like a horse? A sheep or a cow?"

Yan Wushi pointed at Shen Qiao. "Him."

The peddler started. "Hah?"

"Make one of him," said Yan Wushi.

Shen Qiao had never been in a romantic relationship before, but the misunderstanding from earlier, combined with the peddler's dubious expression, was enough for him to know where the peddler had gone wrong.

He said to the peddler, "She's only joking. How about a sheep?"

"No," said Yan Wushi. "I want you." Then he asked the peddler, "Is that all right?"

The peddler seemed to sense a burning gaze beneath the veil. He quickly said, "Yes, of course! Of course it's all right!"

Shen Qiao held his forehead.

The peddler was indeed quite skilled. His hands moved as he talked, and within fifteen minutes, a lively tangren was born right before their eyes.

Since it'd been shaped from molten syrup, the facial features remained indistinct, but its pose and bearing—walking forward with a long cloth bag over its back—really did capture some of Shen Qiao's charm.

Shen Qiao laughed. "As expected of a professional! This level of craftsmanship must have taken at least ten years to hone!"

The peddler let out a small laugh, pleased with the praise. "Not at all!"

Yan Wushi took the tangren and brought it before his veil. Then he bit the head off with a snap and started crunching it inside his mouth.

Shen Qiao could only watch in silence.

To avoid attracting too much of the peddler's curiosity and attention, Shen Qiao handed over the money, then quickly hauled Yan Wushi away.

Zhou vanquishing Qi meant that the north would soon be unified. Neither the Chen Dynasty nor the Göktürk Khaganate would want to see Zhou grow larger without opposition—they'd definitely want to kill Yuwen Yong by any means possible. This was because the crown prince, Yuwen Yun, showed no signs of being an enlightened ruler even now. If Yuwen Yong died, Zhou would become a dragon without a head, a nation without a leader, and it would soon scatter like sand.

Following this speculation, Yan Wushi had to appear in Chang'an as quickly as possible. He had to show up at Yuwen Yong's side and demonstrate to everyone that he was still alive.

Yan Wushi coming out unscathed and healthy after an ambush by five of the world's best martial artists would raise his reputation to new heights. Whether it was a good or bad reputation didn't matter—everyone would hesitate in fear of his might, and no one would dare make an attempt on Yuwen Yong's life lightly.

However, the problem was that the current Yan Wushi—though not dead—had been gravely injured. The flaw in his demonic core was still there, but the bigger issue was his massive personality shift. He'd even split off into multiple personalities, and some of those actually spoke ill of himself. Ordinary people could be deceived, but when it came to the smarter ones, there was a decent chance they'd notice. As for brilliant men like Dou Yanshan and Duan Wenyang, that went without saying—a single glance would be enough for them to realize that something was wrong.

While Shen Qiao pondered this, Yan Wushi had already finished gnawing at the tangren's waist and was moving on to the thighs.

Seeing him like this, who would believe that this was Yan Wushi? If he acted like this in front of Duan Wenyang and the others, they'd definitely beat him until even the dregs were gone.

Shen Qiao couldn't resist heaving a sigh and pulled him into a tavern. Once they were seated, he asked, "You heard what that man said just now. Any thoughts?"

Yan Wushi lifted the veil and shoved the rest of the tangren into his mouth, crunching. He expressionlessly looked at Shen Qiao, his cheeks moving as he chewed.

Even Shen Qiao, with his incredible self-restraint, couldn't help how his mouth twitched at the sight. "Even if you're Xie Ling right now, you should still understand my words, right?"

Yan Wushi made a sound of assent.

"Then what are your plans? Should I take you directly back to Chang'an and look for your disciples?"

"No," said Yan Wushi. He seemed very unwilling to talk and was even frowning because of it. After some time, he finally said, "Send them...a message."

Shen Qiao nodded. "All right. We can wait for Bian Yanmei to receive your message before meeting up with him. Then you can discuss a plan of action together. Huanyue Sect has a fair amount of influence in Qi. Once we enter Qi, we should be able to find one of your members, right? How should we go about sending the message?"

"I don't remember," said Yan Wushi.

Meaning that Xie Ling didn't remember.

Once again, Shen Qiao wanted to sigh. "Never mind. This matter can wait until later. It won't be too late to discuss it after we return to Northern Zhou."

While they were talking, the waiter had already brought over the food. This place was much nicer than the small town they'd stayed at earlier, and there was more than just lamb soup and fried flatbread to order. It was the middle of winter, yet there was a hint of Manchurian wild rice on their plates—a rare sight.

The tavern sat in the middle of the market, and their seats were near the second-floor window. When they looked down, they saw a great many people buying and selling, all calling out their prices. And right below them was a street performer, holding a giant weasel-hair brush in his arms. As he flipped and leapt, the wet brush tip left light and graceful marks over the ground. A closer look showed that he was mimicking the calligraphy from the *Orchid Pavilion*, by the Western Jin Dynasty's Wang Xizhi.

The performance was both refreshing and unique. Soon, it'd drawn in many people, who all gathered to watch. Not everyone could read or understand the contents, but the performer's moves were elegant and nimble, and each of them elicited a chorus of cheers.

Shen Qiao saw that Yan Wushi was watching attentively, so he too tossed the performer a careless glance. However, when he saw the writing left by the weasel-hair brush dragging over the ground, it plucked at something in his heart. Suddenly, he made a mental connection, and a flash of insight came over him.

The man's performance couldn't be considered martial arts—they were only some rough street moves, with punches and kicks. But the man was clever, and he'd combined them with the dance styles of the Western Regions. The result was that he seemed to be danc-ing, but also to be performing tricks, all while writing characters in between. The bystanders found it refreshing and amusing. Even if the richer ones only gave a few coppers, it was still enough to feed a performer for the day.

But the man didn't just put on a perfunctory and half-hearted performance because the crowd was only watching for fun. The *Orchid Pavilion* characters he wrote out on the uneven ground using the weasel-hair brush were quite mediocre—if this had been the Central Plains, countless professional calligraphers would have instantly appeared to sneer at him. However, he wrote every stroke with complete focus, to the point of forgetting himself. He was completely immersed within his own dance, and he stared unswervingly at the ground, paying careful attention to the strength behind each stroke and the structure of each character.

The martial path was incredibly profound and abstruse. It selected for talent, diligence, and even more for comprehension. Sometimes, days or even years of painstaking training would bring no progress, but there would be moments of great advancement too, when understanding would dawn, and the practitioner would instantly enter a new echelon.

And right now, as Shen Qiao watched that performer's every movement, a scene automatically sprang to his mind.

In this scene, the performer had become Shen Qiao, and within his hand wasn't a brush but a sword.

The greatest virtue is like water—water benefits all things without demanding anything in return. It resides in places disliked by men, and therefore it comes closest to the Dao.

The waves of the oceans, the crags of the mountains—the great Dao exists everywhere, melded formlessly into the secular world.

Like drifting clouds or flowing waters, he danced through a set of sword techniques. The moves were incredibly close to the Azure Waves Sword Techniques, but Shen Qiao knew very well that they were different—they were techniques he'd created himself.

Slowly, that set of sword techniques took form in his mind, and Shen Qiao almost forgot everything around him. He even forgot that he was still inside a tavern, forgot that Yan Wushi was still beside him. He immediately leapt to his feet and bounded outside, sweeping toward the city outskirts with such speed, he practically flew.

He could already wait no longer! He had to actualize this set of sword techniques.

# Comprehending
# the Sword

FOR SOMEONE who'd achieved the pinnacle of martial arts, even fallen leaves and drifting flowers could become weapons. So once they reached a certain echelon, the moves themselves became extraneous—they might no longer be the key to victory.

But that didn't mean that the moves were entirely dispensable. As the saying went, "words are the voice of the mind." Internal and external cultivation came as a pair. Possessing only a body of peerless internal cultivation was equivalent to having a mountain of treasures without knowing how to use them.

Qi Fengge was a martial prodigy of his generation, and he keenly understood that knowing too many moves would confuse and overwhelm a swordsman. They wouldn't know where to start using them. It was better to abstract them, reducing the complicated to the simple. Hence, he'd taken all the swordplay techniques of Xuandu Mountain and consolidated them, and in the end only two sets remained. One of them was the famous Azure Waves sword technique.

Xuandu Mountain's sword moves integrated the Daoist concepts of spiritual stillness and non-interference, as well as the Daoist principle of nature. It emphasized agility and elegance, using stillness to defeat movement, and that counterattacking was the key to victory. Shen Qiao's disposition just happened to be a perfect match for these, allowing him to achieve fantastic results with minimal practice.

But after he began cultivating with the *Zhuyang Strategy*'s true qi, his original sword moves gradually became a poor fit. The *Zhuyang Strategy*'s true qi didn't consist of Daoist principles alone but also the essence of Confucianism and Buddhism—intelligent efficiency from the Confucians, and unyielding vigor from the Buddhists. Yet the Azure Waves sword techniques couldn't express either of these.

However, while all things in the world had their differences, they still shared some similarities. Just now, when he'd been watching the performer's dancing and calligraphy, Shen Qiao noticed that though the man was in a busy market and performing for money, he'd seemed unconcerned with appealing to the audience. Instead, he was wholeheartedly immersed in what he was doing, completely engrossed as he danced up a storm. The dance styles of the Western Regions were bold and unrestrained, but calligraphy was a delicate art. By combining the two, he'd created a strange harmony of strength and softness. Onlookers might only find his movements lovely to look at, but Shen Qiao had used them to attain further understanding, realizing an entirely new set of sword techniques.

At this moment, he rose as his sword fell, his sword glare blazing freely. It was winter, and the trees stood bare, all things in a state of wither and decay. But this man and his sword swept and scoured, twisting and turning. Sometimes they were like the drizzling spring winds, so soft they seemed insubstantial; other times they were more unyielding than even a vajra, ferocious and harsh.

The warm spring sun, the clear summer moon, were all contained within.

The whistling autumn breeze, the bleak winter grass, were inconspicuous and unharmed.

The withered mountains and streams, the surging Yangtze and Han, were all conceived by nature.

Ethereal light rippled, converging and diverging—at times dark, at times bright. Within this he danced, poised like a crane on the verge of taking flight.

*The heart is within the sword, and the sword is within the man. Forgetting both myself and the world, I achieve perfect clarity.*

As if the withered trees around him had sensed this, wherever the sword qi touched, they fell one after another, and within the cold, hardened mud beneath him was scored slash after slash of sword qi: some deep and some shallow, some short and some long. Occasionally, the dead leaves, as if intimidated by the sword qi, would flutter from the branches, but they did not fall to the ground—instead, they whirled around the sword qi.

Suddenly, the tip of his sword trembled, and the dead leaves quivered alongside it. Then, one after another, they shot forward with tremendous speed, all straight into the trunk of a tree ten yards away, embedded so deep within that no part of them was visible.

A martial expert channeling their true qi into fallen leaves and flowers wasn't unusual. However, manipulating leaves with the sword went a level beyond that.

Shanhe Tongbei droned and hummed, seemingly in accordance with its master's rippling emotions. Faintly within lay the majestic mountains and rivers, the roar of galloping tempests. Its sword glare wasn't blinding, but only wrapped thinly around the blade, much gentler than it had been before. But this fine veneer of sword glare moved with Shen Qiao's will—at times present, at times hidden, fluttering alongside it.

Having gone through the entire set of techniques, Shen Qiao sheathed his sword and straightened, then released a long breath. The agitation within his heart had yet to subside, and blood roiled within his stomach. He was close to nausea.

He knew very well that this was because his echelon of "sword heart" was still unstable. His internal energy wasn't in harmony with his movements, so the sword qi had backlashed.

During his duel with Kunye, his achieving the echelon of sword heart had stunned and terrified his opponent, but it'd been much like a shooting star streaking through the night—a flash and it was gone. Sometimes he'd been able see it, yet he was unable to grasp it properly. Only now, after great difficulty, did he get his first true glimpse of the gate.

Martial art practitioners had but one lifelong quest: to make continual progress and achieve the next level. Hence, the unskilled looked up to the experts, and the experts wished to climb ever higher. When there was no end to knowledge, how could there be an end to the martial path? There were four echelons of the sword: sword qi, sword intent, sword heart, and sword spirit. To many people, "sword spirit" only existed in legend. Other than Gan Jiang and Mo Ye of the Warring States Period, who'd thrown away their lives for the sword, attaining the echelon of sword spirit in exchange for their lives, no one had been able to achieve this echelon since ancient times.

As for the echelon of sword heart, in the last few decades, Tao Hongjing and Qi Fengge were the only ones to achieve this in the entire world.

And both of them were gone. In the end, Tao Hongjing and Qi Fengge had passed on into history.

But Shen Qiao was still alive in the present.

Shen Qiao sheathed his sword and stood in place, slowly adjusting his disordered breathing. The carefree, intoxicating sensation slowly faded, and he suddenly remembered a very important matter: he'd left Yan Wushi at the restaurant.

*Oh no,* thought Shen Qiao, and he immediately dashed back to the city.

Yan Wushi didn't have even a single copper. With Shen Qiao gone, if the waiter came up and asked him to pay, even if the relatively harmless Xie Ling were in charge, it was still difficult to predict how he'd react.

With this in mind, Shen Qiao quickened his pace further. In the blink of an eye, he'd returned to that tavern.

Sure enough, near the second-floor window, seven or eight people stood around where he'd been sitting. Among them was the tavern keeper and waiters, along with other customers.

Yan Wushi was surrounded by gazes, but he remained completely still. His expression wasn't visible beneath the veil, but at a glance, it seemed like he was meekly standing there after being scolded, too afraid to move.

Shen Qiao quickly walked toward them. "I'm terribly sorry. Something suddenly came up just now and I had to leave for a moment. How much is it? I'll pay!"

The tavern keeper was an ethnic Han. He looked at Shen Qiao the way one would look at their savior, and said with a pained expression, "My good gentleman, we're only a small business. Being in a foreign nation is already hard for us, so we really didn't want to stir up any trouble. This little lady didn't bring any money and you weren't back yet, so my lowly self decided to write it off as bad luck and let it go. But then the little lady refused to leave, and the moment we asked, she...she..."

Shen Qiao followed the tavern owner's finger to look at the table to see the cup shattered into fine powder and the pair of chopsticks stabbed deep into the wood. The corner of his lips twitched.

Faced with this scene, he didn't know whether to laugh or cry. He apologized over and over before paying for both the meal and the ruined tableware. Then he dragged Yan Wushi away.

"You...you're still Xie Ling, correct?" Shen Qiao asked.

"Mm."

Shen Qiao gave a light cough. "Sorry, when I saw that man dance, I suddenly gained a new insight."

He brought Yan Wushi downstairs. That man was still dancing, and though it was a freezing winter day, his face was soaked in sweat. One could see how hard he was working.

Unfortunately, the copper bowl before him held only a scant few coins. The number of onlookers had dropped as well.

Shen Qiao took out almost half the coppers he had on him and placed them into the bowl. The man gaped and repeatedly bowed to them. Shen Qiao gave him a slight nod, then left with Yan Wushi.

After a couple of steps, Yan Wushi suddenly said, "You gave too much."

Shen Qiao laughed. "'It's the unknowingly planted willow that grants one shade.' If anything, I feel like I gave too little. But we don't have much money on us right now, so this is all I could give."

Yan Wushi said no more.

He spoke even less than usual. Shen Qiao wondered if he was unhappy and panicked due to his abandonment earlier. After all, Xie Ling was still different from the real Yan Wushi. Shen Qiao smiled and apologized. "Are you still angry? Don't be upset. I was wrong. I shouldn't have left you like that. I was completely focused on my new insight and wanted to realize those techniques right away, so I became negligent. Would you like something to eat or play with? I'll buy it for you."

Yan Wushi was silent for a moment, then said, "Tangren."

That single word gave Shen Qiao pause.

The moment he said "tangren," Shen Qiao began to regret what he'd said, but this was a grave he'd dug for himself—since he made the suggestion, he had to fulfill it. So, he could only bring Yan Wushi back to the original tangren stall. The peddler recognized them and smiled, surprised. "You're back? Do you want another tangren?"

Shen Qiao said awkwardly, "Yes. Please give us another."

"Two," said Yan Wushi.

Shen Qiao acceded. "Then two, please."

No one would refuse money when it came knocking on their door, so the peddler beamed and, in a flurry of movements, two tangren were shaped and born.

Yan Wushi held one in each hand, crunching as he ate. All Shen Qiao could do was pretend he heard nothing as he brought Yan Wushi to an inn.

He requested a main room. As before, Yan Wushi slept on the bed while Shen Qiao sat and meditated. Shen Qiao's strength was gradually recovering, so whenever he had the time, he'd substitute meditation for sleep, as the former gave him the opportunity to practice martial arts on top of resting.

Shen Qiao said to Yan Wushi, "Since that silk piece can be used to repair the demonic core, you should..."

Halfway through, he found himself unable to continue.

Because Yan Wushi—veil already removed—had finished one tangren and was now licking the "head" of the other one. He licked until the head and face of the "Shen Qiao" tangren was glistening bright.

"...What are you doing?"

"I'm a little full," said Yan Wushi innocently. "So I'll eat this one... slowly."

It wasn't like Shen Qiao could say, "Can you not lick it?" Because that would sound even stranger. After all, the other person was eating candy—Shen Qiao would just come off as oversensitive.

He could only choose to not look—what you couldn't see couldn't hurt you—and finish the rest of his sentence. "The Central Plains are different from the Western Regions. Once we enter Zhou, our whereabouts will be exposed sooner or later. Now that you have the silk piece, repairing your demonic core is only a matter of time. You should ponder it whenever you're free."

After he finished, he couldn't help but shake his head and laugh a little. "Well, if you were the real Yan Wushi, you wouldn't need me to press you about this."

"If the demonic core is repaired," said Yan Wushi suddenly, "Xie Ling may vanish."

Shen Qiao withdrew his smile and became quiet too. A long moment after, he sighed. "But you can't stay like this for the rest of your life. Maybe Xie Ling is willing, but Yan Wushi might not be."

Xie Ling was a part of Yan Wushi, but Yan Wushi would never have returned to save Shen Qiao after freeing himself from danger.

Perhaps deep within every stonehearted person was hidden a trace of gentleness, and even though it was infinitesimally small, that gentleness had been allotted to Xie Ling, and he'd concentrated all of it on Shen Qiao, the person he trusted the most.

However, when the day came that Xie Ling had to vanish, would that trace of gentleness also disappear into nothing?

And would Yan Wushi remain that selfish, detached Huanyue Sect Leader, who couldn't be swayed by anything?

The other man watched him with pitch-black eyes, his single-minded attention evident, untainted by impurities. This was something Shen Qiao had never seen in any of Yan Wushi's other personalities.

That was Xie Ling, not Yan Wushi.

He told that to himself, then walked over to him and lightly caressed the top of his head.

The man let him do it. He only raised his chin a little, as if rubbing back against Shen Qiao.

This was something only Xie Ling would do.

Shen Qiao's heart suddenly melted, turning tender. And within its tenderness surged an inexplicable sorrow.

Under the effects of the jade cistanche, his head injury had begun to gradually heal, but repairing the damaged meridians within his body wasn't something that could be achieved in such a short amount of time. Right now, Yan Wushi's personality was unstable, so he couldn't focus on cultivating. For example, when Xie Ling's personality was dominating his body, like now, his desires would drop to their lowest, and even his thinking seemed to become simpler—a single tangren was enough to satisfy him.

"Do you still have the silk piece with you?" asked Shen Qiao. "Let me see."

The other man pulled out the silk from his lapel and handed it to him.

Shen Qiao took it and observed it intently, his eyes narrowed.

The words written upon it were indeed related to the martial arts of the demonic sects. Back then, Tao Hongjing might have read Riyue Sect's martial arts records. It was around a thousand characters long, and most of it was commentary on their martial arts along with his own realizations. There were no specific tricks or secrets on how to train with the demonic arts. Due to his poor vision, after he'd managed to finish reading using the feeble candlelight, his eyes were sore and painful, almost to the point of tears.

"There's nothing here about repairing the demonic core's flaw, right?" A little confused, he passed the silk piece back.

"There is," said Yan Wushi.

"Where?" asked Shen Qiao.

Yan Wushi shook his head. After a moment, he added, "I don't know, but *he* does."

Meaning that Xie Ling didn't know, but his original self did.

Shen Qiao nodded and didn't press further. Once Yan Wushi was asleep, he found a mattress and crossed his legs for meditation.

Moonlight poured down like water. It was getting late.

Even the baying of dogs in the distance had disappeared. As the world sank into slumber, a tranquil quiet spread forth, from within to without.

On the bed, the occupant's sleep was fitful. Occasionally, his body would struggle a little.

Shen Qiao noticed his movements and opened his eyes. He walked up to examine him.

"Xie Ling?" he called quietly.

The man's brows were tightly pinched. It seemed like he was deep within a nightmare.

Shen Qiao reached out to check his forehead, but before he could touch the skin, the man's eyes suddenly snapped open.

This wasn't Xie Ling!

Seeing his gaze, Shen Qiao immediately became alarmed. He withdrew his hand and backed up.

But Yan Wushi moved far faster than he'd expected. His body shot up like a demon, and he made a lightning-quick grab for Shen Qiao's face!

"Sect Leader Yan, it's me!" Shen Qiao shouted.

But it was to no avail. The other man ignored him, attacking viciously and with deadly ruthlessness.

Yan Wushi might have been heavily injured, but that didn't mean he'd lost his martial arts. Shen Qiao suddenly became aware of this point. Because Yan Wushi rarely attacked before, it'd given him the wrong impression.

However, even if it were the real Yan Wushi, he wouldn't start attacking someone without regard to their identity the moment he opened his eyes. He was obviously confused and mentally disoriented.

Shen Qiao suddenly recalled Banna mentioning that Yan Wushi had once strangled her. But afterward, Shen Qiao never saw him demonstrate such a vicious, irrational side, so he'd gradually forgotten about that incident.

Could this be the manifestation of yet another personality?

He helplessly exchanged several blows with Yan Wushi. The current Yan Wushi wasn't Shen Qiao's match, but the way he fought without regard for his life made Shen Qiao apprehensive. There was no way Shen Qiao could take his life, but to avoid being too loud and alarming the other guests in the inn, Shen Qiao searched for an opportunity, then sealed his acupoints.

Unable to fight back, Yan Wushi collapsed forward. Shen Qiao quickly caught him, noticing as he did that his face was suddenly flushed red with blood. He rushed to feel his pulse and realized that Yan Wushi's internal energy was in chaos, rampaging throughout his body—a clear sign of qi deviation. Shocked despite himself, Shen Qiao quickly undid his acupoint.

But the moment he did, Yan Wushi abruptly seized Shen Qiao's neck, then he threw himself closer and bit down on his lips!

In pain, Shen Qiao snaked his arm around Yan Wushi's neck and struck hard. The other man fell limply on top of him.

It was finally quiet.

Shen Qiao let out a sigh of relief. He picked up Yan Wushi's wrist and felt it, then let out a gasp of surprise.

If the man had just been in the throes of qi deviation earlier, then now, only a short time later, his pulse had completely calmed. In contrast, his life force even seemed to be thriving?

# The Real Yan Wushi

Y AN WUSHI'S CURRENT SITUATION was a hundred times more troublesome than Shen Qiao's own had been back then.

Shen Qiao might have fallen from a cliff and sustained grave injuries, then been plagued with lingering illnesses, but that was due to Joyful Reunion's poison flaring up in his body. His damaged meridians had since been repaired by the *Zhuyang Strategy's* true qi, and the remnant poison from Joyful Reunion had also dissolved when he destroyed his martial arts. Though his eyes were still affected and hadn't fully recovered, the *Zhuyang Strategy* had already rebuilt his foundations. He had to completely relearn his martial arts, but all the disastrous factors within him were gone.

But this wasn't true for Yan Wushi. The flaw in his demonic core had been there from the beginning: it was an innate problem. Guang Lingsan had even discovered it and exploited it using an ambush together with the other experts. He'd aggravated the flaw, and when combined with that head injury, Yan Wushi's entire body's meridians and internal breathing had fallen into disorder. This in turn affected his state of mind, causing massive changes to his personality.

Therefore, they had to heal at least three things before he could recover. One was the head injury, which was no longer a problem now that they had the jade cistanche. Second was to sort out his meridians, and third was to patch the demonic core. The second and third were interlinked: fixing one would fix the other. Each day the flaw remained unrepaired was a day with the risk of qi deviation or disordered meridians. And the problem with his meridians would also impede the recovery of his martial arts.

Currently, the pulse Shen Qiao was feeling might not be indicative of Yan Wushi's true situation. Rather, it could be a sign of "calm without and a storm within." But it was at least a good start. After all, Yan Wushi was a blessed genius. Since he'd said that the silk piece could repair the flaw in his demonic core, it must be true. It was only a matter of time and effectiveness.

Shen Qiao laid him flat on the bed, then pulled a white item out of his sleeve.

This was the jade cistanche that Xie Ling had given him back in Ruoqiang's ancient capital. The cuts the apes had left Shen Qiao then were mostly healed, so he'd never consumed it. Though the jade cistanche could regulate qi and ease breathing, since he now had the assistance of *Zhuyang Strategy*'s true qi, it wasn't too useful for him.

Shen Qiao held the cistanche in his hand, then brought over an empty cup. With a squeeze, the cistanche's powder streamed down from between his fingers. Soon, it filled half the cup, and he added some warm water. Then he gripped Yan Wushi's chin and pried his mouth open before pouring in the cistanche-water mixture.

This object was exalted for its curative powers, so naturally, it possessed some miraculous effects. Even the imperial palaces normally wouldn't have any; one had to go somewhere beneath the Gobi Desert, like Ruoqiang's ancient city, to find one. That it was precious went without saying. Those apes feeding on them year in and year out had been granted incredible strength, and over the years, they'd even developed intelligence. That was why they'd been the martial artists' match in battle.

At that time, Yan Wushi had plucked four fruits and discarded the rest in order to threaten Chen Gong. Afterward, he'd eaten two himself, then given Shen Qiao one. He probably didn't imagine that, in the end, that last fruit would still end up being used on himself.

If it had been anyone else, even if eating it themselves would have little effect, they probably still wouldn't give it to another person for free.

After he drank the jade cistanche water-mixture, Yan Wushi's complexion really did improve quite a bit. Shen Qiao put down the cup and returned to meditating. At the same time, he pondered the matters concerning the *Zhuyang Strategy*.

The *Zhuyang Strategy* had five volumes in total, and one of those was related to the martial arts from the demonic discipline. It was also precisely the contents of the piece of silk that Yan Wushi had seized from Chen Gong. Shen Qiao had read it as well. Being only a couple thousand characters, it was concise yet profound, and the entire thing really was a commentary on Riyue Sect's martial arts in the past. There wasn't any point in Shen Qiao spending more time on it since he cultivated a Daoist core—it had nothing to do with him.

Of the remaining four volumes that concerned the martial arts of the three schools, Shen Qiao had read two: one of them from his venerable master Qi Fengge, and the other inside Chuyun Temple. He'd recited the latter personally before everyone, then Yan Wushi had destroyed it.

As for the two final volumes, one was hidden within Zhou's inner palace, and the other was in Tiantai Sect.

Due to the *Zhuyang Strategy*'s reputation, everyone believed it to be the most wondrous book in the world, and they all vied to see it. Back then, Dou Yanshan had managed to obtain the whereabouts of one scroll, so he'd ordered Deputy Leader Yun Fuyi to purchase it from its owner, then bring it back to him under the pretense of escorting cargo. Who could have known that Yan Wushi would intercept and eventually end up destroying it? As a result, Dou Yanshan hated Yan Wushi to the bone, so him joining in the ambush wasn't strange either. Anyone else would agree that Yan Wushi's actions deserved that kind of hate.

However, though many people knew the *Zhuyang Strategy* to be great, they didn't actually know how it was great. They even assumed that some kind of peerless martial arts must be recorded within, where practicing it would make you number one in the world. Even Qi Fengge of the past and Yan Wushi in the present had been unable to decipher it completely. Only after Shen Qiao lost his martial arts did he understand what was wondrous about the *Zhuyang Strategy*: the ability to reconstruct foundations. The *Zhuyang Strategy*'s true qi integrated the strengths of the three schools—so its practitioners started out a level higher than anyone else—their breadth of vision were entirely different. Due to this, the level of their future achievements would naturally differ as well.

However, even if numerous martial experts realized this, they still wouldn't throw away their martial arts to start over with the *Zhuyang Strategy*. Furthermore, those who had already read the *Zhuyang Strategy* would become attached to it, so most of them wouldn't readily share it with others. Hence, when one took into account the entire world, the number of people who could truly understand the *Zhuyang Strategy*'s essence would probably be in the single digits.

Currently, it was as if Shen Qiao were standing halfway up a mountain. There, he had a sense of how vast the world was, that nothing was impossible. But he was still inferior to someone standing at the mountain summit. Each of the *Zhuyang Strategy*'s volumes were complete and independent books by themselves, but ultimately, they were still connected to each other. So right now, he'd sometimes practice to a certain point and find that he didn't understand, that he couldn't find the answer, leaving him to fumble around on his own. Perhaps once he finished reading the other two volumes, this situation would be completely turned around.

The scroll hidden within Zhou's inner palace was still feasible. With how their previous meeting went, Yuwen Yong might be willing to lend it to him.

But Tiantai Sect's was much more difficult. The Buddhist and Daoist sects couldn't really be considered friendly with one another. The world's sects were still fighting for dominance: each supported their own enlightened ruler as they fought without end. Tiantai Sect could never lend their treasure to an unrelated person without a good reason.

Shen Qiao pondered this until it was past midnight, and he unknowingly grew drowsy, falling into a shallow sleep.

Only once dawn's light broke through the early morning sky did he fully awaken.

He hadn't slept deeply, but Shen Qiao had followed Daoist practices from childhood, so he'd always been disinterested in worldly matters. He'd never been met with any insurmountable obstacles and resolved to carry a clear conscience always. This naturally meant that he never spent days plagued with worry, so even if his sleep had been shallow, it was still restful.

It was just that his past disinterest had carried a slight naivete. However, after experiencing all sorts of ups and downs, this naivete had also gradually subsided. While he still treated people with the same naked sincerity, he'd also slowly learned to differentiate people's thoughts and intentions. Thus, he was no longer so easily deceived.

Even before he opened his eyes, he could sense when a gaze from the bed landed upon him.

He already knew who it was without looking, but he didn't know which personality would be awakening with him this time. If he was as violent as the previous night, Shen Qiao would have to knock him unconscious again. Then he might as well rent a carriage and toss him inside before continuing their journey—that would save him a great deal of trouble too.

Shen Qiao's thoughts turned quickly, and he slowly opened his eyes. They weren't far from each other—he could see the expression on the other man's face.

But Yan Wushi's face was unruffled, his eyes unreadable. His heart gave a thump. "Sect Leader Yan?" he asked. He didn't feel particularly happy.

Yan Wushi smiled, his manner thoughtful. "What, you seem a little unhappy to see me?"

Shen Qiao's eyelids dropped a little. "Not at all."

"These women's clothes I have on...you put them on me, didn't you?"

"Urgent matters require unorthodox methods," said Shen Qiao. "This also saves us from much scrutiny and will help Sect Leader Yan return to Chang'an sooner."

Yan Wushi didn't seem to mind; he even touched the bun on his head, then his sleeves, with great interest. Then he said to Shen Qiao, "If you're going to use a disguise, make it a good one. Most women have long fingernails, and even if they don't, they'll paint them. Otherwise, the moment an observant person sees how prominent my knuckles are, they'll immediately know that I'm a man disguised as a woman."

The corner of Shen Qiao's mouth twitched as he thought, *How am I supposed to know something like that? I've never disguised myself as one before.*

But what he said was: "Sect Leader Yan is right. If you'd like some nail paint, I can purchase some for you."

Yan Wushi raised an eyebrow and smiled. "You seem rather unwilling to talk to me. What's wrong? Xie Ling is but a fragment of my soul, yet you favor him so much and treat him so gently. But when it's me, you're so blunt instead. Could A-Qiao have forgotten which one is the real Yan Wushi?"

When Shen Qiao had made his decision to save Yan Wushi, he hadn't done it to make him repent, and certainly not to win his gratitude. Who could have known that Yan Wushi's personality would fracture? Him meeting Xie Ling and A-Yan had been entirely unexpected. Otherwise, he didn't wish to get involved with this person at all. Best if he could never see his face again; he eagerly anticipated it.

"Xie Ling is Xie Ling. Yan Wushi is Yan Wushi. No matter what happens, I could never dare to forget Sect Leader Yan," said Shen Qiao coolly.

Yan Wushi's gaze landed on his wounded lip, and he laughed in surprise. "What, did Xie Ling even forget how to kiss someone after losing most of my memories? He was so impatient he even bit you?"

Only with this reminder did Shen Qiao become aware of a slight pain in his lip. But as he'd never been good at sarcastic retorts, he simply remained silent and refused to answer.

Yan Wushi didn't seem to mind. Instead, he continued while smiling, "Since we found the piece of silk, the day the flaw in my demonic core is repaired will soon arrive. I truly must thank you for this. If you hadn't brought me to Ruoqiang, I could never have obtained that silk from Chen Gong. A-Qiao, you repaying evil with virtue has even made me a little remorseful about delivering you to Sang Jingxing that day!"

He said he was remorseful, but his tone didn't carry the slightest bit of remorse at all. This was the real Yan Wushi. With his character and actions, even if he owed the entire world, he still would never feel any remorse. Even if they turned back time, he'd make the exact same choice in order to force out Shen Qiao's last, uncrossable line.

In the end, it was as Yan Wushi said. He didn't need friends, only opponents. And the opponent had to be his equal, someone capable of standing shoulder to shoulder with him. Everything else had been Shen Qiao's miscalculations and his own wishful thoughts.

How could Shen Qiao not understand this point by now? So he didn't respond to Yan Wushi's words and instead asked about important matters: "Once we leave the royal capital for the Central Plains, the risk of your identity being exposed grows greater. With your current level of cultivation, you probably don't wish to confront the likes of Buddhist Master Xueting head-on, at least for now. Right now, everyone's bows are pointed at you—you're surrounded by enemies on all sides. If you are discovered, you'll be beset by endless troubles. But the journey back to Chang'an won't be a short one, so what do you plan to do?"

Yan Wushi could see the lack of interest in his expression. It was obvious that Shen Qiao didn't wish to follow his digressions. But that freshly injured lip ruined his ascetic impression a little—like the statue of an immortal that'd been stained with the dust of the secular world. Yan Wushi immediately found it entertaining and continued his mockery. "You have no connection with Northern Zhou. Surely a single meeting with Yuwen Yong isn't enough for you to willingly stand by him and help me? Let me guess: perhaps you've harbored some secret feelings for me since long ago? Then I broke your heart by handing you to Sang Jingxing, but you couldn't let go of those old feelings, and Xie Ling's appearance rekindled them. You even had me wear a woman's outfit. Maybe you wanted to take advantage of the times where I'm delirious in order to do something irreversible to me, so as to make me pledge myself to you?"

Even with Shen Qiao keeping a serious demeanor, Yan Wushi's narcissistic comments still left him reeling and at a loss. "If Sect Leader Yan is unwilling to discuss the important things, then I can just knock you unconscious and deliver you to Chang'an that way. It does not make a difference to me."

Yan Wushi sputtered a laugh. "All right, all right. Don't be mad! We won't head straight back to Chang'an. Wei Province first."

He'd always been capricious. In the past, during his good moods, it wasn't uncommon to see him beaming or coaxing others tenderly.

Shen Qiao frowned. "Why?"

"Like you said, my martial arts have yet to recover, and my reappearance would be far too ostentatious. The Liuhe Guild, the Buddhists, Hehuan Sect, Fajing Sect, even the Khaganate—all of them want me dead. You won't be able to protect me with your current abilities."

*And whose fault is that?* thought Shen Qiao. *You have enemies everywhere, and that's not something everyone can pull off. If not for my concern over the big picture, which prevents me from picking a bone with you, I, too, would have joined the ranks of people trying to kill you.*

Yan Wushi couldn't hear his silent criticism, but Shen Qiao's expression betrayed his thoughts. Yan Wushi found this greatly amusing. He stared at him for a long while, then finally asked, "Has there been any news from Chang'an?"

"I heard that the Northern Zhou army marched right in without a challenge. Northern Qi didn't have the strength to resist. If everything went as expected, they should have already taken Yecheng."

Yan Wushi made a sound of agreement. "I've arranged for some people to stay by Yuwen Yong. He should be fine for the time being. If something does happen, we wouldn't make it in time even if we rushed there now. Huanyue Sect has an official residence in Wei Province. Let's stop there first, then find a way to send a message to Chang'an."

Since he'd already decided, Shen Qiao didn't object. "Then you rest for a while first," he said.

"Where are you going?"

"To buy you nail paint."

For the first time in his life, Yan Wushi was rendered speechless.

The two of them stayed in Tuyuhun's capital for a few days before setting off for Northern Zhou.

Before they left, Shen Qiao had secretly taken a trip to Banna's house. Chen Gong had kept his promise: her grandfather truly had returned. Grandfather and grandchild were both safe and sound. Only then did Shen Qiao's heart settle down, and he quietly turned and left.

Yan Wushi's personalities still showed signs of instability, but his mind was clear more often. Shen Qiao noticed that the first personality to be reintegrated was the violent one that attacked at the first hint of disagreement. The other three personalities rarely came out during the day, but they'd alternate showing up at night.

In other words, during the daytime, Yan Wushi was no different from his past self.

However, whenever Xie Ling emerged, he always showed great dependence on Shen Qiao, to the point that he refused to sleep the entire night in favor of watching him. This was something the original Yan Wushi had no control over. Hence, Yan Wushi spent most of his daytimes rather fatigued, and he often needed to meditate for rest.

In early February, they arrived at the capital of Wei Province.

And the crisis, too, had quietly crept closer.

# Wei Province Capital

EI PROVINCE had been established during the Northern Wei Dynasty. It was located at the source of the Wei River, hence the name "Wei Province." In reality, the seat of its local government was called Xiangwu, but everyone had long gotten used to associating it with Wei River, so they referred to it as "Wei Province capital."

The city couldn't compare with Chang'an, but it was still a city of strategic importance for the western areas. If war broke out between Northern Zhou and Tuyuhun, it would be at the front lines. Still, this danger didn't exist for the time being; spring had yet to arrive and the weather hadn't warmed, which meant fewer traveling merchants. So Wei Province's capital was as calm and tranquil as ever.

Early in the morning, A-Qing walked to the entrance holding a broom.

It'd just snowed yesterday, so naturally he had to clear it properly, otherwise Uncle Wu would definitely slip and fall when he went out for groceries later.

He hummed an off-key tune that only he could follow, thinking that he had to quickly clear away the snow. He also needed to head to the backyard and check if that orange cat was there. The last couple of days, it'd often run into the woodshed to hide from the cold. If it was there, he'd bring it something to eat.

After the heavy snowfall yesterday, the entrance was unsurprisingly blanketed in a thick layer of snow. Sometimes, mounds of snow would slide from the roofs with a soft splat.

By this time, A-Qing had already given the courtyard a thorough sweep. There was a faint sheen of sweat over his skin, but he didn't feel cold, just a little breathless. He stopped to rest for a while.

He automatically looked up and saw two people walking toward him from the street.

A-Qing first noticed the man in blue. He was still a distance away, so he couldn't see his face clearly, but just his movements and demeanor gave off the aura of someone extraordinary. A-Qing found it hard to find a fitting word to describe him. He could only think of the cold rice pudding he often ate during the summer: snow-white and translucent, cool and refreshing. Just looking at it would give him a sense of indescribable soothing, let alone finishing it.

As the man walked over, he realized that his association with cool rice pudding was truly most fitting. A-Qing had never seen such a handsome man before—for a moment he was stunned, still staring, until he noticed that those two people were walking toward him, getting closer and closer. Only then did he quickly return to himself.

"Cold Rice Pudding"—ah no, the man carrying the long cloth bag—walked up to him, cupping his hands at A-Qing. "May I ask if this is the Xie residence?"

In the past, A-Qing would have definitely replied, "The words 'Xie Residence' are right up there, and real big too. Are you blind? Can't you read? Why ask the obvious?"

But he didn't say those caustic words; he even blushed instead. His usual witty speech seemed to have flown away. He actually stammered, "But I...I don't know you?"

"Is this young gentleman also a member of this residence?" the man asked politely with a smile.

A-Qing felt like half of the bones in his body had gone limp.

Right at that moment, a sneer came from beside the man in blue. "A-Qiao, if you're going to ask that slowly, when will we finally get our answer? Just call Lao-Wu out. Tell him that his master has returned."

Only then did A-Qing pay attention to the woman in yellow who accompanied the man in blue. She wore a veil, so he couldn't see her face. However, most woman near the border were slender, while slender couldn't be used to describe this lady at all. She pretty much possessed the height and figure of a man, which was truly a rare sight.

On top of that, though her voice wasn't unpleasant, it also lacked the mellow gentleness common to women.

A-Qing was bewildered for a moment. "Did you make a mistake? We don't have a master here. The lord of Xie residence left to travel a couple of years ago, and he's yet to return!"

Shen Qiao was about to inquire further when he saw Yan Wushi toss the youth something.

A-Qing caught it and looked down. It was a piece of yellow jade, less than half the size of his palm. But the engravings upon it were exquisite: the bright moon over cassia branches, together with the mist-cloaked Kunlun Mountains.

"Give it to Wu Mi and have him come see me," said the "woman" who wasn't like a woman at all.

A-Qing suddenly shivered. Remembering what Uncle Wu had told him before, he realized just who the person standing before him was. He turned without another word and ran inside, closing the gates in the process and locking Shen Qiao and Yan Wushi outside.

He was surprisingly vigilant, but as he lacked the proper training, his various actions would only look childish in the eyes of others.

The two of them stood outside for a long time before the gates opened once more. An old man of around sixty years came out, the youth from before following behind him.

The old man's gaze swept past Shen Qiao and landed on Yan Wushi, still wearing his veil. "Master?" he asked doubtfully.

Yan Wushi gave him a sound of confirmation.

Only one sound, but it was unmistakable to the old man. He was so overjoyed, he almost rushed forward to bow, but after taking a couple of steps, he managed to restrain himself and quickly let them inside instead.

"Come in, come in! We can talk afterward!"

A-Qing followed behind Uncle Wu and scrutinized the two people curiously.

He wasn't from Huanyue Sect, but an orphan whom Uncle Wu had taken in at a young age. Since then, he stayed inside his small house to keep Uncle Wu company and help him with housekeeping. Uncle Wu hadn't told him much, but A-Qing vaguely understood that this house did have a master, and that Uncle Wu was only looking after it for him. But they didn't know where the master was, or even when he'd return. Perhaps he'd return in a couple of years, or perhaps he wouldn't return in their lifetime.

Before, A-Qing had assumed that the master who was "traveling far away," as Uncle Wu put it, had probably passed away in some accident already. Never had he thought that this man would suddenly appear before them one day—and dressed as a woman, even.

"A-Qing," Uncle Wu called him. "Go to the kitchen and prepare some congee, then make a few side dishes. Master is back from what was surely a long and arduous journey, so he must eat something to warm up first."

"Ah, I'm going!" A-Qing dutifully listened to Uncle Wu. He agreed at once and quickly scampered off.

Yan Wushi glanced at his retreating back, then removed his veil. "His foundations aren't bad, but he's a little stupid. Huanyue Sect needs people who are agile of mind and excellent with people. He doesn't qualify."

Uncle Wu quickly replied, "My lowly self only took him in because I was bored, so I let him accompany me! I could never think such presumptuous thoughts!"

Originally, this house was one of Huanyue Sect's bases. Bian Yanmei had purchased it in his name, and because the aliases of Huanyue Sect's disciples all used the surname Xie, these houses were collectively known as "Xie residences." Uncle Wu oversaw this one, and after several years together, he'd indeed grown to love A-Qing a little and had thought about giving him the opportunity to enter Huanyue Sect.

However, he would never dare to bring such an idea to Yan Wushi. Originally, he'd wanted to wait until Bian Yanmei or Yu Shenyang came over to make his request. He could never have expected that neither of the two would show up, and instead the "Great Buddha" himself had. Now he dared not even mention it.

Shen Qiao suddenly said, "Being 'stupid' means that worldly possessions won't easily tempt him, and it doesn't necessarily mean he can't put his heart into practicing martial arts. I find that child pure and simple myself, which is very good. If he has no connections to Huanyue Sect and is willing to learn martial arts, I can recommend him instead."

At that moment, he was thinking of Bixia Sect. After that tragic incident, their sect had waned greatly, and even finding gifted young successors wasn't easy. Yan Wushi was a grandmaster with sky-high expectations, so he might think little of A-Qing's talents, but the boy could still have a bright future in Bixia Sect.

Yan Wushi burst out with a chuckle. "Oh, A-Qiao, I haven't seen you take such a liking to anyone our entire trip! If we're talking about talent and foundations, wasn't the boy we encountered earlier on the road better? Surely you aren't only saying this because you saw how he kept staring at you, infatuated with your face, hm?"

"Sect Leader Yan, just because you yourself are lustful, you believe everyone else to be the same as you."

Before, he hadn't wanted to pay attention to Yan Wushi, because whenever they argued, he lost more than he won. So whenever Yan Wushi returned to his original self, he'd try to limit how much he talked to him. But while he'd endured it the whole journey, he finally lost it here.

Rather predictably, Yan Wushi laughed. "Lust is as hunger: part of human nature. Everyone is like this. It's true that I like your face, but I love your cold indifference to me more. What's wrong with admitting that? You're so gentle toward Xie Ling and A-Yan, but you won't say even half a word to me when I appear. Still, in the end, both Xie Ling and A-Yan are just facets of me, Yan Wushi. And if Xie Ling and A-Yan were using Wu Mi's old face instead and tried to approach you that way, would you still treat them with the same special favor?"

The innocent Uncle Wu had been dragged into this mess. He couldn't figure out Shen Qiao and Yan Wushi's relationship, so he didn't dare speak and just gave a strained smile.

Shen Qiao made a non-committal sound. "It's true that just seeing you annoys me. I'd rather speak even more to Xie Ling than talk with you."

Though Yan Wushi was still smiling, that smile had become somewhat dangerous.

Uncle Wu wanted to leave, yet couldn't, but staying around was terribly awkward. As he listened to them talk, he wished that he could turn invisible.

In the past, he'd followed Yan Wushi for a while. He knew that every time the man revealed this smile, someone was going to suffer.

But surprisingly, after the smile was gone, Yan Wushi said gently, "All right, let's just say I misspoke. I let you dress me up like a woman for the entire journey without complaint, and I did my best to cooperate. Is that still not enough to earn some good humor from you? Our great Sect Leader Shen is magnanimous; I trust you won't hold it against me."

With how arrogant the Huanyue Sect Leader was, how many people had ever seen him lower himself and apologize? Not only was Uncle Wu alarmed, even Shen Qiao was somewhat surprised.

Though Shen Qiao didn't reply, when he opened his mouth again, his tone had softened slightly. "You and Uncle Wu must have much to discuss. I won't disturb you any longer. If there are guest rooms, I'd like to rest a while."

Seeing that Yan Wushi didn't object, Uncle Wu quickly said, "There are. We keep them tidy all throughout the year, so they're always ready for guests. I'll take your esteemed self there."

He took Shen Qiao over and helped him settle in, then rushed back to pay respects to Yan Wushi.

"What good fortune that the Sect Leader is safe and sound! This lowly one heard that you were...were...I didn't dare believe it. It really was just a rumor!"

Yan Wushi sneered. "Not really a rumor. I indeed sustained some injuries and have yet to fully recover."

"Ah," said Uncle Wu. "Then the man just now was…"

"His family name is Shen," said Yan Wushi. "While he's here, treat him as you would treat me."

Uncle Wu quickly gave his assent, too afraid to ask further.

"What's been happening outside lately?" asked Yan Wushi.

"News of your death has already spread through the jianghu," said Uncle Wu. "This lowly one refused to believe it and even sent a message to Chang'an, but Da-langjun has yet to reply. Word is that Hehuan Sect has taken the chance to cause us many problems, but this lowly one remembered your instructions. I've cautiously kept a low profile, so this location remains a secret."

"What about Yuwen Yong?"

"The Lord of Zhou personally went to battle and vanquished Qi. Right now, his reputation is at its peak, like the sun at high noon; even the Khaganate and Southern Chen fear a direct confrontation with him. After the Lord of Zhou heard the news about you, he apparently sent men to torment your murderers, but only the Liuhe Guild had surface forces that could be tracked down; the whereabouts of the rest are unknown. Their various sects aren't within Zhou, and the Lord of Zhou isn't someone of the jianghu either—the power of the imperial court wasn't enough. In the end, he could only seal off several of the Liuhe Guild's branches within Zhou."

"When did you send that message to Chang'an?" asked Yan Wushi.

"Last year, on the twenty-fifth of the final month."

Sending a letter and receiving a reply did take some time, but it was also possible that something had happened with Bian Yanmei.

"I'll stay here for a few days and wait for a response from Chang'an. Go and make arrangements. Make sure that no unrelated persons leak any information."

Uncle Wu hastily said, "Yes, Master can rest assured! A-Qing doesn't know this lowly one's identity, but that child is good at keeping secrets, and his background is clean. He definitely won't cause any trouble."

He personally brought Yan Wushi to his room to rest. As Uncle Wu left the backyard, he saw A-Qing walking over with the freshly made food.

"Uncle, the food is ready. Should I take it to them now?"

Uncle Wu nodded. "Remember not to say too much. Don't ask about things you shouldn't. Chattering on in front of me is fine, but you can't do that in front of Master. He dislikes people who are talkative."

A-Qing promised, but then he couldn't resist asking curiously, "Uncle, is your master...the lord of this house...are they a man or a woman?"

Uncle Wu's face went dark. "Of course he's a man. You can't even tell men and women apart?"

"How should I know," A-Qing muttered. "Maybe he has some special hobbies. I find the gentleman who came with him easier to get along with."

Though his voice was very quiet, Uncle Wu still heard him, and he sent the boy a smack on the back of his head. "What are you muttering? Hurry up and bring them their food! And keep quiet! Those who talk too much err the most; don't you know that silence is golden!"

"Ow!"

# Tranquility

A-QING WAS FAIRLY YOUNG and had grown up in Wei Province. He was satisfied with his current life and had never seen the outside world, but with two extra people in the house, he naturally grew a little curious. Though Uncle had repeatedly warned him to not disturb them unless there was something important, he still took the chance to speak with Shen Qiao sometimes when delivering their meals.

Of course, he didn't dare strike up a conversation with Yan Wushi—not even if he were ten times braver. Youths possessed an instinct akin to that of animals: he knew very well whom he could speak to, and whom he shouldn't provoke.

Today, like always, he knocked on the door of Shen Qiao's room with a hot meal.

There was no response, but A-Qing was used to this. After waking up at dawn, Shen Qiao spent most of the day outside in the courtyard practicing the sword. A-Qing opened the door and entered, then he placed the chopsticks on the table before taking out the congee and side dishes one by one.

Footsteps sounded behind him, and A-Qing grinned as he looked back. "Shen-langjun, you're back! Just in time..."

Halfway through, though, he suddenly stopped, almost choking on his own saliva. He quickly clambered to his feet, and his bright smile instantly transformed into a reserved and strained one. "Hello, Master."

"You look as if you didn't want to see me," Yan Wushi said, eyebrow raised. He walked in, as composed as ever.

He no longer wore the woman's outfit he had on when he arrived. Even the hair at his temples had returned to its original color. He was dressed in dark blue, the shadow of a smile on his face—poised and charming.

But A-Qing inexplicably became afraid, to the point he couldn't meet Yan Wushi's eyes. The casual air about him vanished as he quickly straightened, hands together. "A-Qing wouldn't dare. Uncle Wu told A-Qing that he must treat Master with the utmost respect and not offend him in any way."

Yan Wushi's thin lips curled up slightly, and he sat down at the table, his posture laid-back. "You're so reserved with me, yet so casual with Shen Qiao. Clearly, you must like him a lot?"

A-Qing stammered, "Shen-langjun...is a very kind person!"

"Mm," said Yan Wushi. "He is indeed kind to everyone. Even if he's being bothered or disturbed, he'd never show it on his face."

In A-Qing's mind, Shen Qiao possessed practically all the qualities of perfection that he yearned for himself: a good temper, good looks, great martial arts, and he treated others kindly. It wasn't just A-Qing: any youth around his age would adore and admire someone like that. In this house, A-Qing only had Uncle Wu for company; he didn't even have playmates his age. Now that Shen Qiao was here, of course he wanted to get close and speak to him more. This was only natural.

But when Yan Wushi said it, there was now a slight implication that it was strange. Hearing these words, A-Qing was both sad and disappointed, and he wondered if his coming to talk to Shen Qiao every day was actually a bother to him.

The youth hung his head. He looked like a dispirited puppy.

But Yan Wushi didn't feel sorry for him in the slightest. Instead, he poured fuel on the flames with a final blow: "So you need to be more self-aware."

"Yes," said A-Qing. His voice was downcast; he seemed almost on the verge of tears.

Just then, Shen Qiao entered with his sword. A faint sheen of sweat shone on his face, but this only made his complexion seem fairer, giving him a faint glow.

"What's wrong?" He looked at the two: one standing, one sitting. He had no idea what was going on.

"Why are you in my room?" The second question was directed at Yan Wushi.

Yan Wushi smiled. "I smelled the aroma of food, so I came to steal some."

Shen Qiao frowned. "Didn't A-Qing bring yours to you?"

"Food tastes better when it's someone else's," said Yan Wushi blithely. "Seeing another person's good appetite makes the food taste even better."

Shen Qiao didn't believe a word he said. He felt that the situation was somewhat off, as if something had happened before he'd entered.

"A-Qing?" Shen Qiao saw his lowered head and gently asked, "What's wrong?"

"No—nothing! Master and Shen-langjun should enjoy their meals. Once you're finished, I'll come clean up!" With that, he quickly turned and dashed out of the room.

Out of the corner of his eye, Shen Qiao saw that the youth's eyes seemed a bit red. He became even more suspicious as he watched A-Qing's retreating back. He turned to Yan Wushi. "What did you say to him just now?"

Yan Wushi was all smiles. "A-Qiao, you sound like an old mother hen protecting her chicks! Don't forget that A-Qing is one of my people. I can treat him however I wish, and no one would bat an eye. He only approached you a little, and that was enough for you to suddenly show him favor? We've traveled together for so long, so why did your attitude toward me never change?"

If Shen Qiao's expression earlier was very ordinary, then now he looked completely devoid of emotion. "It's not as though my attitude means anything to Sect Leader Yan."

Whenever his flaw was exposed and his personality shifted, Yan Wushi could feel it. It was like he'd grown another pair of eyes and was watching the outside, but he could only watch, unable to control his body.

So he could "see" how Shen Qiao interacted with his other personalities. Shen Qiao maintained some wariness toward even the sincerely gentle A-Yan. There was only one exception. Back in Ruoqiang, Xie Ling—who shouldn't have awakened at that time—had used all his strength to seize control of his body and return to find Shen Qiao. At that time, though Yan Wushi had been in a deep slumber, he'd coolly watched as Shen Qiao had smiled at Xie Ling, and he'd also felt the tremors within Shen Qiao's heart.

That man was tenderhearted by nature: if someone gave him one thing, he'd return to them ten. If any other person went through what he had with Chen Gong and Yu Ai, even if they weren't left seething with hatred, it would at least make them disheartened and dispassionate. But Shen Qiao instead cherished kindness even more, even if that kindness looked trivial in the eyes of others.

That was why Shen Qiao had started to show Xie Ling favor.

Perhaps, from that moment forward, Shen Qiao really had begun to treat Xie Ling as his own person. Only when in front of Xie Ling did Shen Qiao separate him from Yan Wushi: however kind he was to the former, he'd be just as cold to the latter.

But the more he did so, the more intrigued Yan Wushi became.

In the past, he'd teased Shen Qiao for two reasons. The first was that he thought this person somewhat ridiculous for never learning his lesson after repeated betrayals—that everyone held evil within their hearts, and the only difference was how deeply they hid it. Shen Qiao himself couldn't be an exception. He'd tried everything to draw out that malice within the depths of his heart. The second was that he wanted to implant the demonic core within Shen Qiao, to see what would happen if one fused a demonic and Daoist core. So, Shen Qiao had been his guinea pig.

But life is unpredictable. Shen Qiao didn't walk in the direction Yan Wushi had set for him—instead, he'd taken a completely different path. Though he'd experienced trial after trial, forced again and again to confront the treacheries of the human heart, this person had refused to change. He was even willing to treat Xie Ling, who'd been born from Yan Wushi himself, with such gentle amiability and sincerity.

Should he call this kind of person foolish or stubborn?

But in Yan Wushi's eyes, whether it was Xie Ling or Yan Wushi didn't matter. Good or evil, painful or wonderful—he alone should be special to Shen Qiao. There was no need for some other random person to partake in that special regard.

Hearing Shen Qiao's words, Yan Wushi laughed. "Who said that it doesn't mean anything? It means a lot to me! If you were willing to split even one-twelfth of what you give Xie Ling to me, who knows how happy I'd be."

Shen Qiao turned a deaf ear. He lowered his head and focused on sipping his congee.

Right now, as long as it wasn't Xie Ling, Shen Qiao only listened to a small fraction of what Yan Wushi said. And he'd pry open that tiny fraction, ponder and analyze it, to avoid committing the same mistakes. It was really quite pathetic to fall into the same pit twice when you ought to have learned to avoid it. Though Shen Qiao acknowledged that he wasn't a smart person, he wasn't that stupid either.

Seeing Shen Qiao's lack of response, Yan Wushi smiled and spoke no further. He picked up his congee and began to eat.

For the two of them, these past few days were the most tranquil and peaceful they'd had yet. Certainly nothing like the hair-raising series of events they'd encountered in Ruoqiang. Ever since they'd left Tuyuhun, Shen Qiao had to deal with his ever-changing personalities—as Yan Wushi's flaw hadn't been eliminated—while also keeping guard against their surroundings. Yan Wushi had enemies all over the world, so Shen Qiao hadn't been able to relax even for a moment. Only after entering this place did he start to feel at ease, and he could focus on cultivating the *Zhuyang Strategy*'s true qi.

As for Yan Wushi, though Shen Qiao didn't make any detailed inquiries, he could see from his behavior that the man's personality was gradually stabilizing. It was rare to see a massive personality shift from him right after waking up. Most likely, the contents of the silk piece had illuminated something to Yan Wushi. With his abilities, it would only be a matter of time before he could patch the flaw in his demonic core, and once that happened, he'd rise to the next level with the *Fenglin Scriptures*. It was possible his martial arts could progress so far that he would be unparalleled in the whole world. Even if he didn't achieve that, he wouldn't be far from it. At that point, even if the five martial experts joined up again, they might not be able to take down Yan Wushi a second time.

It was just a pity that Xie Ling... A faint melancholy flashed through Shen Qiao's heart. He sighed to himself.

Yan Wushi suddenly asked, "Why do you show A-Qing such favor? Surely it's not because he resembles Xie Ling, and hence you're projecting onto him?"

When in front of him, Shen Qiao was even more reticent than usual. If he didn't need to speak with him, he wouldn't. But Yan Wushi seemed to have guessed his mood, for he smiled. "You like him, but I find him a nuisance. If you don't tell me the reason, I'll have Uncle Wu drive him out after you leave."

Shen Qiao refused to play along. "Sect Leader Yan, you've always done as you please. Why would I have any say in what you choose to do?"

Yan Wushi laughed. "All right, then I won't drive him out. Can you please tell me? I'm pleading with you."

A true man knew when to bend. Sect Leader Yan was unscrupulous in achieving his goals, and he'd never cared for anything like "moral integrity." He was a mighty martial artist, a grandmaster, but he could even say words like "I'm pleading." It didn't bother him, but as the listener, Shen Qiao couldn't take it.

Shen Qiao could be coaxed, but not cowed. Yan Wushi had learned this long ago. In any case, wheedling a little wouldn't hurt him. Other people might think it'd damage their dignity or integrity to act like this, but demonic practitioners placed little importance on such things.

To no surprise, though Shen Qiao looked slightly uncomfortable, he still said, "A-Qing is a little like the disciple I accepted."

Yan Wushi smiled. "Why didn't I know that you accepted a disciple?"

"You know him as well," Shen Qiao said flatly. "It's Bailong Monastery's Shiwu."

The moment he said this, he inevitably recalled the abbot and Chuyi and how they'd died. As he blamed himself, any good humor he had for Yan Wushi vanished as well.

All right, so he was picking at Shen Qiao's scabs. Yan Wushi was highly intelligent, and he wasn't crazy right now. Of course he could figure out what had happened.

But he acted like he hadn't seen the refusal on Shen Qiao's face, which practically screamed, "I don't want to talk to you anymore." Instead, he kept smiling and talking. "I've indeed seen Shiwu before. It's true that his foundations and aptitude are both quite good. If he meets a wise master, he might see great accomplishments in the future."

This level of shameless behavior... Shen Qiao really had to hand it to him.

He was just about to toss his guest out when faint knocking sounded from outside the residence.

There were two hallways and one courtyard between them and the front gates, but martial artists had fantastic hearing, so they both heard A-Qing's "I'm coming," as he jogged over to open them.

The Xie residence had always been quiet; they had few visitors. When Uncle Wu left to buy groceries, he'd usually take the back gates. He almost never left from the main gates.

At once, the sense that something was amiss surged within Shen Qiao and Yan Wushi—it was an indescribably mysterious feeling, almost like they'd read each other's minds. Only martial artists who had attained a certain level would have this reaction.

Shanhe Tongbei was close by. As A-Qing opened the door, Shen Qiao's hand was already on top of the sheath.

"Who is it?" A-Qing's voice drifted from afar.

"I hope you are well, young benefactor. May I ask if this is the Xie residence?"

The moment he heard this voice, Shen Qiao's expression shifted.

Though he hadn't interacted much with this man, how could he fail to recognize him?

But they'd been so careful the entire journey—of course they couldn't have been completely flawless, but they'd done their best to leave no traces. How did Buddhist Master Xueting find them so quickly?

*Could it be Chen Gong's doing...?*

The two of them shared a glance. Yan Wushi's face was surprisingly composed. In fact, his expression had barely changed.

"Go hide first," Shen Qiao said sternly. "I'll meet with him."

With their present cultivation, neither of them were Xueting's match. But Xueting's target wasn't Shen Qiao, so even if he couldn't defeat him, Shen Qiao could still escape.

Yan Wushi raised an eyebrow. "I fear it's too late."

As soon as these words left his mouth, Xueting's voice came from the courtyard. "Sect Leader Yan is truly remarkable. This humble monk admires him greatly."

In the blink of an eye, the man had moved from the gates to the courtyard outside their room. A-Qing was still shouting up a storm, panting as he chased after him. But he couldn't even keep up with Xueting's shadow, much less with the edge of his robe.

Very few people in the jianghu could achieve this level of speed, where "the land seemed to shrink down to mere inches, and the dust couldn't even cling to their feet."

The door to their room wasn't closed in the first place. Where Shen Qiao and Yan Wushi were standing, they could see that a monk clothed in black had appeared.

Yan Wushi sneered. "So persistent, you bald old donkey! You're like an evil spirit! I haven't even repaid you for bringing a bunch of capering clowns to conspire against me that day! You sure have some nerve, showing up here!"

Buddhist Master Xueting brought his hands together in greeting and said, "This humble monk, too, did not expect Sect Leader Yan to be so powerful. You were ambushed by five great martial experts, yet you managed to deceive everyone and came out safe and sound."

Then he greeted Shen Qiao as well. "Daoist Master Shen is also here. What a coincidence."

Buddhist Master Xueting's voice was placid, without even a hint of anger. As for whether that "what a coincidence" contained any sarcasm, only he himself would know.

Yan Wushi burst out laughing. "Other than you, you bald donkey Xueting, everyone else was mediocre. You couldn't even kill me fighting five-on-one! Bunch of trash! And they have the nerve to call themselves *experts*? Xueting, to think that you'd be willing to lower yourself so far that you'd lump yourself in with them! Really, the longer you live, the more you regress!"

Buddhist Master Xueting didn't grow the slightest bit angry. He looked at Yan Wushi with a placid expression—even his gaze held no hostility. "The new generation shall replace the old. This humble monk is advanced in years; sooner or later, he will yield his spot to more talented successors. With more time, Benefactor Duan and Benefactor Dou may not remain inferior to this humble monk.

"Sect Leader Yan came back to life and is the same as ever. This humble monk must admit that this is most admirable. Sect Leader Yan has to know as well: the farther one walks along the martial path, the more difficult it is to meet an opponent of equal skill. If there were a choice, this humble monk, too, would rather drink tea and play weiqi with Sect Leader Yan, spar and exchange pointers. To be friends as well as opponents.

"However, extraordinary circumstances require extraordinary methods. Each day that Sect Leader Yan is here, Yuwen Yong will behave without scruples and oppress Buddhism further. In order for Buddhism to flourish, this humble monk can only resort to such actions. It's not due to any personal grudges, so he asks for Sect Leader Yan's forgiveness."

There was an implication within his words. Since he'd come here today, he would not leave empty-handed—there must have been a proper conclusion.

"May I ask the Great Master," said Shen Qiao, "how did you know that Yan Wushi was here?"

"Monks do not lie," said Xueting. "To tell the truth, this humble monk met Chen Gong at Chang'an. As Hehuan Sect's Yan Shou had once injured my disciple, and Chen Gong is also close to Hehuan Sect, I wanted to obtain Yan Shou's whereabouts from him. Chen Gong said he didn't know, and to extricate himself, he told me that Sect Leader Yan was still alive and that he'd even obtained a *Zhuyang Strategy* scroll."

Before he'd left, Chen Gong had promised Shen Qiao to not divulge Yan Wushi's whereabouts, but Shen Qiao had never placed much faith in that promise. Hearing this from Xueting, he actually had the feeling that this was expected.

"But between Chang'an and Tuyuhun are many other provincial cities. It's impossible for Chen Gong to know where we'd go or stop."

"Correct," said Xueting. "This humble monk searched for him the entire journey from Chang'an. I stopped in Wei Province and had planned on leaving tomorrow. But then I unexpectedly overheard a conversation between two people; one claimed to be a vendor who goes about selling vegetables to each household every day. There was one household that had inexplicably doubled their demand, so he was very happy."

Shen Qiao sighed. "The Great Master is truly meticulous and observant. If he could use this ability to arrest thieves and settle disputes, it would be enough to render the world free of injustices."

"Thank you for your praise, Daoist Master Shen. Today, this humble monk has taken the liberty to visit due to Sect Leader Yan. Daoist Master Shen is an unrelated party, so I ask that you not involve yourself, lest you meet with some accidental injury."

"What a coincidence," Shen Qiao said. "The Great Master wishes to kill him, but I wish to protect him."

Buddhist Master Xueting's face betrayed a trace of astonishment. "As far as this humble monk knows, the demonic and Daoist sects have never been close. And Sect Leader Yan has time and again shown Daoist Master Shen much ingratitude, repaying your kindness with evil. Why would Daoist Master Shen still try to protect him?"

"It's as the Great Master says," said Shen Qiao. "Each day that he's there, Yuwen Yong will remain safe and sound. Looking at all the nations, Qi is already gone. Only the two kingdoms of Zhou and Chen can be called strong. But Southern Chen is protected by the Confucians, so there's no room for Buddhism there. The Great Master's continuous attempts to kill Yan Wushi are paving the way for the Göktürks to encroach on the Central Plains, are they not?"

Xueting gave a chant. "Is Daoist Master Shen saying that he's also on the Lord of Zhou's side?"

"Correct," said Shen Qiao.

Xueting gave a slight sigh. "Then it seems that today, this humble monk must pass through Daoist Master Shen first."

When his final word fell, his golden staff lightly struck the dark stone tiles beneath them, and a heavy sound seemed to explode in Shen Qiao's ears.

At the same time, Shanhe Tongbei exited its sheath with a clang. Shen Qiao sprang up, and sword and staff met in midair. In an instant, flashes of light and shadow interweaved, while internal energy spread outward from their points of contact. Anyone like A-Qing, without any martial arts foundations, was instantly blasted by the shock waves. He cried out, his ears ringing with pain, and was forced to stumble back. Only after hiding behind the wall did he feel a little better.

Shen Qiao had thought that Yan Wushi, being skilled at assessing situations, who possessed little of the burdens of the usual grandmaster, would see no reason to involve himself. Surely, upon seeing Shen Qiao obstructing Xueting, he'd turn around and leave first. But instead, even after Shen Qiao had exchanged several blows with Xueting, he saw Yan Wushi still standing motionless in place out of the corner of his eye.

"Why aren't you leaving?!" Shen Qiao shouted, enraged. "Don't just stand there!"

"A-Qiao, calm down. I do want to leave, but you should ask that bald old donkey if he'll let me." The corners of Yan Wushi's lips curled up a little, but his eyes weren't smiling in the slightest.

As if in response to his words, two young monks appeared at the east and the west, both bareheaded and dressed in black monk's robes, standing upon the roof tiles.

"This humble monk is Liansheng."

"This humble monk is Lianmie."

The two of them said in unison, "We greet Sect Leader Yan!"

# 74

# Buddhist Master Xueting

T HE REASON Buddhist Master Xueting could rank within the world's top three was definitely not because he was good at calling over friends to help him ambush his opponents, but because he was indeed very strong.

Shen Qiao had never doubted this. The moment Buddhist Master Xueting had appeared, he'd already foreseen that there'd be a fierce battle today.

Buddhist Master Xueting wasn't that much younger than Qi Fengge, but once a martial artist achieved a certain echelon, their appearance would be preserved—their rate of aging would be slower than an ordinary person's. When Qi Fengge had passed, he only looked around thirty or forty. No one could have guessed that his real age had already been pushing one hundred.

So, when the average person looked at Buddhist Master Xueting's handsome face, if it weren't for his complete lack of hair, they'd definitely take him as the young master of a rich family. However, he was calm and composed, his beautiful appearance dignified. There was no hint of the secular world upon him.

Shen Qiao, too, carried an immortal's lofty indifference to material gain, but he also had a very tender heart. Whenever he saw the young or the weak, he'd want to reach out and help them. Hence, sometimes he seemed even more sentimental than most. When comparing him to Xueting, Daoist against Buddhist, Xueting was like a buddha statue within a temple: mouth and heart as hard as iron, lacking even a trace of mercy. Shen Qiao, on the other hand, was more like an azure pond: tranquil in appearance, but when a swan so much as skimmed the surface, it'd leave many sentimental ripples in its wake.

The first of the Acala Seals: "Form is Emptiness." The countless forms of physical phenomena are only layer upon layer of false embellishments. The common people cannot recognize this, so they are easily trapped within, unable to free themselves. Only by maintaining a heart as clear as glaze can one forsake falsehoods for truth and disregard Mara, remaining true to oneself.

The seals came from all directions, surrounding Shen Qiao with layers upon layers of palm strikes. As Xueting's snow-white, flawless right hand swelled infinitely, they became like the seals of Vajrapani, capable of felling monsters and demons, unavoidable and inescapable.

But Shen Qiao remained firmly in place, his left hand behind his back, while he gave his right a slight flick. Shanhe Tongbei tremored at his side, its song like weeping, an ode or a cry: drawn-out and remote. It cleaved through the mass of seals, glimpsing the truth from the countless afterimages, striking directly at Xueting's right hand!

Xueting shifted from an open palm to a sweeping gesture. His fingertips were like willow leaves in the wind, so graceful and beautiful that it was impossible to look away. When compared with the relentless momentum of his previous attack, it was as if the icy winds over acres of frozen, snowy fields had suddenly transformed into a river in spring, reflecting the clouds suspended high in the boundless sky. There were geese and orioles, peach blossoms dangling over the water—indescribably graceful and wondrous.

But Shen Qiao didn't press his advantage; he immediately withdrew and retreated instead. Wherever Xueting's palm brushed, his true qi overflowing, the stones on the floor began to crack and splinter. Even A-Qing, several yards away, could feel a strange pain on his face, like a sharp blade was scraping against it.

Using "A Rainbow Stretches across the Heavens," Shen Qiao drifted like floating dust as he swept back several yards. Then he suddenly leapt up again. Suspended upside down in midair, he and his sword transformed into a band of white silk, his sword qi pouring down from above like a cascade grounded in the heavens, its spray akin to thousands of snow lions bounding forth. Accompanying it was a thundering tempest—the blade point pierced forth with oppressive momentum, unstoppable in its advance!

This series of moves had taken place in the twinkling of an eye. Xueting's face, normally as still as deep water unmoved by waves, finally betrayed a trace of astonishment. Like a cyclone, the sword qi engulfed him from above.

At that moment, Xueting had a number of options available to him, but breaking out of the sword qi wasn't one of them. It whirled a few inches away, and when he raised his left hand, the golden staff met with the sword qi as they both exploded with a thunderous roar. Their breaths seemed to freeze, leaving both unable to advance even an inch. Instead, they were blasted away, sending both men reeling back several steps.

"It's only been several months, yet Daoist Master Shen's martial arts seem to have advanced another level! This is truly a commendable feat!" Buddhist Master Xueting's expression was grave. He no longer spared any attention for Liansheng and Lianmie's situation but instead devoted all his focus to Shen Qiao.

But this wasn't good news for Shen Qiao. Though he'd indeed made progress, that didn't mean Xueting had been idle.

For a martial artist grandmaster like Buddhist Master Xueting, progressing further was very difficult, but he could still practice martial arts, and he could still attain further mental enlightenment. The more honed and perfected one's state of mind was, the more formidable their martial arts would become.

Shen Qiao had concluded this previously: before being injured, he could have fought Guang Lingsan, Duan Wenyang and the others to a draw, but if it were Buddhist Master Xueting, he'd likely find himself lacking. Therefore, in his present state, he was at a sure disadvantage. He'd rebuilt his body using the might of the *Zhuyang Strategy*, and now his foundations integrated the strengths of the three schools—one could say the foundations of his future house would be several times stronger than other people's. But this didn't mean that he could build the house itself any faster. Shen Qiao had already achieved the echelon of sword heart, and was merely a step away from sword spirit, but his internal energy was only seven-tenths of what it had been. He was completely unable to use his sword heart to the fullest.

And against an expert like Xueting, there was absolutely no chance for a fluke.

Therefore, Shen Qiao couldn't allow the other man to discover these details, for if he did, that would mean no one on the scene could stop Xueting.

Shen Qiao let his blade hang as he stood in place. "In the end," he said slowly, "the Buddhist sects do not bear any grudges against Huanyue Sect, and the Great Master has already killed Sect Leader Yan once. So why must he continue pursuing him relentlessly? Even if there is no Sect Leader Yan, no Huanyue Sect, as long as Yuwen

Yong is emperor, there will be other powers that will support him as well. The Great Master is farsighted and wise, so he must understand this, correct?"

On the other end, Yan Wushi was fighting two against one, but he took the time to say, "A-Qiao, it must be thanks to my venerable self, but your mouth has really improved! You've even left that bald old donkey speechless! I'm sure he's so ashamed he'll torment you further out of rage!"

Before, even ten Lianshengs and ten Lianmies wouldn't be Yan Wushi's match, let alone one of each. However, that couldn't be the case now. Xueting knew this too, and that's why he'd brought his disciples.

And even if Liansheng and Lianmei couldn't bring down Yan Wushi this time, they could still stall him.

Xueting saw through Shen Qiao's intentions. He shook his head and said, "Daoist Master Shen should know that this concerns the survival of Buddhism. There is no point in speaking any further. Today, this humble monk came here for Sect Leader Yan alone. If Daoist Master Shen is willing to withdraw and not involve himself, this humble monk will be infinitely grateful."

This man was truly interesting. Though he held the upper hand, he was still so courteous to Shen Qiao, showing no trace of annoyance or anger. He was as indifferent as a light breeze—he truly possessed the demeanor of a grandmaster.

Were the two of them not firmly opposed to each other, Shen Qiao would much rather sit down to discuss theory with him than face him like this—swords drawn and bows nocked, the sparks of war imminent.

But Yan Wushi seemed to be rather displeased with Shen Qiao's new view of Buddhist Master Xueting. As if determined to break his perception of him, he said, "A-Qiao, that question was really too foolish. How could the bald old donkey not know that killing Yuwen Yong is the solution to all his problems? He pursues me relentlessly because Buddhism needs to maintain its just and honorable image, which can't be stained with the crime of regicide. Even if they want to kill him, they must send someone else to do it, thereby keeping their own hands clean and free of the slightest speck of dust. Isn't that right, bald old donkey?"

Xueting had no interest in wasting words on him. He chanted a quiet "Amitabha," then coolly said, "Daoist Master Shen is unwilling to stand down; he insists on protecting Yan Wushi to the end. Therefore, this humble monk can only commit this offense!"

As he spoke, he took but a single step, yet he was already in front of Shen Qiao. A jade chime accompanied him, its tinkling sweet and unending, and his golden staff flitted toward Shen Qiao's chest.

His movements were very slow, to the point that others could see every little detail, yet somehow, at the same time, so terrifyingly fast that there was no time to react.

Shen Qiao realized with a shock that his own martial abilities were simply too inferior. He could predict where Xueting's hands were going, but his body still couldn't respond soon enough. By the time he'd raised his sword, a heavy blow had struck him on the chest. Pain rapidly spread from that point, and Shen Qiao couldn't stop himself from flying backward, his throat gurgling with a salty-sweet taste. After his momentary daze, he spat out a huge mouthful of blood and slammed heavily into a colonnade pillar!

But Shen Qiao didn't pause for even an instant. Using the pillar, his sword glare became as moonlight entering water, accompanying the ebb and flow of the river tides. A split second later, its light grew lustrous and brilliant, overlapping like layers upon layers of splendid brocade, before surging toward Buddhist Master Xueting. Even with Xueting's cultivation, for a moment he was unable to distinguish man from sword.

Meanwhile, Liansheng and Lianmie worked in tandem. They seemed to understand each other naturally, their thoughts and actions in perfect sync. Yan Wushi's martial prowess was far below that of his past self, and he'd yet to finish patching the flaw in his demonic core; there'd always be some leeway within his attacks, which the pair could take advantage of. With one on offense and one on defense, Liansheng and Lianmie encircled Yan Wushi. They didn't attempt to kill him, but they moved seamlessly together like Yin and Yang, with no openings to speak of.

It was obvious they'd received Xueting's instructions beforehand. They knew their own strength—even if Yan Wushi's martial abilities had greatly diminished, killing him would be quite difficult. So they only sought to stall Yan Wushi, waiting for Xueting to defeat Shen Qiao. Then, he could come and assist them.

Unfortunately, after all that waiting and having exchanged several hundred blows in the meantime, both of their foreheads shone with sweat. Xueting was still being held up by Shen Qiao, completely unable to disengage.

Liansheng grew anxious. As his shidi Lianmie attacked Yan Wushi, he couldn't resist glancing over at his shizun.

And with just this glance, the situation suddenly changed!

Yan Wushi had been on the defensive the entire time, but now he suddenly attacked. Using his finger as a sword, he struck at the center of Lianmie's palm. Lianmie had witnessed Yan Wushi's unimpressive showing earlier and ended up underestimating him despite himself, thinking that this was all the Huanyue Sect Leader amounted to. And yet, just as this thought arose, he felt a stabbing pain within his palm, as if a scalding iron rod had pierced through it.

He couldn't help but scream, reeling back reflexively. A glance at his palm showed that a bloody hole had been gored through it, and fresh blood gurgled out. He could faintly see the muscles and white bones within.

Liansheng heard the noises and quickly turned back. He couldn't help but be shocked at what he saw, but before he could react, a sword glare suddenly swept toward his face.

"Go!" yelled Shen Qiao. With that one word, he grabbed Yan Wushi's arm and swept toward the southeast.

Shen Qiao dared not take Xueting lightly. He pushed "A Rainbow Stretches across the Heavens" to the utmost.

Other people would have seen Shen Qiao and Yan Wushi, dragged behind him, transform into two afterimages on the wind—but still Shen Qiao was worried that it wasn't enough. Terrified that Xueting would catch up to them, he soared forward without stopping, the trees on either side becoming mere shadows as they streaked by him at top speed. He never slowed down in the slightest.

Though he didn't look back, Shen Qiao could clearly sense a menacing presence constantly behind them, both near and far as it followed, like a blade against his back. It was obviously Xueting giving chase, unwilling to give up. Even if Shen Qiao were a step faster, he couldn't shake Xueting off so quickly.

Shen Qiao hauled Yan Wushi outside the city, then bounded toward Guojian Mountain next to Wei Province.

At the foot of the mountain was a dense forest, easy to hide in, but Yan Wushi said, "Go up the mountain."

Shen Qiao didn't give it further thought. He charged up the mountain without stopping.

It was early spring. The frozen rivers had thawed, hundreds of flowers were in bloom, the mountains filled with birdsong. Everything was brimming with life. The forest trees twisted and snarled, the mountain rocks were craggy, the mountain path steep. There was no good foothold—standing at the halfway point and looking down, the pencil-straight cliff walls, the curling clouds and mist, accentuated the precipitous nature even further.

Around halfway up the mountain, Shen Qiao discovered a cave obscured by a thicket. It was dark and winding on the inside, with a small stream that gurgled through it. The cave was quite deep—after the two of them entered, they walked many yards before it opened up, becoming bright and spacious. The stone walls here were smooth and glossy, the area about the size of a wealthy family's main hall.

Looking upward, Shen Qiao realized that there was no rocky ceiling overhead. The sunlight spilled through the gaps within the complex weave of branches, dappling the dead leaves by their feet.

"Here is fine," said Yan Wushi. "Xueting would only think that we'd hide within the mountain's forests. He absolutely would not expect us to climb up here."

Shen Qiao finally relaxed the guard he'd kept raised, but what followed wasn't the relief of relaxation, rather a giant mouthful of blood as he bent over.

This was from the internal injuries he'd sustained during his battle with Xueting. When he'd fled with Yan Wushi, his chest had begun to throb unbearably, but he'd been afraid that opening his mouth would cause him to lose his breath, and his last push with it. So he hadn't even spoken until now.

Not many people could withstand a strike from one of the three best grandmasters in the world. Shen Qiao's martial strength had yet to fully recover, yet he'd been able to battle Xueting for such a long period of time, and then escape from him with Yan Wushi in tow. It was all thanks to his still-immature echelon of sword heart. But applying an echelon upon one's sword wasn't something that could be sustained endlessly, unlike internal energy or true qi. Even before their battle, Shen Qiao had never thought about fighting Buddhist Master Xueting to the bitter end—he'd already been prepared to retreat at any time.

Escaping from right beneath Buddhist Master Xueting's nose was no easy task, especially while carrying a "load," but Shen Qiao had pulled it off.

Though the two of them hadn't discussed the idea of retreating in any depth, it was obvious that Yan Wushi had held similar thoughts on the matter. So, they'd been able to achieve a tacit understanding and consensus despite exchanging no words.

With this mouthful of blood, Shen Qiao's head swam and his vision blurred. He barely had the strength to stand. Overcome by his overtaxed martial strength and internal injuries, his sight faded and his ears rang as he collapsed forward.

Yan Wushi caught him without hesitation. He even smiled and said, "A-Qiao, I know you like me, but you don't have to throw yourself into my arms like this!"

His voice was lacking in vitality—it was obvious he'd also been injured. But that did absolutely nothing to diminish the wanton teasing in his tone.

As soon as he said this, Shen Qiao hacked up another huge mouthful of blood. Practically half his body weight was now leaning on the crook of Yan Wushi's elbow. His face was stark white, as if he were about to breathe his last.

Yan Wushi clicked his tongue once. "Surely you're not coughing up blood in anger from just this?"

Of course, Shen Qiao wasn't coughing up blood out of anger, but he didn't have the strength to retort. He only said weakly, "Now that we're gone, what will happen to Uncle Wu and A-Qing?"

"Xueting isn't Sang Jingxing," said Yan Wushi. "He still needs to uphold Buddhism's image, and besides, he knows that he can't threaten me with those two anyway. Naturally, he won't do anything pointless."

Shen Qiao nodded. Blood still stained his lips, making their cold paleness starker and the crimson more vivid. Yan Wushi used his thumb to wipe it away.

There was a muffled, unbearable pain in Shen Qiao's chest. Even his breathing was shallow; he was completely unable to focus his energies on anything around him. His senses had become sluggish as well, and he was caught off guard when Yan Wushi shoved something small into his mouth and covered it with his hand, preventing Shen Qiao from spitting it out. His eyes widened, but his body had already performed the reasonable reaction of swallowing the object.

His throat was so dry and painful, he almost choked to death. He began coughing violently, which aggravated his internal injuries, and even his eyes grew a little moist.

"Jade...cistanche?"

# Dreamscape

"WHO TOLD YOU this was jade cistanche?" said Yan Wushi deliberately. "It's obviously poison."

Despite his internal injuries, which left him without even the strength to speak, Shen Qiao could still differentiate poison and medicine.

"The jade cistanche can only heal external injuries; it won't be very effective on me..."

That strike from Xueting had broken one of his ribs. Now even the rise and fall of his chest was accompanied by a stabbing pain. But to martial artists, this kind of external injury was fairly common. Shen Qiao had suffered injuries too numerous to count—especially in his duel with Kunye—so something like a broken rib wasn't even worth mentioning. The internal injuries were more troubling.

"Then spit it out," Yan Wushi countered lazily.

It was already inside Shen Qiao's stomach—how could he spit it out?

Reality once again proved that arguing with Yan Wushi was completely pointless. Shen Qiao simply closed his mouth, and after a while, he drifted off.

He didn't sleep for long—even if his eyes were closed, his body remained in a vigilant state, suspended between dreams and consciousness. He woke when it was just past noon. Looking around, Yan Wushi was nowhere to be found.

A thought surfaced in Shen Qiao's mind: had Yan Wushi left by himself?

He sat up against the wall with great effort, doing his best not to aggravate his wound. Moist vines hung down from overhead, and water droplets fell onto his cheek, bringing a touch of icy coldness.

The stabbing pain in his chest had transformed into a dull ache—it was clear that the jade cistanche still had some effect. Shen Qiao sat cross-legged, circulating his energy to heal his injuries. After one full revolution, his true qi had flowed through his entire body, causing his limbs and bones to tingle with a warm numbness. Even the state of his internal injuries seemed to have improved.

When he opened his eyes, faint footsteps sounded from the narrow passage leading to the cavern entrance.

Shen Qiao didn't rise, having already identified who the person was from the cadence of those steps—ever since his eyes had deteriorated, he'd purposely honed his hearing, even contemplating the slight differences in each person's footfalls. Over time, his ears had grown quite a bit sharper than those of the average martial artist.

Sure enough, Yan Wushi walked in, carrying a skewer of sparrows.

"You went out?" asked Shen Qiao.

"Mm," said Yan Wushi. "Lend me Shanhe Tongbei for a moment."

Shen Qiao naturally didn't think that Yan Wushi would use it to kill him, so he passed him the sword he always kept close while asking, "You didn't encounter Xueting outside, did you?"

The moment he said this, he noticed that the Yan Wushi was using his sword to remove the sparrows' feathers.

"What are you doing?!" he snapped.

Surprised, Yan Wushi countered, "Do you eat sparrows with their feathers?"

Shen Qiao's qi and blood roiled; he almost spat out another mouthful of blood. "That's the Shanhe Tongbei Shizun left to me!"

Yan Wushi was unfazed. "Why is A-Qiao getting so angry? Careful, you'll cough up more blood. Qi Fengge is practically a god in your eyes, but he still had to eat. Perhaps he used this to shave behind your back. How would you know?"

As he talked, the feathers of several sparrows had already been scraped clean. Using a longsword for a dagger's job was no simple task, yet Yan Wushi handled it with ease.

He then lowered the sword into the stream, washing off the sparrow feathers on the surface, before sheathing it and handing it back to Shen Qiao. He even used his chilled hands to stroke Shen Qiao's cheek. "All right, Qi Fengge has been dead for ages. Even if you do use it to shave, it's not like he can pop out and yell at you. The sword exists within the heart, not outside your body. Only you'd treasure it this much—look at Yu Ai! I broke his Junzi Buqi, and he switched to a new sword without a word. You don't see him running to Qi Fengge's grave to wail and bawl."

Shen Qiao was so furious, he didn't want to speak to him anymore. It was a good thing he'd circulated his qi earlier, or he really would have coughed up blood.

Yan Wushi, on the other hand, seemed to be in a good mood. He found a patch of dry ground, piled up some dead leaves and twigs, then lit it with a fire starter and began roasting the skewer of sparrows.

Soon, the fragrance of searing meat fanned out.

He turned to look at Shen Qiao, whose eyes were closed as he circulated his qi. His profile was like white jade, turning gentle and radiant beneath the sunlight. His blue collar enclosed the beautiful line of his neck, causing that near-austere aloofness to betray a hint of imperceptible warmth.

Yan Wushi had seen countless beauties in his life. There'd been no lack of untouchable types among them, like flowers growing on the highest peaks, but not one had been like the man before him now: resembling a god or buddha with his eyes closed yet brimming with the tenderness of the mortal world when his eyes were open.

Just as he thought this, Shen Qiao opened his eyes. "Once night comes, I'll return to check on Uncle Wu and A-Qing."

Yan Wushi nonchalantly pulled the sparrows off the branch, one by one. "As I already said, Xueting needs to maintain the glorious image of Buddhism, so he can't lay his hands on them openly. The moment Xueting showed up, that residence was compromised. Wu Mi knows how to deal with this."

By nature, he was a cold and indifferent person who rarely took the fates of others to heart. In his eyes, Wu Mi belonged to Huanyue Sect, so dying for Huanyue Sect was a proper ending for him. As for A-Qing, Yan Wushi would never afford him even the slightest hint of sympathy or compassion. However, he knew very well the kind of person Shen Qiao was. If he said any of this, the man would immediately run back to check.

In the past, Yan Wushi would have just stood by and watched. But today, he instead chose to resolve Shen Qiao's doubts.

"Do you know why I brought back six sparrows?" asked Yan Wushi.

Shen Qiao started; he didn't understand why Yan Wushi would suddenly ask this. Thinking that there was some deeper meaning to it, he tilted his head a little and began to ponder it seriously.

Yan Wushi peeled off a piece of bark from somewhere, then placed the roasted sparrows on top.

As Shen Qiao looked at them, he immediately found it difficult to keep his mouth from twitching.

Upon that piece of bark, six sparrows were neatly laid out, with one in the center and five arranged evenly around it.

"This dish is called 'Plum Blossom Sparrows.'"

Shen Qiao bit his tongue. *You came up with the name yourself, didn't you?*

"You have to eat the one in the center first before you can eat the ones outside."

"...Why?"

"Because it looks better that way. If you eat the ones on the outside first, the 'plum blossom' will be ruined."

Shen Qiao was speechless. Suspecting that one of Yan Wushi's episodes was flaring up again, he couldn't help but shoot him a glance of concern.

Yan Wushi's expression remained composed. He even smiled at him and said gently, "A-Qiao. This is a token of my appreciation. Do you really have the heart to waste it?"

Shen Qiao had never expected gratitude for risking his life to save Yan Wushi, but this method of thanking someone...was really too strange!

But when he considered Yan Wushi's way of doing things, Shen Qiao thought that him conjuring up some "Pear Blossom Sparrows" or "Peach Blossom Sparrows" next time wouldn't be too much of a surprise either.

After all, not everyone would be bored enough to line up every single green bean on their plate while they were enjoying a meal at a tavern.

Shen Qiao dithered for a moment before finally picking up the sparrow in the center and taking a bite.

Apart from it being unsalted, the taste was quite decent.

"How are your injuries?" asked Shen Qiao.

Yan Wushi smiled. "You'll know if you feel it."

As he talked, he extended his wrist to Shen Qiao without the slightest hesitation.

The acupoint upon the wrist was also one of the "gates of life."[9] Regardless of martial prowess, anyone who was grasped here couldn't afford to make any rash moments. It wouldn't have been out of the ordinary for "Xie Ling" to do something like this, but Shen Qiao knew it wasn't him.

He repressed the strange feeling in his heart, then placed his hand over Yan Wushi's wrist. After a moment of silence, he said, "You still have some internal injuries, but they're not serious. One or two days of rest should be enough. This mountain is cold, damp, and inconvenient; hiding for a couple of days is fine, but we can't remain here much longer. What are your plans?"

"Head to Hanzhong first, then Chang'an," said Yan Wushi.

Shen Qiao was taken aback. That would mean they would have traveled in a circle.

"I thought that you'd go straight to Chang'an," said Shen Qiao. "After entering Chang'an, you'd have Huanyue Sect's influence and the Lord of Zhou's protection. Then Xueting wouldn't dare do anything rash."

Yan Wushi said, "Since Xueting already knows I'm alive, even if the others don't yet, they will in a few days. If you thought of returning to Chang'an, they definitely thought of it as well. The road we'd have to take from here to Chang'an will definitely be full of countless ambushes and hurdles."

"Mm," said Shen Qiao. He'd also thought of this much.

Yan Wushi sneered, "Xueting and the rest wanted to kill me, but did you really think I was their only target?"

---

9    命门. Traditionally used to refer to an important acupoint on the lower back, but here it means one of a series of vital acupoints that connects to the owner's life.

"Their true target should be the Lord of Zhou."

"Correct," said Yan Wushi. "As I said before, the Buddhists wish to expand their influence, which can only be done through a ruler, so they absolutely must not stain their hands with regicide. Otherwise, even if Yuwen Yong is gone, regardless of who the future emperor is, they won't uplift Buddhism. And if they had the likes of the Göktürks, Liuhe Guild, or Fajing Sect do it, not only would the action be seen as unjustified and unreasonable, it'd also bring them countless troubles. It'd be faster to let the people close to Yuwen Yong take action."

Yan Wushi's words were like a flash of lightning—they illuminated something that had never occurred to Shen Qiao. "The empress Lady Ashina is a Göktürk!"

"My, what a quick learner you are," teased Yan Wushi. "Lady Ashina has been neglected by Yuwen Yong for a long time; naturally, she'd be willing to help Duan Wenyang and add fuel to the fire. There's also the crown prince. He hates work and loves play; he spends all day amusing himself and never strives for improvement. The Emperor has long been dissatisfied with him, and the crown prince knows this as well. If he doesn't act first before his father decides to depose him, he won't be able to keep his seat as crown prince."

Shen Qiao was shocked. After a long pause, he finally said, "The crown prince is his son, he wouldn't go that far..."

Halfway through his sentence, he found himself unable to continue. Shen Qiao suddenly thought of Yu Ai. Could the affection they'd shared be much less than the familial bond between the emperor and crown prince? But Yu Ai had still mercilessly poisoned him with Joyful Reunion. Royal families had always been famed for their ruthlessness. The Crown Prince might really be capable of patricide.

Yan Wushi sighed. "A-Qiao, you're not stupid. But your tender heart holds you back. You're always so optimistic when it comes to interpersonal matters, and you never suspect a dark side to them. What would you do if I weren't here?"

*If you weren't here, my days would definitely go a hundred times more smoothly!* Shen Qiao almost blurted out.

But he was a kind and upright gentleman, so he couldn't say such things. Instead, he turned his attention back to the original topic. Following their conjectures, it seemed that this game of chess was truly fraught with danger, and everything was deeply intertwined.

After what had happened to Yan Wushi, Huanyue Sect was without a leader. The other two demonic sects would be unable to contain themselves and come looking for trouble. Bian Yanmei would be pressed to take care of himself and was sure to overlook things on Yuwen Yong's end. The empress was his wife, and the crown prince his son. No matter how capable Bian Yanmei was, he couldn't accompany the Emperor at all times. If they wanted to do something to him, that something would indeed be simpler and easier to pull off than having martial artists assassinate him.

Shen Qiao coughed twice. "Then what of Hanzhong?"

"The Prince of Qi, Yuwen Xian, lives in Hanzhong. He also has some troops. We'll go there first to scope out the situation, then head to Chang'an."

Shen Qiao understood.

Yan Wushi thought Yuwen Yong's situation didn't look too good, so he was planning out a path of retreat in advance. The Crown Prince was Buddhist and had no fondness for Huanyue Sect—nor Yan Wushi for the prince—so he'd decided to bet on Yuwen Xian. Even before now, Huanyue Sect must have invested a great deal of time into him.

Xueting thought that they'd head to Chang'an, and everyone else would think so as well. Probably no one would expect that they'd instead go to Hanzhong.

"The crafty hare keeps three burrows." No one understood this concept better than Yan Wushi.

Nights seemed to come quicker in the mountains—as the sun set in the west, the densely packed canopy of leaves above them absorbed the last rays of sunlight.

Inside the cave, the firewood crackled along, finally driving away the spring night's chill.

Shen Qiao didn't circulate his qi. Instead, he slept.

He'd been wounded quite seriously in his battle with Xueting. Even with the *Zhuyang Strategy*'s true qi protecting him, he was still a flesh and blood mortal, and at present, there was a fair gap between him and Xueting. It was impossible for his injuries to heal in a couple of days. At night, he burned with fever, his forehead boiling hot as he descended into a nightmare.

His dreams were fantastical and bizarre, with all sorts of people making their appearances. Shen Qiao was trapped in this illusion, unable to free himself.

The shizun he admired the most was holding Shanhe Tongbei, which was also covered in feathers. He asked A-Qiao why he'd used the sword to clean away feathers, and Shen Qiao said, hurt, "Shizun, Yan Wushi did it."

Qi Fengge gripped Shen Qiao's chin and held the sword up to his face. "What else do you see here?"

Shen Qiao stared blankly, then discovered that the blade was covered in tiny black hairs. He immediately blurted, "Shizun, do you really use Shanhe Tongbei to shave?"

"Nonsense!" said Qi Fengge angrily. "You clearly took this master's sword to play with, and now you're blaming someone else! It was only yesterday that I just taught you the character for 'honesty'; you should know better, but now you've gone and done this! It seems you must be punished!"

Frightened, Shen Qiao subconsciously blurted out, "This disciple knows he was wrong!"

But Qi Fengge didn't seem to have heard him admit his wrong-doings. Instead, he ordered him to lie down, then picked up a large rock and placed it on top of him. "Since you were wrong, you must be punished. Stay here like this. You're not allowed to stand unless this master says so."

Shen Qiao didn't know how his master had come up with such a bizarre punishment. His chest felt both stifled and painful from the pressure, and he could barely breathe. He couldn't help but hurriedly plead, "Shizun, please move the stone away!"

But Qi Fengge turned a deaf ear before turning around and leaving. He grew farther and farther away until he finally vanished without a trace.

"This disciple was wrong... Shizun, don't go..."

Shen Qiao's eyes were shut, his eyebrows tightly knitted. "My chest hurts..."

Hearing his murmurs, Yan Wushi opened his eyes and looked down at him. Beneath the firelight, he saw faint tear tracks at the corners of his eyes—he'd actually cried within his dream.

Yan Wushi reached out and touched the wet stains. He'd thought the fresh tears would be warm, but instead, they were ice-cold.

This person must have been pampered and doted on as a child, otherwise he couldn't have developed such a soft and tender heart.

As Yan Wushi thought about this, he heard Shen Qiao, who was within some fretful dream, suddenly mutter two words: "Xie Ling..."

Yan Wushi startled, then a strange cruelty rose to his face, as if a mask had suddenly broken.

Very quickly, all sorts of emotions flashed across his face—some savage, some estranged, some gentle—as though tens of thousands of faces were fighting for dominance, wanting to take control of his expression. It was a chilling sight.

The qi within his body began to rampage, much like the warning signs for the countless times he'd entered qi deviation. Yan Wushi quickly shut his eyes!

After a moment, he opened them again, reaching down to carefully stroke Shen Qiao's cheek. Then his hand meandered to the back to grasp his nape, pulling him up a little. Finally, he lowered his own head and swallowed each one of those incessant murmurs, taking them into his mouth.

# Xie Ling Has Passed

D AZED AND GROGGY, Shen Qiao felt like there was a
bowstring stretched taut in his mind, clamoring for him
to wake up. But his eyelids were incredibly heavy; no
matter how he tried, he couldn't open them.

And from over his lips came a strange warmth—it felt like something was violently invading. He struggled for a while, a feeble moan
escaping his mouth, before he finally forced his eyes open.

Having burned for half the night, the fire had gradually dimmed,
and someone was holding him in their arms, their bodies only separated by a thin layer of clothing. The entire situation caused a sort
of indolence to seep forth from his bones, making him wish to just
sink into slumber and sleep until the end of time.

Shen Qiao suddenly felt a little breathless. However, this stifling
sensation originated not from his chest wound but from his nose
and mouth.

"To think the mighty Sect Leader of Xuandu Mountain has even
forgotten how to breathe? If word gets out, people would laugh
themselves to death, wouldn't they?" A mocking voice drifted over,
sounding both near yet far, but in truth it'd been spoken from next
to his ear. Their faces were pressed together, and the other man's
tongue was currently pulling out from his own slightly opened
mouth. He even pressed a leisurely kiss to Shen Qiao's lips, before

finally putting some distance between them. Then he pinched Shen Qiao's cheeks and tugged. "Did you go stupid?"

A shred of reason finally returned to that bewildered gaze, and Shen Qiao slapped Yan Wushi. The latter yelped and retreated. "A-Qiao, it's me, Xie Ling!"

Shen Qiao ceased his movements and stared at him, frowning.

Yan Wushi moved forward again to hug him. He said gently, "I'm Xie Ling. Don't you recognize me?"

Shen Qiao didn't say anything. He raised his hand, ready to slap him again.

Yan Wushi nimbly caught his hand and said, surprised, "Did you sleep yourself into a muddle? You'd hit even Xie Ling?"

Shen Qiao was disgruntled. "Why would Xie Ling call me A-Qiao?!"

Yan Wushi sputtered a laugh. "That's right, I forgot. He calls you 'Meiren-gege.' But I can't bring myself to call you that at all. To think that you used your good looks to take advantage of me for this long. Every time Xie Ling called you that, were you secretly happy deep down and not letting it show?"

Shen Qiao turned his head away. "Utter nonsense!"

Yan Wushi kissed the side of his face, but before Shen Qiao could react, he withdrew so that he was three feet away from him, knowing that he'd gone far enough.

Shen Qiao wanted to sit up, but the movement aggravated his internal injuries. He held his chest, coughing incessantly until the pain slowly lessened.

He could only yell angrily, "Look at our situation—and you're still doing this!"

Yan Wushi couldn't help bursting into laughter. "A-Qiao, you're way too cute! You don't even know how to curse people! What does that mean, 'doing this?' I'll teach you: this is called 'lustful thoughts arise when material comfort is had!'"

The beauty's rage and coughing fit had flushed his entire face red, and his eyes glistened with moisture. The firelight danced over the tears that were on the verge of falling. On Yan Wushi's side, he saw a perfect beauty sent by the heavens, a feast for the eyes. A shame that he could only look and not partake.

When he realized that Yan Wushi was deliberately enraging him for the sake of entertaining himself, Shen Qiao slowly calmed down. "If you anger me again, my injuries will heal more slowly, and if someone comes after your life while we're on the road, I might not be able to protect you."

Yan Wushi laughed. "That's fine too. I have a genius plan."

Shen Qiao was unconvinced. "What genius plan?"

"Last time you disguised me as a woman; it was quite an ingenious method. This time, let's both disguise ourselves as women. We'll take a carriage and pretend we're going to Hanzhong to live with our relatives. Surely we'll be able to fool even the emperor that way."

Hearing this, Shen Qiao knew that he still held a grudge.

Back then, Yan Wushi had still been ill, so the person who'd dressed up was "Xie Ling." But they shared the same body, so Yan Wushi couldn't have been unaware.

Shen Qiao blinked, then avoided the topic entirely. "How are you feeling?"

"You're asking about Xie Ling, aren't you?" said Yan Wushi.

Shen Qiao was silent for a moment, then made a quiet sound of assent.

He suddenly remembered his dream from earlier. The first half had been about Shizun. Probably due to his chest injury, he'd dreamt of Shizun placing a rock on top of him—it was both disturbing and hilarious. But in the end, it was all due to how dearly he missed his shizun in his heart. Though his training on Xuandu Mountain had been hard, Shizun's protection had been like a towering tree: he'd blotted out all the human evils of the outside world, up until Shen Qiao finally went through his own repeated experiences of hardship. Recalling those years made him nostalgic for the past, when Shizun had been still alive, when his martial siblings had been as close as real family, full of fraternal love for each other. When he hadn't needed to worry about anything beyond advancing his martial arts. It'd truly been a carefree time, without a single worry.

As for the second half of the dream, it'd consisted purely of various projections from his life since that time. All sorts of people had appeared one after another, and the only one he could still remember after waking up was Xie Ling.

Yan Wushi asked, "A-Qiao, do you wish for Xie Ling to be here still? Or do you wish for him to be gone?"

In the first place, Xie Ling was a personality that had split off due to Yan Wushi's qi deviation. If he were still around, that naturally proved that Yan Wushi had yet to fully recover.

Shen Qiao seemed to be at a loss on how to answer. Yan Wushi gave a slight smile at this. "If it were the former, then I must disappoint you. Though the flaw in my demonic core hasn't fully repaired, the personality shifts caused by the qi deviation have already been suppressed. From this point on, Xie Ling will no longer exist."

Shen Qiao froze a little, then spoke no more. But a look of sorrow slowly surfaced within his eyes.

Gathering the outer robe covering his body, he sat and stared blankly, looking both alone and bereaved, both pitiful and lovable.

However, Yan Wushi knew very well that beneath this seemingly weak and soft appearance lay a spine of steel that would never bend, no matter the storms and tempests.

If this had been the past, malice would have welled up inside him. He would attempt to peel off this person's outer shell to look at the tender flesh hidden inside, to see whether it was still the same even after all the setbacks.

But now, within his heart was born a strange, indescribable feeling.

Though Xie Ling had already been smothered, had his dissatisfaction left an imprint within his heart?

Yan Wushi smiled coldly to himself. *Even if you had, what's the point? The Shen Qiao whom you love so much will eventually forget your existence. You'll never be close to him ever again.*

Shen Qiao had no way of knowing what he was thinking. After a long time, he gave a quiet sigh, then said only one thing: "I'm tired. I'll sleep for a while."

He lay down wearily. His outer robes were thin, so he curled up a little—his illness had left him somewhat vulnerable to the cold. His back faced Yan Wushi, hiding his expression.

Yan Wushi walked over to him, but Shen Qiao did not react.

He reached out to touch him, and though Shen Qiao slapped away his hand, his fingertips still grazed some slight moisture.

"You're crying?" Yan Wushi was a bit stunned, thinking it incomprehensible. "What is there to cry about? Xie Ling was merely a fragment of my soul, not even a person."

Shen Qiao said dully, "He might have been a fragment to you, but to me, he was once a living person."

Yan Wushi sneered. "Just because he came back to look for you underground?"

But Shen Qiao ignored him.

In Yan Wushi's eyes, among his personalities, Xie Ling was the weakest and easiest to take advantage of—and the least like himself. Yet Shen Qiao actually liked him the most.

When he thought about this, a sneer of displeasure marred his expression. "You're so weak and soft, yet you said you wanted to become my opponent, to duel me. If you keep on with this mindset, I fear you'll never reach the martial summit."

After a long period of dead quiet, Shen Qiao suddenly asked, "What does Sect Leader Yan believe to be the martial summit? Is it my shizun Qi Fengge? Is it Cui Youwang? Or is it Tao Hongjing?"

When calling out "Xie Ling," his voice was gentle and affectionate. But now, though they were face-to-face and only a few inches apart, it was an utterly emotionless "Sect Leader Yan."

Yan Wushi suppressed his displeasure and coldly answered, "As great as their martial arts were, they still cannot be considered the summit."

If it had been anyone else who'd said this, they'd come off as overconfident, but before Yan Wushi had entered qi deviation, he'd indeed been qualified to say so, even if there'd still been a gap between him and those three.

"That's right," said Shen Qiao. "The martial path is endless, so how can there be a summit? This humble Daoist may be untalented, but he still knows that a weak or soft personality has nothing to do with martial prowess. Sect Leader Yan has his own Dao, and I have mine. Don't impose upon others what you don't wish upon yourself. What does me mourning an old friend have to do with you? I ask that you respect yourself more."

He'd only known him for a number of days, and only for a scant few meetings. He didn't even know why Xie Ling was called Xie Ling, and he'd already become an old friend?

Yan Wushi laughed coldly within his mind, but his frosty expression melted completely. "All right, our survival depends on each other here," he said gently. "It's only some idle chitchat, so why are you getting angry?"

Shen Qiao answered by yanking his outer robe over his head, refusing any further conversation.

Yan Wushi did not press further.

The night passed in silence.

Shen Qiao woke up very early the next day. Yan Wushi had already returned from washing his face in the cavern's stream. When he saw Shen Qiao looking at him, he smiled brightly. "A-Qiao, lend me Shanhe Tongbei."

His expression was gentle, his mood excellent. It was as though the displeasure yesterday had never occurred.

Shen Qiao said warily, "You didn't clean the feathers well last night. I had a stomachache afterward."

"Oh," said Yan Wushi. "That's because I realized that feathers ought to be plucked by hand. I won't use it to clean any feathers this time."

Shen Qiao's suspicions remained. "What are you hunting? I'll go instead."

The moment he stood, a dull pain throbbed through his sternum.

Yan Wushi watched him with a frown, then said gently, "You were injured because of me, so I'll go. In any case, I won't use it to clean feathers."

Shen Qiao refused to believe that, in the span of one night, Sect Leader Yan would suddenly gain a heart full of gratitude. But his martial arts were greatly diminished; if he did meet with danger, at least he wouldn't be completely defenseless as long as he had the sword. After thinking for a bit, Shen Qiao handed it over.

Yan Wushi left with the sword. Before he did, using rolled-up leaves, he considerately scooped some water for Shen Qiao to wash his face with.

With the early spring climate, the cool water against his cheek cleared his mind at once. The jade cistanche's effect was truly extraordinary—his sternum hadn't healed completely, but it'd already greatly improved after a night's sleep. Even the pain that came with breathing had eased greatly.

He sat cross-legged, circulating his qi. He had been doing this for a long time when Yan Wushi returned.

"You left the mountain?" asked Shen Qiao, surprised.

"No," said Yan Wushi. "I just went around to observe the situation a little. If everything goes as expected, we should be able to leave the mountain tonight."

Shen Qiao nodded, then noticed he was carrying a tree branch. Two fish were skewered upon it. "Where did you get such large fish?"

"Spring brings a lot of rain, so the fish are naturally fresh and tasty."

Shen Qiao suddenly had a bad feeling about this. "How did you gut and scale them?"

Yan Wushi didn't even look up. "I used the sword, naturally."

"I didn't lend you Shanhe Tongbei so you could scale fish!" said Shen Qiao angrily.

Yan Wushi sighed. "A-Qiao, you're so unreasonable. You said I couldn't use it to clean feathers, and I promise not to. But you didn't say I couldn't use it to scale fish. Besides, isn't half of the fish going to end up in your stomach anyway? Or don't tell me you won't be able to use the echelon of sword heart if your sword smells like fish?"

The "you're making trouble out of nothing, but fortunately I'm magnanimous and forgiving" expression on his face made Shen Qiao so angry, he almost picked up a nearby rock and flung it at him.

# Enemies

WHEN IT CAME to tailor shops, He Ji was probably the most famous throughout Tonggu County.

Anyone would agree. He Ji's owner, Madam Fang, also thought so.

She wasn't very old—not even thirty—but she'd already been a widow for over ten years. She'd only been married into her husband's family for two years when he suddenly fell sick and died. At that time, Madam Fang had been pregnant with his child. Her parents-in-law had felt guilty, so they gave her the money to open the tailor shop. Afterward, her parents-in-law also passed away one after the other, with her husband's younger brother inheriting the family business. Unfortunately, her brother-in-law was incompetent, and he squandered all the wealth and property completely within a couple of years. Instead, it was Madam Fang's shop that prospered, growing ever-larger. It wasn't only in Tonggu County—He Ji even had branches in the capital of Feng Province in Liangquan County.

But Madam Fang was attached to her hometown. Even though she owned property in Liangquan County, she remained in Tonggu.

She'd risen early today to inspect one of her stores. When the shopkeeper heard that the owner had come, he quickly ran out to greet her.

At this time, another person arrived at their door.

"I apologize to this customer," said the shopworker, walking over to the newcomer while smiling. "Our owner has come to inspect the accounts, so at the moment, we're not..."

Only halfway through his sentence, intimidated by the newcomer's appearance and aura, he found himself unable to continue speaking.

Yan Wushi raised an eyebrow. "You're not doing business?"

Madam Fang pushed past the shopworker and smiled sweetly. "We're open and welcome customers; why wouldn't we be doing business? My worker was impolite; I apologize to the gentleman on his behalf. May I ask what kind of fabric the gentleman wishes to purchase? We also sell ready-made clothes in many styles. If you wish to select a fabric and have it custom-made, we can have it prepared in as little as two days."

She'd been a merchant for more than ten years, so she considered her knowledge and experience far beyond the average married woman who stayed in their chambers. But who could have known that in front of this man, she felt as ignorant as if she'd spent her life looking up at the sky from a well?

The man's face and bearing were both exceptional. Forget their county magistrates, even the provincial officials couldn't compare.

Merchants opened shops to do business—there was no reason to refuse customers at their door. Especially not such an outstanding character as this man. After seeing him, which woman wouldn't feel a little on edge, her maiden's heart blossoming?

Even Madam Fang's smile had become a few touches more genuine.

Originally, Yan Wushi had wanted to pick out two outfits, but after hearing her words, he had another idea. "In other words, you also sell ready-made outfits for women?"

"Yes, of course!" Madam Fang's smile didn't change, but she couldn't help feeling somewhat disappointed inside.

He was such a handsome gentleman and looked so arrogant and unyielding—definitely not the type who could be ordered around by a docile woman. Yet he'd personally come to purchase clothes for one?

Half a month ago, Shen Qiao and Yan Wushi had left the mountain cavern. They'd traveled continuously south until yesterday, when they arrived and stopped at Tonggu County in Feng Province, not that far from Hanzhong.

Shen Qiao liked the quiet. Whenever he had time, he'd practice martial arts in the inn, never finding it dull. So, Yan Wushi went out on his own.

To err on the side of caution, it would be best if they kept to themselves before they arrived in Chang'an, so as to avoid encountering anyone, but this was impossible—just meals and lodging required them to enter an inn, for starters. Besides, if he were to cower in fear at any sign of potential danger, then he wouldn't be Yan Wushi.

He'd originally wanted to purchase two outfits as changes of clothes, but after hearing Madam Fang's words, he'd changed his mind.

"Is the gentleman purchasing it for his sweetheart, his sister, or a senior relative?" asked Madam Fang.

"What's the difference?" asked Yan Wushi.

A giggle escaped Madam Fang. "I can tell that the gentleman has never purchased clothes for a woman before. There's naturally a science here. For older relatives, the color must not be too bright; it's better to be a bit more modest, and the embroidery less fashionable. If it's for your sister, you can choose colors like pale pink or willow green, with butterflies or roses for the skirt patterns. If you gave that to a senior, such designs would be much too frivolous."

"And what if it's for a sweetheart?" asked Yan Wushi.

Madam Fang suppressed a flicker of disappointment. "If it's for your sweetheart, then you can just select the colors and patterns she likes. What color does your sweetheart prefer?"

Yan Wushi thought for a while. "Perhaps sky blue?"

"Sky blue is a difficult color to wear," said Madam Fang, "unless her skin is very fair."

Yan Wushi smiled briefly. "Well, it is indeed quite fair."

"Then does your esteemed self wish to purchase a ready-made outfit or some fabric for a custom-made one? If you want something ready-made, we have various measurements available. How tall is the lady?"

Yan Wushi only wanted to take a bit of revenge on Shen Qiao, to give him a taste of dressing up as a woman. But when he heard Madam Fang's words, he grew a little interested.

"About half a head shorter than me, and a bit thinner."

Madam Fang was shocked. "Half a head shorter than you? Then that woman is incredibly tall! Please let me send someone to look; I'm not sure if our shop has a garment in the measurements you need. How about the style? What kind of shape would you like the blouse and skirt to have?"

Yan Wushi raised an eyebrow, then looked her over from all sides. "Shape? I think what you have is quite nice."

Madam Fang's heart was pounding from his gaze. Her eyes grew soft and liquid as she bit her lip and smiled. "The gentleman likes what I have?"

They were only a breath apart, nearly touching.

The shopkeeper and worker were clearly accustomed to their owner's flirtatious behavior. They'd already closed the doors of the shop and gone to hide somewhere else.

Yan Wushi smiled slightly, then lifted her chin. He lowered his head to examine her closely, as if he were about to kiss her.

Madam Fang was filled with anticipation, her cheeks flushed red as her slender body went soft and limp. Ever her breaths became searing hot.

"A pity that your clothes are quite nice, yet your face is nothing special. Such a waste of good clothing," said Yan Wushi.

Madam Fang's face went blank, as if she were unable to process what he had said. Only after Yan Wushi took a few steps back did she suddenly come to her senses. Her face alternated between green and white, and she gritted her teeth. "This shop is not open for business today. The gentleman should leave!" What could be more intolerable to a woman than calling her ugly? She'd originally wanted to tell him to get lost, but amiability was the key to prosperity for a merchant. Madam Fang also didn't want to cause herself any trouble—the fewer complications the better. But beneath her blouse, her chest was rising and falling slightly; it was obvious she was incensed.

Yan Wushi sneered a little. "Your courting attempt failed, so your shame enraged you?"

He fished out a heavy purse and placed it on the table. "If you want to run a business, being too quick to anger isn't good. And if you keep frowning like that, won't you age faster?"

Madam Fang yelled angrily, "Such a venomous mouth! Your sweetheart must be suffering from eight lives' worth of misfortune to have caught the eye of someone like you!"

After saying this, she picked up the purse, wanting to throw it at him. However, the moment she lifted it, her expression faltered.

On the mahogany table beneath the purse was a slight concave imprint—left by the purse.

The table was of solid wood and construction. Even placing a large stone atop it might not crush it, let alone a purse of silver. Only now did Madam Fang realize she'd encountered someone extraordinary. Her expression cycled through a kaleidoscope of changes, and in the end, she forced a smile. "The great gentleman is most magnanimous; please don't hold anything against an insignificant woman. Your esteemed self wanted a set of sky-blue clothing, ready-made? This one will have someone look for some!"

So she said, but her heart had long filled with loathing toward Yan Wushi. She couldn't stop herself from cursing him, wishing for his sweetheart to prove fickle soon and cast him aside.

Of course, Yan Wushi couldn't tell what Madam Fang was thinking, and even if he could, he wouldn't care. Once he finished purchasing the clothes, he had someone send them to the inn. Then he left the shop empty-handed, leaving Madam Fang gnashing her teeth behind him.

The streets of a county town couldn't be as lively as those of a provincial capital, but there were still people coming and going. After walking several dozen steps, Yan Wushi suddenly stopped.

He laughed quietly. "Whose mice are you? Skulking about and afraid to show yourselves?"

His words were soft and slow, but they suddenly seemed to explode in the ears of everyone nearby.

The common people had no idea what was going on. After their initial shock, they naturally all ran a good distance away so as not to invite disaster upon themselves.

Yan Wushi stood with his hands behind his back. He lifted his head to watch the birds sweeping over the horizon, carefree and content, yet completely unmoving.

"Some time ago we heard that Sect Leader Yan had been killed in an ambush by five great martial artists! My shizun even felt sorry for so long. To think Sect Leader Yan really was so extraordinary he could survive even such a situation as that! Truly worthy of admiration!"

The delicate laugh was sweet and pleasing to the ear, seemingly both near yet far as it drifted about, but the moment that "admiration" fell, a woman dressed in red suddenly appeared atop the roof to the right of Yan Wushi.

Yan Wushi didn't glance at her but said coolly, "You're already here, but you still try to hide. This is all Hehuan Sect's members are good at—no wonder you sought support from Qi. Now that Qi's been destroyed, you've all become stray dogs. To whom will you enslave yourself next?"

"Sect Leader Yan's words are so funny! Those who did not know better would even think Huanyue Sect virtuous and noble! But in the end, isn't Huanyue Sect also the slave of Yuwen Yong? Pity that Yuwen Yong won't be alive for long! Without your protection, your disciples and subordinates are now even more wretched than some stray dogs!"

Accompanied by a cold laugh, another person appeared before Yan Wushi.

If Shen Qiao were here, he'd recognize him at a glance.

"If they're that incapable and require my protection for everything, then they should just die earlier and save me the trouble!" Yan Wushi looked at Xiao Se, shaking his head. "On the contrary, my venerable self truly pities Yuan Xiuxiu. She accepted an ingrate as a disciple, and then he goes and spends all his time hanging out with Sang Jingxing's bunch. But Sang Jingxing doesn't have an eye for people either. His old disciple Huo Xijing might have been completely brainless, but at least his martial arts were passable. However, not only are you brainless, your martial arts are complete garbage. Seems like Hehuan Sect grows worse with each generation."

Xiao Se was so angry, he laughed instead. "Sect Leader Yan truly has the nimblest of tongues! Don't kneel and beg for mercy later!"

With their abilities, Xiao Se and Bai Rong could be considered first-rate within the jianghu. If the two of them joined forces, it would be difficult for Yan Wushi to beat them back in his current condition. But Yan Wushi's focus wasn't on either of them at the moment. Instead, it was on the man slowly approaching him from behind.

"How long did you all wait here before this venerable one finally appeared?" he asked.

Bai Rong replied sweetly, "We heard that Buddhist Master Xueting had a chance encounter with Sect Leader Yan in Wei Province, then he lost track of Sect Leader Yan's whereabouts afterward. Elder Yan said that Sect Leader Yan would definitely return to Chang'an, but for the sake of avoiding his enemies, he wouldn't take the shortest route. So we specially took a detour and waited in Feng Province. Little did we expect that it really was as Elder Yan predicted."

"However, Sect Leader Yan, you need not be upset, because even if you'd taken a different detour, it'd still be the same. Hanzhong has the Liuhe Guild, Yang Province has the Göktürks. You're trapped no matter where you go, and there's nowhere to escape to. If you want to blame something, blame the fact that you have too many enemies. Since the heavens themselves wish for your destruction, even the gods coming to your aid won't save you."

The one who said this was Yan Shou. He walked toward Yan Wushi, step by step, his footfalls incredibly slow and steady. But his gaze never left Yan Wushi for even half a moment, as if he were a cheetah in wait, ready to pounce at any moment and tear its enemy apart with its sharp teeth.

Yan Wushi burst into loud laughter. "Gods? This venerable one has never believed in gods!"

As soon as these words left his mouth, he moved!

# Fleeing for One's Life

SIMPLY THE NAME "Yan Wushi" carried an invisible, intimidating force. They knew that after the five great experts' ambush, even if he hadn't lost all his martial arts, his strength must be greatly reduced. Even without Sang Jingxing here, the three of them together should be more than enough to bring him down.

But though they knew this in their minds, their bodies still didn't move. An undercurrent surged up within Hehuan Sect. It was visible just from the movements of Xiao Se and the others.

Yan Shou had once lost to Yan Wushi in the past, and it'd been a terribly miserable defeat. The reason he'd come this time wasn't to eradicate a formidable foe for Hehuan Sect but for the *Zhuyang Strategy* scroll that was rumored to be in Yan Wushi's hand. However, that horrible defeat had left a deep impression on Yan Shou, and when he witnessed how calm and composed Yan Wushi was, uncertainty arose within his heart.

Xiao Se was Yuan Xiuxiu's disciple, but he wanted to bring Yan Wushi's head to Sang Jingxing to earn merits. However, when he saw that no one else was moving, he didn't budge either.

Because of this, the four of them entered a strange stand-off. Hehuan Sect clearly held the upper hand, but not one of them chose to make the first move.

Yan Shou narrowed his eyes, carefully observing Yan Wushi's every breath, waiting for him to reveal an opening.

Yan Wushi finally moved.

But he didn't target Xiao Se and Bai Rong before him, nor did he turn to leap on Yan Shou. Instead, his sleeves billowed as he soared into the sky, like a white crane in flight!

Xiao Se's expression fell. "This is bad!"

Who'd have expected that the mighty Huanyue Sect Leader would put on a "come at me" act to confound his opponents?

Xiao Se normally considered himself a graceful and elegant young master, but at this moment he couldn't stop himself from swearing loudly. "If you have the balls, don't run!"

Airborne laughter drifted to them. "As you wish!"

Yan Wushi's figure suddenly reversed in midair. Within the blink of an eye, he was already in front of Xiao Se, and before Xiao Se could get a clear glimpse of Yan Wushi's attack, the wind from the man's palm was already slamming into his chest!

Xiao Se was astounded, but it was too late to dodge; he could only take it head-on. The two of them fought in close combat, and Yan Wushi's true qi was like the rise and fall of the river tide, violent and turbulent as it almost engulfed Xiao Se's. It was as overbearing and arrogant as its owner, to the point of being shocking.

They'd heard that when the five great experts had ambushed Yan Wushi, Guang Lingsan had exploited his flaw, seriously injuring him. Could it be that after obtaining the scroll, he'd managed to repair his flaw within such a short amount of time, propelling his martial arts to the next level?

This thought flashed through Xiao Se's mind, and his heart jolted. A sharp pain lanced through his arm, and he screamed despite himself as he wrenched backward. However, his right arm was already shattered, and the injury affected even his chest; it was as if he'd been viciously struck by a hammer. Blood sprayed from Xiao Se's mouth as he collapsed to the ground. When he turned his head, another couple of crimson mouthfuls splattered onto the ground.

"Xiao-shixiong, are you all right?!" Bai Rong cried out in alarm as she flew over to support him.

Demonic practitioners were all selfish and self-serving, and there was even a long-standing conflict between Xiao Se and Bai Rong. Normally, Bai Rong would have been full of schadenfreude over his misfortune, even kick him while he was down. Coming forward to help him up really wasn't her style—but right now, doing so meant that she could avoid a direct confrontation with Yan Wushi, so she didn't mind expressing some fraternal affection.

Xiao Se's setback caused Yan Shou, who'd been preparing to strike, to slow a little as well, but he still ran after him and blocked his path.

"Why is Sect Leader Yan in such a hurry to leave? When old friends meet, shouldn't they reminisce a little about the past?"

"I also wish to reminisce about the past with Elder Yan. May I ask if Elder Yan can spare the time?"

The one who'd answered naturally wasn't Yan Wushi but someone behind Yan Shou.

Yan Shou didn't turn upon hearing these words; instead, he flew right onto the roof, then looked down at the newcomer from above.

"So, if it isn't another stray dog," he said with disdain.

Shen Qiao strolled over from the other end of the street, sword on his back.

Black hair and blue clothes, his figure tall and elegant—like a beautiful, graceful immortal.

"Elder Yan owes two lives to this humble Daoist since that day at Bailong monastery," said Shen Qiao. "Does he still remember?"

"I've long heard that Xuandu Mountain's former sect leader inherited Qi Fengge's mantle and that his martial arts were unrivaled in all the jianghu. Unfortunately, a blow from Kunye knocked him off the cliff, and he's been on the decline over since, forced to rely on Yan Wushi's protection. Looking at things now, it seems the rumors may not have been false."

Shen Qiao said coolly, "Then I wonder if Elder Yan has heard the rumor that Kunye went up Mount Tai to provoke Bixia Sect, but failed, and that he's already fallen to my blade?"

Yan Shou's face betrayed his faint astonishment.

Bixia Sect had collapsed under their internal strife and were busy struggling, trying to rally their strength even after Kunye's death, while the Göktürks themselves certainly wouldn't go around proclaiming the news. Thus, Kunye's death had been effectively concealed, and everyone thought that he'd returned to the Khaganate—no one could have imagined that he'd died at Shen Qiao's hands.

Bai Rong laughed sweetly. "It's only been a few months, but Shen-lang's martial arts have again soared—truly a commendable feat. However, our sect leader has already ordered us to seize the *Zhuyang Strategy* scroll, and Elders Sang and Baoyun are already on their way here. No matter how amazing your martial arts are, I'm afraid you still can't take on all of Hehuan Sect. Since this matter has nothing to do with you anyway, why not just stand aside and watch?"

Yan Shou hmphed. "As you've already arrived, there's no need to leave. You might as well stay!"

Yan Shou's moniker was "The Buddha with the Bloodstained Hand." His martial arts also leaned toward the insidious and cruel, and he crooked his fingers and clawed at Shen Qiao. In the twinkling of an eye, an ill wind blasted his opponent's face, shrieking and wailing. Mountains of corpses and seas of blood seemed to fill the world around them, transforming it into the deepest of hells. The expansive blood glow was about to engulf him, bringing forth swelling despair and terror.

Shen Qiao soared backward as he drew Shanhe Tongbei. Immediately, his sword qi arced like a rainbow, its light overflowing and quickly overriding most of Yan Shou's surging might.

Yan Shou pursued him relentlessly, his palms neutralizing all of Shen Qiao's attacks before he sent out three or four more blows, each as quick as lightning. It made for a dizzying, overwhelming sight.

Every strike pelted down like a mighty ocean wave, rising and falling like a set of heavenly stairs. Each wave was more powerful than the last, leaving his opponent absolutely no time to react!

Yan Shou wasn't within the top ten, but that didn't mean that he was only an average martial artist. In the ten years Yan Wushi spent in seclusion, Huanyue Sect had concentrated their operations on the imperial court of Zhou while Fajing Sect had departed for the distant Tuyuhun. Only Hehuan Sect remained in the Central Plains, and their influence in Qi especially had greatly exploded. And Yan Shou had managed to stake out a spot for himself among Hehuan Sect's throng of talented members, to the point that he was equal with Sang Jingxing. This was certainly not due to his good looks.

Sword in hand, Shen Qiao slashed the air horizontally. A brilliant sword glare was born, as rippling and reflective as river water, but as harsh as snow and frost. Whirling with chill, it swept forward, accompanied by murderous intent!

With the battle going strong on that end, those on the other end weren't slacking either. Xiao Se and Bai Rong surged forward side by side, hampering Yan Wushi from the front and the back, preventing him from disengaging.

While Shen Qiao dueled Yan Shou, he took the time to glance at Bai Rong and Xiao Se's attacks. He couldn't help but frown to himself.

The two of them were martial experts from Hehuan Sect's younger generation. Aside from the various elders, they were among the strongest in martial arts. The Xiao-Bai pair were immensely talented—every time he saw them, their martial arts always seemed to have improved by leaps and bounds, especially Bai Rong. The first time he met her, she'd only just ascended to the ranks of first-rate martial experts, and now, as she gave her all to catch up, her "Blue Lotus Seals" had been honed to perfection. Her posture was lithe and graceful with murderous intent lurking beneath, impossible to completely guard against.

Shen Qiao knew very well that Bai Rong had showed him great mercy several times. Earlier, under the pretext of elucidating their strength to Shen Qiao, she'd notified him that Sang Jingxing would be coming, telling Shen Qiao not to meddle. However, the trace of tenderness she had for Shen Qiao would definitely not be extended to Yan Wushi. At this moment she and Xiao Se worked in tandem, their every move poised to kill. It was like an inescapable, all-encompassing net, their tacit understanding flawless as they entrapped Yan Wushi between them.

Due to the heavy injuries Yan Wushi had suddenly inflicted on Xiao Se earlier, both were filled with apprehension and caution, leaving them unwilling to use their full strength. But only Shen Qiao knew that Yan Wushi's current martial strength was limited, that it hadn't even recovered to half of his peak. Seriously wounding Xiao Se was already the most he could do. Forcing him to also face off against Bai Rong—who'd improved massively—was an arduous struggle. If the battle dragged on and the two of them realized this, they'd no longer hesitate to use their full strength against Yan Wushi. And because Shen Qiao needed to handle Yan Shou, he wouldn't be able to attend to him either.

Having thought this far, Shen Qiao hesitated no longer: he pushed his martial strength to the limit, eliminated all his stray thoughts, and directly entered the echelon of sword heart.

In an instant, his sword glare became boundless, painting the heavens and earth together. It started with a raging momentum like thunder, then transitioned to the clear calm of light rippling over the water's surface, all concentrated within this one sword.

*The man exists apart from the sword, but the sword exists within his heart. Where the sword heart reaches, all existence becomes emptiness!*

Yan Shou's expression suddenly faltered, and he quickly withdrew and retreated, not daring to even brush the sword glare's edge. But now that Shen Qiao had released the sword glare, he had no reason to retract it again. Wrapped in white light, the sword qi chased Yan Shou in hot pursuit, firmly binding itself to him. Accompanied by rumbling thunder and galloping rapids, though the sword heart was immature and its manifestation unstable, its slash already showed the hint of a power that could bring peace to the land.

Shen Qiao didn't withdraw but rather swept straight over to Bai Rong with a swing of his blade.

Bai Rong, Xiao Se and Yan Wushi were at an impasse, forming a precarious balance. With Yan Wushi's original martial strength, he should have been able to crush them, and this deadlock could never have happened. As it stretched on, Xiao Se and Bai Rong grew suspicious, but suddenly a blue shadow glided past them and took Yan Wushi away.

When they saw this, the three of them naturally gave chase, though Xiao Se's injuries meant he couldn't keep up. But Yan Shou pressed close behind, unwilling to let them go so easily.

"You go on first! Get to that forest we passed before entering the city! I'll hold them back!" Shen Qiao's words came incredibly fast, and the instant he finished, he shoved Yan Wushi forward. Without waiting for a response, he grabbed his sword and turned toward their three pursuers.

Yan Wushi looked back, his gaze intent. Then he turned and left without a word.

Their target was getting farther and farther away, but Shen Qiao blocked their path. Even Yan Shou grew impatient, and his palm blasts seemed to transform into bloody shadows as he aimed each and every one at Shen Qiao.

But Shen Qiao remained perfectly in order, and his swordplay grew steadier, more composed. In the face of Yan Shou's frenzied gale of attacks, without Yan Wushi here, he could instead focus his full attention on the situation before him. Shanhe Tongbei roared in the wind, and Shen Qiao's blue robes lent him an immortal grace. As he wielded the Azure Waves sword techniques that he'd improved, a majestic display arose and swept forth, unhindered. It was like a thousand flowers in bloom, the light flooding the world. For a time, the three pursuers were barred outside the sword glare, unable to advance an inch.

Yan Shou gave a muffled humph, and his movements grew faster and faster, his figure flickering through poses until it was impossible to discern what was real and what wasn't. His slender fingers were like sharp blades, and wherever they touched, oceans of blood and skeletons seemed to emerge, wave upon wave. His bare hand even pierced the sword screen and directly grabbed Shen Qiao's hand, still on the hilt!

• • •

Shen Qiao soared forward, his figure now a blue shadow. Like a dragonfly flitting across the water's surface, he barely landed before flying forward more, his toes almost never touching the ground. He pushed "A Rainbow Stretches across the Heaven," Xuandu Mountain's special qinggong, to the epitome of perfection. If Qi Fengge were here, he'd be unable to suppress his praise.

Against such an incredible level of qinggong, the trees on either side were cast far behind him, hazy and indistinct. They blurred together with the enemies in hot pursuit, until everything disappeared without a trace.

But Shen Qiao didn't let down his guard. He drew a breath as his sleeves fluttered, his steps picking up nary a speck of dust. Even a frightened, soaring bird would be lacking in comparison.

The journey took little time. First, he up the mountain outside the city, so as to obfuscate his tracks. Then he followed a hidden path off the mountain, stopping in a small forest at its foot that lay along the road to the city.

The grove wasn't very large, but because it was at the foot of the mountain, it was lush and verdant, practically a world of its own with its densely entangled vines and rugged terrain. An ordinary person entering would find themselves seemingly engulfed by the forest, and it would take a long time to find a way out.

Shen Qiao supported himself with the tree trunks as he walked further in. Though he'd slowed his pace, his feet still left no imprint behind him. Even if an enemy chased him here, they'd be unable to tell whether he'd entered the forest.

After about half an hour of walking, he saw that he'd entered the forest's depths and had almost reached the jungle at the foot of the mountain. Then, finally unable to push himself any longer, he stopped for a short rest.

A hand suddenly reached out beside him and grabbed his wrist.

On alert, Shen Qiao immediately sensed the movement. He yanked his hand back and retreated, but upon seeing the newcomer's face, he immediately stopped and breathed a sigh of relief.

"It's me," said Yan Wushi. He caught his wrist again as his other hand moved to support Shen Qiao's waist, and he walked him further into the forest. "Why did you take so long to get rid of them?"

At this point, Shen Qiao's strength was already exhausted, so he let Yan Wushi support him, gingerly leaning half his weight onto the man.

"There's naturally nothing to worry about if it were only the three of them," said Shen Qiao. "I'd originally wanted to kill Yan Shou to avenge the abbot and Chuyi, but then someone else came. He was dressed like a monk and looked younger than Bai Rong, yet he was on par with Yan Shou in strength. An extended battle isn't favorable to me, so I was forced to find a chance to disengage."

He didn't know that man's identity, but Yan Wushi knew right away. "You're talking about Baoyun, one of the Hehuan Sect's elders. He likes to disguise himself as a monk and wanders about preaching scriptures. He uses that to deceive female worshippers so he can sleep with them. The Buddhists hate him for sullying their reputation, and in recent years, they've repeatedly tried to hunt him down and kill him. He doesn't appear in public much, but martially he's no weaker than Yan Shou."

Hearing about the man's actions, Shen Qiao frowned despite himself, his face betraying his disgust. "Bai Rong said just now that Sang Jingxing and Baoyun were following behind," he said. "If Baoyun is here, then Sang Jingxing shouldn't be far either. We must leave as soon as possible. Otherwise, with that many people they may find us."

"Can you still walk?"

Shen Qiao gave a strained smile and shook his head.

"I have a plan," said Yan Wushi.

"Hm?"

Yan Wushi reached out to touch his cheek, which was pallid from exhaustion. Shen Qiao turned away to evade him, but Yan Wushi still managed to stroke it once. He couldn't help but glare at Yan Wushi, who smiled slightly. "Sang Jingxing was heavily wounded by you, so he naturally hates you to the bone," Yan Wushi said. "But the other members of Hehuan Sect don't possess that kind of bone-deep hostility toward you; instead, they fear you greatly. Leave by yourself and don't worry about me. Then you'll be able to shake them off, and you won't have the extra burden of me to deal with."

Shen Qiao sighed. "Here I thought that you'd actually suggest a good plan. Enough with the nonsense. Let's head up the mountain."

"Is it not a good plan?" asked Yan Wushi.

"If I was going to abandon you, why would I have waited until now? If I'm going to save someone, I'll save them to the end. 'Escort the buddha the entire journey west.' I've already involved myself from the start; I must give it my all."

The two of them continued forward. Shen Qiao had forced his qinggong to its limit just before, and now he felt like every step took momentous effort. He couldn't help but say, "I really can't walk anymore. You go on ahead; I'll cover for you."

Yan Wushi laughed. "A-Qiao, you're really so cute. You want to cover for me the way you are now? If Sang Jingxing arrives, he'll swallow you whole, bones and all."

Before Shen Qiao could respond, he felt his feet leave the ground—Yan Wushi was carrying him on his back.

# Sacrifice

S HEN QIAO had not anticipated Yan Wushi's actions at all, and for a moment, he was stupefied.

Yan Wushi's steps were graceful and swift. It took only an instant for him to cut through the forest and reach the foot of the mountain, then he followed the mountain path upward, circling around to the other side.

Shen Qiao remained stunned for a long while before finally asking, "We're heading up the mountain?"

"On the back side of the mountain is a temple. It's hidden deep within the forest and has been abandoned for many years."

Confused, Shen Qiao said, "You seem to be familiar with this area?"

"In the past, after I battled Cui Youwang, I came to this mountain for secluded cultivation."

Understanding dawned on Shen Qiao, and he didn't press further. He truly was a little tired—he'd just fought hard against four people. Apart from Xiao Se, whom Yan Wushi had injured, Bai Rong, Yan Shou, and Baoyun were each stronger than the last. With Shen Qiao's current internal energy, if it weren't for the support of his sword heart, he could never have retreated safely.

Though Yan Wushi walked quickly, his steps were steady. Shen Qiao could feel the warmth of his skin through their clothing.

Lacking the strength to think any more, he unknowingly drifted off to sleep.

The next time he opened his eyes, he found he was no longer surrounded by a jungle but inside a Buddhist temple.

Because of its age, it had been a long time since the temple had known incense, and even the burners were nowhere to be seen. The statue of Buddha was damaged and missing parts of its body, and everything was covered in dust and spiderwebs. However, the place Shen Qiao had been laid was clean, and there was even a cloth drape beneath him for padding, ripped from two nearby pillars. Though it was tattered, it was still better than sleeping directly on the cold stone floor.

He rested his back against the wall for a while. He hadn't suffered any serious injuries earlier, but ever since his battle with Xueting, he'd been slowly accumulating internal injuries. This left him unable to utilize his full strength and was one of the reasons why he'd failed to kill Yan Shou. When Baoyun joined in, he'd lost his chance completely.

Shen Qiao held his groggy head and let out a light sigh.

A hand stroked him. Caught off guard, Shen Qiao was startled by the icy sensation, and he couldn't help but shiver.

"Why are you sighing?" Yan Wushi was sitting next to him. He was reading a piece of silk that he held in his hand.

Shen Qiao squinted at the silk for a moment, scrutinizing it, before he confirmed that it was the *Zhuyang Strategy* scroll that Yan Wushi had seized from Chen Gong.

He was about to speak when he saw Yan Wushi's hand flip over. The silk fluttered right into the fire and was swallowed by the flames in an instant.

Shen Qiao's words caught in his throat.

Yan Wushi turned his head and saw his expression and answered the unspoken question. "I've already memorized the contents. What's the point of keeping it?"

"You could have given it to Hehuan Sect as a last resort in order to extricate yourself," said Shen Qiao. "You won't even leave yourself a way out?"

"Even if I give them the silk, do you think they'd believe this is the real scroll?"

Shen Qiao frowned in response.

Yan Wushi sneered a little. "In the past, Riyue Sect had a secret technique. Even you probably haven't heard of it. Bluntly speaking, when Demonic Persuasion is honed to the pinnacle of perfection, you can use it to control other people's minds and actions, forcing them to speak the truth without realizing. If I were in their place, I, too, would rather use this method to obtain the testimony I want instead of believing in a piece of silk covered in words."

"So, Yan Shou and the others wanted to take advantage of your greatly reduced cultivation to capture you, then force you to tell them the scroll's contents."

"Correct," said Yan Wushi. "My value to them isn't as a corpse, but in the *Zhuyang Strategy* and my identity as Huanyue Sect's leader. With me in hand, they can easily take command of Huanyue Sect."

To Shen Qiao's knowledge, Yan Wushi had already read three out of five of the *Zhuyang Strategy* scrolls, most notably the one from Ruoqiang underground. That one recorded information on how to improve and repair the *Fenglin Scriptures*. Sang Jingxing and Yuan Xiuxiu also cultivated with the *Fenglin Scriptures*, so they'd naturally understand the effects caused by the flaw in the demonic core. Each day the flaw went unrepaired was a day they couldn't attain ultimate perfection with regards to the *Fenglin Scriptures*. They wished to obtain this information more than anyone else.

In the past, Yan Wushi would have naturally been far above them, leaving them too afraid to act rashly. But the current Yan Wushi had been ambushed by the five great experts and crawled back from the jaws of death. His martial abilities were significantly diminished. If they didn't act now, then when?

Shen Qiao couldn't be clearer on the methods demonic practitioners used.

Back then, because Shen Qiao had killed Sang Jingxing's disciple Huo Xijing, Sang Jingxing had wanted to destroy his martial arts and then break all his limbs to make him his toy. First, he'd wanted to play with Shen Qiao wantonly, then toss him to the rest of Hehuan Sect to be ravaged. Given the long-standing antagonism between Huanyue Sect and Hehuan Sect—as well as Yan Wushi's cutting demeanor and self-indulgent actions—the moment he fell into Hehuan Sect's hands, his fate certainly wouldn't be any better than Shen Qiao's.

Considering this, Shen Qiao's brows knitted tighter and tighter. "If that's the case, we must set out quickly, lest they catch up."

Yan Wushi laughed. "You're being so considerate toward me. Is it because you want me to shed tears of gratitude and pledge myself to you?"

Shen Qiao ignored his mocking words. Instead, he said solemnly, "I know that Sect Leader Yan has never deemed anyone worthy of his attention, but this is a matter of life and death. Your flaw is still there, your strength inadequate. It'd be one thing if it were only Yan Shou's group, but if Sang Jingxing arrives, even I won't be able to ward him off. It's better to be cautious."

But Yan Wushi didn't seem the slightest bit alarmed. He nonchalantly tossed a nearby stick into the fire, the flames leaping higher as a result. Then he suddenly changed the subject: "If you could start over from the beginning, would you choose to not be saved by me at Banbu Peak?"

Shen Qiao started, then shook his head. "I'm afraid I'd have no say to that."

"So, you're saying that even if you already knew that you'd end up completely entangled with me, and that I'd personally deliver you to Sang Jingxing, you still wouldn't regret it?"

"There is no cure for regrets in this world," said Shen Qiao. "We can never alter the events of the past. Instead of clinging to resentment, ensuring I can never get free, I'd much rather thank you for teaching me how to view the world and the hearts of people."

The firelight illuminated his earnest expression, revealing a trace of unique gentleness.

Yan Wushi suddenly began to laugh. "Foolish A-Qiao," he said gently. "When have I ever been good to you?"

He reached over, as if wanting to stroke Shen Qiao's cheek. Shen Qiao leaned back to avoid it while raising a hand to block, but he didn't expect that Yan Wushi would raise his other hand too. It wasn't to attack, though; he only swept his sleeve before Shen Qiao's eyes.

Smelling something strange, Shen Qiao tried to halt his breathing, but he'd already inhaled some. His already weak body went limp entirely, and the other man took the chance to tap his acupoints.

"When are you going to fix your bad habit of leaving yourself unguarded?" Yan Wushi shook his head. "Or, do you already consider me someone you can trust, deep down?"

He ignored Shen Qiao's glare and lowered his head to kiss the tip of his nose. Then he lifted Shen Qiao in his arms, carrying him horizontally to the back of the buddha statue.

Only then did Shen Qiao notice that there was a large, recessed opening in the back of the statue. The inside was neither large nor small, but just enough to fit a cross-legged person within.

Yan Wushi even had the leisure to explain to him. "Casting a buddha statue is quite expensive. Many temples will hollow out the back of their statues to save on costs. I've been to this temple before, and this statue is quite crudely made—even the cavity's construction is sloppy. They only carved the front to look good, but now you'll get something big for no cost at all!"

Shen Qiao frowned. "Exactly what are you planning to do?!"

Yan Wushi said languidly, "I've also read the *Zhuyang Strategy* scroll within the Imperial Palace of Northern Zhou. But as we're in a hurry now, I don't have time to recite it for you. If you want it, you can go to Chang'an to look for Yuwen Yong. He's met you before and thinks highly of you, so I'm sure he'll be happy to let you read it. Also, tell Bian Yanmei not to worry about me. He should first take advantage of Qi's annexation by Zhou to expand Huanyue Sect's influence in Qi."

Shen Qiao's expression faltered. "I'm not from Huanyue Sect. You shouldn't be telling me this. What does it have to do with me?"

Yan Wushi smiled but didn't answer. He stroked Shen Qiao's face, purposely drawing out his movements, as if enjoying the sensation of Shen Qiao's skin against his fingers. The atmosphere took on a hint of indescribable intimacy, and Yan Wushi watched as Shen Qiao's cheeks slowly and predictably flushed with a soft, indignant red.

"Our A-Qiao is so good-looking!" he sighed. "No wonder that chit Bai Rong fell for you. With her around, even if she suspects something, she'll definitely help to keep you concealed and prevent you from falling into the hands of Yan Shou and the rest."

If Shen Qiao still failed to understand what Yan Wushi wanted to do even after he had said all this, he really would be too stupid.

"Yan Wushi, I didn't go through so much to help you escape just to let you leap straight into a trap!"

Yan Wushi laughed. "I've never regretted handing you to Sang Jingxing, even up to today. Now, you have the chance to witness my misfortune, yet you look like you're mourning your mother! A-Qiao, oh, A-Qiao, you've really disappointed me so! You should be reveling in my misfortune right now, you should be rejoicing inside. How can you wear such a pitiful expression? I won't be able to resist getting more intimate!"

After he said this, he gripped Shen Qiao's chin and lowered his head, invading him with his lips and tongue. He only stopped once Shen Qiao's breaths became disordered, his eyes glistening with moisture.

"I've always done as I pleased without a single regret. This isn't for atonement, much less something as laughable as guilt. You don't need to feel indebted to me, or go as far as to harbor some self-serving, wishful thoughts about the meaning of it all. That would only make me want to throw up."

He used his thumb to wipe away the shine from Shen Qiao's lip and chuckled softly. "This venerable one is waiting for you to make good on your promise one day. Become a worthy opponent. Then perhaps this venerable one will deem you worthy of a second look."

Shen Qiao tried with all his might to force open his acupoints, but Yan Wushi's technique was far too artful. He kept trying to no avail, until his forehead carried a sheen of sweat, his face growing even redder. It seemed Yan Wushi's words had left him both ashamed and furious.

When Yan Wushi released him and attempted to stand, Shen Qiao was so anxious that even the pitch of his voice changed. "Stop right there!"

Yan Wushi really did stop, but then he reached out again and simply tapped Shen Qiao's acupoint to mute him.

Shen Qiao's chest heaved up and down, his eyes brimming with unshed tears. His gaze shimmered, wet and glistening—a sight that could move anyone.

"Don't show this kind of expression to anyone." A soft laugh escaped Yan Wushi as he bent down to whisper in his ear. "Otherwise even I won't be able to hold back, much less Sang Jingxing."

Once he'd finished talking, he sent the statue skittering into the wall with a strike. Shen Qiao's hiding place was now pressed tightly against the wall and thus much harder to discover.

He then put out the fire, and with a wave of his sleeve, the place where Shen Qiao had been sitting was now covered in collapsed debris, erasing all trace of his presence.

Yan Wushi had just finished when he felt a sense of forewarning: it was as though murderous intent was closing in from afar.

When one had attained a certain level of martial prowess, they'd possess a deeply profound intuition for danger.

A slight sneer twisted Yan Wushi's face. He strode out of the temple and swept forward, his figure instantly vanishing into the night.

A ray of moonlight trickled through the ruined roof tiles and walls, bleeding into the temple, giving the person within the statue a glimmer of light as well.

The moisture finally condensed into teardrops, which fell from Shen Qiao's eyes.

Some time later, he heard someone outside say, "With his martial prowess, how could Elder Sang be unable to catch up to one insignificant Yan Wushi?"

"'One insignificant Yan Wushi?'" Bai Rong sneered. "Xiao-shixiong, do you dare say that to Yan Wushi's face?"

"Enough!" Yan Shou had no patience for their noise. He frowned. "Yan Wushi left by himself without Shen Qiao. Perhaps Shen Qiao is still hiding nearby. He just battled us earlier; his strength should be spent, and he couldn't have gotten far! Search this place first!"

# Breakthrough

AFTER YAN WUSHI HAD LEFT, Shen Qiao urgently tried to break through his sealed acupoints. He was worried about what tortures Yan Wushi would suffer if he fell into Sang Jingxing's hands with his current martial prowess. The true qi in his meridians surged without restraint, almost trying to burst out of his body. He could feel his heart alternating between blazing hot, like it was being broiled, and freezing cold, like it'd fallen into an icy cavern. His entire person was dazed and muddled, numb even to the flow of time outside. It was as if he'd fallen into a dreamlike state, but one that was still grounded in reality.

On one hand, his body was being tormented by the alternating heat and cold; on the other hand, his consciousness seemed to be wandering about outside. It was as though his soul wished to tear itself away from his body, but a single thread tethered it firmly to his mortal shell, forcing it to rampage along with his disordered true qi. His chest throbbed dully from the disturbance, his four limbs were entirely numb, and he wanted to vomit.

The first half of Shen Qiao's life had been smooth sailing. Xuandu Mountain had been like a barrier, sealing its inhabitants off from all the treacheries of the outside world.

Both him and everyone else on Xuandu Mountain—including the greatly ambitious Yu Ai—had already partially detached from the secular world. Their views on people and their worldly matters all inevitably carried a trace of naivety and presumptuousness, that this was how things should be. However, because there'd been Xuandu Mountain and Qi Fengge standing at the forefront, acting as their shield, none of them had realized what the world below the mountain was like.

After that, Banbu Peak seemed to have split Shen Qiao's life into two clear halves. The peacefulness of the first half juxtaposed against the turbulence of what came after.

He'd experienced many fates worse than death, and he'd witnessed both the kindness and evil within the human hearts in the world. But ultimately, no trace of rage or hatred remained in his heart—and even if there had, the deaths of the abbot and Chuyi, gaining his own disciple in Shiwu, his shared advance and retreat together with Bixia Sect, Yan Wushi's act of luring away Sang Jingxing, even bidding farewell to him in that manner... With all those events, any anger or hatred would have dissipated like smoke, leaving no trace behind.

This thought was like a drop of ice water; slowly, it fanned out from his forehead and through his entire self.

At that moment, his consciousness seemed to completely escape his mortal shell, escaped the buddha statue sheltering him, fled the little temple, and arrived in an unknown world, vast and indescribable. All his pains gradually left his body, and soon, he felt them no longer. However, a sudden flash of understanding bloomed and opened before his eyes, and it was like the moon and sun suspended high in the sky, illuminating the mountains and oceans below, while fish leapt among the waves and the rain reflected the starry heavens above.

His sealed acupoints slowly opened, the true qi flowing through his body like warm streams, slowly allowing his numb, aching limbs to regain their strength.

Shen Qiao felt as though he'd been transformed into a little fish. With a swish of his tail, he leapt into the boundless universe and its star-filled skies. Above his head came the steady noise of dripping. Unable to withstand the weight of the dew droplets, the leaf stalks bent, and the dew, eager to be free of the leaves, slid off and fell before melding into the deep pond and shattering its tranquility.

He raised his head, watching the outside world through the transparent, rippling pond water. It was a profound and mysterious feeling; one that could be experienced but not described.

That droplet of dew fell into the pond, but it seemed more like it'd fallen inside his heart.

And the entire world shifted with it.

Suddenly, harsh winter transformed into balmy spring, and the waters flowing around him too grew warm. In his vicinity, countless similar little fishes darted past him, shaking their heads and swishing their tails as they merrily swam forward. The stars and moon were strewn over the pond surface, and they sent their lustrous brilliance into the waters below, causing everything around them to glisten and glow, as if this were the Milky Way.

Shen Qiao closed his eyes. He felt like he'd already gone through the entire life span of a fish, and now he'd been reborn as this pond, so deep and vast. Day after day, he waited for the rain to fill him to the brim, waited for the pondside flowers to bloom and whisper to him their troubles, then waited for the blooms to fall and inter themselves within the water. For spring to shape the clouds, then for autumn to bring the rains, for the clear bell to ring from afar, for the trees to fill with blooming peach blossoms.

He suddenly recalled a line from the *Zhuyang Strategy*.

*Outside of the self, there is no other.*

Shen Qiao still remembered the first time he'd seen this line, back when Shizun had given him that *Zhuyang Strategy* scroll. Although he'd used the *Zhuyang Strategy*'s true qi to rebuild his meridians with his rebirth, after fighting his way out of certain death, he still hadn't fully comprehended every line within the *Zhuyang Strategy*.

At that time, there'd been another line before this one: *When the self enters the heart of the other, one will be free of all hindrances.*

This line was much easier to understand. Bluntly speaking, studying the sword required fathoming the sword's heart, and studying the saber required fathoming the saber's heart. *When facing an enemy, you must know both yourself and the enemy.* Only then could you be invincible in battle.

But in this way, the "other" and the "self" would become one. Then why separate them out again and say, "Outside of the self, there is no other"?

Once, Shen Qiao had thought that it must be an error, or that Tao Hongjing hadn't thought it through enough when writing it.

However, at this very moment, he suddenly understood the meaning of this line. It was like he'd fallen into a rut with his previous thinking, misleading him.

Humans exist in the space between heaven and earth. First comes the "self," and only after can there be an "other." Humans judge both other people and other things through the self, so if the self has no joy, then heaven and earth have no joy. If the self has no sorrow, then heaven and earth have no sorrow. When the self's heart is full of cheer, even plain words will give birth to spring. When the self's heart is full of grief, even the mountains and rivers will fade away.

With this realization, not only did Shen Qiao's mind immediately open up, even his body seemed to expand without limit, as if it could now hold a boundless, infinite amount of true qi. Like the sea that embraced hundreds of rivers, magnanimous and forgiving. His meridians dilated from the true qi, and with this dilation, his true qi was now free and unfettered, the worries of congestion or blockages cast away.

Shanhe Tongbei quivered slightly, as if it'd sensed its master's mind and progress. Too excited to compose itself, it seemed ready to leave its sheath and sweep through its enemies.

But at this time, the four people outside the buddha statue had just entered the small temple.

Yan Shou said coldly, "Search everything."

Because Xiao Se had been wounded, his steps were heavy, his gait somewhat slow. Bai Rong didn't seem interested in diving into the task either, though, despite being unharmed; she only followed behind Xiao Se.

The two of them circled around the back of the temple once. Xiao Se returned and said, "Elder Yan, there are no traces of Shen Qiao. Could he have seen our greater numbers and abandoned Yan Wushi to leave first?"

"That's impossible," said Yan Shou. "He was already exhausted after fighting us. To recover in such a short amount of time is beyond difficult; even if he did run, he couldn't have gotten far. Since he didn't leave with Yan Wushi, he must have found somewhere to hide first, and this place is quite suitable. Have you already searched everything?"

"We have," said Xiao Se. "This temple is very small, and there's only a single room at the back, without anywhere to hide. The well is still functional—there's water at the bottom, so he can't hide there either. Furthermore, there are no mechanisms that lead to secret rooms or underground passages."

He shot a glance at Bai Rong. "But Bai-shimei has shown much mercy to Shen Qiao, it seems. She's always hindering us and urging us to keep going. I wonder what her intentions are."

"Xiao-shixiong really spends every moment badmouthing me!" Bai Rong said sweetly. "Do you think that Shizun will start favoring you if you get rid of me? Don't forget that you belong under Sect Leader Yuan. If you wish to switch factions, you'll need to display your sincerity. What's the point of picking on a little girl like me?"

Suddenly, Baoyun spoke up from where he was standing next to Yan Shou. "You haven't even found him and you're already fighting amongst yourselves. Is this what Sect Leader Yuan and Elder Sang teach their disciples?"

His tone was dark and sinister, completely incongruent with a monk's solemn, dignified appearance.

But it was evidently quite effective—both Bai Rong and Xiao Se closed their mouths and said no more.

Yan Shou looked all around him before his gaze finally fell on that giant buddha statue. He paused for a moment, then walked toward it.

His movements drew everyone else's attention. Even Baoyun made a sound of surprise. "This statue is incredibly large. If it's hollow in the center, it could conceal a person."

Yan Shou surveyed the statue from top to bottom, starting from the top of its head down to its stone platform. Then he suddenly pulled away the fabric upon that platform, and his gaze landed on the marks left under the draping. With a cold laugh, he sent a palm strike at the statue!

The force from his blow struck the statue right in the center. Cracks snaked up the statue with lightning speed, then it split open with a rumble!

There was indeed someone inside!

Everyone could see the silhouette of the person concealed within the statue. Yan Shou burst out laughing, then leapt into the air. Like an eagle swooping down on its prey, he immediately pounced at Shen Qiao!

His palm blast rolled to his target before him, quick as a raging tempest, filling the skies with a blood shadow and pelting down with bone-piercing cold. It left no time to guard; anyone trying to defend against it would only feel their entire body being engulfed by the blood shadow of his palm blast, without the slightest gap or even the chance to escape. It left one trembling in fear, hearts overtaken by despair.

Shen Qiao was already exhausted after fighting one-on-four, but even if some of his strength still remained, Yan Shou's all-encompassing palm strike would be certain to catch him unprepared.

Previously, during their battle, Yan Shou had been fearful of Shen Qiao's echelon of sword heart, but he'd also probed out Shen Qiao's true condition and realized that his internal energy was completely insufficient to sustain that echelon. In short, he'd advanced too quickly in swordplay, and his foundations of internal energy couldn't catch up. It was impossible for this fatal drawback to have changed within such a short period of time.

Therefore, he'd believed that even if he couldn't seriously injure him, this strike would be enough to firmly hold Shen Qiao in place, forcing him to take the defensive.

While this thought flashed through him, his palm blast had already slammed into Shen Qiao. Yan Shou and Shen Qiao were only a short distance away from each other, and his opponent didn't even have time to turn around and defend himself!

Then a white light suddenly swelled before him, as murderous intent, sinister and cold, rushed at him head-on. It actually suppressed Yan Shou's palm blast, and the sword qi even overwhelmed the blood shadow to press on toward Yan Shou's face!

"Careful, Elder Yan!" Xiao Se yelled.

Yan Shou didn't need his shout at all; he'd already rushed to retreat.

The others didn't stand by and watch either. Baoyun leapt into the air and grabbed at Shen Qiao from a different direction.

Shen Qiao swung his sword horizontally, and sword qi burst out along the blade. As his true qi swept forth, his blue robes fluttered, and he transformed into a blue arc which interphased with the sword glare, shining. It left the eyes dazzled and confused, unable to distinguish what was what.

Yan Shou's face flickered between expressions, and his one retreat took him back ten steps, pressing his back to the temple wall, leaving him no room to retreat further.

He'd managed to make it out: Shen Qiao was clearly rushing toward him while leaving Baoyun aside. The man had used his sword qi to weave a sword screen, which directly walled off everyone else's attacks, allowing him to focus his entire attention on Yan Shou.

But Shen Qiao had clearly exhausted all his strength before. How had he recovered so much in such a short period of time?!

Yan Shou didn't have time for careful thought. He soared straight into the air, smashing through the roof tiles with a palm strike as Shen Qiao followed in close pursuit.

The two of them fought from inside the temple to up on the roof. Their silhouettes drifted about like wraiths, wrapped in sword glares and palm blasts. Harsh as a roiling tempest, or the cold of the dead of winter, when the trees and grasses withered, and all things fell silent. The moment Yan Shou's palm of blood struck forth, bloody rains accompanied it, cold and gloomy, with wave upon wave of murderous intent. However, the sword glare suddenly rose, as brilliant as the red-gold clouds of dusk, spraying forth like spring waters splashing upon rocks. It emptied a flood of divine light, and all faded before its radiance.

In contrast, even the bright moon seemed to have lost some color, and it ducked shyly behind the clouds, never to reappear.

In all of heaven and earth, only the sword glare existed. The mountains and rivers grieved in tandem, as metal and stone released their wail!

Xiao Se found that he couldn't intervene, and he didn't force himself. Instead, he stood by and watched. Out of the corner of his eye, he saw that Bai Rong was also completely still. "Does Bai-shimei still hold lingering feelings for Shen Qiao, to the point she can't even bear to personally fight him herself?" he couldn't help but say coldly.

Bai Rong was all smiles. "Even the combined efforts of Elders Yan and Baoyun can't bring him down! If I attacked as well, I'd just be adding to the confusion. If Xiao-shixiong is capable, your little sister is perfectly happy to hold the line for you!"

These weren't empty words. Shen Qiao was holding his own even fighting one against two. Not only was Baoyun helpless against him, even Yan Shou was betraying signs of impending defeat.

How could a single person suddenly grow so strong?

Xiao Se was bewildered and confused; he even suspected that Yan Wushi must have copied Hehuan Sect's pair cultivation techniques. But even if they had pair cultivated, they couldn't have finished in such a short amount of time.

He gave a cold huff, completely uninterested in squabbling with Bai Rong. Instead, he glanced up at the battle on the roof.

In the time they'd spoken those short words, however, it was already clear which of the two would be the victor and who would be defeated.

# 81

# The Emperor's Funeral

THE HEARTS OF THE MEMBERS of Hehuan Sect weren't unified, and the clues were obvious from Shen Qiao and Yan Shou's battle.

Shen Qiao had just forced open his acupoints, but it wasn't possible for his martial strength to suddenly improve by leaps and bounds to the point of reaching the pinnacle in one day. At best, he'd only been able to dilate his meridians and recover some strength. With his original level of strength, he and Yan Shou should have been evenly matched, but facing both Yan Shou and Baoyun together was much more strenuous.

However, when Baoyun saw Shen Qiao focus on dealing with Yan Shou, he gradually stopped interfering. He let Shen Qiao hold the upper hand while Yan Shou was pushed to the end of his tether.

Yan Shou's heart secretly filled with hatred—even more, he didn't want to be looked down upon. He used all his strength, vowing that he'd kill Shen Qiao beneath his palm.

But who could have expected that the current Shen Qiao would be so different from the past one? His Shanhe Tongbei was enough to prevent anyone from approaching him. More than once, Yan Shou wanted to change from defense to offense, but his fear of Shen Qiao's sword screen forced him to shift back to defense. Among the dense sword glares, the once mighty and awe-inspiring

"Buddha with the Bloodstained Hand" had actually been suppressed to the point he couldn't release a single strike. His eyebrows were tightly furrowed on his frosty face and sweat beaded on his forehead.

When forced into a difficult situation, one would inevitably reveal some openings. And right at this time, Shanhe Tongbei's sword glare flooded forth, sweeping right toward the center of Yan Shou's forehead.

Of course, Baoyun couldn't just sit and watch Yan Shou lose his life in front of him, else he'd have a hard time explaining himself once he returned to Hehuan Sect.

He yelled at Xiao Se and Bai Rong, "Why are you just watching?!"

At the same time, he raised a palm to strike at Shen Qiao.

Xiao Se and Bai Rong couldn't continue watching from the sidelines. They immediately entered the circle of battle and attacked Shen Qiao one after the other.

However, when martial experts battle, anything can happen in an instant. The moment they attacked, they heard Yan Shou scream miserably, and blood sprayed from amid the sword screen before splattering on the ground once the sword glare faded.

An arm tumbled from the roof onto the ground. Everyone stared at it—Yan Shou had lost his arm. He stumbled backward, almost falling from the roof, his face contorted in hideous agony as he sealed an acupoint to stem the blood flow. Naturally, he could no longer continue the fight.

Baoyun exchanged several blows with Shen Qiao, then realized with a shock that Shen Qiao hadn't exhausted his strength even after his battle with Yan Shou. His sword qi remained abundant, continuous, and unending. Baoyun considered the pros and cons, then decided that even if he could win this match, it'd be a costly win. Moreover, he didn't hold any deep-seated grudges toward Shen Qiao, and killing him wouldn't benefit him much either. So he only used around half his strength to prevent Shen Qiao from killing Yan Shou, and they fought each other for a while.

Until Xiao Se shouted from his end, "Elder Baoyun, Elder Yan isn't looking good!"

Aside from losing his arm, Yan Shou's body was riddled with injuries, both large and small, internal and external. He'd lost far too much blood. Even though he'd sealed his acupoint to try to stem the bleeding, even redirected his qi and regulated his breaths, he was still unable to slow the blood loss enough. Even more fatal was that in Yan Shou's moniker of "Buddha with the Bloodstained Hand," the "bloodstained hand" referred to his now-severed right one. Without this right arm, even if he could keep his life, his martial prowess would plummet—to a martial arts practitioner, this was the most fatal of blows.

On top of his loathing for Shen Qiao, he also hated Baoyun and the rest for just standing by and watching. Under the weight of his combined rage and panic, he simply passed out.

Hearing Xiao Se's words, Baoyun took the chance to withdraw. "Shen Qiao, you now owe us a debt for injuring an elder of our Hehuan Sect. Hehuan Sect will definitely do everything in our power to collect on it!"

"There's no time like the present," said Shen Qiao coolly. "Why choose another day when we can settle the accounts now?"

Upon saying this, he swept toward Yan Shou with his sword—he wanted to kill him while the man was helpless to defend himself!

Baoyun was stunned; he hadn't expected this level of persistence from Shen Qiao. He immediately chased after him, sending a palm strike in his direction.

Bai Rong had flown over as well, and she shaped her slender hands into blue lotus blossoms, her demeanor exquisite and charming, almost too lovely to take in.

However, Shen Qiao swung his sword horizontally, and his sword screen suddenly shifted through a myriad of transformations. It dissolved Baoyun and Bai Rong's attacks, and even knocked Bai Rong's palm strike off course to hit Baoyun.

Baoyun yelled angrily, "Bai Rong!"

"Oh no!" Bai Rong said sweetly, "Elder Baoyun, please forgive me! It was this hateful scoundrel's fault!"

Her steps were as graceful as a swaying lotus, her sleeves like their flourishing blooms. Phantoms emerged one after another, growing densely around Shen Qiao as they blossomed forth. It was a gorgeous scene, but a glance was enough for those in the know to realize that this dense field of lotuses was actually a dense field of true qi. This was what made the "Blue Lotus Seals" so formidable: if the user possessed great martial strength, each "lotus" would contain a terrifying amount of true qi, their attacks surging like the tide, unceasing and endless as the waves in the back drove the ones in the front, each more powerful than the last.

Bai Rong's Blue Lotus Seals looked powerful beyond compare, but Shen Qiao, within touching distance, could sense that the true qi within her every strike held not even half of the internal energy she'd used the first time he'd seen this technique.

Baoyun had no plans to fight Shen Qiao any longer. While Bai Rong and Xiao Se were hampering their opponent, he picked up the unconscious Yan Shou and made to leave. From a great distance off came his final words: "Hehuan Sect will seek your guidance another day!"

Being injured, Xiao Se had never had the desire to fight in the first place. When he saw Baoyun leave, he wanted to leave as well, but Shen Qiao had already turned his attention to him, and Shanhe Tongbei followed right after. Another slash carved itself into his back, and fresh blood gurgled forth, dyeing his clothes red. With a cry of pain, he pushed his qinggong to its utmost without looking back. In the blink of an eye, he'd already melded into the boundless night, and his silhouette vanished completely.

Shen Qiao wanted to pursue him, but Bai Rong obstructed him, and he was unable to disengage. They were on completely different sides, and she'd taken no small number of lives, but she'd shown mercy to Shen Qiao two or three times, especially back at Bailong Monastery. If she hadn't impeded Xiao Se then, perhaps Shen Qiao and Shiwu could never have escaped and survived.

As such, Shen Qiao refused to consider her fondness for him, but he couldn't be too cold to her either. Right now, Bai Rong was stalling him, preventing him from pursuing Baoyun and the others, but he couldn't attack her seriously. He inevitably grew sullen and frustrated.

Seeing his expression, Bai Rong burst into giggles, then ceased her attacks.

Shen Qiao saw that she'd suddenly come to a standstill, and he also withdrew his sword and pulled back.

"Since we parted beneath Bixia Sect, this one has been tossing and turning in bed every night, yearning to see you again," said Bai Rong, beaming. "Today I see that Shen-lang's martial arts have greatly improved, enough that no one can push you around ever again. Only then was I comforted. But even though I'm this infatuated with you, and I've shown you mercy and support time and again, you're so rough and violent whenever you see me! How heartless of you!"

There wasn't even a hint of sorrow or surprise in her expression, so it was difficult to tell how genuine her words were.

Shen Qiao said earnestly, "I shall always keep your kindness in my mind. I will never forget it."

Bai Rong covered her mouth as she laughed. "I was just saying it because I could, yet you actually took it so seriously! Still, you're so good-looking no matter what you do! Even I can't help but wish for more intimacy with you!"

She made to come forward, startling Shen Qiao. He took three large steps back, but Bai Rong stopped in her tracks and giggled.

Shen Qiao only felt that her thoughts were as impossible to read as Yan Wushi's. Truly, they proved themselves to be from the same demonic discipline—they certainly had some things in common.

"Do you know where Yan Wushi is luring Sang Jingxing?" he asked.

Bai Rong nodded. "I do. They were heading toward the foot of the mountain. If my guess is correct, Yan Wushi most likely wants to use the city walls as cover to shake off Sang Jingxing!"

Shen Qiao was anxious to chase after them; he turned right around to leave.

But Bai Rong wouldn't let him go. "We haven't seen each other in so long. Is this the kind of attitude you should show your savior?"

"Thank you for the information," said Shen Qiao. "If there's anything else, let's leave it for another day!"

"Shen Qiao!"

When he heard her yell out his full name, he halted his steps and looked back.

Bai Rong's smile had already left her face, and complicated emotions lurked in her lovely, peach blossom-shaped eyes as she gazed straight at him. "I haven't thanked you yet," she said. "In Hehuan Sect, Yan Shou has never liked me. Now that you've injured him gravely, I'll have one less powerful enemy within the sect. However, Shen-lang, in the end, I'm still a member of Hehuan Sect. Next time we meet, if you continue to oppose Hehuan Sect, I can no longer show you any mercy."

Shen Qiao was silent for a moment. "You wish to become the leader of Hehuan Sect?"

Bai Rong was a bit taken aback, but she immediately returned to being sweet. "And I thought Shen-lang was completely indifferent to me. I didn't expect you'd guess this."

Shen Qiao sighed, thinking of the unceasing internal strife within Hehuan Sect, of how their members were all cruel and heartless. There were many things he wanted to say to dissuade her, but in the end he held his tongue. He only cupped his hands at her instead. "I wish you all the best and hope that you take care of yourself. May we meet again."

Bai Rong watched his retreating figure in the distance, then stuck out her tongue. "Foolish Shen-lang!"

As he run, Shen Qiao executed his qinggong to the utmost, his body flying ahead. But even after spending over half the night in pursuit, he still saw no trace of Yan Wushi or Sang Jingxing.

Logically speaking, Yan Wushi's martial arts had yet to recover, so Sang Jingxing must have been able to catch up to him after giving chase for so long. Even if the two of them had run as they fought, it was impossible that Shen Qiao still hadn't caught up to them after over half a night with the speed of his qinggong. By now, Shen Qiao had realized that Bai Rong had probably tricked him. She'd pointed him in completely the wrong direction, deliberately making him waste his efforts.

But even if he returned to that small temple now to seek payback, Bai Rong would not be there.

Shen Qiao stopped, panting slightly. He lowered his head to look at Shanhe Tongbei in his hand, then looked up and gazed into the distance.

After wasting over half the night, and with no idea where to go, what hope did he have of finding a single person?

Shen Qiao remembered the words Yan Wushi had spoken before he'd left. He closed his eyes and forcibly suppressed his churning emotions.

As if it could sense its master's complicated, ineffable feelings, Shanhe Tongbei began to rattle in its sheath.

Dawn arrived as a trace of milky white creeping over the vast and boundless horizon, as if eager to break free of the abyss in order to bring light to all the world.

One word silently surfaced within Shen Qiao's heart:

Chang'an.

• • •

The northward journey to Chang'an wasn't a long one. Shen Qiao's pace was fairly brisk, but because he didn't travel both day and night, it still took him several days.

As he neared Chang'an, Shen Qiao had already sensed that something was amiss.

From time to time on the official roads leading into the capital, he'd find exiled families of guilty officials heading away from the city. There were also some conscripted laborers and convicts being sent to Chang'an on the orders of government officials. He'd seen such things in the past as well, but they hadn't been common. To see two waves of this on the same day was definitely out of the ordinary.

While resting at a tea pavilion, Shen Qiao saw a family whose hands and feet were shackled. Led by soldiers on horseback, they stumbled along, looking rather wretched.

The soldiers escorting them wanted to rest, so the group stopped to take a seat at the tea pavilion. But no such treatment was afforded to the exiled family—they remained sitting outside the tea pavilion without even a drink of water.

Shen Qiao whispered a few words to the pavilion's waiter, then walked to the table where the soldiers were sitting.

"Meetings are ordained by fate. This humble Daoist wishes to treat the two gentlemen to a cup of water. Would the two be willing to accept this favor?"

At this time, Shen Qiao had already changed back into the fluttering fabric of his Daoist robes. Even without speaking, he resembled an eminent master of great enlightenment, and when he did, his voice was gentle and pleasant, giving him an aura that drew people in. Yuwen Yong had prohibited both Buddhism and Daoism, but the common folk's high regard for both schools had never been extinguished. Furthermore, a glance at Shen Qiao was enough to tell that he wasn't an ordinary Daoist at all. The two soldiers didn't dare put on airs, but immediately rose to return the greeting. "How could we let this Daoist master treat us? How about he sit down, and we can chat instead?"

This had been Shen Qiao's intention in the first place. He took the opportunity to say, "This humble Daoist vowed before the venerable immortals to earn ninety-nine merits within three years, and at this time he lacks only one. Would the two gentlemen help him accomplish this by letting him offer some tea to the people outside as well, so that they may quench their thirst?"

The soldiers smiled. "The Daoist Master is so compassionate. Please, go ahead."

Shen Qiao asked the waiter to send the tea over, and the criminal family was of course moved to tears. He then took the opportunity to ask, "On this humble Daoist's return to the capital, he has seen many families of guilty officials being exiled. Has something significant happened within the city? Or did those officials offend His Majesty?"

"Oh," said a soldier. "They've indeed offended His Majesty. His Majesty wanted to renovate the imperial palace. The fathers, brothers, or husbands of these people were court officials who came up to raise their objections. They infuriated His Majesty and brought this disaster upon themselves."

Shen Qiao was confused. "Renovate the palace? From what this humble Daoist knows, His Majesty is hardworking and frugal, as well as very strict on himself. He doesn't seem like one who'd indulge in comfort and pleasure."

But the soldier replied nervously, "I must offer you some advice, Daoist Master. You must not say these words after entering the city! The previous emperor was indeed frugal and compassionate toward the people, but the current emperor is different. His Majesty did not even observe his father's death for a month, and he forbade the people as well. There's even less to be said about the ones who raised their objections!"

Hearing these words, Shen Qiao's expression fell completely, his heart thumping in his chest.

Yuwen Yong had died?!

# 82

# The New Emperor

THE SOLDIER SAW the great change in Shen Qiao's expression but took it as him being unable to accept the truth so quickly. He consoled him: "The previous emperor never liked Buddhism or Daoism, but now that His Majesty has ascended to the throne, the restrictions on Buddhism and Daoism have been relaxed. He's even redesignated Buddhism as the state religion. You'll be able to walk about freely in Chang'an, Daoist Master. You no longer need worry about being interrogated."

Shen Qiao gave a wry smile. Was this what they meant by "every cloud has a silver lining"?

"Then why wasn't His Majesty willing to observe his father's death?"

The moment he asked this, the two soldiers immediately grew nervous. They glanced around them, checking that no one was paying attention, then whispered, "How could we know something like that? It's better not to ask too much about it, Daoist Master!"

Shen Qiao asked further, "Then do you know what's happening with the Prince of Qi, Yuwen Xian?"

Both soldiers shook their head, indicating that they didn't.

As soldiers, they were on the bottom rung. The Prince of Qi's whereabouts indeed wasn't something they should be concerned with.

Since that was the case, there wasn't much Shen Qiao could ask. He thanked the two men and finished his tea. On seeing them prepare to resume their journey with the family of the guilty, he bid them farewell. He then loosened the reins he'd tied to a nearby fence and vaulted onto his horse before riding in the direction of Chang'an.

Shen Qiao didn't notice too much change upon entering Chang'an. It was still as hectic and bustling as ever, with people coming to and fro in endless streams. Compared to the other provincial capitals he'd visited, it was many times more prosperous. The only difference was that there were more government officials on the streets, especially on the main roads to the imperial city. Some were patrolling, others were escorting criminals. There were both male and female criminals, young and old, just as Shen Qiao had seen outside the city. Fearful worry was written all over their faces, making them seem somewhat incongruent within the lively city.

Shen Qiao stopped to watch them for a while. There were children in the group, and he found their crying and wailing hard to take. But he knew very well that even if he did rescue them, even if the family had been wrongly accused, he'd have no place to relocate them to. In the end, it might cause them to suffer even more.

On top of that, in the future, there'd probably be even more people who'd end up in similar situations.

Saving one family was easy. Saving all the people of this world was hard.

He sighed to himself and averted his gaze, then turned and left.

He first went to the Junior Preceptor's residence, Yan Wushi's original residence in the capital. He didn't approach the building—only gazed at it from afar. Unsurprisingly, the manor had already been sealed off. The gates were locked, the yard before the main building deserted. Land in the capital was enormously expensive, and this was the only area that even the carriages avoided, as though everyone were afraid that they'd be implicated in a crime and so kept their distance.

Though there were a couple of vegetable sellers nearby with people purchasing from them, a close look at their expressions was enough to tell that something was off. They didn't seem like normal vendors but more like they were purposely loitering in the area.

In the past, Shen Qiao wouldn't have thought twice about approaching these people and asking questions, but now, having spent enough time with Yan Wushi, he'd been subconsciously influenced. He also knew it best to observe all the minutiae. At this time, he'd sensed that something was amiss, so he didn't approach them further.

Bian Yanmei had two houses in the capital. One was the official mansion gifted by Yuwen Yong, similar to the Junior Preceptor's residence, while the second was a private manor few people knew about—though it still wasn't a secret. Last time Shen Qiao had been in Chang'an, Bian Yanmei had misunderstood his relationship with Yan Wushi and personally showed him the place, then warmly welcomed Shen Qiao inside as a guest. Shen Qiao hadn't known whether to laugh or to cry.

The official mansion was like the Junior Preceptor's residence: it'd been sealed off, and there were people in disguise around it, secretly monitoring the area.

However, the private residence was still there, and though the gates were shut, they weren't locked.

This private manor of Bian Yanmei's was located in the depths of an alley in the west of the city. Those living nearby were mostly gentry scholars with modest family properties. Lacking the endless streams of senior officials' carriages or the din of a merchant market-place, it made for an excellent hiding place.

Shen Qiao didn't open the gates; instead, he vaulted over the wall.

With his martial arts, even this leap was made soundlessly, his pose confident and graceful.

The manor was rather tidy and clean, the plants neatly arranged. There wasn't a speck of dust anywhere, but it was cold and deserted, without a trace of life.

Shen Qiao walked around the interior once, pushing open every door and entering each building, but found nothing.

Where had Bian Yanmei gone?

In recent years, Huanyue Sect's influence had been coupled with the regime of Northern Zhou. Yuwen Yong had granted them a lofty position and relied on them like his left and right limbs. Chang'an was equivalent to Huanyue Sect's main headquarters, but of the three demonic sects, Huanyue Sect was a bit special. Yan Wushi had only accepted two disciples, Bian Yanmei and Yu Shengyan, while the rest of their forces were scattered across different locations, giving the impression that they were lacking in manpower. Now that everyone had left the capital, hunting for them was like searching for a needle within the ocean.

A small sound suddenly came from the eastern wing. It was very faint and sounded like someone had accidentally bumped into a table.

And it just happened to come from the last building that Shen Qiao had yet to investigate.

The person in the house seemed to be suppressing their breathing as much as possible, but with Shen Qiao's ears, he could still hear them clearly.

He pushed the door open and slowly walked toward the folding screen.

The sound of stifled breathing grew heavier and heavier. Shen Qiao stopped in front of the bed, then bent down and reached out.

A surprised shout came from beneath the bed. Before Shen Qiao could touch the other person, a small figure had already scampered out, running toward the door.

But she hadn't gotten very far when she suddenly halted in place, and even her mute acupoint had been tapped, leaving her unable to make a sound. She could only show an expression of great terror.

"Don't be afraid," she heard someone say.

"I came here in search of an old friend, but I didn't expect my old friend's entire family to have moved away," the handsome, almost otherworldly Daoist explained gently as he circled to stand in front of her. "That's why I entered to take a look. Who are you?"

Someone like this didn't seem like a bad person, no matter how she looked at it. Her heartbeat slowly calmed down.

Shen Qiao unsealed her mute acupoint.

The girl was quite young, and the dust all over her face failed to conceal the fair skin beneath. Judging by her clothing, she should be from a wealthy aristocratic family, a child who'd been pampered from birth. He had no idea why she'd run here.

"Who are you?" the girl gathered her courage to ask back.

Shen Qiao smiled. "My name is Shen Qiao. I'm a Daoist priest from Xuandu Mountain."

"Shen Qiao?" The girl seemed to be pondering it. "'Shen' as in elm sap, from the *Book of Rites*? And 'Qiao' as in Mount Yuanqiao, from the *Liezi: Questions of Tang*?"

"Yes, precisely those two characters." Shen Qiao marveled at this girl's depth of knowledge at so young an age. "And which family are you from? Why are you hiding here?"

Ultimately, the girl was still small—regardless of how mature she seemed, she couldn't maintain the image for too long. When she heard his words, her face washed over with relief. "I've heard Uncle mention Daoist Master Shen before. Daoist Master Shen wasn't ordered to find me, was he?"

Shen Qiao was left a bit confused by her digression. "Who's your uncle? And who would have ordered me?"

"I'm A-Yan from the Dou family. My mother is Princess Xiangyang."

Shen Qiao finally understood. "So your uncle should be the previous emperor?"

Dou Yan nodded. "My home is being monitored. Those people wanted to enter the palace and meet His Majesty, so I had to secretly run away. At first, I planned to come here and look for Uncle Bian, but I didn't find anyone. And there are people looking for me outside, so I'm too scared to leave..."

Shen Qiao frowned. "Just what is going on? Your mother is the previous emperor's older sister and the current emperor's aunt. Who would dare to make things difficult for you?"

Just as he said these words, he realized: other than the emperor, who'd dare to make things difficult for them? So it had to be the emperor, didn't it?

Dou Yan bit her lip, as if she found it hard to talk about. Shen Qiao decided not to keep pressing her for answers. Instead, he gently said, "I'm afraid the people here have long left already. It's pointless to stay here waiting for them. Why don't you head home first. With your mother there, surely His Majesty wouldn't dare do anything..."

"No, no! I can't go home!" Dou Yan repeatedly shook her head. "If I go home, His Majesty will summon me to the palace, and Mother and Father won't be able to stop him. My life will be in danger!"

THOUSAND AUTUMNS

Hearing the seriousness of the situation from her words, Shen Qiao was also temporarily at a loss. He was about to ask about her plans now when a loud burst of noise came from outside. Footsteps soon followed, coming in their direction. Then, right after, there was the sound of the manor's gates being forcefully shoved open.

"This isn't an important location. Its residents have probably already left. There's no need for your lot to come in; I can go in and check by myself."

The voice saying these words was somewhat familiar, and after Shen Qiao thought hard for a while, he recalled a person.

Puliuru Jian.

Alarmed, Dou Yan hid behind him and tugged at his sleeve. "Let's go, hurry! Let's go!"

When she saw that Shen Qiao didn't move, she paused her steps, then directly ran back into the first building. She'd probably gone to hide beneath that bed again.

Dou Yan had just run inside when Puliuru Jian strode over, and he just happened to come face-to-face with Shen Qiao, still in the courtyard.

Shen Qiao's expression was placid. Instead, it was Puliuru Jian who was stunned at the sight of him.

"You..." He'd just managed to say that one word when he immediately shut his mouth again. He sent a glance outside, then gestured at Shen Qiao, signaling at him to stay quiet.

Shen Qiao understood the hint and nodded his head, waiting for Puliuru Jian to speak first.

Puliuru Jian's eyebrows knitted tighter and tighter, as various expressions flickered over his face. It seemed like he was hesitating over what to say.

Instead, it was Dou Yan who moved first. When she heard no further sounds from within the building, she couldn't help but tiptoe out, plastering herself against the wall to peek outside. But though she thought she was being sneaky, Puliuru Jian noticed her. Surprise came over his face as he walked forward. Dou Yan was so frightened she almost ran back inside.

"Does Daoist Master Shen know where Bian-dafu[10] has gone?" He put all his effort into keeping his voice as low as possible, but he spoke at a rapid-fire pace.

Of course, Shen Qiao shook his head.

"I have received a request that I'm unable to fulfill at present," said Puliuru Jian. "So, I can only trouble Daoist Master Shen to lend me a hand. Please help me escort the Dou family's young lady to the Su family for refuge!"

*Su family?* Shen Qiao's face betrayed his puzzlement.

"The Duke of Meiyang County's residence!"

Right at this moment, a loud voice came from outside. "Dare this one ask if the Duke of Sui has found anything? Does he require this lowly one's assistance?"

Puliuru Jian quickly replied in a loud voice, "No need! I'm coming out now!"

He was unable to explain further and could only cup his hands at Shen Qiao, before turning and leaving in a hurry.

The faint sounds of conversation came from the gates. After a moment, the entire group left, and the gates were closed and locked once more.

Dou Yan poked her head out of the building, her expression anxious.

---

10    大夫. A general suffix for court officials.

Shen Qiao said to her, "Everyone's left. The Duke of Sui asked me to bring you to the residence of the Duke of Meiyang County first, to take refuge there. What do you think?"

Dou Yan thought for a while. "That will do. The Duke of Meiyang County has always been on good terms with Father. Father should have made the request. Then I must trouble Daoist Master Shen. Will this be a burden on you?"

Shen Qiao smiled. "No, not at all. It is no harder than lifting a finger."

He picked up Dou Yan, lightly vaulted over the wall, and followed her directions, taking the side roads to the Su residence. Dou Yan had never seen such perfected qinggong before, and she spent the entire journey gaping in astonishment. By the time they arrived at the Su residence's back gates, her gaze toward Shen Qiao was filled with awe and reverence.

Shen Qiao couldn't help but stroke her head with its double buns. Then he entered the Su residence by once again vaulting over the wall by the back gates.

Dou Yan whispered the directions to him. "After we pass this courtyard, the second building ahead of us is the study. I've gone there with Father before. The Duke of Meiyang County is usually there during the daytime..."

With Shen Qiao's abilities, infiltrating the Su residence was a bit like using a sledgehammer to crack a nut. Su Wei was perfectly at peace, reading in his study, when two figures, one large and one small, suddenly shoved the doors open and entered. Caught off guard, he almost yelled in shock.

Fortunately, he did recognize Shen Qiao and Dou Yan, and he forced down the words he'd been about to blurt out before switching to a more normal tone. "Daoist Master Shen? Dou-erniang?"[11]

---

11   二娘. Literally "second daughter," can be seen as the female counterpart to erlang.

Dou Yan slid down from Shen Qiao's arms and said crisply, "Uncle, please don't be alarmed. A-Yan didn't come here with any ill intentions!"

Su Wei quickly rose and opened the door, peering outside. When he'd determined that no one was eavesdropping, he closed it again, then asked behind him, "Why did you come here? A-Yan, I heard that the Dou residence has been surrounded by His Majesty's people—they're looking for you."

Dou Yan spoke, downcast. "Yes. It's my fault. I brought so much trouble to my parents. His Majesty fears that my parents have hidden me away, so now he's currently keeping a close eye on my family. I can't return for now. I can only come and plead for Uncle to protect me."

"I met the Duke of Sui at the Bian residence," Shen Qiao said. "He was the one who asked us to come find Duke Su."

Su Wei sighed. "Very well. Come with me."

He didn't ask for more details. He must have already known about the situation beforehand. Instead, it was Shen Qiao who felt like everything had been outside of his expectations since he'd entered Chang'an. All he could do now was take things as they came.

Su Wei stood to push aside a bookshelf, revealing the secret entrance hidden behind it. Then he led them through the door and through a hidden passage until they finally arrived in another building.

This building wasn't dark—sunlight could enter through the windows, which were shaded on the outside by a tree. The rays filtered faintly through the leaves and into the building. If it were summer, the building would be an excellent place to spend a vacation in, but in the same way, its location was well concealed and difficult to discover.

Next to the window stood a man, facing away from them with his arms behind his back. When Su Wei pushed the door open to enter, the man turned and saw Dou Yan. He couldn't help his astonishment. "Erniang?"

Dou Yan's behavior the entire trip had been rather precocious, but when she saw this man, she couldn't stop herself from wailing, "Fifth Uncle! My uncle, the previous emperor, was killed by my cousin!"

All three men's faces paled with shock.

# Alarming Danger

"E RNIANG, do you know what you're saying?" Yuwen Xian almost suspected his ears had failed him.

Dou Yan sniffled. "I saw everything, I was just to the side. His Majesty was on the bed, gravely ill. Then Cousin came over, and he said...he said..."

Having suddenly met her close family member, she was a little agitated and flustered, unable to even form complete sentences.

Yuwen Xian placed a firm hand on her shoulder and helped her sit. "Don't panic," he said. "Take your time."

Su Wei personally poured some water and handed it to her.

Holding the warm cup, Dou Yan gradually regained the strength to speak. "Cousin came over to visit His Majesty," she said, "but then he said to him: 'Why haven't you died yet? The sooner you die, the sooner I can succeed the throne. Each day you linger is another day I can't relax. I went to all this trouble to get you bedbound in the first place, yet you just won't stop breathing! Tormenting me for no reason!'"

Dou Yan was a precocious child and well versed in the classics, so it wasn't difficult for her to repeat this conversation word for word. Previously, she'd even admonished Yuwen Yong, telling him to uphold his responsibilities toward the country even in the face of slander and to not treat Empress Ashina so coldly. Yuwen Yong adored this niece of his very much, even lamenting that she hadn't been born a man. He'd raised her since she was small, keeping her close by—when Dou Yan was even younger, she'd spent several years in the palace. Though she returned home later, she could still enter and leave the palace freely, without needing to pass through layers of checkpoints like most other people.

Dou Yan was renowned for her intelligence in the imperial family. Yuwen Xian didn't doubt the veracity of her words in the slightest, and his shock and outrage were plain on his face. "He really said something like that?"

Dou Yan nodded. "After His Majesty fell ill, Cousin's long-repressed temper gradually began to reveal itself. I didn't want to meet him too much, so when I heard that he was coming, I found myself a place to hide within the bedchamber. That's how I heard Cousin say that to His Majesty... His Majesty was furious and called him unfilial and insolent. He even wanted to have someone draft an imperial edict to remove the crown prince, but Cousin told His Majesty not to waste his efforts, and then...then..."

Her hands clenched around the cup and her face was pale—she was unable to conceal her terror. It was as if she'd returned to the scene on that day, when she'd hidden behind the thick curtain and saw, through a gap in the drapes, Yuwen Yun standing next to the emperor's bed. He'd leaned over, drawn up the blankets covering Yuwen Yun's body, and then...

"He smothered His Majesty! Yuwen Yun smothered His Majesty! I saw it all!" Dou Yan began to sob, unable to stop herself.

For a time, no one in the room spoke. There were only the sounds of heavy breathing and Dou Yan's weeping.

Yuwen Xian's expression flickered like the shifting clouds. He was frozen in place, stunned into silence.

Su Wei held a look of unfading horror. He'd always done his best to avoid court politics, to live peacefully away from any government offices. He'd refused to take up any official position no matter the invitations Yuwen Yong sent. The only reason he'd taken the risk to shelter Yuwen Xian was due to his close personal relationships with the likes of him and Puliuru Jian. He'd never expected to hear such an earth-shattering inside story about a treasonous plot for imperial power.

Fathers and sons slaughtering each other within the imperial household was no shocking news, but Yuwen Yun had already been instated as crown prince for a long time—the imperial throne was set to pass into his hands, sooner or later. If even under these circumstances, Yuwen Yun had been so impatient, so eager to kill his father, he was truly devoid of all conscience.

Shen Qiao asked Dou Yan, "Yuwen Yun knew that you overheard him? Is that why he's seeking to capture you?"

Dou Yan nodded, her eyes red. "As I was hiding inside, I didn't dare to move even a little. I was terrified that Yuwen Yun would find me, so I only came out after he left. When he went outside and announced the news of His Majesty's death, I took advantage of the chaos to rush out. But Yuwen Yun saw me and suspected that I saw him murder His Majesty, so he sent people to my house to tell me he wanted me to enter the palace, under the pretext of wishing to reminisce with his cousin."

"Do your father and Princess Xiangyang know about this?" asked Su Wei.

"Cousin has always been paranoid," she replied. "I was afraid that if they knew what happened, they'd let something slip in front of him, so I dared not reveal anything to them. Father and Mother believe I am only wracked with grief over the previous emperor's passing. Cousin sent people to our house as soon as he ended the national mourning period. I was afraid that Father and Mother wouldn't be able to stop him, so I secretly ran away by myself. I wanted to go the Bian residence and seek help there, but it turned out everyone was already gone."

At this moment, there came the sound of knocking. Su Wei opened the door and went out; a moment later, he returned with a bowl of piping-hot noodle soup.

"A-Yan must be hungry," he said. "Eat something first."

Dou Yan was only a young child after all, not yet even ten. Regardless of how bright and composed she was, she had gone without meals for some time. When she saw that bowl of noodle soup, she couldn't stop herself from drooling. She lowered her head and began to eat without a second word, the composure from her lavish upbringing vanishing without a trace as she practically wolfed the soup down.

Yuwen Xian's heart ached at the sight. He couldn't help but say, "Eat slowly, lest you choke."

"Did the former emperor fail to realize that Yuwen Yun was such a person?" asked Shen Qiao. He too had met Yuwen Yong once, and the man hadn't seemed like he'd be so foolish.

Su Wei realized that he'd yet to introduce Shen Qiao, so he said to Yuwen Xian, "Your Highness the Prince of Qi, this is Daoist Master Shen, from Xuandu Mountain."

Yuwen Xian sighed. "Daoist Master Shen might not be aware, but back when the former emperor was still alive, he was very strict in disciplining the crown prince. He knew that the crown prince was an alcoholic, so he forbade so much as a drop of alcohol from entering the Eastern Palace. The crown prince had been dissatisfied for a long time, but as long as the former emperor was alive, he could only buckle down and endure it."

He didn't need to say anything more; Shen Qiao already understood.

Because Yuwen Yun had repressed himself for so long, his nature had inevitably become twisted, turning him tyrannical and murderous. But his father had been in his prime, and he didn't know when he'd be able to succeed the throne. Unable to wait any longer, he went in for the kill.

As for whether Yuwen Yun would have been able to assassinate Yuwen Yong by himself, even considering his status as crown prince, that question was irrelevant at the moment. Yuwen Yong had prohibited Buddhism and Daoism, vanquished Northern Qi, and he'd been preparing to go to war with the Göktürks. His enemies were everywhere, and there were many who'd have been willing to work with Yuwen Yun to bring him down. Even considering only Empress Ashina, who was conveniently in the position closest to Yuwen Yong, she would have had far more opportunities than most.

Shen Qiao suddenly thought of Yan Wushi and his previous evaluation of Yuwen Xian, his inferences on Northern Zhou's imperial court and its situation. Right now, one by one, they were coming true.

When he recalled that scene within the small temple, his heart trembled slightly, and he couldn't help but draw in a deep breath to forcibly suppress it.

"I heard outside the city that Yuwen Yun has been busy erecting new buildings and constructing palaces," he added. "And that he's also arrested many people who submitted memorials advising him against this?"

Shen Qiao wasn't a citizen from Zhou, and Yuwen Yun was also very unpopular. No one thought it inappropriate that he'd addressed the emperor by name.

"It's a long story," said Su Wei. "After the former emperor passed away, in accordance with the rites, he should have been in mourning for over a month. But His Majesty only observed it for a dozen or so days before he declared the mourning period over. Many people from the court submitted their advice at that time, asking His Majesty to observe filial piety, but His Majesty said that since the ancestors of the Yuwen clan were Xianbei people, there was no need to observe Han etiquette, and that the ministers shouldn't babble nonsense about the affairs of the imperial family. If anyone tried to advise him afterward, he unilaterally declared them rebels and traitors, then punished them with flogging and exiled their entire families from the capital."

"His Majesty also complained that the palace he's currently living in is too cramped and lacks the splendor appropriate of the imperial family," Yuwen Xian added. "Therefore, he wanted to renovate the palace and build a garden outside it for members of the royal family to hunt in. The previous leadership's conquest of Qi had already exhausted a fair amount of both manpower and finances, but the former emperor refused to impose heavier taxes on the common folk. Instead, he had his people confiscate all the valuables obtained from the Qi palace and placed them in the national treasury. But the moment His Majesty ascended the throne, he took these valuables and transferred them into his personal treasury..."

He smiled bitterly. "Many people submitted memorials because of this and were quashed by His Majesty."

Shen Qiao frowned. "A brilliant father, yet an unworthy son! Such a pity!"

Would the Zhou Dynasty's fortunes, that had seemed to be rising like the sun, truly come to an end in his son's hands?

Yuwen Xian shook his head. "The Daoist master is focused on the martial path, so he may not understand the intrigue and infighting that takes place within the imperial court. With this move, His Majesty appears to be diverting funds for his own use, but in truth, he's using the opportunity to eliminate dissidents and probe out the people who are truly loyal to him. Those strongly attached to the previous emperor, or those who are unwilling to wholeheartedly follow His Majesty—His Majesty will naturally take the initiative to uproot them, lest he leave behind any lurking perils. After all, His Majesty spent many years as the crown prince, so he's naturally experienced when it comes to plotting and scheming like a ruler."

"Indeed," said Su Wei icily. "He's completely ignorant in the matters of statesmanship, but a born genius when it comes to eliminating dissidents—to the point His Highness the Prince of Qi was forced to seek me out for refuge!"

Yuwen Xian let loose a bitter chuckle.

Recalling how Yan Wushi once spoke of wishing to support Yuwen Xian, Shen Qiao said, "If this humble Daoist may speak frankly, there goes an old saying: just causes will garner great support, while unjust ones find little. I fear that Yuwen Yun's perverse actions have rendered the previous emperor's blood and sweat to naught, and the Zhou Dynasty's excellent prospects will also be ruined as a result. Now that Qi has been annexed, it's on shaky footing. The Göktürks are also eyeing the situation covetously as they wait for an opportunity to take action, but the Prince of Qi has always been a man of prestige..."

Yuwen Xian gestured his acknowledgment. He didn't put on any act of being alarmed or bewildered; rather, he said with a dejected expression, "I know what Daoist Master Shen wishes to say. After His Majesty ascended the throne, he confiscated my military authority and ordered others to monitor my residence day and night. My entire household, both young and old, are being held under house arrest. Leaving aside the great kindness the previous emperor showed me, I've never possessed such intentions. If I really did conspire against the state, wouldn't I be doing exactly as he wants and making it easy for him to brand me a rebel and traitor?"

"Daoist Master Shen might be unaware," said Su Wei, "but after the previous emperor passed, His Majesty began removing the bans he'd imposed, one by one. He also reinstated Buddhist Master Xueting as state preceptor—the Noble Consort Yuan currently by his side is also a lay disciple of the Buddhist Master's."

With a great buddha like Xueting overseeing things, eliminating Yuwen Yun through assassination would be completely impossible. To say it more directly, as someone who held little leverage, Yuwen Xian was unwilling to start an open conflict over this issue.

Dou Yan had long finished her noodles. Her complexion had become rosy again as she listened intently to the conversation.

Yuwen Xian took notice of this and smiled. "I haven't thanked the Daoist master for escorting A-Yan here."

"It was no hardship," said Shen Qiao. "The Prince of Qi need not dwell on it."

"Did you come here for important matters in Chang'an, Daoist Master?" Yuwen Xian asked.

"I was entrusted with something by an old friend," said Shen Qiao. "I'd come to the capital wanting to see how the former emperor was doing, but unexpectedly, I was a step too late."

"This old friend you speak of, is it Junior Preceptor Yan?"

"Correct. Even as early as the group ambush, Sect Leader Yan had already foreseen that great changes might suddenly descend upon the capital. Before, he said to me that if anything should happen to the former emperor, I should look for the Prince of Qi."

Yuwen Xian smiled bitterly. "I understand what Sect Leader Yan meant, but he overestimated me. As of now, I hold very little military authority. What would I gain from starting a war, other than creating rivers of blood and causing innocent people to lose their lives?"

"But Your Highness surely cannot simply sit idle and wait for your demise?" Su Wei protested. "You've led troops for many years and hold incredible prestige among the military. You may have no soldiers now, but if you rise and sound the call, many people will answer. At that point, there may still be a chance to turn things around."

"And what if that Yuwen Yun holds my family hostage?" Yuwen Xian said angrily. "What can I do then? Are you saying that I should disregard their lives and focus only on achieving the throne? Then what difference would there be between Yuwen Yun and myself? Such actions are neither reasonable nor justifiable. Yuwen Yun is the rightful successor; even if he really did that to the previous emperor, how many people could know? If I bring my men and charge into the palace, with Xueting there, he could easily take Yuwen Yun and retreat. Then they could declare him king in some other place, and the Zhou imperial court would be plagued with internal strife once more. The north we managed to unify with such difficulty would vanish completely. Those were the things my brothers and I laboriously fought for all these years. How can watch myself become the criminal who plunged the Zhou Dynasty into turmoil?"

Su Wei said nothing.

Dou Yan seemed to understand. Tears on the verge of falling glimmered in her eyes.

Shen Qiao couldn't hold back yet another sigh.

Some people were bound from birth to be kind and tenderhearted.

It didn't matter whether they'd killed before, or even how many they might have killed. During these times of turmoil, these types could never become conquerors of great and ruthless ambition. Even if Yuwen Xian knew what to do, he still wouldn't be able to do it.

"Wuwei, you've always been reluctant to interact with the imperial clan," he went on. "The reason we can be so amicable and close is because I'm different from the imperial clan members who place so little importance on human life. But now you're actually urging me to take that road?"

Su Wei gave a long sigh, then cupped his hands in a bow. "I was the one who misspoke. Please forgive me, Your Highness!"

Yuwen Xian stopped him. "You're the one who understands me best. Others might say that I was born a rich aristocrat with military power, that I galloped across the battlefields and slaughtered countless enemies, but if I had a choice, I would never have joined the army. I'd rather find a place with verdant hills and crystal waters, take my entire household there and do some gardening. Now that would be a true paradise on earth!"

But the heavens toy with men—now the mighty Prince of Qi, renowned throughout the land, could only hide here and languish.

Seeing everyone in low spirits, Yuwen Xian instead took the initiative to ask Shen Qiao, "What does the Daoist master intend to do?"

Shen Qiao thought for a moment. "Does the Prince of Qi know where Bian Yanmei went?"

Yuwen Xian shook his head. "After the previous emperor passed, the Bian residence was vacated overnight. No one knows where they went. I suppose Bian-xiong must have long anticipated the current disaster, so he fled very early on. He's much more far-sighted than I am."

"If Daoist Master Shen doesn't mind," said Su Wei, "why not stay at our Su residence for now? You did us a great favor in the past, and it's often on my mother's mind. My younger brother also admires Daoist Master Shen's moral character and martial arts. Now that this coincidence has occurred, I can also bring my mother and brother to pay you a proper visit."

Yuwen Yong had died and Bian Yanmei had disappeared. Though Shen Qiao wished to find Yan Wushi quickly, he had no idea where to start searching. He could only slowly make inquiries about Huanyue Sect's or Hehuan Sect's activities. Chang'an was well connected as a location—news arrived here much faster than it did in other places, so staying here temporarily wouldn't be a bad choice.

With this in mind, Shen Qiao replied, "Then I'll be troubling the Duke of Meiyang County."

Su Wei smiled. "You need not be so courteous, Daoist Master. You can simply call me Wuwei."

They were still talking when they heard a knock from outside. Su Wei went to open the door and was greeted by a trusted maid standing beyond it. "Sir, two people have arrived at the back door, one adult and one child. The former said that he was a personal soldier of the Prince of Qi, named Yan Ying. He said that he's come with the youngest master from the Prince of Qi's residence and wishes to speak with Your Highness."

Su Wei frowned. "How did they know that the Prince of Qi was here with me?"

But Yuwen Xian answered. "If it's Yan Ying, he truly is one of my right-hand men in my army. Perhaps it was my princess consort who told him to bring Qilang here for refuge. Let's allow them in first. I'll go meet them."

Su Wei led them through the dark passage they'd taken earlier, moving from the study to the guest hall, where the maid hurriedly left to deliver his message. After a moment, a young man entered, followed by the maid with a young boy in his arms.

Yuwen Xian was both surprised and delighted. "Yan Ying! You brought Qilang with you?"

The other man fell to his knees with a thud, his eyes filled with hot tears. "Your Highness, you've worried Yan Ying so much!"

"Rise, rise!" said Yuwen Xian brightly. "Men should not shed tears so easily! Why are you kneeling; stand up!"

He took the little boy from Yan Ying's arms, and the child held Yuwen Xian's face with both hands. After staring at him intently for a while, he suddenly said, "Father, you've lost weight."

Yuwen Xian hugged him tightly. It was a long time before he finally let go. "How did you find this place?" he asked.

"Ever since Your Highness vanished, the capital has been flooded with rumors, saying that the bastard Yuwen Yun was..." He trailed off under Yuwen Xian's stare. Reluctantly, he amended, "...That the emperor was keeping you under house arrest in the palace. The Prince of Qi's residence has been surrounded for many days, so we were all beside ourselves with worry. But without your word, we dared not take any action. Wei Xu said that we must act in case something happens at the residence, so he had me seek out the princess consort to ask for your whereabouts, then bring all the little masters out one by one and escort them somewhere safe in case the emperor does something in a rage!"

"So the princess consort had you take Qilang away?" Yuwen Xian said.

"Yes," said Yan Ying. "She said that Qilang is the youngest and has yet to be registered in the genealogy records, so even if something happens, he'd be hard to track down. That's why she had me bring Qilang to you."

His own princess consort had already thought of the worst-case scenario. Yuwen Xian's heart ached, and he could only clutch the little boy tighter.

But Su Wei's face was grave. "Tell us: Was it Wu Xian who told you to do this? Did anyone follow or see you when you were making your way over with Qilang?"

Yan Ying thought long and hard. "There shouldn't be," he said. "I was very careful..."

He'd just finished speaking when Shen Qiao's expression shifted, and suddenly he stood up.

Everyone couldn't help but look at him. "Daoist Master Shen?"

"There are many soldiers on horses coming this way, right now!"

Everyone's expressions abruptly filled with alarm. Su Wei roared, "Quick, into the secret passage!"

But Yuwen Xian said, "It's too late. They must have tailed Yan Ying here and surrounded the Su residence in a bid to catch everyone in one go. If the Su residence doesn't turn anyone over, His Majesty will never let this go!"

Yan Ying slapped his thigh in frustration. "Could it be? Did that bastard Wei Xu predict the princess consort would trust me and tell me your whereabouts? Is that why he told me to seek her out, so that he could tail me here?"

As they spoke, a large troop of soldiers on horses had already arrived outside the Su residence, and they pounded thunderously on the gates like a raging flood. It could even be heard in the guest hall, far as it was.

The Su residence's steward rushed over to report. "Master, we're in trouble! There are a lot of people outside, and they say that they're to apprehend the Prince of Qi on His Majesty's orders. If we don't open the gates, they'll storm right in. What should we do?!"

Yuwen Xian gave a long sigh. "Fortune and misfortune are both determined by fate. What's ordained to come, must come. Fate has ordained that I'm unable to escape. Go open the residence gates; I'll depart with them. They must not hurt anyone in the Su family!"

Su Wei stopped in his tracks. "What do you mean, go?! Even if you don't go, my Su family will still be indicted for harboring a fugitive! Why worry so much? You go hide first and I'll go deal with them—surely they won't dare to tear down our house!"

"It seems that the Duke of Meiyang County has no respect for His Majesty whatsoever. He'd rather harbor a fugitive and bring down his entire family!" A cold laugh drifted over from afar, yet it was crisp and clear.

Su Wei, who had no internal cultivation at all, suddenly felt each of those words drumming against his heart, making it jolt hard.

At the head of the people who'd entered was Yuwen Qing, whom Shen Qiao had traveled to Chen with. But he wasn't the one who had spoken; it was someone behind him.

This man was no stranger to Shen Qiao either. When he saw Shen Qiao, a slight expression of surprise crossed his face—then he immediately sneered. "Daoist Master Shen, what a small world. How come I always meet you wherever I go?"

"Murong Qin," Shen Qiao said coolly. "Is Chen Gong well?"

Murong Qin smiled. "Naturally, he's doing very well. I forgot to tell Daoist Master Shen—His Majesty has already named my master the Duke of Zhao, for his great service of bringing him the Tai'e Sword."

# 84

# Kill to the Last

C HENG GONG had split open Tai'e's hilt with carnelian back underground in Ruoqiang, retrieving the Zhuyang Strategy scroll inside. To think that he'd bring the sword back with him and have it reforged! It was a famous sword from the Warring States period, and its reputation had swelled because of Qin Shi Huang:[12] it was as though anyone possessing that sword would become the ruler of the entire world. It no longer had any use to Chen Gong, but gifting it to Yuwen Yun was obviously an attempt at pleasing him, and he'd succeeded.

Since Chen Gong could take to being Gao Wei's subordinate like a fish to water, it was little trouble to him to deal with Yuwen Yun, who was a similar kind of man.

As they watched a large group of men on horses surge in from outside, enclosing the Su residence within a watertight circle, the faces in the room took on a myriad of expressions—some terrified, some enraged, and some collected.

Su Wei's mother, Madam Qin, had also seen the disturbance. She walked out, accompanied by her second son Su Qiao. Su Qiao had spent much time wandering the jianghu and didn't possess the same restraint as those involved in government: the moment he saw what was going on, his tone froze over. "What are you trying to do,

---

12 秦始皇. The first emperor of unified China, who established the Qin Dynasty.

Yuwen Qing? My Su family has done nothing wrong nor offended anyone. Why are you bringing all these strays here?"

At the implication that he was a "stray," anger flashed across Murong Qin's face, but he immediately suppressed it.

Yuwen Qing seemed to have been suddenly assigned to this task and absolutely didn't want any clashes with the Su family; hearing these words, he smiled. "Su-erlang, it's been a while. A few days ago, I heard that you went to Qingcheng Mountain. I didn't expect you to return so soon."

Then he turned and greeted Yuwen Xian, Su Wei, and Madam Qin one by one. He also spoke to Shen Qiao like a familiar friend. "Daoist Master Shen, since our last parting, this Qing has often kept you in his thoughts. I trust that your health has improved greatly?"

Shen Qiao inclined his head. "Thank you for your concern. I've gotten much better."

"That's good, that's good." Thanks to Yuwen Qing's quick thinking, the tense atmosphere instantly relaxed quite a bit.

Only now did Yuwen Qing cup his hands at Yuwen Xian, getting down to business. "Someone has accused the Prince of Qi," he explained. "They said that the Prince of Qi was involved in the previous emperor's illness and passing. His Majesty is furious and has ordered me to bring you to the palace so you can explain yourself. If it's a wrongful accusation, you will receive justice."

"Nonsense!" Yan Ying was the first to snap. "His Highness the Prince of Qi was devoted and loyal! How could he harm the previous emperor? This is no more than an unfounded attack!"

Shen Qiao couldn't help but glance to the side. Dou Yan was hiding behind Yuwen Xian, and there was both alarm and surprise on her face.

He'd always been slow when it came to scheming and plotting, and he'd always been willing to take others in complete good faith. But after everything he'd been through, Shen Qiao too had begun to follow Yan Wushi's ways when it came to approaching problems.

Yuwen Yun knew that Dou Yan had seen his act of patricide. And his uncle had also held much military power for a long time, with a whole slew of impressive military achievements. Terrified that Yuwen Xian would become a threat, he'd simply opted to land the first strike by pinning the crime on Yuwen Xian. Whether people believed it was not a concern. Dou Yan was just a little girl; even if she did speak the truth, it would only become one of many rumors.

After all, he was Yuwen Yong's son. No matter how foolish he was, there was no shortage of methods he could employ as the ruler. In comparison, Yuwen Xian was too passive.

Today's events were unlikely to end well.

Naturally, everything Shen Qiao could think of, Yuwen Xian could too. Within the span of a moment, many thoughts passed through Yuwen Xian's mind.

In truth, back during Yuwen Yong's reign, Yan Wushi had sought him out. He'd told him clearly that he was willing to use Huanyue Sect's power and influence to support him in accomplishing great things, replacing Yuwen Yun as the crown prince. But Yuwen Xian hadn't agreed. Later, when Yuwen Yong suddenly became bedridden from serious illness, Bian Yanmei too had insinuated that he needed to start making preparations. But at that time, Yuwen Xian still hadn't made up his mind, and in the end, he was unwilling to do something so subversive to heaven's will.

Bian Yanmei didn't urge him any further. In the end, after Yuwen Yong passed, everyone within the Bian residence vanished without a trace in the span of a night. In contrast, thanks to that one mistake of his, Yuwen Xian had fallen into the situation Yan Wushi predicted.

Yan Wushi had once told him that the moment Yuwen Yong passed, Yuwen Yun would definitely move against his uncle.

And now, things had proceeded exactly as he said.

Yuwen Xian heaved a sigh. With an indescribable emotion twisting in his heart, he turned to Yuwen Qing and said, "I am completely loyal to our sovereigns; the sun and moon can bear witness. The previous emperor knew this, and His Majesty knows this. The entirety of the court and military knows this as well. The day His Majesty passed away, I indeed visited the palace, but at that time, His Majesty was drowsing, so I left within fifteen minutes. I only knew of His Majesty's passing afterward, so how could I be involved?"

Yuwen Qing's expression was uncomfortable. "Your esteemed words should be said before His Majesty, Prince of Qi. I'm only here as the messenger; I have no authority!"

"If the Prince of Qi enters the palace," said Su Wei coldly, "will he be able to leave in one piece?"

Yuwen Qing's mouth snapped shut, and he didn't speak. In truth, there was no need to answer this question: everyone already knew the answer.

"Yuwen-dafu," Murong Qin said suddenly. "When we left the palace, His Majesty told us that this matter cannot be delayed. The faster we finish, the better!"

Displeasure surfaced on Yuwen Qing's face, but in the end, he didn't refute Murong Qin. Instead, he said to Yuwen Xian, "You heard him too, Prince of Qi. I must ask your esteemed self to please come with me."

"Your Highness, you must not go," said Yan Ying anxiously. "There's no coming back. Everyone in the world knows that this is an unjust accusation, but the emperor will never let your esteemed self go. If you give my lowly self but a single command, I will stake my life on fighting our way out of this encirclement!"

Murong Qin sneered. "His Majesty has already ensured that there will be no escape, wherever you go. Martial experts are lying in ambush all the way from here to outside the city. Even if you manage to leave this place, leaving the capital is impossible! Let's look at the bigger picture now. Everyone in the Prince of Qi's family, both young and old, is still within your residence. Is your esteemed self so callous as to watch them lose their lives?"

Yan Ying roared, "Murong Qin, you despicable scoundrel! You wretched backstabber! What right do you have to say such things!"

Madam Qin suddenly said, "For many generations, my Su family has upheld a great and illustrious reputation. Moral character is ingrained within our bones, and we lack any cowards or reprobates. The Prince of Qi has galloped across the battlefield and made great contributions in establishing the Zhou Dynasty. Everyone knows this, and the common people hold him in great respect. How can you reduce him to a prisoner based on a single false charge? If His Majesty has any doubts, I'm willing to use the Su family's name to guarantee the Prince of Qi's innocence!"

"That's right," Su Wei said as well, "Our Su family is willing to testify on behalf of the Prince of Qi!"

"Whether you testify or not," said Murong Qin icily, "you'll have to tell that to His Majesty himself. Don't obstruct us in our official duties. Today, we will take Yuwen Xian with us. The rest of you need not say any more!"

Su Qiao glared at him, furious. "And what if we refuse to let you take him away?"

Murong Qin slowly drew his saber from its sheath. "Then I have no choice but to commit this offense."

"Murong-xiansheng!" Yuwen Qing's words were filled with warning. "This is the Su family's second son, but he's also the personal disciple of Chunyang Monastery's Daoist Master Yi, on Qingcheng Mountain!" He turned to Yuwen Xian. "Murong-xiansheng's words were indeed correct, Prince of Qi. Even if your esteemed self escapes, the people within the Prince of Qi's residence cannot. I beseech you to consider this carefully."

"And if I don't escape, will His Majesty let the people from my residence off?" Yuwen Xian gave a miserable smile and then put Yuwen Song down. He turned to Madam Qin and the others, then suddenly gave a deep bow. "Yuwen Xian gave your esteemed residence much trouble these last few days. I ask the Madam to forgive me. I'm grateful for your protection, but one must bear the consequences of their own actions. I will leave with them today—don't implicate yourselves because of one Yuwen Xian."

"Prince of Qi..." said Madam Qin.

Yuwen Xian took several steps forward and held out his hands to be arrested. Yuwen Qing waved his hand, and the soldiers on either side immediately came forth to grab him.

"Your Highness!" cried Yan Ying.

"Please take care of Qilang, Yan Ying," said Yuwen Xian. "Take him away from the capital, to his uncle's house..."

Yet Murong Qin said, "The Prince of Qi worries too much. Whether it's your esteemed self's children or your subordinates, not a single person from the Prince of Qi's residence will be able to leave the city without the emperor's permission."

Yuwen Xian's face fell in horror. "I've already surrendered myself for arrest, but His Majesty still does this to us? Does he wish to kill us to the last?!"

Murong Qin paid him no heed. "Soldiers, seize Yuwen-qilang as well!"

Yan Ying placed himself before Yuwen Song, shielding him, as though he were ready to protect the child even at the cost of his life.

As if Murong Qin would take him seriously. He pushed aside the soldiers next to him, his saber flickering alongside him. Within three moves, Yan Ying was already on the ground. With an expression of contempt, Murong Qin reached out to snatch Yuwen Song.

A sword suddenly appeared before him.

The hand holding that sword was incredibly lovely, fair, and slender. As perfect as jade, without a single flaw.

Murong Qin was in no mood to admire it. Without thinking, he reached out to grab the sheath. But the moment he was about to grasp that sheath, he suddenly recognized the sword, and realized the identity of its wielder.

And then he recalled a scene within the Ruoqiang ruins, when Shen Qiao had fought the pack of apes alone.

He couldn't help but pause for a moment.

And this momentary lapse meant that the sheath was no longer within his reach. Murong Qin quickly stepped backward, evading the wind from the sword as it swept toward his face.

Looking at him properly, Shen Qiao hadn't even drawn his sword.

His Daoist robes fluttered, and he looked like an immortal: elegant and graceful, detached from the world. He looked more harmless than anyone else present.

However, Murong Qin knew that it was a sham. Even if he'd looked down on Shen Qiao before, after Ruoqiang, he could never

be contemptuous of the incredible strength within this Daoist ever again.

He composed himself and said coldly, "Daoist Master Shen, were you born in the year of the dog? Why is it that every time I meet you, you're always sticking your nose where it doesn't belong?"

"You haven't even reached a conclusive verdict on whether the Prince of Qi is guilty, yet you're dragging in a child?" Shen Qiao said.

Murong Qin sneered. "He had the guts to assassinate the previous emperor. Naturally, his entire family must pay the price."

Dou Yan couldn't take it anymore. She yelled shrilly, "The Prince of Qi didn't hurt the previous emperor! He was killed by Yuwen Yun!"

Other than Su Wei and Shen Qiao, who already knew the story, everyone's expressions filled with alarm.

Yuwen Qing couldn't help blurting out, "What did you say?!"

"Misleading others with heresy!" bellowed Murong Qin. "Capture her, don't let any of them escape!"

At his words, Tuoba Liangzhe and Murong Xun also swept in from outside. One of them grabbed at Dou Yan, the other leapt at Yuwen Song.

The two children were utterly powerless to put up a fight. They couldn't even see their attackers' movements clearly and could only watch helplessly as they closed in.

However, neither Tuoba Liangzhe nor Murong Xun managed to make contact.

A sword glare swept over to the two men, brimming with true qi. Like the wind gusting through the towers before a mountain storm, it was forceful enough that the two of them reeled back several steps.

"Who dares to lay a hand on them while I'm here?" said Shen Qiao.

His every word was tranquil and calm, yet within them was a pressure that seemed to weigh a thousand tons.

Murong Qin gave a savage smile. "Let me see, then, Shen Qiao. How are you going to protect them all by yourself!"

His sword slashed in a horizontal arc as he charged forward, sweeping toward Shen Qiao.

"Who said that he'll be by himself?!" yelled Su Qiao.

He blocked Murong Qin with his sword, then turned his head to shout to Shen Qiao, "Hurry, take them away!"

"So, your Su family intends a rebellion?!" raged Murong Qin.

"What we want is not rebellion but justice!" Madam Qin's sandalwood wooden cane thudded heavily into the ground. The cane instantly split into two, and she pulled out a longsword from within. Its blade was like autumn water and infused with murderous intent. A single glance was enough to tell that the weapon was renowned and precious.

Su Wei hadn't known that the cane always by his mother's side had held such an incredible secret. For a moment, he was dumbstruck.

The two sides immediately fell into a disordered mass of fighting, and the Su residence transformed into a battlefield. Yan Ying still wanted to rescue Yuwen Xian, but Yuwen Xian yelled, "If I leave with you, it will serve to confirm my guilt in plotting the previous emperor's murder! Take Qilang and leave with Daoist Master Shen. Run as far as you can and never come back!"

"Your Highness!" Yan Ying's eyes bulged with rage—he couldn't accept this.

Instead, it was Yuwen Song who spoke. "Father wishes to use his death as an admonishment, to clear the emperor's mind? That way this chaos will abate too."

"Exactly, now hurry up and go!" Yuwen Xian was both gratified and sorrowful. Gratified at how wise and clear-minded his youngest

son was at such a tender age—in the future, he would be outstanding within his generation. But he was sorrowful that he would never
have the chance to see him grow up. "If you take me with you, you'll
never be able to leave. Furthermore, I cannot abandon everyone still
at the Prince of Qi's residence!"

Yuwen Song suddenly fell to his knees and kowtowed thrice at
Yuwen Xian.

Tears flowing down his cheeks like rain, Yuwen Xian turned his
head away.

Yan Ying's eyes were bloodshot. He gritted his teeth and quickly
ran forward to pick up Yuwen Song, then ran over to meet up with
Shen Qiao, who was carrying Dou Yan. With the help of the cover
provided by Su Qiao and the others, the two of them rushed out of
the Su residence in the direction of the city gates.

A scream came from behind them, closely followed by Murong
Qin's callous voice. "In the event that Yuwen Xian resists, His
Majesty has commanded that he be killed on the spot to serve as a
warning to others."

While Murong Xun and Tuoba Liangzhe were holding off
Madam Qin and the others, Murong Qin had taken the opportunity
to kill Yuwen Xian. He'd even deliberately made more noise, letting
Shen Qiao and the others hear it.

"Bastard!" Yan Ying was so enraged, he halted. In his arms, Yuwen
Song had tears streaming down his face.

"Don't turn back!" yelled Shen Qiao. "We need to get out first!"

Murong Qin had already caught up to them from behind.
Holding Dou Yan in one arm, Shen Qiao turned around and slashed.
However, Murong Qin had once been the number one martial expert
in Qi, and now he was also Chen Gong's right-hand man—naturally,
a single slash wouldn't be enough. His figure flitted swiftly, and his

swordplay was unpredictable—he excelled at discerning and striking at his opponents' weak points. But Murong Qin knew very well that Shen Qiao was no longer someone he could kill, so he kept close to him and only targeted Dou Yan. This would distract Shen Qiao by forcing him to protect Dou Yan, thus revealing openings. At the same time, it'd slow Shen Qiao down.

Surrounded by the flash of weapons, Dou Yan's face was full of terror, yet she said nothing. She only clung tightly to Shen Qiao's neck so as not to distract him for even a moment.

Murong Qin said severely, "Shen Qiao, you're carrying a little child, and on top of that you need to tend to those two. Waiting for you on the road from here to outside the city gates are martial experts even stronger than I am. How far do you think you can get by yourself?!"

Shen Qiao remained unmoved. "With the Dao, even tens of thousands of enemies will be unable to cease my advance."

His sword qi surged, and Murong Qin was unable to withstand it—as if he'd been struck heavily on the chest, he spat out a mouthful of blood.

However, he didn't cower away from the fight but laughed instead, the sound full of mockery. "Dao? And just what is this Dao of yours? During these tumultuous times, only might makes right! If your Dao were of any use, why did you suffer setback after setback? Why did you lose even your position as Xuandu Mountain's sect leader? If your Dao were of any use, why has the 'enlightened ruler' you so believed in yet to appear?"

At these words, Shen Qiao gave a faint smile.

This smile was like a breeze caressing spring waves, stirring up ripples within people's hearts. It seemed capable of placating even the rage of the rivers and mountains.

The nearby Dou Yan stared at him in a trance. Suddenly, she forgot her fear, forgot that she was in danger and surrounded on all sides. Many decades later, she would still never forget this smile.

However, Shen Qiao spoke not a word, for concealed within this smile were thousands of words of meaning.

Those who'd understand would understand. As for those who didn't, what point was there in wasting your words?

People of different Dao must go their separate ways.

The falling leaves rustled, the chill wind whistled. His once stolid and majestic swordplay underwent a dramatic change, suddenly filling with destructive force. This was the new set of sword techniques that Shen Qiao had created after the battle with Kunye at Bixia Sect, born from him merging his comprehension of the sword into his swordplay. Every single move was simple and straightforward, without any fancy tricks, and Murong Qin too thought that he'd parried them. But somehow, every time he tried to block and counter, his saber would involuntarily veer off or simply fail to achieve the desired effect. Instead, it felt like Shen Qiao was leading him around by the nose.

Shen Qiao held Dou Yan with one arm, fending away his opponent with the other. Yet he still managed to force Murong Qin into a situation where he was helpless to fight back!

Another mouthful of blood spilled forth. Murong Qin slammed hard into the wall behind him, and before he could react, the tip of Shen Qiao's sword quivered once, and his sword qi turned substantial, striking an important acupoint in his shoulder and leaving him unable to move.

Shen Qiao had no desire to fight, so he didn't pause for even a moment. With a tap of his toes, he swept toward Yan Ying.

At this moment, Yan Ying had brought Yuwen Song almost to the city gates. Having come from a military background, his martial skills lay in the life-or-death struggles found on the battlefield—his qinggong wasn't particularly advanced. At this moment, he mustered up his entire strength, hoping that he could dash out of the city and take Yuwen Song far away from the danger, to fulfill the Prince of Qi's final request.

Something whistled through the air.

He tilted his head to avoid the arrow shooting over from atop the nearby city gates.

As expected, it was as Murong Qin had said: soldiers had been lying in ambush for a while. Every single one of them had their arrows nocked. As long as they released thousands of arrows in tandem, Yan Ying and Yuwen Song would be perforated like honeycomb.

Yan Ying didn't pause for a moment; instead, he sped up. Dropping his chin, he said to Yuwen Song, "Qilang, you must listen to me. In the next moment, I shall shield you. Once this shower of arrows abates, they'll need to re-nock their arrows. Take this short respite to run along the city walls. There lies a small door that is unlocked. I'll guard your back—only think about running forward. Daoist Master Shen is right behind us, and he'll catch up very soon. At that time, just follow him. Pay no heed to anything else, and whatever you do, don't look back! Do you understand?!"

Yuwen Xian had dearly loved Yuwen Song from a young age, believing him to be the most promising of all the Yuwen family's children, and this was proof of how intelligent he was. How could he fail to understand the implication behind Yan Ying's words? Hearing these words, he gritted his teeth hard. "Uncle Yan!"

Yan Ying knew he'd understood. His lips stretched in a grimace as he evaded the arrows pelting down from above. A short while later, his back was pierced through with arrows, but he only grabbed Yuwen Song harder, his feet not slowing for even an instant.

He raced toward the unlocked side door while carrying Yuwen Song. Many soldiers wielding spears came to impede him, but he beat each of them back.

"Go! Hurry up and go! Run outside!" he yelled and released Yuwen Song.

"Don't shoot, hold!" A figure dashed atop the city gates, stopping the soldiers who were preparing to fire a second volley of arrows.

When the gate guards saw who the newcomer was, none of them dared to act rashly. However, the person next to the guards said, "Continue shooting. Without my command, no one's allowed to stop!"

"Hold!" Puliuru Jian yelled. "Commander-in-Chief, His Majesty didn't order you to kill the Prince of Qi's entire family. Why are you doing this?"

Liu Fang laughed. "Duke of Sui, I remember that the Prince of Qi, Yuwen Xian, once advised the previous emperor to be wary of you. Yet you don't hate him—instead, you're stepping forward to speak for him? What is the logic here?"

"The Prince of Qi's advice to the former emperor was simply him carrying out his duties," said Puliuru Jian. "It was his desire to help the public. I'm not so wretched that I lack even this tiny amount of tolerance. But this child is innocent—why not let him go, Commander-in-Chief? Consider it a good deed!"

Liu Fang reconsidered. Yuwen Xian held incredible prestige with both the court and the common folk. Now, the emperor's attack had been too abrupt, so many people were caught off guard and unable to respond. Once this storm passed, there would certainly be many people coming forth to plead on behalf of the Prince of Qi's family. So why should Liu Fang involve himself in something so inauspicious?

"Very well," he said. "I'll leave the Duke of Sui some face. However, I must remind you that it's useless even if I show mercy. His Majesty has already dispatched martial experts to lie in ambush outside the city. Even if this child manages to leave these gates, only death awaits him still."

Puliuru Jian's heart thumped once, and he couldn't resist turning to look at the area beyond the city.

From high up, he saw, crystal-clear, Yuwen Song stumble out of the city gates, but three people were already walking toward him.

One was bald.

One was missing an arm.

And the last had all his limbs, an impressive air about him.

Any of those three would count as top-class martial artists within the jianghu. Using them to surround a little child was truly like cracking a nut with a sledgehammer.

Puliuru Jian didn't recognize the bald man, nor the one-armed one, but he did recognize the leftmost one.

"Chen Gong? His Majesty places so much importance on Yuwen Song that he sent even Chen Gong?"

Everyone knew that Duke of Zhao, Chen Gong, had won the emperor over and was his new favorite official. He'd presented him with Tai'e and introduced Hehuan Sect to him, thus diluting the authority of the Buddhist discipline. While they were at it, Hehuan Sect also replaced the influence Huanyue Sect once had in their close relationship with the crown. Yuwen Yun was leaping to establish a system of checks and balances, and so Chen Gong garnering his favor had gone as smoothly as water flowing through a canal.

At Puliuru Jian's side, Liu Fang said, "One must pull the grass up by the roots. Everyone speaks of how gifted and intelligent Yuwen-qilang is. His Majesty fears that letting him go will be like returning a tiger to its lair, thus planting latent threats for himself in the future."

During their conversation, Yuwen Song had already stopped in his tracks. He stared at the three people before him, as if he didn't know how to respond.

Baoyun smiled at him. "Yuwen-qilang, I advise you not to run anymore. His Majesty ordered us to capture you, dead or alive. If you listen and return with us, you'll save yourself much physical suffering."

Puliuru Jian watched from afar and sighed to himself. Was even the last of the Yuwen family bloodline doomed to vanish here?

As he thought this, he saw a man's silhouette flit over from within the city. When the man saw that the gates were shut, he simply leapt into the air. As if he were treading on clouds, he soared up and up—before anyone on the wall could react, he'd already flown past them and was drifting downward, now below the walls.

Like a river nymph stepping gracefully on the waves, his feet picked up nary a mote of dust. A rainbow stretching across the heavens, scattering into the distant winds.

This level of qinggong had truly achieved transcendence. Even those like Liu Fang and Puliuru Jian were already dumbstruck, let alone the other soldiers.

"Addressing the three gentlemen who lost to me. Please forgive this humble Daoist for arriving late."

As if he'd descended from heaven, Shen Qiao landed before the trio, holding Dou Yan in his arms.

# A Radiant Showing

EVERYONE HAD ALREADY been long acquainted with each other. No introductions were needed for their reunion this time. One of Yan Shou's arms had been lost at Shen Qiao's hands, so the moment he saw him, his murderous intent surged. More than anyone else here, he wished to kill Shen Qiao and satisfy his hatred.

But Chen Gong still managed to smile. "It's been a while since we parted at Ruoqiang. Has Daoist Master Shen been well?"

Shen Qiao seemed unwilling to speak with him—he didn't even bother with a perfunctory response.

In the past, Chen Gong had possessed an astonishingly high sense of pride. Whenever he encountered someone looking down on him, he'd explode into a rage, rolling up his sleeves to brawl with them without a second word. However, times had changed. Now he held great power and standing, so his outlook and mind had expanded to match. Not only did Shen Qiao's cold shoulder fail to anger him, he instead began to persuade him with a pleasant smile. "Daoist Master Shen, Buddhism and Daoism were prohibited for a long time, but the moment His Majesty ascended, he removed those bans. Does the Daoist Master understand what this means?"

Shen Qiao still remembered. Back then at the broken-down temple, Chen Gong had regarded even a single donkey-meat sandwich as a treasure, and he'd barely been able to read. Yet now, he was talking to Shen Qiao about the emperor's goal in lifting the bans of Buddhism and Daoism. In all likelihood, the stepmother who'd thrown Chen Gong out of the house would scarcely be able to dream what her stepson had become in the present. When he compared the two, Shen Qiao could only feel that life was truly unpredictable and unfathomable, especially during turbulent times. As long as a person was willing to throw away their shame and ethics, as long as they were ambitious, bold, and unscrupulous enough, they could become like Chen Gong: a role model who'd encourage others to advance themselves to greater heights.

"What does it mean?" Shen Qiao asked indifferently.

Chen Gong smiled. "It means that His Majesty holds no prejudices toward Buddhism and Daoism," he said. "Regardless of which discipline, as long as they're willing to pledge allegiance to the court, His Majesty will extend to them fair and equal treatment. Daoist Master Shen is from Xuandu Mountain—once, you were chosen as its sect leader, one who was absolutely dutiful. Yet villains took advantage of you and stole your position. If you wish, His Majesty is willing to fully support you in recovering your position. Currently, Xuandu Mountain's standing within the Daoist discipline is gradually being supplanted by Qingcheng Mountain, but with the court's support, regaining its glory as the world's foremost Daoist Sect would be as simple as snapping one's fingers. What does Daoist Master Shen think?"

Dou Yan was bright. Though what he was saying about the various power factions within the jianghu was beyond her knowledge, she could discern the intent at persuasion within Chen Gong's words. The other side had three people, yet they seemed so terrified of the strength of this Daoist master carrying her that they'd rather try luring him in with benefits first than come to blows with him.

*Was this enough to persuade Shen Qiao?* Dou Yan was a little anxious, and she couldn't help but clutch his lapels a little tighter.

Out of the corner of her eye, she saw Yuwen Song, whose hand was currently in Shen Qiao's. Though his face was stiff, his gaze too revealed some anxiousness—he was clearly worried about the same thing.

Baoyun joined in. "That's right, Daoist Master Shen. Eternal friends don't exist in this world, and neither do eternal enemies. Hehuan Sect has offended you in the past, but that was because we were on different sides, serving our own masters. Before, Sang Jingxing told me that the reason you fell into his hands back then was that Yan Wushi restrained you and served you to him, then lured him in with his words. That's why he made such an oversight. In the end, our common enemy should be Yan Wushi. His Majesty wishes to draw in talent from all over the world. Our Hehuan Sect was at odds with the Buddhist sects in the past, but now we are all willing to dedicate ourselves to His Majesty. If the Daoist sects join in as well, it would make for an even more wonderful story. Once the world is unified, Daoism's standing will surge like a boat on rising waters. With how much His Majesty values Daoism, His Majesty would be absolutely delighted to grant you even the position of state preceptor, never mind Xuandu Mountain's sect leader."

He'd already witnessed Shen Qiao's strength that day—Yan Shou's arm had been severed before his eyes. Baoyun had assessed that even if he fought Shen Qiao, his fate wouldn't be much better than Yan Shou's.

As for Yan Shou, he wished to exact revenge for his arm, but he was not blinded by hatred—against such a powerful opponent, he naturally couldn't take him on alone.

If Bai Rong were here, she would certainly be filled with awe.

When she'd first met Shen Qiao, he had been blind and downtrodden, without even a shred of martial arts. He could only lie down to be trampled by others. Yet within the short span of a few years, Shen Qiao, who'd once had nothing, whom everyone could walk over, had climbed back up, step by step, to the point where even Hehuan Sect elders wouldn't be willing to battle him without preparation.

"When the previous emperor was alive, I once entered the palace and met him," Shen Qiao said. "At that time, he already mentioned his willingness to lend me a hand, to make Xuandu Violet Mountain a cornerstone of Daoism. If I were going to agree, I'd have agreed back then. Why would I wait until now? If we were to discuss prestige and integrity, surely the previous emperor was more reliable than Yuwen Yun."

His contempt for Yuwen Yun was clear in his words.

"Very well," said Chen Gong. "It seems like Daoist Master Shen would rather risk himself for these two utterly unrelated little children. This Chen will give you a reminder out of consideration for our past friendship. To do this is to directly oppose the court. From now on, the Buddhists, Hehuan Sect, and even members of the court itself will never accept you. Once the Zhou Dynasty unifies the world, you'll become the common enemy of everyone beneath heaven. Have you thought it through carefully?"

Shen Qiao showed an expression of slight astonishment. "Friendship?" he repeated. "What friendship do we have? The friendship whereby you sold me out for personal gain, where in order to avoid becoming Mu Tipo's male concubine, you directed the disaster to me?"

To think a day would come where this kind gentleman could jeer at someone. If not for Chen Gong's utter shamelessness, and his terrible impression of Hehuan Sect, Shen Qiao wouldn't have spoken these words either.

At this mention of the past, a strange expression flashed over Chen Gong's face—there was embarrassment, guilt, as well as rage. It was like his face had been physically ripped off; he seethed with pain.

"You're always behind the times, Shen Qiao," he sneered. "Since that's the case, you can't blame me."

Yan Shou had been gnashing his teeth at Shen Qiao for a while. In his eyes, Baoyun's and Chen Gong's words were utter drivel. In the jianghu, agency was given according to one's fists—the one who punched the hardest, whose martial arts were the strongest, had the final say. The loss of his arm that day was a deep shame, one that he'd never forget his entire life. Regardless of whether Shen Qiao agreed to Chen Gong's persuading, he would kill him. So as soon as those words were out of Chen Gong's mouth, Yan Shou suddenly sprang forth, throwing himself at Yuwen Song next to Shen Qiao with the speed of lightning.

His goal was clear: he'd attack Yuwen Song, distracting Shen Qiao by forcing him to protect him and reveal a weak point.

Yan Shou's speed was immense. His plan had only just formed, and his hand had already reached Yuwen Song, just about to graze his hair. As expected, Shen Qiao lifted his sword to block, and Yan Shou had already predicted this—he suddenly twisted to strike at Dou Yan within Shen Qiao's arms!

If this blow connected, landing right on the crown of Dou Yan's head, it was certain the girl's skull would split open and she'd die, hemorrhaging all over her face.

Naturally, Baoyun and Chen Gong didn't just sit back—the moment Yan Shou attacked, the two of them moved as well, attacking Shen Qiao from separate directions.

Chen Gong's martial skills seemed to have improved again since Ruoqiang. His sword moved like the rolling waves, as swiftly as a poisonous snake, accompanied by layers of rippling true qi. A careful study revealed that his martial arts contained extraordinary multitudes—they were the amalgamation of the strengths of multiple schools.

Chen Gong began as a court favorite. Shen Qiao had given him a glimpse of the martial path, but the one who'd personally taught him martial arts was Mu Tipo. However, Mu Tipo's martial prowess could only be considered second-rate, and Chen Gong quickly realized that what he could learn from him was limited. With his incredible talent and perfect memory, he began to set ever-grander goals. After he began following the Emperor of Qi, Gao Wei, Chen Gong was naturally able to meet even more of Qi's martial experts. Among these were Murong Qin and the people of Hehuan Sect. Chen Gong integrated the martial arts he'd learned from the Zhuyang Strategy scroll that he'd unconsciously memorized, and unbeknownst to himself, he began to climb higher and higher up the martial path.

As someone this gifted, akin to fine jade, he might not be inferior to the likes of Shen Qiao or Yan Wushi—he could even surpass them. If Tao Hongjing were here, he'd also have praised him, declaring him a heaven-blessed prodigy. Tumultuous times produced not only heroes but ambitious conquerors as well. This world had given Chen Gong plenty of space to extend himself. He was destined to be extraordinary.

Here and now, the sword move he struck against Shen Qiao seemed to contain a modified version of Murong Qin's saber techniques but also a branch of Zhongnan Sect's sword techniques. It carried both the severe imperiousness of the saber as well as the flitting agility of Zhongnan Sect's sword. The sword qi rose in flurries, like white snow or fluttering catkins, drifting down flake by flake. They seemed everywhere yet almost imperceptible, and so they were difficult for an opponent to read.

Yan Shou was filled with loathing, while Baoyun was waiting for a chance to strike Shen Qiao unawares. On top of that, Chen Gong kept oppressively close with every step he took. None of the three were easy pickings, yet Shen Qiao used only one arm to fend them off, still holding Dou Yan in the other. Furthermore, he needed to protect Yuwen Song. All while facing attacks pelting down at him from every direction, like an all-encompassing net that left him no room for escape.

But Shen Qiao didn't run.

In fact, he didn't even back up.

He drew his sword from its sheath, then slashed horizontally at the three enemies approaching from three directions.

He only used a single move, and it was one without flourish, plain and ordinary.

However, atop the city gates and sweating in fear, Puliuru Jian could faintly hear the sound of roaring waves, almost as though they were rolling in from the distant horizon. Yet they also sounded like a rumbling coming from deep within the earth.

He could see very clearly that as Shen Qiao's sword swept outward, the blade seemed to transform into white waves that undulated outward instantly, one by one.

When filled with true strength, all things become ephemeral. True art is unassuming, and simplicity is the greatest sophistication.

Chen Gong, Yan Shou, and Baoyun—the white waves engulfed all three of them. And though there was clearly only one Shen Qiao, he seemed to have split into many. All three of his assailants felt an incomparable oppressiveness, and not only were their attacks nullified, they rebounded back to the men, forcing them to suffer their own techniques.

Liu Fang was no stranger to martial arts, and he immediately shouted in alarm, "Is that Shen Qiao a monster? How did he suddenly split himself into innumerable copies?"

"That's a type of illusion," explained Puliuru Jian, "derived from his echelon of the sword. When it comes to the path of his sword, Shen Qiao's achievements there have already attained the pinnacle of perfection. I fear that even if you compared him to the Qi Fengge of the past, he has already surpassed his master!"

Even Liu Fang had heard of Qi Fengge before. There were only a few grandmaster-level martial artists in the world, but each of those grandmasters could doubtlessly enter the midst of thousands of horseback soldiers, behead a specific person, and then leave without issue. The court would do everything to win them over. Even someone as headstrong as Yuwen Yong had relied heavily on Yan Wushi, and he'd never put on an emperor's airs before him.

Currently, Shen Qiao might lack tempering compared to a true grandmaster, but this tempering wouldn't take eight or ten years to achieve. Hearing this, Liu Fang became somewhat afraid, and he said hurriedly, "Just now, I didn't order them to shoot at Shen Qiao. You saw that too, Duke of Sui. We were under the emperor's orders; we had no choice. If Shen...ahem, Daoist Master Shen misunderstands anything, you must help me clear it up!"

Puliuru Jian agreed. "Yes, the Commander-in-Chief had his official duties and possessed no personal motives. Jian naturally understands."

Liu Fang inwardly breathed a sigh of relief. His gaze was drawn back to the fighting beneath them. "Do you think Chen Gong's group can win?"

They weren't the only people watching the fight. The solders atop the gates were staring fixedly at this peerlessly marvelous altercation. Beneath their gazes, weapons danced and flashed, murderous intent surging in all directions. Shen Qiao continued to protect the two little children, yet despite this burden he was able to move with ease. The soldiers couldn't help but show expressions of great admiration.

The people of these times valued heroes. Although they were hampered by the emperor's orders and forced to attack Yuwen Song, Yuwen Xian had always possessed great prestige within the military. Shen Qiao should have had nothing to do with this, yet he was willing to place himself in danger for two small children. How could the common person, seeing this level of broad-mindedness and sentimentality, not be filled with deep veneration?

The day Shen Qiao had killed Kunye, only the members of Bixia Sect had been present. Though it was an earthshaking scene, very few people knew about it. But at this time, all eyes were on him as he fought against heavy odds, singlehandedly overcoming greater numbers.

With this battle, his name was destined to shake the world itself!

Shen Qiao shielded Yuwen Song behind him as he held Dou Yan in one arm.

He constructed layer upon layer of sword screens, temporarily warding off Chen Gong and Baoyun. The blade's edge quivered. Then, like the bright moon piercing through the clouds, its radiance overflowed as it thrust viciously at Yan Shou.

Yan Shou sent out three palm strikes in succession, yet they all rebounded off the sword qi, forcing him to fall back several steps. He'd thought that with Chen Gong and Baoyun's participation, Shen Qiao would be overwhelmed and unable to pay attention to him. Never did he imagine that Shen Qiao would ignore the other two entirely. The sword qi swept forth with a force that could overturn rivers and seas, rolling toward him.

He quickly raised his palm to meet it, but the instant he raised his arm, he felt an unbearable, piercing pain—the sword glare had already reached his face!

His entire hand was engulfed within the boundless white light. The pain was like the day he'd lost his arm. He couldn't help the terror surging within his heart, and for the first time in his life, he wanted to turn tail and flee.

His will to fight vanished, his murderous intent forcibly wiped clean. At this moment, all Yan Shou could think of was escaping in one piece. But he'd forgotten: the moment the thought of retreat had arisen, he'd already lost.

The boundless sword glare monopolized his vision, but there was only one sword, and what pierced through Yan Shou's back and into his heart was also only that one sword.

Yan Shou lowered his head. He saw the point of Shanhe Tongbei, already dyed red.

That was his blood.

The bloodstained Shanhe Tongbei continued to hum. It was a very quiet sound, but Yan Shou strangely found that he could hear it, and very clearly at that.

Perhaps because the blade was buried inside his body.

Before he could even confirm this, Shen Qiao had already yanked the sword out of his back. Yan Shou stumbled forward several steps, then collapsed to his knees with a thud.

Behind him, the fight continued, but his participation was no longer required.

Filled with awe, Puliuru Jian couldn't help but yell from atop the city gates. "A true hero indeed!"

Though the people around him said nothing, their expressions clearly showed that they felt the same.

No matter the time and place, such an illustrious hero would be praised and admired.

Below the city walls, Yan Shou's death filled Baoyun and Chen Gong's faces with alarm, but they didn't cease their attack. Instead, with the cutting fierceness of a tempest, they both chose to avoid a direct confrontation with Shen Qiao, instead targeting Dou Yan and Yuwen Song.

Since Shen Qiao had chosen to make these two children his weak spots, attacking these children sent a message: in matters of life and death, all that was important was victory or defeat, and regardless of the means.

If they couldn't kill Shen Qiao today, he would definitely become a fatal calamity to them in the future!

This thought surfaced almost simultaneously within Chen Gong and Baoyun's minds.

Chen Gong's blade was incredibly swift, but Baoyun's moves were more of the uncanny kind. One attacked from the left and the other from the right as they worked in tandem. Both knew that, regardless of how powerful Shen Qiao's sword qi was, it couldn't flow ceaselessly like an inexhaustible river.

Shen Qiao also sprinted toward Yuwen Song, but it wasn't to shield him. Instead, he tossed Dou Yan to him.

Even without his instructions, Yuwen Song understood what he was doing in an instant. He stretched out both arms and caught Dou Yan, who was a full head shorter than him.

With a furl of his sleeves, Shen Qiao flung the two of them several yards away, then turned around and swept back.

He charged with the force of a great, surging wave, his figure like an arching stone bridge, surging upward as it displayed itself. One could vaguely see the might of a king descending from the heavens, a complete reversal from the unbiased and tranquil energy released by his sword in the past.

Chen Gong dissolved this momentum entirely, then stabbed his blade into Shen Qiao's sword screen, his movements confident and smooth. Delight surged within him, but that same instant, he was stunned to realize that his target had somehow become Baoyun.

*Behind him!*

His sense of vigilance elicited, he abruptly turned his head and saw a blast of sword qi soar outward.

But Baoyun had also encountered the same misdirection, and he couldn't pull back in time. His palm struck toward Chen Gong.

Chen Gong, halfway through his sword move, was forced to hurriedly withdraw. He leaned to one side to avoid the blast from Baoyun's palm.

Yet Shen Qiao neither swayed nor moved—he became one with his sword as he rushed toward Baoyun.

When two tigers fought, one must inevitably fall.

Initially, Baoyun had used all his strength in this palm strike but was forced to withdraw half his internal energy when his target suddenly became Chen Gong. However, now that he'd already struck out, it was difficult to restrain his momentum. Together with his sword glare, Shen Qiao charged toward him like an outpouring of raging waves, carrying the momentum of a thousand tons.

Fresh blood spurted from Baoyun's body—in the blink of an eye, a bloody hole had opened in his throat.

To think that two elders from Hehuan Sect had died at Shen Qiao's sword, one after the other, was unbelievable.

Chen Gong could see that the situation was dire. Right as Shen Qiao had stabbed his sword at Baoyun just now, he'd turned around and begun sprinting toward the two children.

Their goal today had always been to detain Yuwen Song. It was Yan Shou who'd moved by himself, dead set on killing Shen Qiao. If he could just bring Yuwen Song away now, his mission would be considered accomplished.

But he'd never expected that Shen Qiao's sword had already attained such heights. Though he had just killed Baoyun, he was already sprinting toward Chen Gong, his qinggong so brilliant that he practically left no trace.

With that speed, even if Chen Gong managed to grab Yuwen Song, he'd still have to fight Shen Qiao directly.

On one hand, the grass must be pulled up by the roots. On the other hand, his life would be in danger. There was no doubt which was more important to Chen Gong.

Chen Gong made his decision promptly: he abandoned Yuwen Song and twisted his body around to sprint toward the city. He pushed his qinggong to the utmost, stepping along the jutting bricks within the wall. In the blink of an eye, he was already atop the gates.

Shen Qiao had no intention of giving chase. Carrying Dou Yan and Yuwen Song, he sprinted in the opposite direction instead.

He sheathed his sword and, with a child in each arm, Shen Qiao sprinted a mile or two in one go, running until they were well out of sight of the city gates. Only then did he stop.

He placed the two children down and stumbled forward several steps before coughing up a large mouthful of blood.

"Daoist Master Shen!" Dou Yan cried out in alarm as she quickly ran up to support him.

Though Yuwen Song didn't speak, he too had grabbed Shen Qiao's other arm as he struggled to support the majority of Shen Qiao's weight.

"It's no problem…" Shen Qiao held his chest as he strenuously tried to comfort the two, his mouth filled with the salty-sweet taste of blood.

Baoyun and the others weren't amateurs. Even if they didn't rank among the top ten, martial experts of the level it took to become an elder within Hehuan sect were still rare within the jianghu. With Shen Qiao's current level of ability, killing two of them in the same breath sounded impressive, but he'd paid quite a steep price as well.

During their fight just now, he'd suffered several palm strikes. Had Chen Gong not been fooled and frightened by the unyielding facade he'd forcibly put on and observed him carefully instead, he wouldn't have found it difficult to realize that Shen Qiao's strength was spent, flagging like an arrow nearing the end of its flight.

Tears welled up in Dou Yan's eyes, but she forcibly held them back.

"You must not cry!" Yuwen Song said to her. "Ahead of us is a pavilion. I've been there before. Let's go there and sit for a while."

Shen Qiao thought about how none of the city's soldiers had come out to pursue them when they'd been fighting earlier. It seemed that quite a few people were secretly sympathizing and assisting regarding Yuwen Xian's affairs. Determining there shouldn't be any danger for now, he didn't force out his true qi to take them away.

Dou Yan quickly nodded, and the two of them supported Shen Qiao as they continued forward.

After a fairly short walk, they turned a corner and saw a small pavilion, as expected.

However, there were two people standing inside.

And there was also a horse tied outside.

"It's Father!" Before Shen Qiao could react, Dou Yan's sharp eyes had already recognized the other man, but she didn't abandon Shen Qiao and kept supporting him until they reached the pavilion. Only when they were inside did she leap over.

"Father!"

"A-Yan!"

Dou Yi grabbed his daughter in a tight embrace, his face full of worry instantly transforming into surprised joy.

Observing this scene, Yuwen Song couldn't help but recall his own father and his tragic death. He had held back his tears as long as he could, but now they finally trickled down his face.

A hand covered his head and gently caressed it, bringing with it warmth.

It was Shen Qiao.

Yuwen Song didn't speak, and he didn't sob. But he couldn't resist pressing closer to Shen Qiao, snuggling up toward him.

Within a short period of time, a sense of wordless trust and tacit understanding had formed between them, something they'd obtained through their life-and-death ordeal.

Dou Yi cupped his hands at Shen Qiao and bowed. "I'm grateful to esteemed Daoist Master Shen for saving my daughter! Yi will never forget this great kindness and virtue for the rest of his life!"

This gratefulness came from the depths of his heart—hence, he'd even used the most respectful title for Daoists when addressing Shen Qiao.

In the past, Shen Qiao's master Qi Fengge, too, had been addressed as "esteemed Daoist Master."

"Dou-langjun need not be so courteous!" Shen Qiao's voice was somewhat hoarse and feeble.

"This lowly one is Zhongnan Sect's Zhangsun Sheng," said the man who stood next to Dou Yi. "I met esteemed Daoist Master Shen once back during the Su family's birthday banquet. Perhaps you still remember me." He fished a small bottle from his lapels. "These are Jade Dew Pills. Zhongnan Sect uses them to heal internal injuries, and they are quite effective. Please take them, esteemed Daoist Master Shen."

Shen Qiao didn't show him any deference—he thanked him and took the bottle.

"The injustice suffered by the Prince of Qi is known to all," said Zhangsun Sheng. "It's unfortunate that his great achievements ended up threatening the emperor, who reacted so perversely— framing your own loyal subject! Everyone is enraged but too afraid to speak. Because Sheng still has his family to take care of, he had many misgivings about what he should do. But seeing the esteemed Daoist Master's deeds today, I am deeply ashamed. Please accept this bow from Sheng!"

Shen Qiao reached out to stop him. "There are thousands of Dao, and the path everyone chooses is different. There was never anything to criticize—if not for your support behind the scenes, I wouldn't have been able to extricate myself so smoothly. The Su family isn't like me—I'm alone in this world, without any attachments. But the entire Su clan, young and old, remain in Chang'an, yet they still fought together with me against Yuwen Yun just now. Will they be all right?"

"Yes," said Zhangsun Sheng. "Please be at ease. I'm from Zhongnan Sect, and the Zhangsun family still has some connections in Chang'an. We can secretly bring the whole Su family over to Zhongnan Sect for refuge. Your esteemed self can also bring Yuwen-qilang up the mountain. Zhongnan Sect may not be a large or famous sect, but we still possess enough courage to face the Lord of Zhou's underlings."

Yet Shen Qiao shook his head. "No, Zhongnan Mountain is too close to Chang'an. If Yuwen Yun wishes to pursue things to the end, we won't be able to stay for that long, in the end. I wish to bring him further away, until we're completely out of danger. Then we'll see."

Zhangsun Sheng and Dou Yi shared a glance. "Very well," said Zhangsun Sheng. "This horse is no winged steed, but it's still a fine mount of the sort that's hard to come by. Your health isn't very good, esteemed Daoist Master, so I believe that riding should be much more convenient than walking!"

**THE STORY CONTINUES IN**
## Thousand Autumns
### VOLUME 4

# Characters and Associated Factions

# CHARACTERS
## AND ASSOCIATED FACTIONS

The identity of certain characters may be a spoiler; use this guide with caution on your first read of the novel.

A sizable portion of *Thousand Autumns'* cast are based on real-life historical figures, though they have all been fictionalized to some degree. The names of those with real-life counterparts but without an entry of their own are indicated by **bold text**.

## MAIN CHARACTERS

### Shen Qiao (沈峤)

**TITLE(S):** Sect Leader of Xuandu's Violet Palace

**CHARACTER BASIS:** Fictional

As the chosen successor of the legendary Qi Fengge, and the reclusive leader of the land's foremost Daoist sect, Shen Qiao seemed to have it all: first-rate talent, a world-class master, a loving family, and a kind heart devoted completely to the tenets of Daoism. But a duel atop Banbu Peak changed everything for him.

The *qiao* in Shen Qiao's name is a rare character, referring to a tall and precipitous mountain peak. He was named after a verse in "Ode to Zhou: On Tour" (周颂·时迈), recorded in the *Shijing*—a song written in commemoration of King Wu of Zhou. The verse extols how he traveled the land after vanquishing the Shang in 11th century B.C.E. He offered sacrifices to the many gods, including those in the rivers and tallest mountains.

## Yan Wushi (晏无师)

**TITLE(S):** Huanyue Sect Leader, Junior Preceptor of the Crown Prince of Zhou, Demon Lord

**CHARACTER BASIS:** Fictional

The egotistical and capricious leader of the demonic Huanyue Sect. A terrifying martial artist who some sources claim was on par with Qi Fengge, Yan Wushi is also ambitious, shrewd, and above all, a committed misanthrope. In Yan Wushi's eyes, there are no good people, only evil people disguised as good people. As far as he's concerned, anyone who thinks otherwise is either a liar or a fool.

Yan Wushi's personal name means "has no master." The *ling* in his old name, Xie Ling (谢岭), means "mountain range."

## XUANDU MOUNTAIN (玄都山)

The world's foremost Daoist sect, located on the border intersection of Northern Qi, Southern Chen, and Northern Zhou. Sect Leader Qi Fengge built their legendary reputation, but despite this prestige and influence, he chose to seclude Xuandu Mountain away from the world, closing its gates and withdrawing from all outside affairs. After his death, his mantle passed to Shen Qiao, who held fast to his shizun's isolationist stance. When Shen Qiao fell during his duel with Kunye, Yu Ai took the reins as Acting Sect Leader.

Officially, Xuandu Mountain is a location—the actual sect is called Xuandu's Violet Palace (玄都紫府, *xuandu zifu*), named after Taishang Laojun's abode on the mythical Daluo Mountain. *Xuandu* ("black city") refers to Daluo Mountain's immortal realm, while *zifu* ("violet residence") refers to the Bajing Palace supposedly located within it. The sect leader of Xuandu's Violet Palace is known as the *zhangjiao* (掌教), a term more specific to Daoism compared to *zongzhu* (宗主), which is how Yan Wushi is addressed in Chinese.

## Qi Fengge (祁凤阁)

**TITLE(S):** Sect Leader of Xuandu's Violet Palace, World's Number One Martial Expert

**CHARACTER BASIS:** Fictional

The number one martial artist in all the land before his passing and Shen Qiao's master, Qi Fengge is held in high esteem by the entire world to this day. Two decades ago, he won a duel with Hulugu of the Göktürks. In lieu of a reward for his victory, he made Hulugu swear to stay out of the Central Plains for the next twenty years. He had five disciples in total: Tan Yuanchun, Shen Qiao, Yu Ai, an unnamed fourth disciple, and Gu Hengbo.

## Yu Ai (郁蔼)

**TITLE(S):** Acting Sect Leader of Xuandu's Violet Palace

**CHARACTER BASIS:** Fictional

One of Qi Fengge's disciples and Shen Qiao's shidi, though two years older than him. Originally the closest to Shen Qiao out of all his martial siblings, he collaborated with Kunye to poison Shen Qiao, which led to Shen Qiao's crushing defeat on Banbu Peak. Afterward, he took over leadership of Xuandu Mountain and involved the sect in the ongoing power struggles of the current regimes, cooperating with Göktürk Khagahate. One of the five martial artists participating in the group ambush on Yan Wushi.

## HUANYUE SECT (浣月宗)

One of the three demonic sects, established and led by Yan Wushi after the collapse of Riyue Sect. Though wealthy and influential, they tend to keep a low profile and are the key supporters of Yuwen Yong's rule in Zhou. Like the rest of the demonic sects, their final goal is to reunite the sects of the demonic discipline.

### Bian Yanmei (边沿梅)

**CHARACTER BASIS:** Fictional

Yan Wushi's first disciple. As shrewd as his master, Bian Yanmei currently juggles both Huanyue Sect logistics and Zhou imperial court duties, serving Yuwen Yong in an official capacity.

## HEHUAN SECT (合欢宗)

One of three demonic sects born from Riyue Sect's fall, Hehuan Sect specializes in charm techniques and parasitic cultivation, where the practitioner drains qi and energy from their sexual partners to strengthen their own martial arts. Hehuan Sect was established and led by Yuan Xiuxiu, but her lover Sang Jingxing is known to hold great power within it as well. Highly influential in Qi.

### Bai Rong (白茸)

**CHARACTER BASIS:** Fictional

One of Hehuan Sect's most prominent disciples under Sang Jingxing. Cunning and devious, she has a very peculiar relationship with Shen Qiao.

## Yuan Xiuxiu (元秀秀)

**TITLE(S):** Hehuan Sect Leader

**CHARACTER BASIS:** Fictional

The leader of Hehuan Sect, rumored to have gotten her position due to her relationship with Sang Jingxing. During Yan Wushi's ten years of seclusion, she led Hehuan Sect in repeated attempts to annex Huanyue Sect.

## Sang Jingxing (桑景行)

**CHARACTER BASIS:** Fictional

An exalted elder in Hehuan Sect, Cui Youwang's disciple, and Yuan Xiuxiu's supposed lover. A twisted martial artist with a horrific reputation, as well as an appetite for beauties and parasitic cultivation. He was grievously injured by Shen Qiao when the latter destroyed his own martial arts to take him down and loathes both Shen Qiao and Yan Wushi.

## Xiao Se (萧瑟)

**CHARACTER BASIS:** Fictional

Yuan Xiuxiu's disciple. Specializes in fighting with fans.

## Yan Shou (阎狩)

**TITLE(S):** The Buddha with the Blood-Soaked Hand

**CHARACTER BASIS:** Fictional

An elder in Hehuan Sect. Keeps his head shaved like a monk's but has a reputation for murder. Became Shen Qiao's nemesis after he killed both Zhu Lengquan and Chuyi at Bailong Monastery.

### Baoyun (宝云)

Character Basis: Fictional
An elder in Hehuan Sect, who enjoys deceiving women by pretending to be a monk.

## FAJING SECT (法镜宗)

One of the three demonic sects born from Riyue Sect's fall. Unable to compete with the other two branches, the sect now primarily operates in Tuyuhun. Their sect leader is Guang Lingsan.

### Guang Lingsan (广陵散)

**TITLE(S):** Fajing Sect Leader
**CHARACTER BASIS:** Fictional
The leader of Fajing Sect, who moved their operations to Tuyuhun ten years ago due to overwhelming pressure from Huanyue Sect and Hehuan Sect. A master of the zither who uses music to harm and confound his opponents, as well as one of the five martial artists participating in the group ambush on Yan Wushi.

## RIYUE SECT (日月宗)

The origin of the "Noble Discipline" (demonic discipline to outsiders). Once located in Fenglin Province, it vanished after splintering into three: Huanyue Sect, Hehuan Sect, and Fajing Sect. Their last sect leader was Sang Jingxing's master, Cui Youwang.

# LIUHE GUILD (六合帮)

One of the largest martial arts organizations in the Central Plains, whose reach extends both north and south of the Yangtze River. Led by guild leader Dou Yanshan and deputy leader Yun Fuyi, they deal in all kinds of business, from escort missions to spy work.

## Dou Yanshan (窦燕山)

**TITLE(S):** Liuhe Guild Leader

**CHARACTER BASIS:** Fictional

The leader of the Liuhe Guild. Harbors a grudge against Yan Wushi, as he destroyed the copy of the Zhuyang Strategy that Dou Yanshan ordered the Liuhe Guild to escort. One of the five martial artists participating in the group ambush on Yan Wushi.

## Yun Fuyi (云拂衣)

**TITLE(S):** Liuhe Guild Deputy Leader

**CHARACTER BASIS:** Fictional

The second-in-command of the Liuhe Guild and a talented martial artist. After losing the Zhuyang Strategy scroll to Yan Wushi, her standing within the Liuhe Guild has grown unstable.

# LINCHUAN ACADEMY (临川学宫)

The leading Confucian sect and the main force backing the Emperor of Chen. Their leader is Academy Master Ruyan Kehui, one of the world's top ten martial artists.

### Ruyan Kehui (汝鄢克惠)

**TITLE(S):** Linchuan Academy Master

**CHARACTER BASIS:** Fictional

The leader of Linchuan Academy. A powerful and cultured martial artist who ranks in the top ten, he believes wholeheartedly in the Han's right to rule, and therefore seeks to undermine Yuwen Yong's Zhou Dynasty. Part of the plot to ambush Yan Wushi.

## QI DYNASTY (齐朝)

Also known as Northern Qi, the country occupies the land northeast of the Yangtze River and was founded by Gao Huan. Originally warlike and powerful, the reign of Gao Huan's successors, especially the incompetent and frivolous Gao Wei, has put the kingdom into a steady decline. Its capital is Yecheng (located at the south of modern-day Hebei).

## ZHOU DYNASTY (周朝)

The country that occupies the region northwest of the Yangtze, also known as Northern Zhou. Its capital is Chang'an (now known as Xi'an). Though it was established by **Yuwen Tai** before his death, for years his nephew **Yuwen Hu** held power as regent, killing off Yuwen Tai's puppet-ruler sons whenever he perceived them as a threat. The third such son, **Yuwen Yong**, managed to feign obedience for years before finally ambushing and killing Yuwen Hu, officially seizing back his imperial authority.

## Xueting (雪庭)

**TITLE(S):** State Preceptor of Zhou (former)

**CHARACTER BASIS:** Fictional

One of the top ten martial artists of the world and a former member of the Buddhist Tiantai Sect. Previously a high-ranking official of Zhou under Yuwen Hu, who honored Buddhism, Emperor Yuwen Yong's anti-Buddhist measures have pushed him into taking drastic measures. One of the five martial artists participating in the group ambush on Yan Wushi.

## Puliuru Jian (普六茹坚)

**TITLE(S):** Duke of Sui

**CHARACTER BASIS:** Historical

A learned, high-ranking official of Zhou whom Shen Qiao met at Madam Qin's birthday banquet.

## Su Wei (苏威)

**TITLE(S):** Duke of Meiyang County

**CHARACTER BASIS:** Historical

The current patriarch of the Su family, Su Wei comes from a distinguished line of scholar-officials and is highly talented himself. His younger brother is Su Qiao, and his mother is Madam Qin.

## Yuwen Xian (宇文宪)

**TITLE(S):** Prince of Qi

**CHARACTER BASIS:** Historical

Brother of Yuwen Yong and a member of the imperial family of Zhou. Once a hero of the Zhou Dynasty with many military exploits under his belt, persecution from his nephew, Yuwen Yun, has driven him into hiding.

### Yuwen Song (宇文诵)

**CHARACTER BASIS:** Fictional

The youngest son of Yuwen Xian.

### Dou Yan (窦言)

**CHARACTER BASIS:** Historical

The young daughter of the noble Dou family and Yuwen Yong's niece. Ran away from home after witnessing a certain crime.

### Qin Shuanghan (秦双含)

**TITLE(S):** Su Matriarch

**CHARACTER BASIS:** Fictional

The matriarch of the prominent Su family of Zhou and mother of the brothers Su Wei and Su Qiao. Unbeknownst to her family, her true identity is Aisaule, a former disciple of Hulugu who absconded with the martial artist's keepsake twenty years ago.

### Yuwen Qing (宇文庆)

**TITLE(S):** Court Councilor

**CHARACTER BASIS:** Historical

An official from the Yuwen family who became Shen Qiao's acquaintance when they traveled south for the alliance treaty between Zhou and Chen.

## CHEN DYNASTY (陈朝)

The country south of the Yangtze River, founded by **Chen Baxian**, also called Southern Chen. Unlike Qi and Zhou where most of the upper class are of Xianbei descent, the Chen Dynasty is dominated by the Han. Its capital is Jiankang (modern-day Nanjing), and the current ruler is Emperor **Chen Xu**.

# GÖKTÜRK KHAGANATE (突厥)

A powerful Turkic empire north of the Great Wall, led by **Taspar Khagan**. Their people have been at odds with the nations of the Central Plains for years—relations between them are uneasy and tinged with hostility.

## Hulugu (狐鹿估)

**CHARACTER BASIS:** Fictional

Once the most powerful martial artist of the Göktürk Khaganate, he was defeated by Qi Fengge twenty years ago. Qi Fengge then made him swear not to set foot in the Central Plains.

## Duan Wenyang (段文鸯)

**CHARACTER BASIS:** Fictional

Hulugu's disciple and Kunye's shixiong, a shrewd and ambitious whip user. One of the five martial artists who participates in the group ambush against Yan Wushi.

# OTHER CHARACTERS

Characters who aren't associated with a particular faction, regardless of where they live.

## Tao Hongjing (陶弘景)

**CHARACTER BASIS:** Historical

The legendary creator of the *Zhuyang Strategy*. Before his death, he was known as a great genius and the one true master of martial arts for his success in marrying the principles of all three schools of thought.

## Chen Gong (陈恭)

**TITLE(S):** Duke of Pengcheng County

**CHARACTER BASIS:** Fictional

Once a homeless youth who Shen Qiao met in Funing County, now a duke and Emperor Gao Wei's new favorite.

## Murong Qin (慕容沁)

**TITLE(S):** Murong Patriarch

**CHARACTER BASIS:** Fictional

Qi Dynasty's strongest martial artist who originally worked as a hired hound for the Qi imperial court, but now follows Chen Gong. Murong Xun's uncle.

# PRONUNCIATION GUIDE

Mandarin Chinese is the official state language of mainland China, and pinyin is the official system of romanization in which it is written. As Mandarin is a tonal language, pinyin uses diacritical marks (e.g., ā, á, ǎ, à) to indicate these tonal inflections. Most words use one of four tones, though some (as in "de" in the title below) are a neutral tone. Furthermore, regional variance can change the way native Chinese speakers pronounce the same word. For those reasons and more, please consider the guide below a simplified introduction to pronunciation of select character names and sounds from the world of *Thousand Autumns*.

More resources are available at sevenseasdanmei.com

**NOTE ON SPELLING:** Romanized Mandarin Chinese words with identical spelling in pinyin—and even pronunciation—may well have different meanings. These words are more easily differentiated in written Chinese, which uses characters.

## CHARACTER NAMES

### Qiān Qiū

Qiān, approximately **chee-yen**, but as a single syllable.
Qiū, as in **cho**ke.

### Shěn Qiáo

Shěn, as in the second half of ma**son**.
Qiáo, as in **chow**.

### Yàn Wúshī

Yàn, as in **yen**.

Wú, as in **oo**.

Shī, a little like **shh**. The **-i** is more of a buzzed continuation for the **sh-** consonant than any equivalent English vowel. See the General Consonants section for more information on the **sh-** consonant.

### Qí Fènggé

Qí, as in **chee**se.

Fèng, a little like **fun**, but with the nasal **ng** one would find in so**ng**.

Gé, a little like **guh**.

### Bái Róng

Bái, as in **bye**.

Róng, a little like the last part of chape**rone**. See the General Consonants section for more information on the **r-** consonant.

## GENERAL CONSONANTS

Some Mandarin Chinese consonants sound very similar, such as z/c/s and zh/ch/sh. Audio samples will provide the best opportunity to learn the difference between them.

X: somewhere between the **sh** in **sh**eep and **s** in **s**ilk

Q: a very aspirated **ch** as in **ch**eat

C: **ts** as in pan**ts**

Z: **ds** as in su**ds**

S: **s** as in **s**ilk

CH: very close to **c-**, but with the tongue rolled up to touch the palate.

ZH: very close to **z-**, but with the tongue rolled up to touch the palate.

SH: very close to **s-**, but with the tongue rolled up to touch the palate. Because of this, it can give the impression of **shh**, but it's a different sound compared to the **x-** consonant.

G: hard **g** as in **g**raphic

R: partway between the **r** in **r**un and the **s** in mea**s**ure. The tongue should be rolled up to touch the palate.

## GENERAL VOWELS

The pronunciation of a vowel may depend on its preceding consonant. For example, the "i" in "shi" is distinct from the "i" in "di," where the first is a buzzed continuation for the sh- consonant and the latter a long e sound. Compound vowels are often—though not always—pronounced as conjoined but separate vowels. You'll find a few of the trickier compounds below.

IU: as in **yo**-yo

IE: **ye** as in **ye**s

UO: **war** as in **war**m

APPENDIX

# Historical Primer

# HISTORICAL PERIOD

While not required reading, this section and those after are intended to offer further context for the historical setting of this story, and give insights into the many concepts and terms utilized throughout the novel. Their goal is to provide a starting point for learning more about the rich culture from which these stories were written.

The following segment is intended to give a brief introduction to the major historical events featured in *Thousand Autumns*.

## THE JIN DYNASTY

In 266 C.E., at the close of the tumultuous **Three Kingdoms** era, the central plains were finally united under Sima Yan, founder of the **Jin Dynasty**, also known as **Western Jin**. But when Sima Yan passed away in 290 C.E., his son and heir was deemed unfit to rule. Conflict broke out among members of the imperial court who vied for the throne. This became known as the **War of the Eight Princes**, after the eight members of the Sima royal family who were the principal players.

## UPRISING OF THE FIVE BARBARIANS AND THE SIXTEEN KINGDOMS PERIOD

Over a period of fifteen years, the repeated clashes and civil wars greatly weakened the Western Jin Dynasty. During this time, most of the royal princes relied on non-Han nomadic minorities to fight for them, in particular Xiongnu and the **Xianbei**. The Han lumped them together with other foreign ethnicities like the Jie, Di, and Qiang, collectively designating them the **Hu**, sometimes translated as "barbarians." As the Jin Dynasty's control over these minority tribes slipped, instances of rebellion combined with local unrest to usher in the **Uprising of the Five Barbarians** in 304 C.E.

Although it began as a revolt spearheaded by the Hu, the Uprising of the Five Barbarians soon led to the complete collapse of Western Jin as its Han upper class fled south of the Yangtze River. This was the mass **southward migration of the Jin** referenced in *Thousand Autumns*. When the old capital of Chang'an fell, the new emperor reestablished the seat of government in Jiankang, heralding the start of the **Eastern Jin Dynasty**. At the same time, north of the Yangtze River, the Di, Qiang, Xiongnu, and Jie each established their own dynastic kingdoms. Thus began a time of great upheaval known as the **Sixteen Kingdoms** period.

During the turmoil of the Sixteen Kingdoms, regimes formed and collapsed in the blink of an eye as they warred with each other and the Eastern Jin. The strife finally abated when the **Northern Wei Dynasty** conquered the other northern kingdoms in 439 C.E. and unified the lands north of the Yangtze. Meanwhile in the south, Liu Yu usurped the emperor of the Eastern Jin Dynasty and founded the **Liu Song Dynasty**. This marked the beginning of the **Northern-Southern Dynasties** period, during which *Thousand Autumns* is set.

## NORTHERN-SOUTHERN DYNASTIES

For a period of almost ninety years, Northern Wei held strong. The first half of their reign was focused on expansion, but when Tuoba Hong rose to power in 471 C.E., he championed the dominance of **Buddhism** and Han culture, going so far as to ban Xianbei clothing from the court and assigning one-character family names to Xianbei nobility (Tuoba Hong himself changed his family name to Yuan).

South of the Yangtze, the regime changed hands three times— from Liu Song to **Southern Qi** to **Liang**, before the **Chen Dynasty** that ruled during *Thousand Autumns* was finally established in 557 C.E.

In the north, Northern Wei held strong for almost ninety years. While the first half of their reign was focused on expansion, when Tuoba Hong rose to power in 471 C.E., he championed the dominance of Buddhism and Han culture, going so far as to ban Xianbei clothing from the court and assigning one-character family names to Xianbei nobility.

A rift slowly developed in Northern Wei between the increasingly Han-acculturated aristocracy and their own armies who adhered more to the traditional, nomadic lifestyle. A series of rebellions escalated into all-out revolt, and by 535 C.E. the kingdom had split in half. **Western Wei** was ruled by Yuwen Tai, and **Eastern Wei** by Gao Huan. In the space of a generation, they would depose the last of the old leadership and become the kingdoms of **Northern Zhou** and **Northern Qi**. In the Zhou Dynasty to the west, rule favored the Han-acculturated nobles, while in the Qi Dynasty to the east, the traditional tribes came into power.

Qi's military superiority over both Zhou and Chen began to diminish due to corruption and incompetence in the ruling class, and particularly that of the emperor's grandson, **Gao Wei**. After a politically turbulent period of regency in Zhou, **Yuwen Yong** took power in 572 C.E. and made a point of bolstering state administration and military affairs.

By 575 C.E., where *Thousand Autumns* begins, a new maelstrom is already brewing...

# THE THREE SCHOOLS OF THOUGHT

This section hopes to provide some basic context as to the major schools of thought that inform the background of *Thousand Autumns*, so that readers may explore the topic in more depth on their own. Note that with their long period of coexistence, the schools have all influenced each other deeply, and their ideals have become rooted in Chinese culture itself, even among non-practitioners.

## Daoism (道)

Daoism revolves around the concept of **Dao**, or "Ways": the courses things follow as they undergo change. Though there are many Dao a human can choose from, there is one primordial "great Dao" (大道), the source of the universe and origin of all things—the void of infinite potential. The course all things in the universe follow is the "heavenly Dao" (天道), the natural order.

According to Daoist principles, by imposing constraints and artifice, humanity strays from the primordial Dao and stagnates.

In particular, the rigid social roles enforced by society are seen as unnatural and an example of degradation. For humans to flourish, they must revert themselves, disengaging from these tendencies in order to return to the primordial Dao. This is sometimes known as "becoming one with heaven" (天人合一). The method of disengaging is called **wuwei** (无为), sometimes translated as inaction or non-interference.

Expanding on this idea, Daoism has the concepts of **Xiantian** (先天, "Early Heaven") and **Houtian** (后天, "Later Heaven"). The prenatal Xiantian state is closer to the primordial Dao, and thus is both purer than and superior to the postnatal Houtian state. The Houtian state is created at birth, along with the **conscious mind** that thinks and perceives and which in turn suppresses the primordial mind. This is what gives rise to sources of suffering: anger, worry, doubt, desire, and fatigue.

The goal of *wuwei* is to reverse the changes brought on by Houtian and return to the primordial state of Xiantian. To conflict with nature is to stray from it, and to intervene in the natural order—as society does—is to perpetuate degradation. Disengaging from all of these influences requires rejecting social conventions and detaching from the mundane world altogether, so seclusion and asceticism are common practices. Emptying oneself of all emotion and freeing oneself from all artifice is the only way to achieve union with heaven and surpass life and death itself.

When it came to politics, Daoism was often seen as a justification for small, *laissez-faire* governments—in fact, *laissez-faire* is one of the possible translations of *wuwei*—supporting low taxes and low intervention. The anti-authority implications of its philosophies were not lost on its followers, nor on their rulers. As a result, it wasn't uncommon for Daoism to struggle to find its footing politically, despite its cultural pervasiveness.

## Buddhism (佛/释)

Founded by Gautama Buddha in India, Buddhism only arrived in China during the Han Dynasty, well after Confucianism and Daoism. Despite early pushback and social friction, its parallels with Daoism eventually helped it gain widespread influence.

Buddhism is rooted in the concepts of reincarnation, karma, and **Maya**—the illusion of existence. Attachment to Maya keeps living beings rooted in the cycle of reincarnation, where they are beholden to the principle of karma that determines their future rebirths. Buddha claimed that this eternal cycle is the root of all suffering and that the only escape is through achieving **Nirvana**, or enlightenment. To achieve enlightenment is to fully accept that all things within existence are false. It then follows that any emotions, attachments, or thoughts that one develops while interacting with and perceiving the world are equally false. This philosophy extends to the attitude toward karma—the ideal Buddhist does good deeds and kind acts without any expectation of reward or satisfaction, material or otherwise.

Despite these selfless ideals, it also wasn't uncommon to see Buddhist temples amass land, authority, and wealth through donations, worship, and the offerings of those seeking better futures or rebirths. Combined with the men who'd leave their homes to join these temples as monks, this sometimes made the relationship between Buddhism and rulers a tricky, precarious one.

## Confucianism (儒)

Unlike Buddhism and Daoism, Confucianism focuses on the moral betterment of the individual as the foundation for the ideal society. The founder Confucius envisioned a rigidly hierarchical system wherein the lower ranks have the moral duty to obey the higher ranks, and those in superior positions likewise have the moral responsibility to care for their subordinates. This social contract is applied to everything from the family unit to the nation itself—the emperor is the father to his people, and they in turn must show him absolute obedience.

To foster such a society, Confucians extol the **five constant virtues** (五常): **benevolence** (仁), **righteousness** (义), **propriety** (礼), **wisdom** (智), and **integrity** (信). Paragons who embody all five virtues are called **junzi** (君子), sometimes translated as "gentlemen" or "noble men," while their direct opposites are *xiaoren*, literally "petty people," and sometimes translated as "scoundrels."

Throughout most of history, mainstream Confucians believed in the goodness inherent in humanity, that people can better themselves through education and learning from their superiors. The ideal ruler must be the ultimate *junzi* himself and lead by example, thereby uplifting all of society. In the same vein, Confucius expected officials to be virtuous parental figures, held to a higher moral standard than ordinary citizens.

Due to its emphasis on social order, Confucianism was easily the most influential and politically favored of the three schools throughout history. Its social contract was so absolute that even dynastic takeovers had to be performed in a way that did not "break it." Usurpers who acted otherwise ran the risk of being seen as illegitimate in the eyes of the people. Famously, the old emperor had to offer the new emperor his position multiple times, with the new ruler declining three times (三让) before finally accepting.

## Bonus: Legalism (法)

Though not regarded as one of the "big three" and although it received far less overt support, Legalism was enormously influential for one key reason: it served as the foundation for the entire Chinese government tradition for two thousand years, regardless of dynasty.

Unlike the three schools, which are each in pursuit of an ideal, Legalism is entirely utilitarian and concerned only with efficacy. This is reflected in its Chinese name, the "house of methods." Core to its beliefs is the idea that human nature is selfish and evil, and so people must be motivated through reward and punishment. Morality is inconsequential, the ends justify the means, and the most effective administration must minimize corruption by restricting its subordinate administrators as much as possible.

It was with these tenets that the first unified Chinese empire, the Qin Dynasty, dismantled the existing feudalist system and established in its place a centralized government overseen by the emperor. After the Qin's collapse—brought about in part due to how harsh a fully Legalist regime was on the people—the succeeding Han Dynasty under Emperor Wu of Han made sure to suppress Legalism as a philosophy. However, they inherited the entire Legalist government structure mostly unchanged, though their policies were softened by a push toward Confucianism. This trend of furtively repackaging Legalist tendencies within the leading school of thought (usually Confucianism) continued almost uninterrupted for this period of two thousand years, and rulers continued to study Legalist texts like the *Han Feizi*.

# OTHER IMPORTANT CONCEPTS

## DAOIST CULTIVATION, THE ZHUYANG STRATEGY, AND THE POWER OF FIVE

In real life, the scholar Tao Hongjing compiled the famous, three-volume *Concealed Instructions for the Ascent to Perfection* (登真隱訣, translated in the novel as "Dengzhen Concealed Instructions"). For *Thousand Autumns*, Meng Xi Shi invented an extra associated manual, called the *Strategy of Vermillion Yang* (朱陽策, translated in the novel as "Zhuyang Strategy") after the real-life Monastery of Vermillion Yang on Mount Mao where Tao Hongjing secluded himself.

The *Zhuyang Strategy* draws heavily from classical concepts of Daoist cultivation and pulls together many ideas from Chinese culture. Primarily, they are based on the *Wuqi Chaoyuan* (五气朝元, roughly "Returning the Five Qi to the Origin"). The first lines of each of the *Zhuyang Strategy*'s five volumes correspond exactly to the *Wuqi Chaoyuan*'s five principles:

1.  The heart conceals the mind; Houtian begets the conscious mind, while Xiantian begets propriety; once emptied of sorrow, the mind is settled, and the Fire from the Crimson Emperor of the South returns to the Origin.

2.  The liver conceals the soul; Houtian begets the lost soul, while Xiantian begets benevolence; once emptied of joy, the soul is settled, and the Wood from the Azure Emperor of the East returns to the Origin.

3. The pancreas conceals the thought; Houtian begets the deluded thought, while Xiantian begets integrity; once emptied of desire, the thought is settled, and the Earth from the Yellow Emperor of the Center returns to the Origin.

4. The lungs conceal the anima; Houtian begets the corrupted anima, while Xiantian begets righteousness; once emptied of rage, the anima is settled, and the Metal from the White Emperor of the West returns to the Origin.

5. The kidneys conceal the essence; Houtian begets the clouded essence, while Xiantian begets wisdom; once emptied of cheer, the will is settled, and the Water from the Black Emperor of the North returns to the Origin.

The traditional Chinese worldview includes the **Five Phases**, the **Deities of the Five Regions** (also known as the **Five Emperors**), the five constant virtues, the **Five Spirits**, and the five major internal organs. The *Wuqi Chaoyuan* links all these ideas together, unifying them into a doctrine that explains how one can achieve immortal status or "godhood." For those who are interested, we provide here a brief introduction to several of these concepts in hopes that readers can further appreciate the world of *Thousand Autumns*.

## THE FIVE PHASES

The **Wuxing** (五行), sometimes translated as Five Agents or Five Elements, are a cornerstone of Daoist philosophy. Unlike the Four Elements proposed by Aristotle, the Five Phases—**Metal** (金), **Wood** (木), **Water** (水), **Fire** (火), and **Earth** (土)—are seen as dynamic, interdependent forces. Each phase can give rise to another (生), or suppress another (克). As Daoism dictates that all entities are bound by the natural order, the Five Phases can be seen as an overarching rule set that governs all aspects of nature. Most things are regarded as corresponding to a certain phase, including but not limited to planets, seasons, cardinal directions, organs, colors, and types of qi.

## FIVE EMPERORS, FIVE REGIONS, FIVE COLORS

In Daoism, the **Wufang Shangdi** (五方上帝), or High Emperors of the Five Regions, are the fivefold manifestation of the **Supreme Emperor of Heaven** (天皇大帝), or simply **Heaven** (天). As they correspond to the Five Phases, each emperor has an associated cardinal direction, as well as a color that informs his namesake.

## FIVE SPIRITS, FIVE ORGANS

The traditional Chinese conception of the spirit divides it into five separate aspects: **mind** (神), **soul** (魂), **thought** (意), **anima** (魄), and **will** (志). These classifications may not be a perfect match with their western definitions. For example, the will—which arises from the **essence** (精)—is responsible for memory, as well as discernment and judgment. A strong will is generally associated with clear-mindedness. In another example, the anima governs instincts, impulses, and reflex reactions, and is said to dissipate on death, unlike the soul.

Each of the five aspects is said to reside in one of the five major internal organs–heart, liver, pancreas (includes the spleen), lungs, and kidneys, which in turn also correspond to the Five Phases. The *Wuqi Chaoyuan* claims that part of ascending to immortality is learning how to "return" the true qi of each aspect to one's Dantian, or "Origin."

## THE FOUR OCCUPATIONS

The 士农工商 classification of citizens as *shi* (eventually **gentry scholars**), *nong* (**farmers**), *gong* (**artisans**), and *shang* (**merchants**), was a cornerstone of ancient Chinese social hierarchy strongly associated with both Confucianism and Legalism.

As the upper class and decision-makers, the *shi* naturally ranked the highest, followed by the peasant farmers who were valued as the backbone of the nation. Merchant businessmen were seen as agents of exploitation who profited from price fluctuations, so they were placed lowest.

In practice, these hierarchical rankings shaped cultural attitudes more than they dictated political clout. Even though merchants were looked down upon, the much-needed cash flow they provided made them far more influential than the artisan and farmer classes. This created a curious situation—merchants were both sought after and derided by the *shi* in charge of governance. In later dynasties some merchants went so far as to purchase positions within the imperial court, making them honorary *shi* and granting them legal protections.

Though the *shi* remained firmly at the top of the social hierarchy regardless of the period, the membership of the class changed over time. Originally, the *shi* were warrior aristocrats not unlike western knights, but they became obsolete when the Warring States period mobilized the common folk for warfare. With the rise of philosophy, the warriors slowly gave way to scholars. Later, during the harsh Legalist regime of the Qin Dynasty, the emperor began assigning administrative responsibilities to learned scholars who showed promise and merit. To weaken the authority of the noble class, he dismantled the existing feudalist system in favor of a centralized bureaucracy of dedicated officials.

Though the Qin's system of governance persisted well after the dynasty's collapse, the importance of family lines meant that prominent scholar-officials effectively became the new aristocracy. Their wealth and influence almost always guaranteed their descendants the resources to land their own positions within the imperial court. *Thousand Autumns* includes examples of powerful clans like the Su and the Xie; one talented ancestor could elevate their entire family for generations to come. It wasn't until the Tang Dynasty that a true merit-based system was introduced—the civil service exams—that would give capable commoners the chance to find their place in governance.

APPENDIX

# Glossary

# GLOSSARY

## GENRES

**DANMEI (耽美, "INDULGENCE IN BEAUTY"):** A Chinese fiction genre focused on romanticized tales of love and attraction between men. It is analogous to the BL (boys' love) genre in Japanese media and is better understood as a genre of plot rather than a genre of setting. For example, though many danmei novels feature wuxia or xianxia settings, others are better understood as tales of sci-fi, fantasy, or horror.

**WUXIA (武侠, "MARTIAL HEROES"):** One of the oldest Chinese literary genres and usually consists of tales of noble heroes fighting evil and injustice. It often follows martial artists, monks, or rogues who live apart from the ruling government. These societal outcasts—both voluntary and otherwise—settle disputes among themselves, adhering to their own moral codes over the law.

Characters in wuxia focus primarily on human concerns, such as political strife between factions and advancing their own personal sense of justice. True wuxia is low on magical or supernatural elements. To Western moviegoers, a well-known example is *Crouching Tiger, Hidden Dragon*.

# NAMES, HONORIFICS, AND TITLES

## Diminutives, nicknames, and name tags

**A-:** Friendly diminutive. Always a prefix. Usually for monosyllabic names, or one syllable out of a two-syllable name.

**DA-:** A prefix meaning "eldest."

**LAO-:** A prefix meaning "old." A casual but still respectful way to address an older man.

**-ER:** A word for "son" or "child." When added to a name as a suffix, it expresses affection.

**XIAO-:** A prefix meaning "small" or "youngest." When added to a name, it expresses affection.

**GE/GEGE:** A word meaning "big brother." When added as a suffix, it becomes an affectionate address for any older male, with the -gege variant expressing even more affection.

## Cultivation Sects

**SHIZUN:** Teacher/master. For one's master in one's own sect. Gender-neutral. Literal meaning is "honored/venerable master" and is a more respectful address, though Shifu is not disrespectful.

**SHIXIONG:** Older martial brother. For senior male members of one's own sect. When not bound by sect, speakers may also append "-xiong" as a suffix for names, as a friendly but courteous way of addressing a man of equal rank.

**SHIJIE:** Older martial sister. For senior female members of one's own sect.

**SHIDI:** Younger martial brother. For junior male members of one's own sect. When not bound by sect, speakers may also append "-di" as a friendly suffix to names, with "-laodi" being a more casual variant.

**SHIMEI:** Younger martial sister. For junior female members of one's own sect.

**SHIZHI:** Martial nephew or niece. For disciples of the speaker's martial sibling.

**QIANBEI:** A respectful title or suffix for someone older, more experienced, or more skilled in a particular discipline. Not to be used for blood relatives.

## Other

**DAFU:** A general but respectful address for court officials.

**GONGZI:** A respectful address for young men, originally only for those from affluent households. Though appropriate in all formal occasions, it's often preferred when the addressee outranks the speaker.

**LANG/LANGJUN:** A general term for "man." "-lang" can be appended as a suffix for a woman's male lover or husband, but it can also be used to politely address a man by pairing it with other characters that denote his place within a certain family. For example, "dalang," "erlang," and "sanlang" mean "eldest son," "second son," and "third son" respectively. "Langjun" is a polite address for any man, similar to "gentleman."

**NIANG/NIANGZI:** A general term for "woman," and has the same pairing rules as "lang." "Niangzi" is a polite address for young women, similar to "maiden."

**XIANSHENG:** A polite address for men, originally only for those of great learning or those who had made significant contributions to society. Sometimes seen as an equivalent to "Mr." in English.

**XIONGZHANG:** A very respectful address for an older man the speaker is close to. Approximately means "esteemed elder brother."

# TERMINOLOGY

**FACE (脸/面子):** A person's face is an important concept in Chinese society. It is a metaphor for someone's reputation or dignity and can be extended into further descriptive metaphors. For example, "having face" refers to having a good reputation and "losing face" refers to having one's reputation damaged.

**INTERNAL CULTIVATION (内功):** Internal cultivation or *neigong* refers to the breathing, qi, and meditation practices a martial artist must undertake in order to properly harness and utilize their "outer cultivation" of combat techniques and footwork. As Daoism considers qi and breathing irrevocably linked, a large part of internal cultivation centers on achieving the advanced state of **internal breathing** (内息). Practitioners focus on regulating and coordinating their breaths until it becomes second nature. This then grants them the ability to freely manipulate their qi with little effort or conscious thought.

In wuxia, the capabilities of internal cultivation are usually exaggerated. Martial artists are often portrayed as being able to fly with qinggong, generate powerful force fields, manipulate objects across space without physical contact, or harden their bodies and make themselves impervious to physical damage.

**JIANGHU (江湖, "RIVERS AND LAKES"):** A staple of wuxia, the jianghu describes the greater underground society of martial artists and associates that spans the entire setting. Members of the jianghu self-govern and settle issues among themselves based on the tenets of strength and honor, though this may not stop them from exerting influence over conventional society too.

**MERIDIANS:** The means by which qi travels through the body, like a bloodstream. Some medical and combat techniques target the meridians at specific points on the body, known as acupoints, which allows them to redirect, manipulate, or halt qi circulation. Halting a cultivator's qi circulation prevents them from using their internal cultivation until the block is lifted.

**NAMES:** When men and women came of age in ancient China, they received a new name for others of the same generation to refer to them by, known as a **courtesy name**. Use of their original or **personal name** was normally reserved only for respected elders and the person themselves—using it otherwise would be very rude and overfamiliar.

Using an emperor's personal name was even more disrespectful. Rulers were usually addressed by the dynasty they led, and they each had a formal title to distinguish themselves from their predecessors or successors. For example, Yuwen Yong's official title was "Emperor Wu of Northern Zhou" (北周武帝).

**PAIR CULTIVATION (双修):** Also translated as dual cultivation, this is a cultivation practice that uses sex between participants to improve cultivation prowess. Can also be used as a simple euphemism for sex.

**PARASITIC CULTIVATION (采补, "HARVEST AND SUPPLEMENT"):** The practice of draining life energy and qi from a host to strengthen one's martial arts. As the bodies of men are believed to hold more *yang* qi while women hold more *yin* qi, the person in question will often "harvest" from the other sex to "supplement" themselves, which gives the practice its association with sexual cultivation.

**QINGGONG (轻功):** A real-life training discipline. In wuxia, the feats of qinggong are highly exaggerated, allowing practitioners to glide through the air, run straight up walls and over water, jump through trees, or travel dozens of steps in an instant.

**SECLUSION (闭关):** Also known as "closed door meditation," seclusion or secluded cultivation is when a martial artist isolates themselves from the rest of the world to meditate and further their internal cultivation for the purpose of healing injuries or taking their martial arts to the next level.

**TRUE QI AND CORES:** True qi (真气) is a more precise term for the "qi" commonly seen in Chinese media. In Daoism, one's true qi or life force is believed to be the fusion of Xiantian qi and Houtian qi.

True qi is refined in the lower Dantian (丹田, "elixir field") within the abdomen, which also holds the foundations of a person's martial arts, called the core. In *Thousand Autumns*, Daoist cores and demonic cores are mentioned, differentiated by the discipline (and hence Dao) the practitioner chose. All internal cultivation and breathing builds off these foundations—losing or destroying them is tantamount to losing all of one's martial arts.

In wuxia, a practitioner with superb internal cultivation can perform superhuman feats with their true qi. On top of what is covered under internal cultivation above, martial artists can channel true qi into swords to generate sword qi, imbue simple movements and objects with destructive energy, project their voices across great distances, heal lesser injuries, or enhance the five senses.

**YIN AND YANG (阴阳):** In Daoism, the concept of *yin* and *yang* is another set of complementary, interdependent forces that govern the cosmos. It represents the duality present in many aspects of nature, such as dark and light, earth and heaven, or female and male. *Yin* is the passive principle, while *yang* is the active one.

**WARRING STATES PERIOD:** An era in ancient Chinese history characterized by heavy military activity between seven dominant states. The rise of schools of thought like Daoism, Confucianism, and Legalism was partially in response to the extreme turmoil and suffering that were rampant during this time. It lasted from around 475 B.C.E. to 221 B.C.E., when the Qin state annexed the rest and established the first unified Chinese empire: the Qin Dynasty.

**WEIQI (围棋):** Also known by its Japanese name, *go*. Sometimes called "Chinese chess," it is the oldest known board game in human history. The board consists of a many-lined grid upon which opponents play unmarked black and white stones as game pieces to claim territory.

**ZOROASTRIANISM:** A religion from ancient Persia founded by the prophet Zoroaster.